D0793940

This special signed edition
is limited to 600 numbered copies
and 26 lettered copies.

This is copy ________.

A Different Vintage

A Different Vintage

Neal Barrett, Jr.

Terry— I know YOU recall the 60s & 70s -- Admit it!

Subterranean Press 2001

First Edition
May 2001

ISBN
1-931081-20-4

Subterranean Press
P.O. Box 190106
Burton, MI 48519

email:
publisher@subterraneanpress.com

website:
www.subterraneanpress.com

CONTENTS

INTRODUCTION

You can't go home again if
they've
plowed the place under where
you
lived
and played
and dug in
the dirt
when you
were a kid
and they built
this enormous fugging concrete
monster that has smothered
your past and
crushed the toy soldiers
you lost in the yard
and even pulverized
the bones of cherished
dogs you
buried there.

THIS IS NOT RIGHT. THERE IS NO GODDAMN EXCUSE FOR THIS AND I WANT EVERYTHING BACK!

Okay, no way, right? Because time marches on, stomps and clomps and craps as it goes, and there's nothing you can do except watch your step or you'll get it all over your shoes and clear up in your soul.

Last year I wrote a chapbook called "The Day the Decorators Came" for *Subterranean Press.* The title story had to do with aliens coming down and redecorating the world in most hideous ways, starting out with Washington, D.C., and generally making a mess everywhere.

I didn't realize this story was unconsciously inspired by a real event in my life until the tale was nearly done. It was then I recalled going back to Oklahoma City on one of those simple-minded trips to relive the "wonder years" of childhood. (Never works, unless childhood was twenty minutes ago, which means the bulldozers are on your ass right now.)

I discovered, to my horror, a gargantuan office complex was crunching its way down the block, and that it had devoured my boyhood home only weeks before, and was now swallowing the houses of snot-nosed pals, and curly-headed sexpots, seven years old.

The house was gone, and so was everything else, except for the precious relics I didn't leave behind: Superman, Batman, Plastic Man, Tarzan, The Green Lantern, The Flash. *Big-Little Books* (ask some old guy what they were) like "Flash Gordon and the Perils of Mongo," "Buck Rogers and the Moons of Saturn," "Alley Oop and the Jungles of Moo."

Some years passed, and some of my literary treasures were lost. but I had enough of them in my head to start writing tales of my own and sending them in to magazines. Don't ask why. If you want to do that, you just do.

At the same time, other people were submitting tales to the same magazines. I wondered if these people had watched their childhood homes get plowed into the ground as well.

People who were sending stories to the magazines I was sending to were Jack Vance, John Brunner, Jack Dann, Philip K. Dick, Cordwainer Smith, Poul Anderson, Ursula K. Le Guin, Clifford Simack, Mack Reynolds, Gordon R. Dickson, Frederick Pohl.

Hey, a pretty nifty group, and a smart bunch, too. Apparently, a lot of them got their books and magazines out of the house in time as well.

Look up "vintage" and the dictionary will tell you "*the crop of a single season,*" or an alternate definition: "*choice.*"

That's the definition I like the best. And I'd like to say that every one of the dozen stories here (from the crop of 1960-1979) is a top-notch example of the storyteller's craft. All right, get off my back, I won't say that, okay?

The thing you *can* say about anyone's vintage stories is that they reflect the state of the art at the time. That doesn't mean we were all writing in the same manner, but it does mean that what we did both formed—and reflected—what was going on in the heads of writers, editors and readers in 1960, say, or 1975.

Some of my stories (I'll speak for myself here, but you know what I mean) hold up well today, while others more fully—and sometimes too well—reflect their own time. But that's the point, of course: that's what they were supposed to do, and that's why the editors bought them.

I don't intend to even try to be humble on this particular point: I *know* I'm a hell of a lot better writer now than I was then, and so are the other writers who were honing their skills at the time.

Hey, I think we honed pretty well. I still like their vintage stuff, and I still like mine. You're going to run across some cigarette smokin' here, and possibly some less than proper attitudes relevant to the times, but live with it, okay?

I did, so can you.

Neal Barrett, Jr.
January 1, 2001

Nightbeat

The wakechimes touched me with the sound of cinnamon. I stretched, turned over, and watched the clockroach play time games against the wall. It marked the spidery minutes in fine script and left crystal duntracks behind.

It was half-past blue, and a lemon moon spilled color into the room. Its light burnished Bethellen's hair to silver and brushed her flesh with coffee shadow.

She stirred once, and I slid quietly away, padded to the shower cage, and let cool spicewater bring me awake. There were cocoacubes where Bethellen had left them, but I passed them by and trotted back to the nightroom. My Copsuit sprang from its hollow with a sunfresh scent, and I slipped into it quickly.

I would have liked to look at myself. A small vanity, but mine own. I take a pride in the uniform. It's a Copsuit in the classical cut—basic whipcord in umber and vermilion, sepia pullover, and fringe-leather vest. The jackboots, gloves, and chainbelt are traditional indigo. The Marshal's Star of David is cadmium-gold, and the Peacemaker by my side is finest quartz and ivory.

Set. Ready to go, and a last look at Bethellen. She had turned in her sleep to catch the moonwaves. Citron limbs bared to an ocher sea. By morning, I'd taste lemon on her lips.

Outside, the prowlbug hummed to electric life. The moon was high now, and a second had joined it—a small saffron tagalong. Lime shadows colored the streetways. The dashglow winked me into service, and I switched the roadlights and moved along.

The street ribboned over soft hills furred with bonebrake, and through dark groves of churnmoss. Raven blossoms hung from high branches nearly to the ground. I swung the prowlbug into Bluewing, whispered through Speaklow, and coasted down the steep circle to Singhill.

There were people all about now. If I listened, I could feel the sound of their sleeping. From Tellbridge I watched lonelights far and away. Not everyone slumbered, then, but all were snug in their homeshells till the day. None would stir before Amberlight polished the world. For that was as it was—the day belongs to us, but not the night.

I have often stopped the prowlbug and dimmed the lights and watched the darklife. In moments, the night fills with chitter-hums and thrashes. A beetlebear stops to sniff the air, pins me with frosty muzzle and razor eyes. For a while there is pink carnage in her heart; then she scutters by clanging husky armor. Jac-Jacs and Grievers wing the dark hollows. A Bloodgroper scatters his kill. There is much to darklife, and few have seen it as it is.

A quarter till yellow. The dashglow hemorrhages, coughs up a number. The prowlbug jerks into motion, whines up the speedscale. Sirens whoopa-whoopa-whoopa through the night, and I switch on the traditional lilac, plum, and scarlet flashers.

There are no strollwalkers to pause and wonder. No other bugs abroad to give me way. Still, there are customs to keep alive, bonds with the past.

The address was nearby. Prowlbug skittered up the snakepath around Henbake. Pressed me tight against the driveseat. Pink lights to port. A homeshell high on Stagperch, minutes away.

Around a corner, and green sparkeyes clustered ahead—nightmates and shadelings hunkered in the streetway. The prowlbug whoopa-ed a warning, and they scattered like windleaves.

They were waiting for me, portal open. A big man with worry lines scribbled on paper features. His handstrobe stitched my path with lightcraters to shoo stray nightlings. The woman was small and pretty. Hands like frightened birds. I moved through them up turnstairs past buffwalls to the boy's room.

I'd been there before, but they didn't remember. No-face in a uniform.

A child in Dreamspasm is not a pretty sight. I punched his record on the bedscreen, scanned it quickly. Twelve and a half. Fifth Dream. Two-year sequence. No complications. I gripped one bony arm and plunged Blue Seven in his veins. The spasms slowed to a quiver. I touched him, wiped foamspittle from his cheeks. His skin was cold, frogdank. Waterblue eyes looked up at nothing. The small mouth sucked air.

"He's all right." The man and woman huddled behind. "Take him in in the morning. Don't think he did internal damage, but it won't hurt to check."

I laid a vial beside the bed. "One if he wakes. I don't think he will."

"Thank you," said the man. "We're grateful." The woman nodded his words.

"No problem." I stopped in the hall and faced them again. "You know he could secondary."

They looked startled, as if they didn't.

"If he does, stay with him."

They frowned questions, and I shook my head. "Punch in if you like, but there's nothing else I can do. He can't have Seven again. And a strong secondary's a good sign." I sent them a Copgrin. "He's old enough. You could be out of the woods."

They gave each other smiles and said things I didn't hear. The prowlbug was turning all my buttons red and shrieking whoopas into the night. I bounded down turnstairs and tore out the portal. No time for strobes and such. If nightlings got underfoot, they'd get a jackboot for their trouble.

The prowlbug scattered gravel, skit-tailed into the streetway. It was wound up and highwhining and I held on and let it have its way. Stagperch faded, and the snakepath dizzied by in black patches. I prayed against sleepy megapedes bunked in on the road ahead. A tin medal for Bethellen. Early insurance.

The dashglow spit data, but I already knew. Bad. Category A and climbing. Name of Lenine Capral and long overdue. First Dream and fifteen.

The Rules say punch before you practice. No way with Lenine Capral. No record, no time, no need. The Dream had her in nighttalons. Down on the dark bottom, and nothing for it. Lost, lost Lenine.

I drew the Peacemaker, pressed the muzzle between her eyes. Her body arched near double, limbs spread-eagled. I pulled back lids and looked. Milkpools. Silverdeath darting about. The little shiverteeth nibbling away.

I tossed my jacket aside. Grabbed a handful of hair and pinned her neck where I wanted it. Put the muzzle low behind the ear and up. This time, shock jerked a small arm and snapped it like crackwood. But nothing snapped Lenine.

I couldn't shoot her again. More would burn her skull bone-dry. And nothing in the little glass tubes. Blue Seven was fine for the boy—about as good as mouse pee for Lenine.

Okay. One deep breath and down to dirty fighting. I ripped the sheet away. Stripped her bare. She was slim and fragile, too close to womantime. I spread her wide, and the motherperson made little noises.

"Out."

The man understood and moved her.

Dreamspasm is a thing of the mind. But that door's closed for helpers. The physical road is the only way. Peacemakers. Blue Seven. Redwing. And after that: physical stimuli to build mental bridges back home. Countershock for young minds. For Lenine Capral, therapeutic rape. Thumb the Peacemaker to lowbuzz and hope this one's led a sheltered life.

Hurt her good.

Whisper uglies in her ear.

Slap and touch and tear. No gentle Peacemaker funsies. Only the bad parts. A child's garden of horrors. Everything mother said would happen if the bad man gets his hands on you.

Orange.

Red-thirty.

Coming up violet. Cream-colored dawn on the windows.

And finally the sound you want. Lenine the wide-eyed screamer. The violated child awake and fighting. Afraid of real things, now. Scared out of Dreamspasm One.

Quickly out and past the hoverfaces. No gushy gratitude here. Mother doesn't thank the Coprapist.

Outside, dawnbreeze turns the sweat clammy cold. A medbug has braved the nightlings all the way from Fryhope. Lenine will get proper patching.

The prowlbug has a homepath in mind, as well it might. Only I am not ready for Bethellen and breakfast. Both are out of temper with the night's affairs. Instead, I brave the prowlbug's grumblings, move past Slowrush, and wind down to Hollow. The road ends, and prowlbug will duly record that I have violated Safecode and am afoot before the dawn. The nightlings don't concern me. They've fed before Firstlight and bear no ill. At the stream I hear their thrums and splashings as they cross back over to find hugburrows for the day.

The stream is swift and shallow and no wider than a childstep. It makes pleasant rillsongs and winds beneath green chumtrees. It has no name. It is simply the stream that divides the world. Dark from light. Night from day.

There is still nightshadow on the other side. The groves are thick and heavy. I watch, wait, and listen to the stream music.

Timebug says half-past violet. While I wait, I polish dun-glasses. Put them on. They help to see what is, and temper what isn't at all.

Wait.

Watch the waterlights.

A blink and a breath and he's there. As if he'd been there all along.

For a moment my stomach does its tightness. But it's not so bad for me. They make teetiny headchanges in policemen. Little slicecuts that go with the Copsuit. But there is still a childmind to remember. Dreamspasms in dark nightrooms.

Through the dun-glasses I can see bristly no-color. Hear his restless flickersounds. See him move with the shape of frostfur. Hear him breathe hot darkness. Sense his crush-heavy limbs.

Only, I cannot see or hear these things at all.

I wonder if he watches, and what he sees of me. I have to look away. And when I look again, he is gone. Nothing has changed in the thickgroves.

What would I say to him? That wouldn't need the saying?

Back to the prowlbug. Ten till indigo now. Amberlight dares the high ridges. Sucks away darkness.

I imagine him. Thromping and shiffing. Dark fengroves away. Safe against the sunstar. And all the young darklings purged of manfear. Only fright-thoughts, now—fading daydemons named Lenine.

Who can tell such a thing? The stream divides the world. Whatever could be said is what he knows. That there are pinchfew places left. That mostly there is nothing. That we will have to make do with what there is to share.

Neal Barrett, Jr. writes:

It is no news that we're running out of bunks on this small green dormitory of ours—a problem we handle, at best, with cautious pessimism and renewed apathy. You are my polite intruder, and I am yours. We have erected dampers and defenses to keep each other at bay. Courteous walls divide your sins from mine, but nothing works too well. For we live perilously close to one another. The aroma of your Big Mac enhances my coq au vin *no at all. Your TV growls ominously at mine. Your lovemaking comes to me in fiberboard fantasies.* I know *that you are there.*

So far, your dreams do not intrude upon mine. But this too may come to pass, with someone/something, on one world or another. Which is what "Nightbeat" is all about.

One could argue the credibility of such a tale. For it is inconceivable, now, that we should ever find ourselves planetary roommates with an alien life form. It's a vast, lonely universe out there; innumerable clusters of ripe green Edens hang on the big galactic bush.

Hopefully, that's the way it is. Certainly the way it ought to be. And if it isn't? Well, we've been wrong before. And we can always take solace in the words of Florida's redoubtable developer, Ponce de Leon, who said: "Just park the trailer anywhere, baby. There's plenty of room for everyone..."

HERO

What I told Colonel Dark was he could shove it all the way up and break it off, for all I cared. I sure wasn't going to ride in no groundhog parade.

"Sergeant Ash, you sure are going to do just that," Dark told me.

"Sir, I'm not. Begging the colonel's pardon."

"It is all set, boy, and I reckon you are."

I looked across the desk at him. You got to check twice to make sure the man is sitting. Jack's seven foot eight in his socks—shoulders wide as rail ties, and a chest like big black sacks of cement. Long-steppin' legs hard as good oak, and fists the size of baby heads. I'm no boy-child, myself—but I'm no Jack Dark, either.

He was dressed the same as me—spit and blister boots, pitch-night skinners, and star-silver piping from shoulder to toe. From the head on up, we're not much alike. Jack's got this black rubber face he's worn since Razoridge—darker'n his own was, and twice as ugly.

"Jack," I told him, "you're 'bout the scariest nigger I ever seen."

"You just remember that, cracker," he said solemnly.

"If I was a little ol' tyke, I'd pee in my pants just looking at you."

"Some do, I hear."

"Aw, shit, Jack." I threw my coonskin cap on his desk and tried to look mean as him. "I ain't going to do it, and that's that. Get someone else. Get old Bluebelly Ripper. Now *there's* an A-number one hero. I seen him on a magazine."

Colonel Dark looked at me with big, sad eyes. "They don't want an everyday space jock up front, Ash. What they want's a real live wormhead. And you're it."

"Well, I ain't, either. You can bust me or whatever. This boy isn't riding in no parade, and you got my honest to God word on it."

I meant it, too, and Dark knew it. In a field situation I wouldn't question an order from Colonel Jack, but this wasn't any field situation or anything like it. And a man's got to stand up for himself when he knows he's right. That goes for soldiers as well as anybody.

I felt like the biggest damn fool on Earth, and likely looked the part. Bands playing and flags flying and paper falling all over—and me riding in a bright red skimmer with Dark and the President and whoever, and enough high brass to start our own little war. And of course our tag-alongs were right close by, his and mine—their pretty red boxes nice and handy. I kept grinning and waving and looking happy as a frog, and Jack sat right there watching, smiling real nice and showing me his fine white teeth.

It was a good parade, I suppose, if you didn't know better. There were lots of drums and pretty costumes and long-legged girls. There were battle trophies and war wagons and even a dead Centaurian in a tank—one of the better-looking varieties. They'd found an old Beta Scout somewhere that'd been rusting out for about ten years and painted it all up and stuck it on a float. Major Bluebelly Ripper was ridin' that, and looked near as miserable as I did.

The worst part, though, were the troopers. I could take all the rest, but that was kind of hard to swallow. There must have been soldiers from half the old units on Earth—every one in fancy dress, all brand-spankin' new and shiny. Jack's Nairobi Lancers were there looking tall and proud, red plumes waving on their big bone helmets. Right behind me were the Swiss High Guards and the Queen's Own, and I could see the green banner of the Virginia Volunteers up ahead, and the Red Russian Eagles after that. And right in front of me, of course, a troop of Tennessee Irregulars, my own outfit. Each and every one in fine buck leather, sporting coal-black beards and coonskin hats.

I didn't know whether to laugh or bust out bawling. What I really wanted to do was hop right out of there and knock me some heads together. Sort of work out the tension, some. Dark looked right at me, once, and I figured he was feeling the same.

The truth is, there wasn't a man there fit to wear those outfits. Not a one had ever been off-planet, and if any two of 'em had been soldiering more than a week, why I'd buy them all the beer they could drink.

There aren't any Tennessee Irregulars any more—haven't been for near twenty years. Maybe me, and three others, from what started. The same goes for Jack's outfit, and the rest. We still come from everywhere, but there isn't much time to think on it, or worry 'bout who's carrying the flag. We're soldiers, and we do what we have to do.

Only, like Jack Dark says, that don't make much of a parade. People get tired reading about a war they never see. I guess you got to give them something to look at now and then, so they'll know we're still out there, fighting for home and mother—and pretty soldiers marching by is about the best thing for it. Folks sure don't want to see much more than that, or think on it any. How we drop a million troopers every couple of years out there and don't get more than a handful back alive. Who's going to do much cheering about that?

There was plenty of noise and shouting, but it sure got awful quiet when I passed by. People looked, all right. They didn't want to miss a real wormhead—there aren't that many to see. But they didn't want to *really* look, not like you look at just anyone. What they'd do is look *at* something else and kind of see me in the bargain. Like maybe starin' straight at me would give 'em warts, or something worse.

I could've done the same. Looked right over them and never seen a thing. I didn't, though. I grinned until my face hurt and caught every one of them right in the eye. Squirm, you bastards, I told them. You ain't sure what I got, but you're *god*damn sure you don't want any…

"Marcus, I'm buying," said the colonel, when we were right near the end.

"Shit, Jack, you haven't *got* enough whiskey to buy out of this one," I told him.

There was a ground-hot major sitting up front, and he didn't much like it—me talking to an officer like that. He started to say something, then didn't. Which was a good idea. I wouldn't ever do anything to embarrass Jack, but he's not near as nice to folks as I am.

There was a banquet somewhere with tin speeches and paper food, and we put up with about fifteen minutes of that before Dark got up and pulled me off to a nearby bar. What we didn't drink we threw at the walls, and we soon had the place to ourselves. When we got into regimental songs about two in the A.M., the tag-alongs cut us off quick. A couple of sober shots, and we were ready to go again, but our keepers said absolutely no. Instead, they called a staff car and packed us off fast to Heroes' Hotel. Dark and I protested—but not much. His tag-along was a lieutenant, and mine a captain, which doesn't mean anything. If you're a wormhead, your tag-along outranks God.

Jack went his way and I went mine. Halfway down the long hall, though, he stopped and called out over his shoulder. "Sergeant! Sleeeeeeep TIGHT!"

"Sir!" I shouted back, "Don't let the BAD bugs bite!"

Captain Willie Brander roused the night crew. They weren't too glad to see me, but no one complained. I'm about all they have to do.

Annie See stripped me down and held me under happy juice. Little Mac Packer scrubbed every hole and hollow with a fine rusty brush.

Bigo Binder glued me up tight.

They dried me and rubbed me and ground me up good, then rolled me in the Sounder. All the little hairs that had dared start growing since yesterday got hummed off quick.

Finally, I lay back flat on the table and let the red rubber jam-jams wrap me up tight. Three hundred thirty-two gold and silver wires dug their little snout noses into my skin. Dewpads shut my eyes and plugged up my ears. Hard rubber clamps spread my jaws so the bright yellow tubes could snake down my gullet. Then, when all was done and checked, they picked me up easy and dropped me down deep in the white foam pool.

I couldn't move an eyelash. Even if I had one.

It was beddy-bye time. But tell that to a wormhead, and he'll come right out of his nightsuit and hand you your ass.

Another wonderful night in Ash's head. All my good bug-buddies were waiting, and we romped and splashed all over and had us a time. The little white teeth were slice-belly sharp and we gutted each other good. There was hot red screaming, and pink things to eat. We ripped and tore and cut through the long wet hours, and the night didn't last more than a couple thousand years.

It doesn't get better, it just gets worse. Like someone who isn't here any more scratched in the bar downstairs:

Hell is where the good guys go.

Only, you got to be a wormhead to know it.

"Sleeeeeeep TIGHT?"

"Damn RIGHT!"

Dark shot us all a big grin and dropped his ugly self down between Miguel Mendoza and me.

"Pleasant dreams, Ash?"

"Hell, yes, Colonel. I'm thinkin' about going on back after breakfast and grabbin' me another couple hours."

Everyone laughed at that, and Jack Dark reached out a big paw and speared about thirty ounces of steak.

"You got the hungries, Jack?" Mendoza asked him.

"Always do after a good night's sleep, Mig."

The chatter went around the table and back again, like it always does with wormheads in the morning. We're so damn glad to be awake there isn't anything doesn't sound funny.

There were thirty-two of us there, all the wormheads on Earth. Off-planet there's more, of course, though not as many as you'd think. The survival factor out there's low enough to be a big dark secret, and so the number of live troopers with kills is lower still. We're the cream of the crop. Or the worst of the lot, whichever. Men with anywhere from 550 to 900 kills on their record, which makes us too hot for the field Sleepers to handle any more. We come from most everywhere, but this bunch is heavy on soldiers from the U.S.A. and the African Republics. No special reason, except maybe there were more of us out there in the beginning. Everyone's in it, now—every male-child over fifteen who can walk, or crawl some. There'd be plenty of women in it, too, if the law would let them. But that'd play hell with making new baby soldiers, and then where'd we be?

I said there were thirty-two of us. There were thirty-three, until last night. Everybody at breakfast knew Hu-cheng had bought it in bed, but wasn't one of us goin' to say anything. What's there to say, that we weren't all thinking anyway?

No one was left except Dark and me, trying to see who could out-hog the other. Jack always wins in the end—he's just got more room to put it than I do. But I give him a fight now and then.

"Jack, I sure want to thank you for yesterday," I told him. "I ain't ever been in a parade before. I get a chance, I'll make it up to you, for certain."

Dark just looked at me and did something in his throat that sounded like thunder.

"I'm dead serious," I said. "That was an opportunity don't come to just every soldier. Ridin' around with officers, wavin' at folks—"

"You just keep talking, Ash."

"Sir, I'm not joking about this—"

"Sergeant." Dark turned on me. "I got work to do, and I sure don't have time to sit here listening to you. However, if you like, I can spend a minute or two thinking up some useful job needs to be done."

"Reckon I'll just freshen up some, then maybe see me some town, Colonel."

Dark looked at me sideways and eased back down in his chair.

"Now just hold her, Jack." I knew what was coming. "I'm a big boy now. Near as big as you."

"You're a wormhead."

"Don't guess I need you to tell me that."

"Sounds like you need someone, Sergeant."

"Well, I don't—and I'm going. Isn't any need to talk about it, sir."

Jack gave me his ugliest look, and I gave it right back to him. Finally, he just got up like he was leaving, but I could feel him standing right behind me. A big black cloud wondering when it ought to rain.

"Maybe you ought to know, Ash," he said quietly. "Hucheng didn't die in bed. He opted out."

That shook me good. Just like he knew it would. Hu was a good man, and more than a friend. And there wasn't anybody'd tried harder to make it go right.

"Colonel," I said, "I'm obliged to you for tellin' me. But I guess I'm going to have to see me some town."

Dark didn't say anything. I just sat there eyeing steak bones and cold gravy for a while, and when I looked up again, he was gone.

We were right in D.C. and it wouldn't have been anything to get a skimmer down to Nashville. I could have hitched a free ride from the base to most anywhere—or rented my own craft, if I wanted. Money's no big problem for a soldier, if he lives long enough. There's no place to spend your pay out on the dung worlds, and I had about ten years coming, plus enough bonus and time to about double that.

I wasn't quite ready for home, though. When I am—if I am—I'll know it. There's something funny about going back where you haven't been since you weren't much more than a kid. You got this picture of it, the way it ought to be. It feels real good that way, all nice and comfortable, and you don't want it any different. Maybe you figure going back will change something, and if it did, it wouldn't be the same in your head any more.

So I did what a man does in a place he doesn't know, that doesn't know him.

Bars haven't changed all that much. I reckon you could go in one a thousand years ago or a thousand from now and know right where you were. This one was dark and cool and served a good whiskey, and the music wasn't bad enough to bother a man's drinking. That's a funny thing about music. It changes when you're out of touch, but if you stay gone long enough, it comes right on back around to where it was.

Poor old tag-along took him a seat and waited and kept a good strong eye on me. I'd have bought him a beer but of course he wouldn't touch it. When you're shaggin' a wormhead, you keep your cool all the time, and you sure don't do any drinking. So old Willie sat loose, trying hard to look like there wasn't anything peculiar about a man hanging dry in a bar, carrying a little red box on one hip and a big .45 on the other. If he was having bad thoughts about damnfool wormheads who had to go roamin' around loose, he kept them to himself.

Sitting still isn't one of my best family traits. So I laid a couple of bills on the counter and drained the last drop. The boy tending bar moved up and shoved the cash right back.

"You're not buying any drinks in here, Sergeant. No way."

I looked him over close, catching what I'd missed the first time 'round.

He was about sixty-percent prosthetic, in all the wrong places. Kind of split down the middle, where the baddies had got him good. Rubber face, pink ears and nice new teeth.

"Where were you, boy?"

"Alpha-two. First landing in twenty-one."

"Shit. I was right next door on that little old mudball, where all the meanies come when you fellas flushed them out."

He grinned at that.

"What's your outfit. Virginians?"

He shook his head and his chin came up real proud. "California Diggers. Second Corps."

"Damn good outfit."

"Was. Nothing much left of 'em now."

I nodded. What's there to say?

"Listen," he told me, "I know who you are, Sergeant." His good eye touched my ribbons and the bald dome under my cap. "You need anything in this man's town, you give a yell. The groundies around here don't much understand why you guys are special. There's some of us do, though."

"I'm obliged," I told him and got myself out of there. He was well meaning and all, but I wasn't figuring on starting any more parades. About one's all I can handle.

The next spot had a fancy name, all red and gold and old-looking inside, with lots of dark wood showing. There wasn't any big surge of patriotism going on here. Nobody'd ever heard of Sergeant Major Marcus Ash, and didn't want to. If you could handle the tab—about four times what whiskey ought to be—why, you were just welcome as could be.

I would have backed on out real quick if it hadn't been for the girl. She just sidled right up and slid on in, easy as you please. I *could* have left after that, but didn't much want to. She was tall and kind of lanky, lazy blue eyes and wheat-colored hair falling easy off her shoulders. She had that special kind of thing some women carry around without really trying. They know who they are and don't need anyone to tell them.

"Care if I sit? It's okay if you don't."

As soon as she opened her mouth, I leaned back and grinned. "Well, if that don't beat all. Where you from, child?"

She looked into me real strong, then came out laughing. "Atlanta, right outside. And you got to be Tennessee."

I slapped the table hard and waved down a waiter. "Nashville, honey, and what are you drinkin'?"

She made it just as clear as could be right off. Worked in an office in Defense, which was about all you could work for now, and wanted me to know she wasn't a pro or anything but she did like to talk and have a drink and that was the best way to get to meet people. If we got along, fine. If not, that was okay, too. Her name was Jennie and she was twenty-three and how long had I been in the army and what was it really like out there?

I told her my name and she didn't seem to know it. That I'd been in the army twenty-one years and was thirty-six now. I skipped the last question, but it didn't matter anyway—she was doing a little quick arithmetic on the age business.

"My God. You were fifteen."

"Close to it."

"That's all your life." She was having trouble swallowing that.

"Well, time really flies when you're havin' fun."

"Can you get out now?"

"Could."

"Don't you want to?"

"And do what?"

"Well—" She waved me off into the ceiling somewhere. "—anything."

"Honey," I told her, "I don't *know* anything else. Last job I had on Earth was cuttin' high school and stealing spoons. Don't much want to do that again."

She laughed and kind of leaned back easy, knowing that I was going to tell the rest of it.

"See, there was this fella run a restaurant down home," I said. "Did a big business all over town, but he didn't much like to buy stuff. He was mostly interested in *selling*. So what he'd do is give us kids next to nothing for all the spoons and knives and forks and whatever we could steal off of somebody else. Hell, he didn't care whether they matched or nothing. Glasses, plates, salt shakers—everything."

"So what happened?"

"So bein' kids, we got ourselves caught, and the judge fella tells our folks they got a new rule on with the war just starting, and we can either go to the county farm for about six months, or join up."

Jennie looked pained. "So you got twenty-one years."

"Uhuh. Cured me of stealing spoons, though."

She laughed, showing me a pretty pink mouth.

"It's the God's truth," I told her and held up a hand to prove it. "Listen, you want another drink or you gettin' hungry?"

She thought about that. "You really want to take me to dinner? You don't have to. I just sat. You didn't ask."

"Know I didn't. But I'd like it, if you would."

"I would. Okay?"

"Okay. Only this is your town, and I haven't got the slightest idea where to start."

Jennie closed one eye. "There're a lot of good places."

"What's the best?"

"For what?"

"Anything."

She stopped a minute. "Are you asking me the best place in *town?*"

"Uhuh."

"That's very nice," she said gently, "but we don't have to do that." What she meant, was I likely couldn't.

"Yeah, but if we did."

"If we did, it'd be The Chalice."

"Food any good?"

She decided to ignore that. "Marcus. I don't even know anyone who's ever been there."

"Well, you will tomorrow," I told her. "Reckon I ought to call?"

"You're kidding. For which month?"

I grinned at her and got up and found a phone. Jack Dark was in a meeting and didn't much like getting out, but he'd do it.

"Done," I told her.

"It is?"

"Uhuh."

"Hey. How about that?" Something hit her and the big pink smile dropped real quick. "Look, friend," she said coolly, "if I'm going to get raped in an alley or something, just say so, okay? But *don't* promise me The Chalice first. I couldn't take that."

I laughed and helped her up and we started out. It was the first chance I'd had to get close to her and smell her hair and feel how soft she was to touch. It did good things to me. You think a lot about girls like Jennie out there. Not just the loving part. Laughing when you want to and going where you want and breathing all the clean air you can hold. There are good and precious times out there when there's no fighting for a while and you know you're most likely going to live through the week. You can get yourself a woman sometimes if you're lucky and go off and share army beer. You remember all that and hold on to it. But it isn't the same thing.

Outside we stopped to blink the bright sun away, and I caught Jennie's gaze going past me, over my shoulder, and saw it happen right in her eyes. It might have ended right there. It should have. Only I didn't want it to.

I'd been waiting for it, knowin' damn well when it'd be; and of course the minute she spotted the tag-along on my heels, it wasn't hard to put together. She just stood there, one hand kind of stiff in front of the little 'o' her mouth was making.

"Look, I never should've let us get going, " I told her. "Forget it, okay?"

She stared at me, not really seeing much. "You're him. My God you really are. I didn't even know."

I felt the heat startin' up my neck. "Yeah, fine. Well you do now!"

"Hey." Concern crossed her face. "What is this? Listen, I'm sorry. I'm a little—well, surprised. I've never been out with a genuine hero before, Marcus."

I studied her real hard. "Jennie. You don't have to play no games with me. I don't know about any hero shit, but I'm something besides that—and if you know who I am, you know what it is."

"What I *know* is I got me an invitation to a fancy restaurant from one Marcus Ash, and if he's figuring on squirming out of that little number, he better have one hell of a good reason."

She looked so damn funny, all pouty and ready to spit needles. That wasn't the end of it. We'd have to take it some further than that. But it was enough, for the moment. "Come on, lady," I told her, "let's get ourselves some supper."

There wasn't much talking on the way to her place. We just sat real quiet, enjoying where we were and not wanting to worry it any. I stayed in the skimmer while she changed. Tag-along Brander was up front with the driver, a kid no more than thirteen or so. No, he didn't mind stopping for a couple of minutes—or forever, if someone was paying.

I couldn't see the boy's eyes—they were locked in on some kind of crap under a pair of those personal vidspecs everybody's wearing. Something they came up with while I was out chasing meanie-bugs. You could see folks everywhere doing it—bars, streets, all over. Looked like a whole stumblin' town full of blind men. I thought about the kid. The draft age is fifteen, now. If there wasn't something real bad wrong with him, he'd be out fighting bugs in a year or so. We were building a world of children and old men, and nothing in between.

What can I say about Jennie? She came back looking straight and tall and shiny, her dress was all shimmery white—kind of there, and kind of not, all at once, like she was walking in smoke. I just stared like a dumb kid somebody'd handed the biggest piece of candy in the world. Jennie finally started turning red all over and said if I kept thinking stuff like I was thinking we weren't ever going to get much dinner. I told her that had sure crossed my mind, and she said it would just have to *stop* crossing because she wasn't going back to work telling everyone how she almost ate dinner at the fanciest place in town.

Washington raced by below as far as you could see, until somewhere up the way it got to be something else with a different name. There was a river, with the last of the sun making whole pools of copper, and I got a glimpse of some kind of monument and wide bands of green places checkered with white buildings. The skimmer gave a little tilt, then straightened, as the driver got hung in heavy patterns and turned the job over to a computer somewhere.

"We've got things to say," Jennie told me. "I'd kind of like to, if we can."

"Good enough," I said, like I really did mean that.

"You were—right, back there," she admitted. "Some, anyway. I *was* surprised to find out who you were, Marcus, and that's most of it. Honest. Only, there was some of the other stuff, too. You saw it and I knew you did and I—didn't know what to do about it. I didn't know because I don't under*stand* it. I—" she dropped her hands in her lap and made little fists.

"Okay. Straight, huh? You read about it, but it doesn't ever say much. I know there are men who've been in the war and they've—what? Got something in their heads that makes them different. I want to know and I want to understand only you don't *have* to, Marcus. It doesn't really make any... difference..."

She just kind of let it trail off, and I reached over and pulled her around. "Hey. Sure it does. You'd be a damn fool if it didn't."

She wouldn't look at me. "Yeah. Damn it, Marcus, it does. Is that—"

"It isn't anything. 'Cept maybe a little plain old human curiosity. How much do you know about what we're fighting? The Centaurians."

"About as much as anyone my age. I don't remember not hearing about the war, Marcus. It's just always been there." She shrugged. "I've seen the pictures a thousand times. And the things they've got in tanks at the museums. I know they're awful."

"Okay. Without gettin' scientific, they're bugs, worms—whatever. About twenty-two hundred varieties, four of 'em dominant. And every one of them meaner than anything Hell's got to offer. If you want to know what happened to me, Jennie, and the others, you got to understand about them. First, there isn't anything even similar between humans and bugs. Nothing. We can't even talk to each other, even if the Centaurians wanted to, and they damn sure don't. Second, and this is something Army don't like to make much out of, but it's true—they're *better'n* we are in most everything that's got to do with fighting. They're faster, better coordinated—everything. And the reason they're better is there isn't anything a Centaurian wants to do but kill something. Us, each other, it don't much matter. They eat and sleep and reproduce and kill. And they do the first three so's they can get on with the fourth. The only reason they haven't whipped us already is a piece of plain old luck. We beat 'em into space about thirty years, and we got us a better drive. We can get there—and they can't get here. Not yet, anyway. If they could, we wouldn't be sittin' here talking about it. We got to kill every last one of them and burn every egg in the system. If we don't—" I ran a quick finger over my throat and Jennie shuddered.

"I'm not telling you anything new, but it's something you got to really see if you're going to understand. What they are, and why, has got just about everything to do with how they affect humans. Only that part's not so easy. Everybody knows about it—but isn't anybody sure what it is."

"You mean, the thing that happened to you."

"To me—but to them, first. What they were makes 'em what they are now. Hasn't anybody had a chance to do much on-hand studying about prehistoric Centaurians, but they got some pretty good guesses. They had to survive, like anything else. Probably there was something eating *them* a couple million years ago. So they developed something to fight back with. Anything ate a big bug got this—picture, image, whatever, and it stayed with him. Something like a stinger that won't come out. And maybe next time he thought twice about goin' after that particular meal."

Jennie bit her lip thoughtfully. "That doesn't *say* anything, Marcus, not if you just leave it there with images and pictures. It's all kind of vague. Like on the holos, when you were in the parade, only I didn't know it was you—"

"So what'd they say?"

"Nothing much more than they *ever* say about anything. You know—'One of our brave troopers who still carries the terrible memories of the war within him blah-blah—dreams of Centaurian warriors blah-blah-blah.' Is that like it is, Marcus? Dreams?"

I didn't look at her; I just studied Willie Brander's head up front like it was real interesting. "Guess it's kind of which words you want to use," I said. "It's not something we can come real close to naming, Jennie. The thing that started out bein' a defense mechanism evolved into something a lot more than that. It's a matter of pride, now. Only it's a natural kind of pride, like breathin'. The top baddie around is the one with more kills to his credit. And he's got the wispies in his head to prove it."

Jennie shuddered. "The what?"

"Wispies. Spookprints, psycho-shadows, whatever. The science fellas have got fancier labels than that."

Jennie went real quiet a minute. The skimmer dipped down out of traffic, and I figured we were getting where we were going.

"Marcus," she said finally, "it's not the same, is it? With people?"

"Well, sort of," I told her. "Not just *exactly* the same, though." Seemed like I was doing a lot of talking to the back of old Willie's head.

I never been many places. Wasn't time to, hitting Earth about twice in twenty years. You don't have to pick up every rock you come to, though, to figure what's under it. A man makes it through about two hundred landings, he gets a fair nose for the terrain up ahead.

The smell I was getting now was money. Dusty bottle money, all fat and lazy—and they smelled me, same as I did them. I was the wrong kind of animal, one they hadn't seen before and didn't much want to. Bald-skinned and big, suited up black as night. A bright shiny girl beside me, and a tag-along behind. It scared the deep hell out of 'em, and I was feeling just pure mean enough to enjoy it.

Jennie didn't smell anything, 'cept what she was supposed to—crystal and silk and candle-shine silver. She took one look at the table, and the menu, and got the panics. "Marcus! I didn't have any *idea*— "

I tried to tell her what kind of money old soldiers have to spend, but she didn't believe that, either.

It was a hell of a place. There were dead-men waiters all over, men with long, gray-powder faces. They moved without walking and you never heard them coming. When food came out it was all secret and covered, and they'd stand around and whisper real serious awhile, then off one'd go, like a doctor wheeling God into surgery.

I don't know what Dark told them to get us in, but in wasn't eating. They were in no big hurry—we were there, but they'd make it hurt if they could. I grabbed one cruising by and told him we were ready, and he gave me this patient little smile and said he'd be glad to get me a menu in English. I grinned right back and told him I'd sure be grateful. When the new menu came, I set it aside without looking and ordered from the old one in Danish, Frisian and a little Pashto. I couldn't see his face, but Jennie could. He wouldn't know more than two of those, and they'd have to run tapes off his little pad recorder and take them off somewhere and get 'em figured.

When he was finished, I stopped him and gave him the look I learned from old Dark. "Boy, you been about this much help, so far," I told him, flipping a U.S. dime on the table. "You get your head on straight real soon, and we'll see about something better, okay?" I took a new eight hundred dollar bill out of my pack and laid it by the dime. He hated himself, but he wanted it, and he took himself out of there quick.

Jennie was eating needles. "That insufferable *bas*tard!"

"Hey, he's just got the sorries, like most everyone else," I told her. "Sorry he's standin' instead of sitting; probably hates every one of these folks and has reason to. We sure goin' to get us some service, though."

"You are not a nice person, Marcus Ash."

"Never get time for it."

She tried a little wine and gave me a crooked grin. "Okay. That cute trick with the languages. Where'd you get time for that?"

I filled up her glass again, and mine. "We got soldiers out there from most everywhere, Jennie. We're all supposed to speak standard Armycom in the field, and we do if there isn't much hurry. You put a man under fire, though, where you got about an eighth of a second to figure which way to duck, your buddy's goin' to say *'watch it, Ash!'* in whatever tongue he was born with. When he does, I don't want to take no time sayin' 'huh?' just because he's Portuguese or Welsh. Besides, there isn't much else to do out there if you're not fighting, 'cept talk. So you learn to do it with whoever's in the same hole. Maybe that's worth a war, I don't know. Maybe when it's over we'll all go back to being just like we were."

The salad came, bright green with some kind of fruit on top I'd never seen before, and a thick white sauce with little specks in it. Whatever it was, I'd ordered it during my big show-off scene, and if I didn't like it, that son of a bitch would sure never know it.

Halfway through the next course I caught Jennie with fork in midair, watching my tag-along. It wasn't the first time. She hadn't got on that yet, but she was thinking about it. Willie was a couple of tables away with a plain glass of water—untouched—trying hard not to look like he was looking.

"Poor guy," she said, shaking her head, "he doesn't have much fun, does he?"

I gave her a real hurt face. "Hey, *I'm* the hero, remember? He isn't supposed to have fun."

"Oh, golly, listen I forgot myself." We both laughed, but she was still thinking. "Does it—bother you any?"

"No. Way it's got to be unless I want to sit around Heroes' Hotel all day." I read her question. "Officially it's RIFETS—Research Institute for Extraterrestrial Studies. Someone dubbed it Heroes' Hotel 'cause it's homebase for troopers with peculiar conditions like mine."

"He goes with you, because something might happen to you." It wasn't a question. There was worry in the tight little corners of her mouth. It kind of did something to me to see it there.

"Hey, you know about the tag-along," I told her. "Something *could* happen, but it's not likely. The wispies I'm draggin' around don't bother you any unless you're sleeping, passed out drunk or otherwise unconscious. I sure as hell don't go to *sleep* on purpose, and we've learned not to booze it up too much. Most of the time. The tag-along's with us for that slim chance you might fall on your head, have a stroke—whatever. He's got all kinds of goodies in that little red box, and he can jolt me full of wake-up real quick if he has to."

I picked up my glass, and she started to say something; then I caught him over the rim, bearing in on us from across the room. Big belly and three or four stars on his tabs—a couple of little ground-hog ribbons on his chest for peeing straight. Whatever he'd been pouring down was working just fine. He was having trouble with his feet and trying to make up for it by walking real slow and serious.

Jennie caught my eyes going small and didn't know why. I stood up slower'n you're supposed to, and he wheeled on over and shot me a big grin.

"Listen, you *sit,* Sergeant." He winked down at Jennie, going over her good and taking his time. "I'm the one ought to be standing, Rafe Hacker." A wet hand came out. "I know who you are, Sergeant Ash. Hey, sit. I mean it."

He had it all figured and so did I. If Ash sits, he sits too, and there we go. He plants himself down awhile, then goes back and tells his buddies he talked to a real one. Maybe he picks up the girl's name in the bargain. Only the whole business wasn't going right, and he was beginning to figure out why. If we kept standing, everybody guesses the general's pullin' rank on the hero sergeant. If he sits—and I don't—it looks a lot worse than that.

"Sergeant, I'd be pleased if you'd let me buy you and the lady a drink." His little eyes are right on me and he knows.

"Thank you, sir. Maybe we could take a raincheck on that."

"Maybe the lady—"

"No, sir. She wouldn't."

The eyes don't move but the grin gets real tight. "Sergeant, I've got a lot of respect for you wormheads, but—"

"Sir. That isn't one of your words. You got no right to it."

His face went slack. "You are out of *line,* Sergeant."

"No, sir. You are. That's our word. We can use it, you can't. Go out and make your kill and get your gray ribbon, and it's yours. Until then, you don't own it. You want my number, sir, it's 775041113.

The red was starting up over his best ugly smile. He was thinking about what ought to happen next and how he ought to bring me up on charges and all, but he wasn't dumb enough to do it. Instead, he showed me the little pig eyes again and hauled himself out of there.

Jennie was trying to crawl under a napkin. "Hey, listen, you're more fun than anyone. Who we gonna kill next?"

"Sorry. I got this thing about ground-hog brass."

"No, really?"

"Okay, let me go. Peace."

"Oh, sure. St. Marcus of Ash."

We laughed together and caught each other just right for a quick second and held it there, then let it go. It'd be there when we came looking for it.

Outside we got us a brand-new high, breathing in all the good night air. It was one of those times anybody watching figures there's another couple of happy drunks running loose—but you see it different from the inside 'cause you've got something circling in around you keeping all the fine stuff going. We were smarter than anybody and saw things nobody'd ever seen before. And of course *every*thing was funny.

We both knew what was coming, that we were about a breath away from bein' there. We held it all back in the skimmer because we knew we couldn't handle it and didn't want to.

"Hey, Marcus Ash."

"Uhuh."

"Got to know. Okay?"

"Got to know what?"

"Dinner. How much that huge goddamn dinner cost. 'Bout a zillion dollars?"

"None of your business."

"Come *on.*"

"All right. Nine hundred somethin'."

"*Dollars?*"

"Well, hell, yes."

"My God. And an *eight* hundred dollar tip. Who's going to believe me? What'd you do this weekend, Jennie? Oh, nothing. Picked me up a war hero and we had us a couple of drinks and 'bout nine hundred dollars' worth of snacks—"

"Hey, now. I didn't say I left that groundie no eight hundred dollars."

"Didn't you?"

"No."

"How much?"

"Half that."

"Four hundred?"

"Hell, no."

"What?"

"*Half* that."

"Listen, you..."

"Goddamn, Jennie, I said half, I meant half." Scrubbing around in my pouch, I found it and gave it to her. She blinked at it a long time, then threw back her head and howled until the tears came.

"Marcus, what's that—*poor* man going to do with half an eight hundred dollar bill? Oh, no!"

We looked at each other and got the funnies goin' and couldn't get 'em stopped. When everything settled down a little, I told her I had something real wonderful for her and gave her the silver spoon I'd stolen from The Chalice. "Don't look like I learned nothing since high school, does it?"

When she looked up at me her hair was making yellow smoke around her head and there were tiny bright points in her eyes. "Hey." She poked one finger at my chin. "I can't make any words, Marcus."

"Maybe it isn't a talkin' kind of time."

"Yeah. Maybe it isn't."

She slid in close all lazy warm and smelling like girl and said something, and I said *what?* and she said whatever it was again and grinned in closer. Past her I could see the city, and it seemed to stretch on forever, like worlds fadin' out to the Rim until there wasn't any place else to go. If I thought about it just right, all the lights turned into stars, and I was out there again, where I didn't ever want to be. This time the whole string ran out, and the billion-to-three odds clicked back to zero. The meanies holed me up in some stink-warren and ripped me good. Snap-claws clipped me down like paper, and all the little razor feet came hummin' in to peel the wrapper…

"Hey, you're off somewhere."

"Right here."

"What you thinking?"

"I was just kind of wondering what those little stringy things was in 'bout the umpty-third course—you know? Right after the duck with sugar peaches…?"

Jennie made a face. "You weren't either."

"Sure I was. What you figure I was thinking about. You?"

"Well, maybe."

"Huh."

"You were thinking about me a minute ago."

"That wasn't thinking."

"Oh? What was that?"

"Doing, mostly."

"Yeah. Was, wasn't it?" She gave another one of those sounds and turned over and propped her chin in her hands, and I leaned back to enjoy the view. We didn't say anything, and she kind of stared out the window and thought about something and then looked back at me again. "What are you going to do, Marcus?"

"About what?"

"You."

She said *you,* but she was thinking you and maybe me.

"What I'm doing now," I told her. "It's a little late to start learning a new trade."

Her head came up. "You mean the army? God, Marcus, you don't have to go out *there* again? They wouldn't send you *back?"*

"Not fighting, no. There's other things."

"You want to do that."

"It's that, or go back to stealin' spoons."

"I'm serious, Marcus." She reached out and touched the little chained medallion on my chest, holding it and turning it in two fingers.

"Sure," I said, "I am, too. The army's not a bad place for a guy like me. It's somewhere I can do some good. If the war keeps on, and I reckon it will, there's going to be plenty of use for a man who's made it through more years than he ought to. When—hey, you listening to me?"

"What? Yes. No, I'm sorry. Marcus, what's this?"

I winked at her and took the medallion from her fingers. "This, is somethin' real important. What it does is let you and me do what we're doing in here without Captain Willie Brander sitting right there on the corner of the bed."

She looked at me without expression, and then it suddenly dawned on her what I was talking about. I laughed and swiped at her hair. "Honey, it doesn't do *pictures*—just stuff like pulse, respiration, BP. Comes through on the little red box."

"Well, if he's any good," she said coolly, "he sure as hell knows what *you're* doing. If I'd known that, I would have made you take the thing off. It's like—peeking."

"No, you wouldn't," I told her. "If I did, old Willie'd come right through that wall, and there wouldn't be no question about *peeking*."

She sat up and stared at me.

"Well, sure. What did you think?"

"My God, I don't know." She shook her head, troubled. "Marcus, you must think I'm an idiot. We talked about this, and here I am asking a bunch of dumb questions again. It's—" She shrugged helplessly. "Yeah, I do know, too. I forget all that when we're—like this."

So do I...

"It doesn't seem important. It's outside somewhere and not in here, and it doesn't have anything to do with us. Oh, damn, Marcus, it *doesn't!*" A little sound stuck in her throat; she came to me quick and held me, and the tears were hot on my chest. "Don't you see? I just want you to *be* here, I want to wake up with you, and I don't—"

She felt what it did to me because she pulled back fast and kind of stared at her hands, like I'd gone all hot and burned her. I grabbed her shoulders hard. "Goddamn. You don't know what you're talking about." I was hurting her bad, but I didn't let go.

"Even if it was bad, I wouldn't care." She just kept shaking her head, not even feeling anything. "If you woke up *screaming,* I'd be there. I'd—"

"Shit." I was already out of bed looking for my stuff in the dark. I could hear her trying to make little noises and feel her movin' all soft-naked behind me, and I shut that out and didn't feel anything.

"Marcus, please!"

I can't hear you any more...

"God, what did I *do?* I want you to *stay* here is all, I don't *care!*" She reached out and found me, and I came around fast and slapped her hard. She made a little cry and fell back. I didn't look at her anywhere else. Just the eyes. There wasn't anything there yet. Only fright and tears and hurt.

"Look," I told her, "you got your belly full of food and some of me under that. You lookin' for more, girl, don't. There ain't nothing you got I can't get somewhere else. You *read* me?"

She didn't want to hear it. She was going to shut it all out and say it wasn't real. So I just stood there a minute, taking my eyes down her slow, leaving dirty where I passed. Then I waited until I could see it happening to her. Like real good glass, coming all apart.

When they snugged me in good and made all the little wires just right, I kept seein' her, only I couldn't much look at her now because all the bad hurt kept looking right back. Jennie, Jennie, I had to kill the tomorrows, or we'd wind up trying to live 'em, and that can't ever be. We *can't* tell folks what it's like inside. We got to say its wispies and nightmare shadows in our heads. There's kids out there with dyin' on their minds, and not much more. They going to *fight* any better, knowing the red screaming baddies in my head are just as real as real can be?

Shall I stay the night and hold you, then, Jennie? I can rest on your pillow with the smell of your hair and the soft-soft sound of your breath – and you can pray good Willie Brander drops me quick when they come and find me sleeping….

Jennie, Jennie, do you see? Old Dark is right, and a wormhead can't be what you want him to. He can drink with all the other fine heroes and think where he'd like to be. But more than that's a bad and hurtful thing…

The Flying Stutzman

Angela always told him at the door, "Lew, you look like a dead person. You didn't sleep on the plane?" And he always said, "No I didn't sleep on the plane, I *can't* sleep on the plane, Angela." Angela wanted to know why and Stutzman didn't know. Ten years on the road, eleven in September, could he remember even a minute sleeping on the plane? "You should try, Lew," she told him. "You should try and get some sleep. You look like a dead person." I *feel* like a dead person, he wanted to tell her.

Stutzman squinted out the little round window. Flat banks of perfectly white clouds covered the earth. He liked to look at clouds. You could look at a cloud all day and not think about anything. Once when he got home he told Angela, "Nobody ever hurt his head, looking at a cloud."

It was maybe the one good thing about flying. The rest was a nothing. And he could give up the clouds, easy. You like clouds, get a picture and put it in the den and look at clouds. An airplane you don't need to see a cloud.

The fat lady in the next seat ate oranges. She had a whole sack of oranges in a little net bag like you get in the store. She would peel an orange and drop the peelings in the pocket on the back of the seat, which was already stuffed to the top. A nice surprise, thought Stutzman, for Miss Stuck-Up the stewardess, who had time, all right, to twitch her ass for Mr. Joe College in the back but no time to get coffee for Stutzman. Fine. She should get a handful of oranges.

Stutzman closed his eyes and thought about being home. He thought quickly past the baggage-limo-taxi part and on to Angela. She would meet him at the door. Maybe she'd wear the evening pajamas he liked, the Halston number, which was a hand-painted three-piece, yellow petals on a silk chiffon and ran about nine-hundred fifty bucks retail. She'd be fresh from the beauty shop with black curls around her face and a little green eyeshadow. A good wife, and a good-looking woman still, thought Stutzman. His family had shaken their heads and told him you marry a girl with Italian blood, she'll go to fat, Lew. But Angela could stand up to any of them. So a little padding around the thighs and tummy, now. What was a fifty-two-year-old woman supposed to look like, a Las Vegas cutie? A chorus girl with pink feathers on her tits, she's going to stay home and fix supper for Stutzman? She could still get in a 12, which was more than you could say for Miss Stuck-Up.

She'd have a little drink ready and then a meal he'd be too tired to eat, but he'd take a few bites to please her. And then they'd go to bed and watch *The Tonight Show* and maybe something nice would happen. Or maybe it wouldn't. Sometimes the miles caught up with him the first night back.

He could never tell Angela, because she wouldn't understand. The best part of getting home wasn't Angela. It was just *getting* there. Peeling off your clothes and dropping in the hot tub and washing off the trip. How could you get so dirty, just flying? You're not looking, they got people sneak around and put soot in your clothes? He'd tried to tell her once about that: "Look, you pack and get out to the airport and get on the plane, okay? Take a shower and a shave and you got your clothes all clean and packed and you get on the plane. So it goes down the runway and they decide to come back, maybe. A wheel's bad or something.You go six blocks on the runway and they come back and you get off and go home. Everything you got on, it's dirty. You need a shave, you smell like an animal in the zoo. Everything in the bag, you didn't even wear it, that's dirty too. Why? I don't know why. Maybe they got girls in a room somewhere, they put dirt in the ticket."

There was that, thought Stutzman, and the pockets. Start out with a wallet and a pencil and take a one-day and back, you got pockets that look like goiters. A millions dollars in nickels hanging to your knees, you bought cigarettes and a Snickers. You got maybe a hundred matches from everywhere. A one-day from Dallas to Houston, you see a customer and come home, you got enough matches and change to fill a truck.

The plane banked and fell into clouds and Miss Stuck-Up said she was glad they'd all gotten to fly together and maybe they could do it again sometime. You should get a pocket full of peelings, thought Stutzman.

People cluttered about the end of the carpeted tunnel, but Stutzman didn't look up. Nobody was waiting for him, and he moved quickly past them to baggage. He didn't look up even when he heard his name. Then he did look up, and there was Bernie Freed. Stutzman frowned at him like he'd never seen him before. "Bernie. What are you doing at the airport?"

Bernie laughed and pumped his hand. "The airport is where the planes come in. What I'm doing is waiting for Stutzman."

"What for?" A terrible thought crossed his mind. "Angela. Something's happened to Angela."

"Nothing has happened to Angela," Bernie assured him. They were making an island in the stream of traffic, and Bernie moved them to a wall.

"*Some*thing has happened," said Stutzman. "Don't tell me nothing has happened." Thirty years, he could read Bernie Freed.

"Okay. So something's happened." Bernie looked up at him. He had to look up to see Stutzman. Stutzman wasn't tall but Bernie was short. A short, jumpy little terrier in a blue blazer, houndstooth pants and white turtleneck. The pencil-thin mustache twitched under water-blue eyes.

"I gotta ask a favor, Lew. Christ, you're gonna hate me. But I gotta ask."

"What?" Stutzman said warily. "You gotta ask what?"

"It's a trip."

"A trip? What kind of a trip? You mean like flying? When?" He already knew when, because Bernie hadn't *said* when.

Bernie didn't answer. He slid back his cuff and darted a glance at his gold Piguet. "Look, we're shorta time. We better move while we talk." He grabbed Stutzman's elbow and guided him toward the escalator. He was looking at everything in the airport. He wasn't looking at Stutzman.

"Bernie. You're not looking at me. Just tell me what it is, okay? And look at me. Where are we going? I got bags back there."

"Lew, the bags are okay."

"How are they okay? Tell me. I'm not there and the bags are okay."

Bernie led him down the escalator into the hot air and through a glass door under the terminal. It was a small, concrete room where you could catch the boxy little Air-trans cars from one airline to another, when the system was working.

It wasn't getting any better and Stutzman didn't like it. "Bernie. Stop a minute. Just stop and talk to me."

Bernie looked at his watch again. Glass doors slid open and one of the cars clacked to a stop. Bernie pushed Stutzman in and the doors hissed together.

"*Bernie*—"

Bernie's mustache twitched. "Lew, it's Neuman."

Stutzman looked blank. "Neuman? So what about Neuman?"

"He's gone crazy or something." Bernie spread his hands in despair. "I don't know him anymore. Twenty years, I don't even *know* him. What happens to people?"

"I don't know what happens to people," Stutzman said patiently. "What's happened to Neuman?"

Bernie's eyes went hard. "He is killing me, is what. He's losing the line everywhere, and it'll take a hundred years to get it back. A hundred? A hundred fifty is closer. Neuman is fucking everything on the east coast. Models, buyers, secretaries—goddamn *poodles* he's fucking. Mostly, he is fucking me. Can you believe? He tries to screw the Saks buyer. Right in her own office. They can't get him *out* of there, he's crying." Bernie looked at the ceiling. "Crying. Can you believe it? Everybody's canceling. I call New York and nobody'll talk to me. Bloomingdale's doesn't know me. Bergdorf is maybe burning our line in the street."

"Neuman is fifty-seven," said Stutzman. "He's got a family."

Bernie glared at him. "He's a hundred and two, what's that? He's killing me!"

The car bobbed to a halt and Bernie stopped talking. A girl got on. She was young, twenty or so, with long straight hair faded yellow in the sun. Small breasts and a lanky figure. Patched jeans and something Stutzman decided were shower clogs. She dropped a green backpack on the floor and took out a paperback and started reading. Stutzman saw the name on the front and made a face. Herman Hesse. Great. Now we got Nazi hippies flying around the country.

"What I got to do," Bernie was telling him, "is straighten this thing out or we're dead. You see where I am, right? I *hate* to do it to you, Lew. Honest to God. I know you been gone a couple weeks. I been on the road, I know how it is."

"Three."

"What?"

"Three weeks. I been gone three weeks. And why me, anyway, Bernie? I'm a salesman. Send a vice-president or something. Send Marvin or Harry." Go yourself, he didn't say.

"Lew." Bernie looked pained. "Marvin and Harry don't know from selling. I got to send someone they'll respect. They know you. You got a name in the business."

Stutzman turned in his seat and looked right at him. "Bernie, where are we? Right now. Just tell me where we are right now."

Bernie looked bewildered. "Lew. You know where we are."

"No, I mean it. What city? Where is this, Bernie? I want you to tell me."

"Lew. It's Dallas. You know where it is. What're you trying to do to me?"

"Dallas." Stutzman nodded. "Okay, I am very pleased to hear that. It's a big load off my mind. Because you know what, Bernie? Sometimes I been out a week maybe and I'm sitting in a motel somewhere, I got to stop and try to figure where I am. I think maybe—okay, this is Atlanta, because it's Wednesday. Only maybe it's not. Maybe I got behind a day and it's Raleigh or Nashville or Charlotte or somewhere. If I watch the TV, I can wait until a program's over and maybe they'll give the town, you know? So I get home once in a while, and you know what? Nothing looks right. It doesn't even smell like a Holiday Inn or a Ramada or anyplace I ever been. I look in the bathroom and I think, what kind of place is this? The glasses aren't wrapped. They don't even have a little paper thing over the pot—which is wrong anyway because the seat's white instead of black. I go around feeling pictures. They aren't screwed in the walls. Nothing's right. And you know why?

I'm *home* is why, and I feel like I broke in a house or something."

The girl looked up over her book at him. Stutzman came right out of his seat and shook a finger in her face. "Just get right back in your dirty book, Miss Dope Smoker," he shouted. "This doesn't concern you!" The girl shrugged and looked away.

"Jesus, Lew." Bernie shook his head. The car came to a stop and he led Stutzman out. "I never heard you talk like this before."

"Maybe I never did before."

"I feel like a son of a bitch."

"Good," said Stutzman, "that's something." At the top of the escalator he stopped. "So where am I going, Bernie? What am I supposed to do? You got the bags coming? Great. I'm leaving town, I got two bags full of dirty shirts and smelly underwear."

"Forget it." Bernie waved him off. He handed over a heavy envelope. "I got all the stuff here. Names, you know most of them. Tell 'em everything's gonna be fine; we're sorry about Neuman, the lousy bastard; we'll give them discounts on top of discounts, whatever. Throw away your goddamn clothes. Get a whole fucking wardrobe. I don't care. *Fix* it, Lew. Okay? I'll never forget it."

"Okay, Bernie."

"No, I mean it." He clutched Stutzman's elbow. "I'll make up for it."

"I got to call Angela. I don't know what the hell I'll tell her, but I got to say something."

He got an angry busy signal and waited a minute and called again. She was still on the phone. He waited and called again, then glumly set the phone back on its hook. He looked at his ticket to see where he was going. New York. On Braniff. Bernie was hopping around from one foot to the other by the gate, like he needed to pee. Stutzman stared morosely out the broad windows. Planes in Braniff's varied colors squatted around the big half loop. Wonderful. So I'll ride a yellow banana to New York. Or maybe an apple or a lettuce. He looked past the planes at the hot summer sky. "Listen, God," he said darkly, "I never said a bad thing about You anytime—so what's the big deal on Stutzman? I don't *need* this trip, and You know it. What I need is a hot bath and a bed. You could make him get someone else easy if You wanted to. You could do it now, I'm still at the airport."

Stutzman waited. Nothing happened.

"Okay. You're pissed off at Stutzman, I'm telling You something. You like it nor not, Stutzman is plenty pissed off at You..."

On the flight he took his attaché case into the cramped restroom and shaved and brushed his teeth and took his shirt off enough to spray under his arms. That didn't make the shirt clean or the underwear either. He had an extra pair of socks in the case but no underwear. He sat on the toilet and changed the socks. The old ones smelled awful. He hated to put them back in the case. He thought about it a minute and then did something he'd never done before. He wadded them up and tossed them in with the paper towels. That made him feel a lot better. Bernie Freed could spring for new socks. Bernie could spring for new everything. He would go to a place he knew in New York and buy wholesale and charge Bernie the retail price and maybe a little on top. Let him scream about it if he wanted to. He didn't like it, he could send one of his nephew vice-presidents to do his dirty work. That'd serve him right, too. He could see Marvin and Harry in Saks and Lord & Taylor and Jordan Marsh. Bernie'd be lucky if he didn't lose the whole east coast.

The more he thought about it, the madder he got. What the hell was he doing here? On another damn airplane to New York? He was a salesman and a good one. This year he'd pull in maybe sixty-five, seventy thousand in commissions. It wasn't his job to clean up after Bernie Freed. So if it wasn't, what was he doing here?

Someone knocked on the door. He muttered to himself and tossed his toothbrush and toothpaste back in the attaché and snapped it shut and opened the door. It was the hippie girl in the jeans. "Listen, you smoke up the place with heroin in there, I'll have you arrested," he told her.

"Fuck you," said the girl.

Stutzman spend two days in New York, mending the company's fences. Bernie hadn't exaggerated about Neuman. Neuman had clearly gone bananas. He had run up and down the eastern seaboard with his pants down. People in the business stopped him on the street. What's with Neuman, they wanted to know? What could happen to such a man, Stutzman wondered? A man with a family and responsibilities? One minute he's okay, the next he's acting like a crazy. He felt sorry for Neuman and his family. But he felt even sorrier for himself. He was unhappy about being in New York, and to make matters worse, he caught a cold the first day in the city. No—when he stepped off the *plane* he got a cold. It was waiting for him there, ready to hop off someone else into his nose. And when he left for Philadelphia, he took the cold with him. He took it to Baltimore and Washington. He took it to Hartford and Boston. When he talked to Angela she said he should get more sleep on the plane and keep his health up. In Richmond he thought about calling Bernie and telling him he could send someone else up to catch diseases. Who needed a trip to catch a cold? You could do it at home and save the money. Only Bernie would think it was a trick of some kind. He would be certain Stutzman had gotten the cold on purpose. Like you could go into Gimbel's maybe and buy a cold.

When he was on the road, Stutzman never counted days or cities. Through years of traveling he had developed the ability to ignore the little counter in his head that kept track of things like that. It was there but he wouldn't look at it. Not until the last day in the last city. Then he would open his black appointment book and take out his pen and mark through all the cities and stores and dates at once. Somehow, that made it easier. Like the trip had only taken that long. Just the time it took to scratch them out.

On the last day in Miami he called Angela and told her he was coming, and then he sat on the edge of his bed at the motel and took out his book and crossed off the list. He crossed off New York and Philadelphia and Baltimore and Washington. He crossed off Hartford and Boston and Richmond. Charlotte and Roanoke and Miami. He crossed off American and Piedmont and Eastern. He closed the book and put it away. Then he took it out and looked at it again.

Now that's peculiar, he thought. In his head he quickly checked the places he'd been and the people he'd seen. Then he did it again and put the book down on the bed and got up and looked at himself in the mirror.

Something was wrong somewhere. For the life of him, he couldn't remember being in either Roanoke or Boston. All the others fell into place, but those two were a blank. He couldn't remember a store or a face. He sat and tried for a long time, but nothing happened. Finally, he turned back to his meeting notes and found them, along with where they'd gone to lunch and how much the taxis cost and where he spent the night. Seeing the notes pushed everything back in place again. But he couldn't forget it had *happened.* Was he a crazy, like Neuman? Maybe that's how it started. You forget where you've been, next minute you're chasing a poodle.

What it was was the goddamn trip, he told himself wearily. One right on top of the other with nothing in between.

You couldn't push a man forever. He had to stop, sometime. Well, Lew Stutzman sure as hell had a stop coming, and Bernie Freed and all his nephews wouldn't get him on the road again soon. He'd take the phone out and lock Angela in the bedroom. Maybe they'd do some things you weren't supposed to if you were over fifty and a respectable person. Why not? If hippies could do any kind of dirty stuff they wanted right out in front of everyone, couldn't a man be a crazy in his own bedroom?

Usually Stutzman stayed in his seat when he couldn't get a nonstop and the plane set down somewhere. In Atlanta, though, they were going to be on the ground for maybe half an hour while something got fixed—he didn't know what, and Miss Smartmouth the stewardess wasn't saying.

He was tired and stiff. If he got up, the time would pass. He took his attaché with him. The girls weren't supposed to touch anything, but who could know what they did when you weren't looking?

By the time he walked up the long tunnel and got cigarettes and a *Newsweek* it was time to get back. He showed his ticket at the gate and strapped himself in and buried his head in the *Newsweek.* There was a story on the economy, which was bad. Such a big surprise, thought Stutzman. Everything was still in turmoil in the Middle East, God should curse the Arabs, and food was up again. He closed the magazine and stuffed it in the seat pocket and glanced out the window. The ground was dropping away and the light was off. He reached for a cigarette and found orange and blue Howard Johnson's matches in his pocket and opened the ashtray and lit a match. He looked at the match a minute and then blew it out. Now *that* was funny. He hadn't noticed it before, but the seat in front of him was the wrong color. It wasn't the way it *had* been before he got off the plane. How could that be? Maybe he was in the wrong seat. He looked up and across the aisle. That wasn't it, either. *All* the seats were the wrong color. Stutzman leaned out and peered up the long aisle. His heart jumped up in his throat. It wasn't even the same kind of stewardess—the uniforms were different!

Stutzman moaned. He felt suddenly weak all over. For Christ's sake, he was on the *wrong* airplane! He'd gotten off and gotten on again on the wrong goddamn plane!

He felt like a complete idiot. How could you *do* a thing like that? He waved frantically until the girl saw him and came briskly down the aisle.

"Yes, sir?"

"Look," Stutzman cleared his throat, "I'm not a crazy or anything, so don't think something. This isn't a Delta, is it? I'm not on an airplane with a Delta."

The girl smiled. "This is Southern, sir. To St. Louis."

"St. *Louis!"* Stutzman was furious . "I'm not flying a Southern—I'm flying a Delta to Dallas!"

The smile didn't change. "May I see your ticket, sir?"

Stutzman fumbled through his coat, cursing to himself, and handed it to her. She looked at it, and then held it up and showed it to Stutzman. Stutzman was appalled. It didn't say Delta on the folder. It said Southern. She opened it up and took out the ticket.

"You're Mister—" she looked down, "—Stutzman?"

"I'm Stutzman, I'm Stutzman."

She closed the packet and handed it back to him. "Your ticket's in order, Mr. Stutzman."

"What do you mean in order!" shouted Stutzman.

"You *are* on the right plane, sir." She opened it up and showed it to him. "Atlanta. Southern to St. Louis."

Stutzman stared at the ticket. Was he going crazy? There was his name. Lew Stutzman. To St. Louis. There wasn't anything about Dallas.

"There's a mistake. I'm not going to St. Louis. I got nothing to do in St. Louis."

"Sir, could you see our agent in St. Louis? I'm sure he can clear things up for you. I'm terribly sorry for the inconvenience." She gave him a look he didn't like and trotted back up the aisle.

Stutzman leaned back and tried to relax. How could such a thing happen? What had they done, switched tickets on him? When, though? The ticket was fine in Miami. Atlanta, then. When he got off the plane. Maybe he took the ticket out somewhere. When he got the *Newsweek* and the cigarettes. He tried to think. Maybe there was another Stutzman. Was the other Stutzman on his way back to Dallas? That didn't make any sense at all. The whole thing gave him a headache.

He lit a cigarette and tried to read the *Newsweek.* After he'd scanned the same paragraph half a dozen times, he wadded up the magazine and jammed it angrily into the seat pocket. Goddamn airlines. He was dead certain, now, what had made Neuman a crazy...

In St. Louis the man at Southern said he was sorry for whatever it was that had happened and directed him to Ozark. He got an Ozark to Dallas and waited for flight time and got in line at the gate. He wanted to phone Angela and tell her what had happened, but he decided not to. Just get there. Just get on the goddamn plane and get home.

The man in front of him moved away, and Stutzman got out his ticket for the agent. The agent took it. Stutzman grabbed it back. The sign above the counter didn't say Ozark. It said TWA. What was he doing at TWA!

"Your ticket, sir?"

"No." Stutzman shook his head. "I'm in the wrong place." What was the *matter* with him? Was he really losing his mind—trying to get on the wrong plane *again?*

The agent took his ticket and smiled. "No, sir. Everything's fine." He tore out a page and picked up a boarding pass. "Smoking or no smoking?"

"Smoking," Stutzman said dully. He looked at the agent in horror. What was he saying that for? He wasn't even *going* on TWA! He jerked back the ticket and stepped out of line, peering down the long corridor for Ozark. There wasn't a sign anywhere. He'd have to go back to the terminal and work his way back and maybe miss the flight. Shit. He'd be stuck forever in St. Louis.

Stutzman put his ticket in his pocket and started back up the corridor. Only he didn't. He started back in his head, but nothing happened. He was thinking all the things you were supposed to think to get moving, but he didn't. He wanted to go. But he couldn't. Nothing worked. All he could do was stand there and look where he wanted to go.

Stutzman had never been so frightened in his life. His heart slammed painfully against his chest. He was hot all over. He could smell the sweat under his arms. I'm dying, he decided. God in Heaven, I'm having a coronary. I'm having a coronary right here in the terminal in St. Louis, and I don't even *know* anyone in St. Louis.

How could he do that, he wondered. Who ever had a coronary standing up? You fell on the floor and turned blue, maybe. You didn't freeze like a pillar of salt in an airport!

He tried to move again—and gave a big sigh of relief. Whatever it was went away, and he was all right again. His feet were moving like feet were supposed to. He was going.

—Only *where* was he going? He stared down helplessly, his heart beating fast again, as his traitorous legs turned him around and walked him past the counter and through the waiting room and onto the TWA that wasn't going to Dallas.

Stutzman sat rigid in his seat, afraid to move. He looked down at the dark landscape and back at his ticket. How could it say that? It should read Stutzman to Dallas on Ozark,—not

Stutzman to Denver on TWA. Why was he going to Denver? What was happening to him? What had they *done* to him!

When they put the tray of food in his lap, he sat and looked at it until the girl took it away. When it was gone, he couldn't even remember what had been on it.

Stutzman knew he had to stay calm. Whatever it was, it was something he could handle. If he was having a breakdown, he'd see someone. There was no disgrace in it. You could get a problem in your head, without being a crazy.

The more he thought about it, though, the more it frightened him. He wanted a drink badly but settled for coffee. Right now, he couldn't afford to screw up his head any more than it was already.

At Denver he ran all the way down the terminal. He was out of breath and sweating all over. He tried to light a cigarette but his hands were shaking and he dropped the match. Okay, he told himself. Just calm down and take it easy, Stutzman. Just do it right this time and get home and get to bed. There were Braniff flights to Dallas every hour. He got a ticket and studied it carefully. It was fine. It was exactly like it was supposed to be. It didn't say Stutzman to somewhere he didn't want to go. It said Stutzman on Braniff to Dallas. He walked back out to the planes, making sure it said Braniff where he turned. There was no line, and they took one of his tickets and gave him a boarding pass, and he got in his seat and strapped himself in. The plane lumbered out to taxi, and he could see the lights blinking on the wing and hear the engine whining up the scale for takeoff. The plane howled down the runway, and the ground blurred away in streaks of light, and they were in the air. He lit a cigarette and looked at his ticket. It was a TWA again and it said Stutzman to San Francisco.

There was blinding sunshine on a blue ocean. Wind whipped the waves frothy white and tossed them angrily against a rocky coast. The plane banked sharply and skimmed in for a landing, tires squealing rubber on the hot runway. Stutzman stared wearily out the window. His head felt like a fuzzball. His legs ached and his body was a sack of rocks. Where was he? On the TWA? In San Francisco, or where? No. He remembered, now. He was off the TWA. The TWA was—what, yesterday? The day before? He wasn't sure which.

The plane taxied up to the terminal, and he saw the other planes sitting there. Fat and round, gleaming in the sun. The terminal said Pacific Southwest and the planes were all painted pink and red and white. They said PSA and there were little smiles painted across their noses.

It came back to him a little at a time. San Francisco and Los Angeles and Hollywood/Burbank and San Diego and wherever. Up and down the coast. Hopping about like rabbits from one city to the other. And how long had that been? It was hard to think. Things happened—but it wasn't easy to say when. Like the watch in his head had stopped running. The whole thing was a terrible nightmare. It wasn't happening. Why were they *doing* this to him?

On the TWA from Denver, Stutzman had tried to talk to people. That had been the most frightening thing of all. It wasn't as if nobody would answer. They just didn't *hear* him right. He told the stewardess he had to get off. She brought him coffee. He pleaded with her. She brought him peanuts. He told a respectable-looking business man he was on the wrong plane and he had to get to Dallas and would he do something to help. "Fine, and you?" said the man.

What was Angela thinking, he wondered. She'd be worried sick. Would she try to do something? They could trace the tickets, maybe. Track him down and find him and make whoever was doing this terrible thing let him go.

He looked down morosely at his suit. It was crumpled and saggy and wrinkled all over. It pulled up tight around his crotch, and his bottom was numb from sitting. He felt like a fat brown lettuce. His face was covered with a scraggly stubble. He smelled and his feet itched. He reached down under his socks and scratched. He could clean up, anyway, and maybe feel better. He still had the attaché with the toothbrush and the razor. He could, he thought angrily, if everyone would just get out of the bathroom.

Stutzman didn't get a chance to clean up until he was on the Canadian Pacific from San Francisco. He brushed his teeth and shaved and took off his clothes and washed all over as well as he could in the cramped little room. He looked at himself in the mirror. A gray, pudgy face with bloodshot eyes looked back at him. He wanted to cry. "Lew, you look like a dead person," Angela said in his head. "So maybe I am," he said back to her.

They landed at Vancouver and Calgary and Edmonton. They stopped at Winnipeg and Ottawa and Montreal. He took something to New York and went on to Chicago and got North Central to Madison and Green Bay and Milwaukee and La Crosse and Grand Rapids. He learned to eat whenever they'd serve him after he got stuck on short hops for two or three days where there was nothing but peanuts.

He took American to Tucson and Phoenix and Las Vegas and even back to Dallas once. That was almost more than he could take. He was right there—and all he could do was go wherever his legs would take him. Angela! Angela!

He went to Seattle and Portland and Anchorage and Fairbanks...

Des Moines and Detroit and Memphis and Wichita...

Nashville and Pittsburgh and Dayton and Kansas City...

He flew Frontier and Capital and Southwest and National...

Northwest and Continental and Eastern and United...

He flew airlines he'd neverd hear of before.

Even though Stutzman missed a meal now and then, he was putting on weight. He couldn't get his pants together anymore. His shirt wouldn't button. All he ever did was sit in the cramped economy seats and eat. There were sores on his thighs and buttocks, now. When he took his standup baths, he cleaned them off as best he could, but they burned worse than ever the minute he sat down again.

He used the toothpaste sparingly but it finally ran out. He started using salt he took from the meal trays. The deodorant was gone. There was still a good blade left, but he wouldn't let himself use it. He kept scratching away with the dull ones, tearing and scraping and making himself bleed. He stubbornly resisted the new blade. It was somehow a symbol of normalcy. Once the blade was gone, Stutzman was certain something terrible would happen.

Washing out the socks and underwear wasn't so bad, except he couldn't leave them out anywhere and they never got dry in the attaché. There was nothing to do about the shirt and the suit. They both smelled like a cat box, but after a while he didn't notice.

He ran out of cigarettes the second day and started robbing ashtrays. Since he always used credit cards and traveler's checks, he only had about twelve dollars cash. He spent it all on drinks, and when it was gone, he watched longingly as his fellow passengers downed bourbons and Scotches and vodkas and beers. Sometimes a passenger would leave the little toy bottles in a seat pocket, and he'd dig them out later and get maybe a drop or two. He was ashamed and embarrassed to do this, but he missed having a drink. It was something. There wasn't much else.

Sometimes on a long night flight, Stutzman sat and stared out the little window and wondered why it had all happened to him. Who was doing this terrible thing? What had *he* ever done to anyone? A family man and a responsible person who minds his own business. A taxpayer and a citizen. So who?

He had a good idea who. It almost had to be God. Who else could handle such a thing? It took a big organization and a lot of tricky business. Like making feet go where they shouldn't and messing around with people's tickets.

Stutzman didn't want to believe it was God. If it was God, he was in for it. You could deal with almost anybody better than Him. Bernie Freed who thinks he knows everything, okay. A Bernie Freed you can handle. A God, though, what're you going to do? A God is a lot cagier than a Bernie Freed.

"This is something we can talk about?" Stutzman asked the dark window. "Whatever it is, it's got to be something we can talk about. There's nothing people can't work out, they sit down and talk together. There's been a misunderstanding, we can do something."

Stutzman paused a moment, considering. He dug around in the ashtray and found a butt that was mostly filter.

"Look, no offense—" he said, "you don't mind me saying, there's plenty You could be doing besides fooling around with Stutzman. So who's Stutzman, a Hitler? Does Stutzman chase around after buyers and poodle dogs? Maybe You already know it, I'm not telling anything new. Bernie Freed cheats like a dog on his taxes. Also, he's got a *shiksa* girlfriend. The one sits in the corner in accounting? You can't miss her, she's got tits out to here."

It wasn't right, thought Stutzman. Bernie was back in Dallas with his home and his gold Piguet watch and his girlfriend with the tits, and Lew Stutzman was flying around like a crazy with no toothpaste. It didn't make sense. What had *he* done so terrible? God could be giving Arabs the clap or something. Why all the trouble with Stutzman?

It might be something that had happened a long time ago, he decided. Something he'd forgotten. That was the thing with God. He could hold a grudge forever. You could read about it in the *Torah*. One little thing. Pow!

"Listen, it's not the business with Mary Shuler's daughter, is it? That's forty years ago! You go back to that, it's only fair

You get Levitch and Greenwaldt, too. I took her out once, maybe twice. She was happy to go, that counts for something."

Other things came back to him when he started thinking. Little things. Okay, a couple of mediums. So who's perfect? The trouble with God was you couldn't tell. He was picky about some things and some things He wasn't.

"Sure," Stutzman said aloud once, "it's easy enough for You. *You* don't have to go out and sell in a bad season when nobody's buying. Try that sometime You got nothing to do!"

Stutzman looked at movies when there was one on the flight until he'd seen most of them twice. He read magazines until his eyes burned. He read *Time* and *Newsweek* and *Sports Illustrated* and the *Reader's Digest*. He read *People* and *Business Week* and *The National Geographic.* He even read things he couldn't stand like *Vogue* and *Ms.* and *Glamour*. There were two things he didn't read. He didn't read magazines that ran pictures of naked girls because it made him feel bad. After a while, he didn't read newspapers, either. Newspapers were terrible reminders of the passage of time. Tormenting calendars that scratched off the slow days of his long trip to nowhere. It was better not to know. He couldn't bear to think about it.

As it was, the days and nights seemed to blur and flow together like two heavy syrups, one never quite becoming the other...

Stutzman didn't imagine it could get any worse, until it did. He wasn't sure how long it was before he realized he wasn't on domestic flights anymore. There were long, endless journeys from New York to Paris...

From London to Los Angeles...

From Frankfurt to Capetown to Dar es Salaam...

From Karachi and Delhi to Osaka and Seattle....

There were strange butts in his ashtrays. Foods he didn't like and magazines he couldn't read and people he couldn't understand.

He flew Air France and Alaska and Alitalia...

El Al and Lufthansa and Varig...

Icelandic, Sabena and Finn-Air...

Mexicana, Garuda and Qantas.

"It was the sales meeting in Tahoe, maybe?" he asked God. "One weekend – You're going to make a big thing out of that?"

He couldn't eat. But he couldn't not eat, either. A deadly cycle began: dreary, constipated days followed by awesome watery nights. His stomach cried out against breakfast in Bangkok, lunch in Zagreb and dinner in Kinshasa. He threw up gazpacho, schnitzel and shad. Rumaki, sevich and rabat loukoum. He had cold chills and hot flashes. For a while, he was too weak to get from his seat to the john. The terrible bed-sores got worse. He itched all over. He didn't even bother about the underwear and the socks anymore. It was too much trouble and he didn't care. If he smelled, he smelled. They didn't like it, they could kick him off the plane.

"So what is it," he cried, "cheating Marty Engel at poker? Eight dollars, I got to fly forever for *that?"*

For some time, God hadn't even bothered with the wrong-ticket business. He got on, he got off. The feet knew where to go, if Stutzman didn't. Sometimes the man didn't look at his ticket. Sometimes he couldn't even remember changing planes. One flight flowed into another, like the days and the nights.

He quit trying to talk to people. Whatever he said, nobody listened. He had a secret horror that they couldn't even see him anymore. A smelly, invisible Stutzman. God could see him. But could anyone else? There was a way to find out. He could talk to someone. If he answered, he was there. He didn't even think about trying. If it was true, he didn't want to know.

The morning the sun came up over somewhere and burned into his eyes and clear through the back of his soul, and he knew why he'd saved the last good blade. There was no fear or sorrow in the knowledge. It was like the moment before lovemaking. The bouquet of a good wine. It was a beautiful and perfect thing. Stutzman didn't hesitate a minute. When it came to him, he was ready. Ready? He couldn't wait to get started.

In the tiny john he crouched on the toilet and took off his coat and rolled up his sleeve. Before he started, he let himself think a moment. About Angela. Only a moment. Any more and he knew he might not do it. It was the only thing that could stop him. She flickered into his consciousness, a little wallet picture, and then she was gone.

The blade was cold in his fingers. Like a melting sliver of ice. Sweat stung his eyes and he closed them hard and shut his mind and sliced quick and deep across his wrist. Stutzman went rigid with fear. The blade didn't hurt, but he felt the horror of its passage in his heart.

It had all happened so fast, the deed coming swiftly on the thought. He hadn't considered what might come after. In the back of his mind somewhere there was a vague projection of peace and darkness and clean boxer shorts. In the picture, there was nothing in between. In actuality, there was much more than that—a long interval of *living* he hadn't counted on. Stutzman was frightened. Death was one thing. Dying was something else again!

He was angry and disgusted. What was he supposed to do now? How would it feel? Would it hurt? Would he just get weaker until he passed out?

So far, it didn't feel like anything. Okay. So what's the matter with that?

He told himself he'd be all right. He could do it. Just sit still and let it happen. Just keep your eyes closed and *don't look.* He knew what it would look like and it was something he didn't want to see. Ever. Jesus—how long had he been *in* here? There'd be blood over everything. It would look awful.

He promised himself all he'd do was open his eyes a *little.* Just enough to let the gray in. Not any more than that. The best thing to do would be start high, and work down. That way, you could stop just before you got to something you didn't want to see. You'd see the edge of it first and you could quit.

He saw the top of the wall. The edge of the sink and part of the door. A piece of his leg. A little spot of white that was the end of a finger. Hold it. Damn, there ought to be something awful by now. Slow, slow. A little further but not much—

Stutzman opened his eyes all the way and stared. *Nothing!* Not even a scratch! How could that be? He picked up the blade and ran it carefully over his finger. Again, harder. Finally, he slashed his palm desperately a dozen times as hard as he could. A terrible cry stuck in his throat, and he dropped the blade and tore at his face with his hands. Hot tears ran down his cheeks. He should have known. He might have guessed God wouldn't let him do it. It was just the kind of dirty trick He'd come up with...

Getting off the foreign run helped for a while. Stutzman was even glad to see *Ms.* and *Popular Science.* He welcomed the toy bags of salt and pepper, and even the seventy-four ways the airlines cooked chicken looked good again.

He flew to Chicago and Des Moines and Corpus Christi...

Omaha and Ft. Smith and Cedar Rapids...

Tulsa and Knoxville and Fargo and St. Petersburg.

For a time, there was a remote sense of day/night/day/night, like the quick frames of a movie flicking by. A numbing rhythm at best, but at least it held the dull hint of one something following another. Then, the beats and flickers blurred into a single, nearly inaudible hum, and for Stutzman there was neither yesterday nor tomorrow, only the terrible, frozen barb of now lost in the temporal wilderness...

He flew to Wichita and Albuquerque and Amarillo...

Austin and Sioux City and St. Paul...

Reno and Bismarck and Boise.

Sometimes he remembered to take off his suit in the tiny washroom and clean himself a little, but even that seemed to take a great effort of will, more than he had to give. He forgot things like that. Or didn't bother when they came to mind. It had been a long time since he'd shaved. Right after God tricked him, he threw the good blade away. A thing like that, a man couldn't put to his face.

One night when his window looked far down on the lights of somewhere, the dreary curtain parted in his mind, and in a rare moment of clarity he remembered things. Things beyond the dull animal sense of simply being a Stutzman, who was hungry and tired sometimes and had a cramp in his foot. He remembered Angela and cobwebs and wine. Grass and pillows and bathtubs. He remembered the hippie girl with the yellow hair and the lady peeling oranges and Neuman's buyers and poodle dogs. He remembered everything there was to remember about Bernie Freed. The blazer and the houndstooth pants and the gold Piguet watch and the mustache that twitched. And in that moment he remembered something else, a thing that had happened right in the airport with Bernie he hadn't remembered before.

"That's the thing, maybe?" he asked God. "A thing like that? Listen, a person gets mad, he says things. It's something you say, you don't mean it like it sounds. Anyway, it's Bernie I'm pissed at, not You. I meant Bernie, I should've said Bernie. I'm sorry. You got nothing to do with it. The whole thing's a mistake. It's somethin'll never happen again, You got Stutzman's word on it."

Stutzman waited, but nothing happened. Maybe it wasn't that at all. Maybe it really was the business with Marty Shuler's daughter and God wouldn't admit it. "I'm supposed to know, You won't talk to me? How can you get along with someone, the someone won't sit down and talk? It's a good thing You got Your own business," Stutzman shouted, "You'd sure as hell never make it working for somebody else!"

He flew to Shreveport and Dayton and New Orleans...

Clearwater and Brownsville and Hartford...

Little Rock and Augusta and Wheeling.

In the beginning he'd put on extra weight, eating rich food and sitting in his seat and doing nothing. Now he hardly ate at all. He wasn't hungry anymore. Trays passed over his lap uneaten, an endless train of plastic and glass and chicken and peas and tarts and butters and coffees.

He didn't read anymore.

Or dig for butts in the ashtrays.

He sat in his seat and looked at nothing, encasing the essence of Stutzman.

He slept more and more, the sleeping and the waking subtly brushing together, until it was hard to tell one from another.

"I still look like a dead person, Angela," he said aloud or dreamed, "but you should be happy—I'm sleeping on the airplane."

He was dimly aware of rain slapping hard against the window. Dirty clouds swept by in quick streaks of gray. The plane hit heavy air and jolted him awake. Stutzman opened bleary eyes and saw the trailing edge of the wing groan down in place for a landing. He felt the wheels shudder from their nests and bite air. He leaned back again and closed his eyes and opened them wide. The plane gave a crazy little tilt. Stutzman's head slammed the window. The belly hit concrete and hot metal howled. The wing showered sparks and clutched earth, clipping bright blue lights like a lawnmower.

From the moment the plane touched ground until the end, only seven quick seconds went by. But Stutzman saw it all, in an instant replay of horror—slow dark honey creeping down a pancake forever.

He saw a gray wing crumple and tear like leftover foil…

He saw the big engine, still whining and angry, pull gently from its place and tumble gracefully through First Class and out the other side…

He saw the bright white wall of fire roll back to swallow Economy and watched the pale-eyed surfers swim against it…

And then in an instant they were gone. He saw dark clouds and felt cold rain on his face. He was alone. No sound, no sight, no touch, no nothing.

In the instant he knew what had happened and understood that he would die in the tiny slice of a second, Stutzman felt a great and terrible fear. Then, a wonderful sense of joy and happiness brushed the fear away, and he saw that God had forgiven him and let him off the hook. No more bedsores and dirty underwear. No more seat belts and peanuts and paper napkins. And in that fragment of a moment before nothing, Stutzman returned the favor and forgave God.

"Jesus!"

Okay, so I'm wrong. You got a Son. Whatever.

"C'mere. This one's alive!"

Alive? What's with alive?

White faces and white coats. White arms lifting and pulling and a white ambulance door and a siren shrieking and red and white and blue.

"Where am I?" said Stutzman.

"You're okay, mister. Got a little burn on your arm is all, you're gonna be okay."

Stutzman stared at him. "I got out? I'm alive? A thing like *that,* nobody's hurt?"

The white face went whiter. "*Hurt?* Shit, man, there ain't nobody *whole* back there! Maybe a hundred fifty poor fuckers all—"

"Hey, he don't want to hear all that," said the other face.

Me, he thought wondrously, just me? Everybody dead, and Stutzman alive? He understood, then. God was sorry for what he'd done. He'd spared Stutzman. It was over. All over and he could see Angela. He could get a drink and take a bath and kick the shit out of Bernie Freed. He could get a little furniture store, maybe a dress shop. You got to go somewhere, you get a bus or a taxi.

"You okay?" said the face.

"I'm okay."

"Can you sit up?"

"I can sit."

The doors opened, and the man helped him out, and he could hear the big engines idling and see the tail of the plane high against the dark and the moisture pebbling its skin. The stewardess got his ticket from his coat and looked at it and smiled, and from the yellow light in the door he could hear the other girl telling everyone how federal regulations require that your seat back and tray table be upright for takeoff and landing and that should the cabin become depressurized oxygen masks would automa—

To Plant a Seed

Gito leaned against his dome and squinted narrowly at the 888 naked vermilion backsides. It's not too often, he mused, one has the opportunity to examine the collective rear of an entire race. Not just the greatest distinction in the world, maybe, but good enough to win a bar bet.

No need to count, he knew—they were all there, the whole population of Sahara III stretched upon the sand, waiting for Lord Sun to rise above the brown horizon.

As an awesome moan rose from 888 throats, Gito automatically reached up and lowered his dark goggles. Then, in unison, 888 heads plunged into the hot sand in penance for yesterday's sins. In answer, Lord Sun burst over the horizon in a flash of white anger. The heads rose again, and moans turned to high-pitched shrieks of gladness.

Gito frowned. It was hard to share the joy of a new dawn when *Posi Frondee,* Lord Sun, turned his eyes into lead marbles even through the thick-lensed goggles. The incandescent eye stared down with unbelievable brightness—each ray a burning wire stretching 8000-million miles to shrivel and desiccate Gito Marachek.

He took one last look. The ceremony was over, and the brick-red figures scurried for their sandy tunnels. Twenty seconds of dawn was sufficient on Sahara III—even for the Kahrii who lived and died there.

Gito sealed the door behind him and pulled in great gulps of cool air. Then he swallowed a heat tablet and chased it with a pint of moderately cold water.

At the beginning of his tour, his nightmares had concentrated on vivid pictures of his foolproof power pack oozing into metallic butter, leaving him to face *Posi Frondee* without air conditioning. The nightmares had stopped, but he still caught himself running an occasional rag or the edge of a sleeve lovingly over the pack's smooth surface. Not that dust could possibly enter the sealed unit—it was just a matter of respect.

The buzzer rang softly. Gito jerked around and frowned suspiciously at the port. Buzzing meant guests—and daytime guests were as common on Sahara III as blizzards.

He stood and moved across the room. Through the slight translucence of the dome a short figure stood outlined against the morning terror of *Posi Frondee*. Gito quickly pressed the door stud. He heard the outer panel slide open, then shut. The temperature lowered as cool air poured in and sucked out the stifling heat. Gito slid back the lock portal and dimmed the lights.

Golsamel-ri dropped his white robe on the floor and stood in naked formality before the entranceway. "Greetings, friend Geetomorrow-shek. Happy dawning to you."

"Happy dawning to you, friend Golsamel-ri," said Gito. "What passes to bring honor to my dwelling?"

Golsamel-ri blinked, his sensitive eyes closed to bare slits even in the dimness of the dome.

"I am not disturbing? You were not preparing for sleep?"

Gito shrugged. "Later, perhaps. Each second of your presence is more dear to me than an hour of sleep-time."

Golsamel-ri acknowledged with a gracious bow, lowering his forehead nearly to the ground. Then he straightened, closed his eyes, and folded his hands carefully over his mouth.

Gito sighed, and relaxed against the back of his chair. Evidently, he had done it again—stumbled onto one of the 8,888 Supreme Compliments, or close enough to count, anyway. It was not too hard, if you spoke any Kahriin at all.

Custom now called for a few moments of meditative silence, and Gito was glad enough to take advantage of the interruption.

He was puzzled over Golsamel-ri's visit. Being at the dome was not unusual—he was a frequent and welcome guest—but his timing was far from normal for a native of Sahara III. A complex set of rules dictated Kahrii behavior—to break one of those rules was something to be considered. Golsamel-ri had come to the dome from the Ceremony, upsetting a lifelong habit that called for silence and sleep until the next waking, when *Posi-Frondee* sank in the west and work resumed on the surface.

What, then, had brought him here? Casting custom aside would cause Golsamel-ri temporary anguish, certainly—but there was also the trip back to his tunnel in the terrifying heat. More than *temporary* anguish could result from that.

Whatever it was, Gito had an idea he wasn't going to like it. He glanced apprehensively at the Kahrii. Standing, Golsamel-ri would have reached slightly above his waist. Now, in his squat-straddle position, the Kahrii's body seemed like a limbless red statue. He was, of course, anything but limbless, Gito knew. The stubby, scoop-shaped feet and hands could pack plenty of power when they needed to.

On another world, they might have been the limbs of a mindless, nocturnal burrower—on Sahara III, the fleshy webbing that covered long splayed fingers ended abruptly beneath the third joint of four-jointed members—allowing free use of fingers that should have been no more than claws, in conjunction with a perfectly respectable thumb. It wasn't much of a difference, Gito reminded himself, but while Golsamel-ri might still be a nocturnal burrower, he was also a thinking, reasoning creature.

Slit eyes opened and blinked at Gito over narrow, short-whiskered jowls.

"I thank you for bestowing honor upon me," Golsamel-ri whispered, "I am undeserving."

The statement required no answer. Gito waited in silence.

"I will not long disturb your privacy," he went on. "May *Posi Frondee* understand and forgive my intrusion. I wish to speak of the other—the female you name Cowezh-a-tir."

Gito's brow lifted. "Arilee? Arilee Colwester? What passes with her? Has she intruded in some way on your being? If she has—"

"*No.*" Golsamel-ri's head shook violently. His eye slits opened wide. "Please, I make no formal accusation against Cowezh-a-tir. This is not lightly done!"

"Yes, of course," Gito covered quickly, "I—understand that."

Golsamel-ri breathed a sigh of genuine relief. "As I say, this thing *concerns* Cowezh-a-tir—but is in no way a criticism. I would go to her myself, but my life thread has not traveled with hers as it has with yours. Also, of course—forgive me—she is a female. I had thought it would be seemly if I spoke to you about the thing—and perhaps you would convey it to Cowezh-a-tir? You are offended by this presumption?"

Gito relaxed imperceptively. Evidently, it wasn't too bad—just another Kahrii ethical entanglement that might be unraveled in a week or two of ceremony.

"No," Gito assured him, "I am in no way offended. On the contrary, I gain much honor by assuming any confidence you might bestow."

Good grief, Gito swallowed, *did I say that?* No question about it, he decided grimly; I've about had it on Sahara III.

"Now. What may I carry to Colwester?"

Golsamel-ri looked away. "I hesitate, good friend. Still, I have spoken with those wiser than myself, and it must be." He straightened himself and took a deep breath. "Dishonor may fall upon me, but Cowezh-a-tir is no longer to be allowed to observe the tunnels of the children of *Posi Frondee.*"

Gito sat very still.

"It is a terrible thing," Golsamel-ri moaned. "We are forced to break the High Rule of Hospitality. I only pray the enormity of our reason is sufficient. There will be an indemnity, of course."

Gito opened his mouth, then caught himself quickly. He bowed his head gravely. "Of course. I will discuss the terms with Colwester."

Golsamel-ri stood, wrapping his white robe about himself in that peculiar manner Gito had never quite been able to duplicate.

"I speak no more of this," he said quietly. "Convey my mortification to Cowezh-a-tir. Good Sleeping, Geetomorrowshek."

"Good Sleeping, Golsamel-ri—my dwelling has been blessed."

With a quick bow, the alien was through the airlock. In a moment, Gito caught a glimpse of him diving for the nearest tunnel mound, *Posi Frondee*'s beneficent rays burning into his vitals.

Gito frowned at the empty desert. He gazed up at the ceiling, tapping one finger thoughtfully against his cheek. Then, cursing himself silently, he walked the few steps to the rear of the dome and stuck his head around the corner.

"Arilee?"

The sleeping quarter's lights were dimmed, and for a moment he could see nothing. He stepped out of the doorway and let the sunlight behind him fall on bare shoulders and wheat-colored hair. He caught an almost imperceptible flinch at the back of a slim, white neck.

Grinning, he sat down beside her.

"You awake?"

"No. Certainly not." Then she turned over toward him and sat up, pulling the thin gown about her just in time—or a particle of a second too late. It was a trick most any well-trained Mistress over a Five could do in her sleep; but Gito could recall none that did it quite as well as Arilee.

She kissed him lightly and brushed a strand of hair from her eyes. "Well," she smiled, "crisis on Sahara III too big for you to handle?"

Gito nodded, looking as firm-and-no-nonsense as he could when he was looking at Arilee.

"Yes, as a matter of fact there is—and I think its name is Arilee—or Cowezh-a-tir, depending on your point of view."

Arilee lifted a brow in question.

"Our friend Golsamel-ri just risked about a 99th degree burn to let me know you've been officially banned from roaming about the tunnels of the Children of the Sun."

Arilee bit her lip. "*Uh-oh.*"

"Yep. Uh-oh it is. Naturally, the whole thing was too mortifying for him to go into—so suppose you fill me in on the details?"

Arilee sighed, wrinkling her face in thought. Then she looked at Gito and nodded slowly.

"Now what is *that* supposed to mean?"

"Just that I am not at all surprised, love. I was—expecting something like this—sort of."

Gito thought her eyes darted away maybe a second too soon. He stood up and looked down at her. "You're trying to tell me something. And I have an idea I'm not going to like it."

"I don't think you are either," she admitted. She paused, then smiled up at him brightly. "Coffee? You—me—talk-talk?"

Arilee was a mimic, and he instantly recognized Innocent Tahitian Beauty Established Rapport With White Trader. He grinned before he remembered to look stern.

"Okay. Coffee is called for. You dress and I'll brew—and I *mean* dress. This is definitely talk-talk."

The coffee was bubbling when she stepped from the sleep quarters, and he remembered with happy resignation that a Mistress always obeys, if not the letter of the law, then the vague spirit of it. The implied order was plainly 'fully dressed and no distractions,' and Arilee complied. Only Arilee was distracting in anything, and Mistress-designed coveralls did a great deal more than cover.

"Very funny," he said acidly, "ha-ha."

She picked a chair and breezed into it with natural and innocent grace. He handed her a steaming mug and she smiled.

Gito settled down across from her and passed a cigarette. "Now—to the point."

"Okay," she nodded, "to the point. I think Golsamel-ri doesn't want me in the tunnels because they're doing something of religious significance."

Gito sighed. "Doll, you are delaying the game. *Everything* they do is of religious significance—and *you* know it."

Arilee shrugged. "Sure. But this is ah—more significantly significant. You ready?"

"I am firmly braced."

She took a deep breath. "Gito, I suspect it is getting close to moving day for the Kahrii."

"Once more, if you please. I don't think I got that."

"Simple. They are leaving the tunnels. Taking off. Make big journey. Gods angry—"

"All right, knock it off." He shook his head and laughed. "You have flipped, Arilee. You are my own living doll and all that but you don't know what the hell you are talking about. I think you've been getting too much sun, or *Posi Frondee,* or whatever you want to call it."

Arilee shrugged. She pursed her lips and peeked at the ceiling. "I didn't *think* you were going to like it."

"Ho-ho," he said flatly, "that does just about sum it up." He leaned forward and took her hands in his. "Now Arilee," he said quietly, "you pulled a little boo-boo and you're too stubborn to admit it. Okay. I've let you roam around down there because I was—frankly—pleased that you were interested in finding out what they were like. In spite of the fact it's against every regulation in the book. Now, you tell me what it was and we'll forget it. Okay?"

She shook her head. "Not okay. Did Golsamel-ri say that?"

"Say what?"

"That I—pulled a boo-boo?"

Gito dropped her hand in mock astonishment. "If you'd dissected his grandmother, would he risk eternal mortification by *complaining* about it? He said he prayed his sin would be forgiven—or something. And there is an indemnity—I suggest twenty-five lengths of Shari cloth."

Arilee cringed. "I don't want any Shari cloth. It itches."

"Arilee—"

She grabbed his wrists and smiled patiently. Gito frowned. "Now don't give me the mother-will-explain bit, Arilee."

She laughed. "Mother's going to *have* to, because I get the strange feeling you don't believe a word I'm saying. Listen—I *mean* it, Gito. I'm *not* just making this up."

He looked at her closely. For a moment, he had the horrified idea that she wasn't.

"One," she said, holding up a finger, "the Shari roots are *not* being worked. They are simply being *sliced off* in portable sections. You see that? *Portable?* As in Going Somewhere?"

"That's all?"

"Nope."

"Then—?"

"They're—nervous. Like they're afraid—or anticipating something."

Gito snorted. "The Kahrii are never nervous. They are incapable of being afraid."

"*These* Kahrii are..." she said haughtily.

Gito ran a hand across his face. "Is that all?"

"No."

"Please, Arilee..."

After a moment, Gito said, "Just slicing the roots?"

"Uh-huh. Slicing."

He tried to consider the intricacies of Kahrii agriculture. "You mean slicing—not just notching for the milk or cutting the polyps?"

Arilee nodded smuggly.

"Hah!" said Gito suddenly. "Doesn't mean a thing. The roots could be cramped—the Kahrii could be thinning them out. They could be diseased, they could—oh, come on, Arilee; you took one little fact and decided the whole race is about to take the Long Trek?" He spread his hands to take in the whole smoldering world outside. "Arilee—where in hell would they *go?*"

Arilee said nothing. And that, thought Gito warily, is disturbing in itself. She just sat there, small hands neatly folded in her lap. He had the uncomfortable feeling she was measuring him for dissection and study.

"Arilee, will you *please* not do that? I'm trying, out of my high regard for your brains, beauty, and assorted charms—not to mention the fact that you're at the head of your class in Gito's Quick Course in Alien Ethics—to give you a fair hearing on this—this—"

She uncurled long legs from her chair and walked over and put her arms around his neck. She kissed him long and soundly.

When she stepped back, her eyes were sparkling. "You have no idea," she said sincerely, "how *relieved* I am to get this foolish idea out of my head. Now that you've explained it to me, I can see it's all just nonsense. And you *won't* let the idea of the Kahrii slicing off the roots of the plant that *keeps them alive* bother you—will you?"

"What? Oh, certainly not."

She walked to the door of their sleeping quarters and raised a hand to the top of her coveralls. Again, it was impossible to tell what she had in mind.

"See?" she said happily. "When you talk things out, it's not so bad, is it?"

Sunset usually pulled Sahara III's temperature down to the low nineties, but Gito seldom left his dome until the local midnight. In the first place, there was no place to go—and nothing to see he hadn't seen before. More particularly, his comfort-oriented logic told him it was pointless to trade his refrigerated 72 for a dry, hot and thirsty 86.

Now, drooping limply in the sandcar, gasping from the short run through the heat of dusk, he waited for the air conditioning to breath him back to life.

Gito had actually witnessed few Saharan sunsets in the open. They left him with the illogical but unshakable conviction that the great molten eye of *Posi Frondee* might reverse itself and rise again, catching him there on the bare surface. It was an unpleasant thought, to say the least—and the image of Arilee curled comfortably in the cool darkness of the dome was no help at all.

In an hour or so she'd be awake, and know damn well he'd taken her seriously enough to have a look on his own. He grinned and shook his head. Being Arilee, she had probably known what he'd do all along anyway.

Arilee Colwester was a Nine, like himself—and while a Nine was average for an experienced Planet Warden, a Mistress classification that high was nothing to sneer at. Not, of course, that he'd ever sneer at Arilee. She had been with him only two out of the eight months of her tour, and already he had a feeling for her he'd never experienced with the others.

Now that he thought back, it hadn't really taken two months—from the moment she stepped off the supply ship there was, well—something—he couldn't put his finger on exactly what it was. It was just there.

And, as he told her, he was frankly and genuinely flattered when she took an interest in the habits of the Kahrii. Gito was perceptive enough to recognize that it *was real* interest; and he had broken a hard and fast rule to allow her to enter the tunnels of Golsamel-ri's people.

And so, brother, he told himself wryly, stretching in the cramped confines of the sandcar, it is your own damn fault you're out here—waiting like an idiot for the natives to take off for Nowhere...

Gito geared the sandcar forward at a snail's pace across the desert floor. The first hint of darkness was beginning to color the landscape, and number one of Sahara's four moons was visible above the horizon.

In a moment, the first pair of bright, luminous eyes peered above ground, then scurried across the sand. Another pair followed—and another. Soon the land seemed covered with darting, bodiless fireflies.

With darkness, work began on the Kahrii's major—and only—occupation: the care and cultivation of the Shari cacti, source of Shari cloth, Shari root, Shari fruit, and a hundred other products of Kahrii existence. It was also the pipeline to Sahara III's rarest molecular combination—water.

What the people of the tunnels actually did with—or to—the Shari, was much of a mystery to Gito. As far as he could see, the cacti were doing a damn good job of surviving without any help. Still, he reasoned, you have to do something. You can dig so many tunnels—then what?

It was, Gito pondered, a strange and rather frightening world. On the whole planet, only the tall and bulbous Shari dared defy *Posi Frondee.* Of the two life forms on Sahara III, the vegetable Shari thrust its silver-gray columns above the surface, while the intelligent bipeds tunneled fearfully beneath it.

For an hour, Gito wormed the sandcar in a wide circle around the night's work area. With the windshield on infrared, Kahrii deviations from the norm stood out like the proverbial sore thumb. The sand-trencher trenched sand in a circle beginning 4 units from the base of the Shari, and the moment the circle was completed the thorn-binder stepped in with 44 lengths of thornbinding, and bound 44 thorns, stepped aside, and allowed the pulp-juicer in to juice pulp—etc., etc., etc.

The fact that Arilee's alleged root slicing had occurred beneath the surface didn't worry him. What happened below would eventually be reflected above. That was the way the Kahrii did things.

The second hour, Gito widened his circle and left the work area behind. Five miles out, the Shari forest thinned, and only a few lone sentinals thrust above the sand. Sahara's four moons rolled crazily across the sky, casting dull spokes from the dark plants.

Gito geared the sandcar into overdrive, and the shielded drive unit whined briefly, then thrummed into silent power. At 130, he eased off and let the treads turtle back into the hull as the lift units took over and inched him off the hard-packed sand on a cushion of air.

At high speeds, there was no sensation of going anywhere at all. The featureless landscape offered no point of reference. The horizon seemed endless, but it was an illusion of darkness Gito was accustomed to. When the star that seemed to hang over the horizon a long fifty miles away suddenly disappeared, he arced the sandcar into the beginning of a slow curve.

Ahead was the great wall that sheltered the Kahrii in their long and narrow valley; a wind-scoured, smooth sandstone barrier 750 feet high and a hundred miles around. Gito had seen it from the air in the few times he had lifted the sandcar over the rim. It was an oddity duplicated maybe a dozen times on the planet; a long scar in the endless sand, a sunken ellipse that partially protected the life of Sahara III from the murderous storms of wind and sand that periodically swept the surface.

The walled valley was the big wrench in Arilee's idea of the Long Trek—even, as he had explained, if the Kahrii *wanted* to leave their tunnels, there was no place to go and no way to get there. Scaling the walls was possible, but it could certainly not be done in a night—and no Kahrii would live to continue his try—not if he had to cling to the wall during the day. So it meant a 25 mile walk to the base of the wall, a few handholds hacked in the stone, then a race against dawn back to the tunnels. About 30 years work for the entire population, Gito figured roughly. And once on top of the rim, nothing but death. The fertile Shari groves of the valley had little in common with their dry and stunted cousins scattered sparsely above.

And no Shari—no Kahrii. It was as simple as that.

He kept the sandcar in a steady climb up the side of the wall, and soon he was skimming round the rim of the valley on a naturally-slanted raceway. To his left was the valley floor, to his right the stars. In a few seconds, he thought, I've gone higher than any Kahrii in a thousand years—or, perhaps, in the whole history of the planet.

No, there might be some significance in the natives' slicing the roots of their life-giving Shari—but whatever it was could not be explained in any terms Arilee had imagined. Her idea had worried him—more than he had let her know. He had seen some strange things happen on the far-flung planets of the galaxy. Still, his ride around the valley had convinced him migration was not the answer to an unexplained deviation in agriculture.

By the time the car's treads touched sand again and began the slow crawl through the Shari, Gito was beginning to feel his ride around the rim through the muscles of his back. Stretching, he took a last look at the Kahrii at work, and locked the sandcar in its dome. There was still another 15 hours of the long night to go; but he had seen nothing in three, and had no intention of sticking around for the rest.

A picture of Arilee asleep in the darkness before him hurried his steps across the still warm sand.

It might have been night; the sleeping quarters' ceiling was still opaqued. Then a ray of intense white glanced from the other room off Arilee's cheek, and he knew *Posi Frondee* had returned to bless Sahara III.

"Gito..."

It was pleasant to hear his name—he liked the way she said it...

"Gito, get UP!"

He jerked, opened his eyes fully, and stared up at her. There was something—something wrong.

"Gito!"

Another look and he sat up straight, grasping her shoulders.

"No," she said tightly, "don't say anything." There was a small line between her brows he hadn't noticed before.

"Arilee, what—"

She shook her head. "No. Don't. Just—look. Just go out there and—and look."

She was beginning to shake, and he was past her before she finished, the hairs rising on the back of his neck. Whatever it was, he thought grimly, he had gone to bed a little too early to catch it. He wasn't at all sure he wanted to know what the Kahrii considered too important to do in his presence.

At the sleeping quarter's door he jerked to a stop, slapping his hand across his face. The dome could be adjusted from opaque to complete transparency, and Arilee had dialed too far. The room was flooded with unreal brightness, and the cooler labored to draw away the heat.

He reached blindly for the dial. The dome darkened, and his vision returned through a maze of whirling spots of color.

He stared, blinking his eyes. The hair rose up the back of his neck again and stayed there. Beside him, Arilee tightened her grip on his arm.

He had been on Sahara III a long time. The scenery was not much—but it was damn well the only scenery he had. Now, it was as if a city of tall buildings had been swallowed overnight, leaving behind an emptiness more terrifying for the memory of the space it had filled.

The Shari were gone. All of them. The dense, protective groves of cacti that nourished the Kahrii, kept them alive on this harsh world, were gone. No, Gito thought, it's worse than that. For the Shari were dead, but *not* gone. A thousand silver corpses lay scattered about the settlement for a hundred yards around the dome.

...*Scattered?* He made a quick, wide circle with his eyes. Arilee saw it too. A gasp caught in her throat.

What in all hell—? thought Gito. No catastrophe had hit the grove. The Shari had been *cut!* Cut, stripped, and sliced into long curved sections. They lay about the landscape in every conceivable variation of the open curve. Where there was a need for big sections, slices had been butted together and laced with tough Shari fiber. There were semi-ovals, near-circles, and half-ellipses of every size and description. The longest one Gito could see was seventy-five feet across the widest point of its arc.

They lay there, staked into position, as if, Gito thought, they had been tortured for some insane vegetable secret and left to dry and shrivel under *Posi Frondee's* glare.

He let out a breath he hadn't realized he'd been holding. He turned to Arilee. "I—believe we could use a drink about now."

She said nothing.

"All right," he said sharply, "what *else* do you suggest?" He closed his eyes and turned from the dome, fists clamped tightly at his side.

Arilee sat on the couch below him, looking suddenly very small. She smiled weakly. "I'm—sorry, Gito." Her voice was a little too high.

Gito took a deep breath, shrugged. "What for? You didn't do it, doll—you just called it." He studied her carefully. "How, I'm not even going to *try* to figure out."

He swore suddenly, slamming his fist against the dome. "What do they think they're *doing* out there? Don't they know—don't they *know...!*" His voice faded. He walked to the wall and frowned at the chaotic landscape.

Arilee mixed drinks in two shaky glasses. Gito turned his up and passed it back to her, then resumed his nervous circle of the dome.

"I hope," he said acidly, "they cut off a lot of those roots. It's a long walk to the next meal."

Arilee looked up questioningly.

"No, of course not," he shook his head. "I'm just raving. They *can't* get there—if it was right on top of the rim they couldn't get there! And it isn't. It's about 2,000 miles away."

Gito bit his lip and closed his eyes. "Two thousand miles... if I could take two at a time in the sandcar, at night...God, that's 444 round trips!...and each two would *have* to start digging the new tunnel...big enough for the next two. Arilee! Arilee—" He shook his head and rubbed a hand across the side of his face. "Good Lord, what am I thinking of? It's too incredible."

She was with him, smiling gently. "Gito..."

He looked up and held her eyes a long moment, then reached out and squeezed her hand. He shrugged and showed her a sad smile. The whole thing was insane, ridiculous—hopeless.

"I'm sorry," he said. "It's just—this is the first world that ever suicided on me..."

He thought about what he'd said, and added a hollow laugh. That's it, he told himself. Laugh at it—and maybe it won't be real...

They were both out of the dome as soon as darkness sent the first Kahrii out of the tunnels. It hasn't been a good day, Gito thought—but it sure as hell has managed to be a long one. They had batted it back and forth, and gotten nowhere. Speculations were easy, and the frayed nerves and quick tempers that followed—but answers were something else.

"Sure," he had told her, "everything the Kahrii do has a basis in religion—but what kind of a rite do you hand down generation after generation that calls for suicide? Self-destruction might be an impressive gesture to the gods—but you can only show that kind of devotion once!"

"—and then," Arilee had finished for him, "what does *Posi Frondee* do for worshippers? It isn't just insane, Gito—it's uneconomical!"

Through it all, Gito became increasingly aware of some very interesting qualities in Arilee—rare, he decided, even in a Class Nine Mistress. He'd had such thoughts before about women, certainly—that nostalgic sadness when they left, often wishing they could extend their tour.

But never like this—this was something else. Before, his thoughts had usually dwelled on a woman's more obvious qualities—thoughts that were generally quickly relegated to shadowy memories by the next Mistress.

Objectively, he told himself that being a perfect companion to a man was just what a Mistress was born and trained to do—was it possible that Arilee Colwester just managed to do that job a little better; mirror his ego, his thoughts, a little more keenly than the others? No. He didn't believe that. She, well, she just couldn't be *that* good an actress.

At least—he fervently *hoped* she wasn't.

After the first pair of Kahrii eyes edged about the ground, they quickly disappeared. Soon, four others emerged, and stayed. When they saw Gito and Arilee, three of them fell flat on their faces and covered their great owlish eyes. Gito thought he could hear high, thin squeaks coming from the huddled trio. He looked at Arilee and motioned her still. It was unnecessary—Arilee had no intention of moving.

The fourth member of the group stared at them a moment, then slipped back into the tunnel. He was back up in a few seconds, and walking straight for them.

Arilee stiffened and Gito took a deep breath. He saw it too, and frowned uneasily.

"Just take it nice and slow," he said softly, not taking his eyes from the white-robed Kahrii.

Gito had recognized Golsamel-ri, and just as quickly identified the thing in his hand. If he had landed that moment on Sahara III he would have known. On Sahara, or any other world—a taboo stick looks the same.

Dyed Shari cloth hung in drab colors from a gnarled Shari root that had been turned into a crude staff. From the top of the staff hung four painted skulls—three adults and a child whose age, health or religious status had made them expendable on those occasions when the population exceeded the ritual number of 888.

Golsamel-ri plunged the taboo stick into the sand and stepped back. the skulls rattled against the dry stick, then stilled. For a long moment they stared across the darkness at each other, Golsamel-ri's unblinking eyes mirroring the moons and stars.

Well, Gito decided, somebody's got to do it. "Friend Golsamel-ri—I wish to speak with you. I do not understand what your people have done."

Golsamel-ri was visibly shaken. Familiarity with the Kahrii had given Gito some knowledge of their facial expressions. Golsamel-ri displayed a comingling of fear and disgust. Hatred was not yet there, but it might break through any moment.

"Please," Gito went on recklessly, "if I ask things that offend you, it can be forgiven by your knowledge of my ignorance. I am unblessed by *Posi Frondee.* Have you not said you desired that I understand your god?"

Golsamel-ri bowed his head a moment, then looked up. His gaze flicked briefly to Arilee, then rested on Gito.

"There is nothing for you to understand," he said softly. "My people do not exist, therefore I can explain nothing about anything they have done—if they existed and were capable of any action. Also, having nonexistence myself, I could not explain their non-act or nonexistence."

Gito swallowed hard. One question was answered, at least. The Kahrii were perfectly aware of what they had done—they already considered themselves dead.

"It remains," Golsamel-ri continued, "for me to deliver this message from the nonliving. This staff signifies a line across which the living must not pass. You are forbidden to disturb the work of the souls of the children of *Posi Frondee.*"

So much, sighed Gito, for the traditional Kahrii courtesy. Less seems to be required from the nonliving.

"One thing remains," said Golsamel-ri. "It nearly escaped my recognition, so much has death clouded my mind. The former Golsamel-ri, during the last days of his life, offended the female Cowezh-a-tir. His ghosts wishes to pay his indemnity, as he has been instructed."

The nonliving Golsamel-ri reached into his robe and drew out a tightly-packed bundle. Gito touched Arilee. She looked up at him, eyes wide. He nodded toward the Kahrii, and she bit her lip and stepped forward. Golsamel-ri extended the bundle, and Gito could tell it was Shari cloth.

"Thank you," said Arilee clearly, "I accept and thank the soul of Golsamel-ri." Gito was proud of her. She stepped back beside him and he squeezed her hand.

Gito fully understood her fear. Arilee had made many friends among the Kahrii, and Gito himself had come as close to Golsamel-ri as a man could to a being born on an alien world. It was nonsense, of course, he told himself—but this was a totally different Golsamel-ri. How, and why, he couldn't say.

"The shade of Golsamel-ri accepts your thanks," said the Kahriin, "for the being formerly surrounding his soul. And now, farewell, Geetomorrow-shek, from my previous self. I will be honored to greet you in the next life."

Then he turned, and walked slowly back to his huddled companions. At a word, they rose and went to their tasks. Behind them, the ghosts of the population of Sahara III slid like wraiths from their tunnels.

Dead or alive, Gito noted solemnly, there still seemed to be a great deal to do.

Gito pressed against the dome wall, straining against the Sahara night. Even with the dome lights darkened, there was little he could see. The fourth moon's rising would improve things somewhat, but he wished fleetingly that there was some way to dismantle the infrared panel from the sandcar.

The area outside the taboo stick had not been forbidden; still, Gito felt uneasy about venturing beyond the dome at all—at least for the time being. Actually, he admitted grimly, with the dome completely surrounded by decapitated Shari, freedom was now something like having the run of a hole in a doughnut.

"Gito," said Arilee testily, "if I'm interrupting, say so, but—"

Gito shrugged. He turned and picked her out in the dark. "Interrupting what? Unfortunately, there's absolutely nothing *to* interrupt." He caught her gaze and held it a moment.

"That—rambling, about airlifting the Kahrii—that's what it was, abstract rambling. I might as well have been figuring ways to save Pompeii." He paused, knowing there was more, knowing she was waiting, too. It was a subject they had skirted, carefully avoided.

She was watching him, and he read a kind of pleading in her eyes.

"Don't make it any harder," he said stonily, turning away.

"I'm sorry—I didn't mean—"

"—to forget the rules? Don't you think I'd *like* to? Don't you think I'd try to save as many as I could?" He shook his head. "We're on a Class C planet, Arilee. Spelled out that means Sahara III is populated by intelligent beings in a stage where my job becomes a matter of being present—and observing. Period. No footnotes. No boosts up the ladder. On a C you stop, look and listen—and make sure no one else gets a finger in the pie. No backdoor traders, no Sportships. Did you know C stands for 'Casual' and 'Critical?' A world in a critical stage of development—calling for casual contact by the Planetary Warden. Namely me. And," he grinned slightly, "in this case, you."

She looked at him. "Will it—I mean, you shouldn't have let me go down there. I know that—"

"No. I shouldn't have. Only it doesn't matter. You didn't do anything. As a Nine you could qualify for an Observer. If it came to that—well, you are now so appointed. Only it won't come to that."

He sat down beside her, and she moved over to make room, then dropped her head on his shoulder.

"Why, Gito?"

"What?" he answered her, but knew what she meant.

"Why did you let me—just because I wanted to. Would—"

He saved her from having to ask. "—Would I let anyone else do that? No. I wouldn't." He turned her head toward him. "As to why—that's a rhetorical-type question, isn't it, Arilee? You have to know the answer before you ask."

She looked up into his eyes. "Yes. I know." She got up quietly and disappeared into the sleeping quarters. She half-closed the door before turning on the dim light. He knew she was combing her hair—which, as far as he was concerned, never needed combing—but it was a task that would keep her away awhile. She had brought up the subject herself, broken the ice. But he knew she wasn't ready to take it any further. Gito was glad. Of course, he had sensed she realized this tour wasn't turning out quite like the others—for either of them. Now, she had answered a question for him, too.

In a moment the door opened and she came back to her place beside him.

"I'm sorry," she said. "Maybe I shouldn't have brought up anything—like that, when there's so much else." She faced him, and he frowned, seeing her eyes slightly wet. "I think that's why I did, Gito, because I know the rules and I don't like to think about them. I—guess I don't understand why they have to die because of a rule. There should be something—there's always something—isn't there?"

He wanted to say yes. He shook his head. "No. There isn't, Arilee. Sure, I could call for help, advice—but they wouldn't give it to me. Not on a C..."

He got up and walked to the darkened wall. "Once, Arilee, there was a planet with a new race. It wasn't even a C. There just seemed to be some slight chance—potential—of intelligence." He turned back toward her. "Have you ever heard a Warden say 'Something Bad on Tsirtsi?' No? Well it means emergency, help, war, planet-wide disaster—and it comes from what happened on that planet with the new race. What happened, I won't say and no other Warden will either. But when something like this happens—what's happening here—a Warden catches himself, and remembers Tsirtsi."

Arilee sat, unmoving, as he paced through the shadows of the dome.

"We found out you can't equate the things an alien *seems* to do, with what you know a human does under similar conditions. We learned the hard way, and we learned there is more diversity in the forms intelligence can take than we had dreamed. What are they doing out there with those circles of rotting cacti? Why did they destroy their food and water source?" He shrugged. "I don't know. So I keep hands off. The Kahrii may die, Arilee. That's something we have to face. But C's aren't allowed the deus ex machina. I don't introduce the miracle drugs, the 'wonders of science'—no matter what."

Arilee frowned somberly. "But Gito, haven't you *already* done that? I mean, they *know* there's something better. They've seen the dome, the—the sandcar, the supply ship, uh—in here, the way we live. It's too late for that, don't you think?"

Gito shook his head. "That sounds right, but it's a fallacy. A C culture doesn't have the background to conceive of an atomic generator or a space drive. It's like taking their picture with a 'magic box.' So what? There's a god in there, with a little power, and that's just fine. They have gods with power, why shouldn't the man from the sky? No, if you want to corrupt them, give the Kahrii a steel knife, or a shovel—or worse yet, introduce trade goods and a system of barter. *Ideas* are the real danger. Why an idea can—can—!"

Gito stopped. He had paused in his pacing to watch the third and fourth moon rise together over the rim of the world, flooding the desert in pale light. He pressed his face hard against the dome.

"Gito, what is it?"

"Come here, Arilee—quick!"

Gito pointed, and Arilee gave a short cry. As they watched, several of the Kahrii attached strong Shari fiber ropes to the open ends of one of the arcs they had sliced and sewn the night before. Gito swore silently. He had made a quick, snap judgment about the cacti—they had not rotted in the sun at all. As one group pulled the ropes, another braced the center of the arc—and the arc raised slowly—*and stiffly*—into the air.

Gito whistled sharply. They knew what they were doing—whatever that was. That the Shari could be dried into a strong, light-weight building material had never crossed his mind.

But, he asked himself, *why?* What would the Kahrii *want* to build?—And above the ground, where they couldn't possibly live even if they had suddenly planned on remaining alive?

After a few precautionary guywires were attached, the arc stood firmly in place. It stood like a giant horseshoe magnet, resting on its back, poles aimed at the stars.

"Maybe it's a—temple, or something," Arilee suggested weakly. "The—last sacrifice to *Posi Frondee?*"

"Huh-uh. If it's a temple, they've got their arches upside down. Besides, where did they get an idea like that? They've lived in tunnels since the race began. Architecture doesn't just spring up overnight." He cut her off as she took in a deep breath. "—And don't say *I* corrupted them with the dome. Whatever it is they're building, they'll never get a dome out of *that!*"

The Kahrii wasted little time admiring their work. In fifteen minutes, they had another arc in place, directly in front, and twenty feet away from the first.

Gito watched in silence. When the third, smaller arc went up, something small and cold dropped heavily into the pit of his stomach. With the fourth and fifth, he knew he was going to be sick…

Gito and Arilee watched off and on, for most of the night. Arilee forgot how many times the coffee pot emptied itself. When they talked at all, they talked of the past, people they had known—anything instead of what was happening outside the dome. To talk about that, they knew, might somehow make it more real than it already was.

By dawn there was little more use pretending the Kahrii project didn't exist. The arcs now stretched 100 yards across the desert. Those near the center, the first to go up, stood alone; the smaller, tightly-curved sections rose on each end to graceful points supported by a cross-hatch of framework. Running the full length of the row, a network of stout Shari beams now connected each arc to the other. A night of coffee had dulled his senses, left him hollow and empty. Now dawn brought the cold weight back to his stomach and left his mouth dry and tinged with acid. He was angry and tired, and he knew he was going to stay angry and tired no matter how much sleep he could manage to get.

He was angry because he was a man who was used to problems, and used to finding reasonable solutions to those problems. Gito didn't like questions without answers, and he knew he was going to knock his head against the dome wall forever without dulling the truth. Nothing he could do would change the fact that the Kahrii, who dug their tunnels in a world of sand and never dreamed of more water than the pitiful droplets that could be sucked from one Shari fruit at a time—had spent the night laying the keel of a ship…

He was awake at dusk. He frowned at, then meekly accepted the cup of hot coffee waiting for him in the main room of the dome. He noted, thankfully, that Arilee had been considerate enough to opaque the dome walls. Maybe, he thought sourly, she has the right idea. If we can't see it, the whole damn thing just might go away.

He glanced at Arilee. She was watching him and he smiled back, weakly.

"Bad?" she asked.

"I dreamed," he said, letting himself sink back into the cushions, "that Golsamel-ri was an Admiral—gold braid and all—and I was walking the plank. Have you ever had the opportunity to drown in *sand?*"

Arilee cringed, holding back a grin. "No water?"

"My imagination," he said wryly, "is not as vivid as that. Even in my dreams I could not conjure up water on Sahara III. Hell, I've been here so long I'm about half Kahrii anyway—I just don't believe in things like oceans. They don't exist."

"They did once," Arilee said quietly. Gito turned slowly.

"You believe that, Arilee?"

She shrugged, getting up to refill her cup. "Are you saying you haven't been thinking about it? There's nothing else *to* think—is there?"

Gito didn't answer. He sat back on the couch and blew smoke at the ceiling. For a moment, he studied the drifting patterns curling toward the vent.

"Gito, I think it's an exciting possibility." She leaned forward. "Just think, how long ago—"

"It doesn't excite me," he snapped. "It worries the hell out of me!"

She went on without him, her eyes sparkling. "If there *were* seas out there once, and they remember—I mean, the story must have been handed down for centuries..."

Gito jumped up, rubbing his hand quickly across his face. "All right. I know where you're going, but look—I'm no geologist, and it'll be quite a few years before one gets here. But Arilee—we're not talking about thousands of years—maybe *millions!* And those beings are still digging tunnels with their—*hands?*" He shook his head violently. "I just can't buy that."

"They didn't always dig tunnels, Gito. Once, when there was a better climate, more water...well, anyway, now all they remember is a *symbol* of what they had. A ship, and no sea to sail it on."

"Very pretty picture. Only," he said patiently, "it just *wasn't that way,* doll. There were never—repeat *never* any oceans on Sahara III."

She caught his eyes and held them and he knew he'd been a little strong. He hadn't meant to carry it that far. He was scared, and now she clearly sensed it.

He was scared because he knew the Kahrii, and knew their religion. It was a hard, practical and basic kind of religion. *Posi Frondee* was not a symbol of God, a representation of light—no subtleties or symbols here. He *was Posi Frondee,* and if you didn't believe he existed, just go stand a moment under his blazing eye and defy his reality.

No, when the Kahrii made a sacrifice, it was a real sacrifice—often enough with real Kahrii. If these beings had built a ship—and God only knew where the idea had come from, the dark past, glimpses of the dim future—if that *was* a ship, then they would sail in it to meet *Posi Frondee.* -And the sea of sand would suck them dry and preserve them in their broiling vessel forever—and that would be all anyone would have to remember of the Kahrii...

Time between dusk and dark passed too slowly—or quickly—Gito couldn't decide which. An endless chain of cigarettes and coffee ticked off the long silence.

Arilee was in no mood for charm or dazzling wit. She could have braced herself—she was well-trained for that—and put on a real performance if it would have done any good. She knew it wouldn't, and Gito was grateful for her awareness. He knew she was there, and the warmth of her presence made extra efforts unnecessary. From the way she moved about the dome, performing small duties that didn't need to be performed, he knew she was sharing his experience.

You can face a thing when it happens, and scream about it and curse it, and even discuss it in sane and reasonable terms. Shock is a sugar coating for a bitter pill. It is a period of experience, not understanding. Now, as the coating dissolved, Gito was jolted by what he saw.

Curiously, he realized, the ship was not a part of it. He no longer feared it because he simply could find no way to accept it. There could *be* no ship, not on Sahara III. He would not let his mind dwell on a history that included dark seas and waterless deserts—and a race that survived and spanned that awful time between the two.

That kind of understanding was too much to handle now—for Gito, the vehicle of Kahrii destruction paled beside the destruction itself. The death of a race repelled him, and the thought that he was going to stand by and watch it chilled him until he fought to keep from fleeing past Arilee and shutting himself in the sleeping quarters.

What the hell kind of job was this, anyway? His anger reached out to pull in all Planet Wardens and the Corps itself. A race, relatively small and unimportant, and certainly unimposing, was going to kill itself. Period.

Was that *all?* Do you just write it off the books? Was it possible to look at it with that kind of cold objectivity?

Then: Did what happened on Tsirtsi have any relation to Sahara III?

But: Could you look at the Kahrii now, and say their loss could ever be related to what we lost on Tsirtsi?

No. But they didn't *know* on Tsirtsi, either, did they? Not until it was over. Not until it was too late.

He slammed a fist painfully into the arm of his chair. If that was the way the system worked, *then the system was wrong!* Just as man had no right to interfere—he also had no right *not* to, didn't he?

When, then, was the time to keep the rule and the time to break it? There was a way, was there not? There *had* to be a way to tell—at least to judge. Playing God halfway just wouldn't work out. Even a backwater planet like Sahara III had a right to their chance at greatness—or anonymity.

But the rule of the Wardens said no one had the right to interfere with that race's decision—even if that race rejected both choices and chose final oblivion.

Arilee touched his arm lightly, a quiet smile on her face. She spoke softly. "Hey, remember me?" It was not a bid for attention. She was asking, with her eyes, to share his thoughts.

He pulled his gaze away from her and glanced apprehensively at the darkening sky.

She pulled him back to her. "No," she said sternly. "It's not time, Gito." She led him to a chair and set a plate before him. "Now eat. They won't do a thing for two hours. You're not going to miss a move."

He looked down at the thick steak and grinned at her. He hadn't even realized he was hungry. He was warmly pleased by her attention, and strangely touched. The scores were adding up, as if there was a kind of game going on between them. There was more here than just an 8-month Mistress with a trim figure and wheat-colored hair. He idly wished for a vague time and place when there would be nothing to keep him from pursuing that line of thought.

Arilee was wrong. The Kahrii emerged from their tunnels long before that two hours was up. Gito's pulse quickened as he pressed against the wall of the dome. Something seemed terribly out of place. He sensed the frantic urgency that had brought the aliens to the surface while the heat of day still waved above the sand.

He thought about the food supply of Shari roots that must be dwindling down to nothing. The roots were not the Kahrii's favorite food, they were a supplement only; they could not possibly sustain 888 workers for long.

He was suddenly struck by the ludicrous, insane logic of the situation. Whatever the Kahrii were building, they were working with back-breaking haste to complete it before starvation set in—they didn't want to starve to death before they had a chance to kill themselves!

When the rolls of thick Shari cloth stretched across the ribs of the ship, Gito was only mildly surprised. Considering the Kahrii were building a seagoing vessel on possibly the driest habitable planet in this end of the galaxy, whey shouldn't they carry the inanity to completion?

They worked in a fever of desperation, and the job of covering the hull went quickly. As soon as one crew stretched material over a section of the ship, another followed with fiber buckets of milky substance which they brushed into the cloth.

For a moment, Gito was puzzled, then realized with a start the Kahrii were applying what must be a *waterproofing* resin to the hull! The hackles on his neck rose at the thought.

"*Why?*" he said aloud, turning to Arilee, "why should they take the trouble to—" He stopped, seeing she wasn't going to answer. Curled up in a tight ball on the couch, she seemed more a small child than a woman. He kissed her lightly, then got up to empty his cold coffee.

While the fresh pot heated, a familiar thought worried its way back to the edge of his consciousness. From the beginning, the Kahrii ship had presented a paradox. He knew it was impossible—all right, so highly improbable as to *be* impossible—for even the ceremony-bound Kahrii to maintain such a link with an incredibly distant past that included oceans on Sahara III. He simply could not accept it.

Still, on the other end of the paradox, there remained the fact that the Kahrii just *did not have the ingenuity or background to symbolize something they had never seen!* It wasn't there, and never had been. Existence was harsh, precarious and deadly dull on Sahara III. As *Posi Frondee* was a real God, one that could literally bring life or death; so was the day to day battle of survival real. There was no time for the niceties of easy symbolism, the fabrication of legends.

Gito poured his coffee, lit another tasteless cigarette, and sank into his chair near the dome window. It didn't figure—it just didn't figure at all. Still, there they were, and the hull of the ship that couldn't be was turning into a very familiar shape. Gito didn't like it at all...

Suddenly, he sat up stiffly. For a moment he thought he had fallen asleep—it was possible, but a glance at his watch assured him no more than ten minutes had passed since he'd last checked.

Gito blinked uncertainly. Something—what was it? He stared hard through the port. Nothing had changed. The routine he had watched half the night continued. The Kahrii swarmed over the surface of their ship attaching the long rolls of Shari cloth to the stiffened ribs, their figures casting odd, multi-shadowed shapes under the swift-running moons, the—? Gito bit his tongue and squeezed the arm of his chair. *Shadows!* That was it, of course. He had been watching so long he hadn't even noticed. The dark silhouette of the Kahrii ship was different—subtly *changed...*

The sides still sloped to the 'deck' level in a gentle arc, but now the curve continued—more Shari lengths had been added and were already partially covered! The chill began at the base of Gito's spine and gained momentum until it reached the top of his head. His scalp was suddenly unbearably tight.

There was no use trying to justify it or explain it or pass it off. If they continued—and he had every reason to believe they would—the Kahrii boat would soon be transformed into a completely covered, long and tapered cylinder.

In the darkness, with the tricky lighting of the four moons masking its imperfections, it looked too much like the thing it was meant to imitate. It was made of dried cactus and covered with coarse cactus fiber. It would never move a fraction of an inch above the surface of Sahara III—much less course out to touch the stars. But it was what it was, and nothing Gito could do would change that...

It was painfully clear in the first hot light of dawn. No one would mistake the Kahrii structure for a working spaceship—but, Gito admitted, no one would hesitate to say it was beginning to *look* like one.

After the first moment of stunned surprise, Gito readily accepted it. He sensed the same reaction, or lack of it, in Arilee. How many times were you *supposed* to start, catch your breath, stare wide-eyed at some new alien madness? For Gito and Arilee, the distance between the impossible and the utterly impossible was easy enough to swallow.

"If they change the damn thing into a cactus-covered nuclear reactor," Gito said darkly, "I don't intend to contribute a batted eyelash."

Arilee showed a small, sad smile and added a sigh of resignation. "My poor Gito. I had no idea warding—is that right? Warding? Wardening? I had no idea there were so many problems."

She was perched on the arm of his chair. He looked up at her. "Neither," he said sourly, "did I." He pulled her down into his lap and held her golden head between his hands.

"Arilee, I am about as drained of useful ideas as I ever believed possible. This business has left me empty of bright thoughts—if I ever had any—and I'm sick of pulling cultural histories out of thin air. It doesn't do any good, or lead anywhere at all unless you can base your fairy tales on something solid. And something solid—pardon the grammar—is what we don't have anything of."

Arilee got up and brushed back a strand of hair from her cheeks. She sat down across from him and rested her chin on two fists.

"You really mean it. You are not going to like it—you *know* that."

Gito grinned. "Every time you say that damned if you're not right. But, yes—go ahead. I've got a good grip on my chair, and I have the added advantage of knowing where you're going this time. And no—I *don't* like it!"

"What else is there, then?" she said softly.

Gito shrugged.

"Okay," she went on, "then we take it straight with no flinching. It's an old story—but it's a *possible* one, isn't it?"

Gito felt he chill get another good grip on the back of his neck. "Yes. It is. And it might as well be, for all we've got to go on. But look, Arilee—" He reared out of his chair and stalked to the edge of the room. "Every second looie in the Corps finds a 'lost race' on his first tour of duty. It's—it's—!"

"I know—and the video picks it up and squeezes it to death. A once mighty race that coursed the stars, then sank to savagery, forgetting their heritage. Worshipping," she said sternly, "at the shrine of Ah-tom and Aye-on, and—"

Gito moaned, slapping his hands to his ears.

"I don't like it," said Arilee, "any more than you do. If you want to hear an elated confession—the more I thought of the boat idea the less I could see *that!* So now—" She shrugged her hands, "—where to, love?"

"We're back," he scowled, "to Ah-tom and Aye-on—that's where we are. I'd like to say I won't buy it; and every time I don't 'buy' something, *they* build it!" He waved his hands wildly in the direction of the desert.

"I don't give a hang about that thing sitting out there. I *know* these people. They have *not,* damnit, 'sunk to savagery.' They never saw a spaceship and their immortal ancestors didn't, either!"

"So?"

"So nothing. If I could ever convince myself I know them as well as I think I do, I wouldn't keep getting that creepy feeling that all the hairs on the back of my neck are marching up the top of my head. One—I don't believe they have carried on some eternally long memory of a high technological culture. Two—and this is what hurts—I also know they simply don't have the inherent ability to think up boats and spaceships out of the blue. The children of *Posi Frondee* are as rigid as day and night.

"You see the paradox, Arilee? They *couldn't* think up anything like this themselves—and the other possibility just *does—not—happen!"*

"You're sure," Arilee said thoughtfully, "you're *certain* they never saw a spaceship?"

He stared puzzedly at her. "What? Oh, you can forget that. We don't introduce that sort of thing at this stage of the game. Everything big and scary stays off-atmosphere. Nothing bigger than a strut and tube platform comes in on a C. Just try to get the mistaken image of an FTL ship out of one of those—in the dead of night, completely out of sight of the settlement. These people think we came from over the ridge somewhere—and they'll continue to think so."

Arilee looked away quickly, and Gito remembered that future tense no longer applied to the Kahrii—not if they boarded their impossible ship for one short and terrifying journey.

Was it possible, then? Was he really taking his knowledge of the Kahrii for granted? Golsamel-ri had said his people were *already* dead—they considered themselves shades of their former selves. But, he remembered, the Kahriin had also expressed his desire to see Gito again when *next they lived!*

A thought flicked on the borders of his mind, then dropped with sudden coldness. Was Golsamel-ri talking about an afterlife—or was he following the narrow and literal pattern of his race—actually intending to *see* Gito again?

Gito turned suddenly. He stared at Arilee but his gaze was far beyond her and she stepped quickly aside, opening her mouth in a question then catching a glance of his eyes and keeping her silence.

Arilee knew men, and for some time she had realized she was making more effort than the job called for to know this one. The thing she saw in his eyes as he rummaged through the small equipment locker kindled a personal fear that rose from a fire she had not known existed. Not for a long time.

It was hot. Gito expected that. Sahara III was no ice-world. He looked back the hundred yards to the dome and felt a moment of panic. It might easily have been a hundred miles. Even with the suit's filtered glass the dome shimmered like a fiery jewel seen through wavering weeds of heat.

The maximum use of the suit was protective comfort. He knew that. It was not designed for survival in the vacuum of space or the poisonous atmosphere of a chlorine world. Of course, neither condition existed here, and the bright foil surface of the suit *should* reflect enough of *Posi Frondee*'s glare—with the help of the built-in air conditioner.

Looking up, he read the small, efficient legend on the inside of his helmet: 'For emergency use on an extremely hot surface—limited endurance.' He scowled grimly. That, he told himself, is about the most unscientific damn description I have ever heard! He wondered what the Corps semantics expert mean by 'limited' this week. The laboring wheeze of the conditioner was helping him to form his own opinion.

A quick glance at the exterior temperature gauge showed 176. Gito swallowed and tried to turn the conditioner knob to maximum. It was already there. The sweat poured down from his hair and stung his eyes.

He paused in the small strip of inadequate shade cast by the Kahrii ship and craned his neck upward. This close, the thing was even more awesome and impossible. He tramped slowly around the side until he found what he was looking for. It was a small hole, less than two feet across, about eight feet off the ground. Reluctantly, he could only think of it as an entry port.

Entry, though, was not going to be easy. The hole was small, with no ladder—it was high, and it was getting hotter. Gito kept his eyes from the temperature gauge, ran back a few yards, and jumped. On the fourth try, his fingers grasped the rough edge of the port and held. For a long moment he hung there, breathing hard. In a split second of panic he thought the air conditioner had stopped. Then he heard its heavy wheezing above the ringing in his ears. Gathering his muscles, he closed his eyes and pulled himself up and over the lip of the port.

He lay flat against the sloping walls of the Kahrii ship, letting the straining unit catch up with his need for air. The strain was considerable—inside the ship the heat was a stifling, breathless hell.

Gito sat up. Light from the open port drilled a bright tube into the opposite wall of the ship. It was a white cylinder filled with dusty strands of coarse Shari fiber. His admiration for the Kahrii rose several points. He had expected the interior to be riddled with stars of sunlight—as far as he could tell there wasn't a single leak. A breath of old fear touched him. *It was thorough – too thorough!* A good imitation of an airtight ship—but what?

Okay, he told himself sharply, this *is* what you came for, isn't it? You wanted to know the truth, whatever it was—didn't you? No, he answered himself solemnly—no, I didn't want any such thing.

Biting his lip, he pulled the flashlight from his belt and aimed it down the long darkness.

A dry and brittle cry left his throat and bounced again and again through the helmet. He turned his shaking hand and flicked the light down the opposite end of the ship. His heart pounded against his chest. It was the same—everywhere! At even intervals, the inside of the ship was ringed with coarse, woven sacks, like cocoons, or—the image forced itself into his mind—shrouds. On each side of the sacks two cords hung loose. Their purpose was too obvious—he could picture one of the Kahrii in each sack, the cords tied securely.

Counting the sacks in one section of the ship he multiplied quickly—knowing he would end somewhere near the figure of 888. Like the ship, the sacks were crude imitations—but their use was clear enough. Gito laughed harshly.

Acceleration couches! My God, what were they going to accelerate *against!*

He was vaguely aware that the heat was rising much too quickly within the suit. The ringing in his ears seemed to drown out the wheeze of the conditioner.

Okay, he reasoned, this is it. You've seen it. Here is a race that has forgotten its past, forgotten everything except the long journey through the vast darkness. And now they would relive that journey—after how many countless eons? Only this time they would not emerge from the darkness—this time the acceleration couches would not cushion their passengers against the harsh shock of death.

Only it isn't going to happen, he thought grimly, forcing himself back through the small entry port. I *can't let* it happen! Not now! The idea had come unbidden, wedging itself into a corner of his consciousness.

He stopped, swaying in the shadow of the ship. The giant, malignant star was higher now, and he could feel its increased heat blazing, burning through his suit. He twisted the conditioner knob frantically. Where was the air—what was wrong? His face, oddly enough, was cold. Why should that be, he wondered vaguely. Bright dots of color swam before his eyes.

He took a step forward. Somewhere, the dome blurred in the distance. He had to reach it now—had to reach it because he knew what he had to do.

Another step—another...The sand wavered dizzily around him. He had to make it, because he knew what the Kahrii were, and he knew the Corps was wrong. The lesson on Tsirtsi was one thing—but that had happened a long time ago and had nothing to do with now, here, on Sahara III.

There had to be a time when rules were broken, and this *was that time!* What they did to him—after—didn't matter. With a faraway sadness, he saw a dream dissolve. He shrugged it off.

What had he been thinking of, anyway? What kind of a love can you have with a Mistress? With a—he said the word—*professional,* someone who had loved others before and would love others after you.

No! It *wasn't* like that—not with Arilee. She had almost told him it wasn't, she—still, he thought slyly, she would, would she not? Wasn't that her *job?*

He gritted his teeth and blinked hot sweat from his face. He was cold all over now. Good—then the conditioner was working again. Everything was going to be all right. He would make it now. *Arilee...I've got to tell you, even if it never means a thing to you...Arilee...Arilee...!*

Out of the raging stars, the bright, exploding moons, the white ghost staggered toward him. He tried to take a breath, but there was no air. It was all right, he didn't really need air, did he? Not now...

The ghost came closer, weaving across the hot sand, its white hood parted to show a pale head topped by long flames of wheat-colored hair. Then the ghost staggered, falling toward him, and there was a comforting blackness...

For a long century the ghost dragged him roughly over the bright sand. Then there was darkness again. Later, coolness, great lungfuls of sweet air, and sleep…

No. NO! He sat up, fighting against the exploding stars. His vision cleared and a great sob broke from his throat. She was on the floor beside him, her body tangled in the white robe. He parted the robe and dropped it with a cry. The velvet flesh was red, seared, blistered and cracked. He jerked to his feet and fell into the supply locker. He ripped the medikit from its rack and nearly fainted again.

He tore the robe away and ripped off the clothes underneath. Tears welled up uncontrollably. He placed the medikit under her left breast and heard it begin its chittering and humming as it began to probe and prick like a benevolent leech.

The blackness was almost upon him again. He tore through the locker again until his hands touched a round surface. The lettering on the spraycan blurred before his eyes. He said a silent prayer that it was the right one and covered her body with the spray, turning her gently, until the can was empty. He had a last, shimmering glimpse of a slim figure covered in a cottony foam. Then the can dropped from his hands.

"That's a hell of a way…to get a suntan," he said weakly. She turned quickly as he opened his eyes. A little cry escaped her as she knelt and buried her face against his shoulder.

"You're…all right?" he said. He grasped her shoulders and held her at arm's length. She winced slightly at his touch and he jerked his hands away.

She shook her head. "No. It just burns a little. Still. But hold me, Gito. Hold me! I thought you were—were—"

He cut her off and pulled her to him, gently. The wheat-colored hair brushed his cheek. A brown shoulder pressed against his chest. He was amazed at the job the spray had done. The medikit had undoubtedly brought her out of shock, but the spray had sucked away the heat and smoothed the damaged cells. Her skin was a golden bronze against the white of her brief costume.

Gito grinned weakly. The spray had brought seared flesh back to gold velvet, but Arilee was gingerly wearing as little as possible, and would be for awhile.

Her deep eyes stared into his, and he remembered the white-robed figure moving toward him under the death-bearing sun.

"Arilee...Arilee..."

She shook her head gently and pressed a finger to his lips. "Hey, now," she said softly, "Don't. I had to go out. What would I do with a fried Planet Warden, anyway?"

When he told her his decision, she said nothing. Outside, the giant ball of *Posi Frondee* once more flattened against the high ridge.

Gito scowled thoughtfully. "I thought maybe you'd have something to say. I'd like to hear it."

Arilee bit her lip. She looked up at him briefly, then her gaze traveled down to the gray-cased weapon on the table.

"I don't know anymore," she said anxiously. "It was easy before—when it was just talk; about saving them, I mean. Now—" She shrugged, reached out for his hand. He moved it away quietly, shaking his head.

"I told you, Arilee, that can't matter." His voice bordered on irritation. He touched the weapon then looked away.

"If I let it be that way, thinking about it afterward, I can pretty quickly decide my life is worth more than 888 of them! I'm human, Arilee. I want something for myself, too. More than ever now. You understand that?"

Her eyes were wet and she nodded quickly before her face contorted and she turned and buried her head in the couch.

Gito closed his eyes hard. Was it right—*that* right? Strange, he thought, that the rightness seems to matter, and I'm not worried about the other part. He knew what the punishment would be—*had* to be. The Corps was humane, certainly, but this couldn't be overlooked. It would be humane—quick, and final.

Still, that wasn't it. He *had* to be right! If he stopped them, prevented them from sacrificing themselves for an insane gesture—could he ever really know? The Kahrii had traveled to this world through the terrible, yawning vastness of space a million years before his own ancestors had learned to speak. Could he decide now, what was right for them?

He paused, following the last rays of *Posi Frondee* into the darkness. Tonight. Yes, he knew that. He couldn't say how. But he knew. The Kahrii would leave their tunnels and crawl into their ship to die. And he could stop them, maybe discover where they had come from, bring them back to greatness—they *must* have reached greatness, long ago, when—

Doubt overtook him again. Doubt, he told himself acidly, or a last attempt to ease out of a decision. The excuses were countless in number, and they had all paraded themselves before him by now. The Kahrii were not an ancient, superior race—they had landed here in a lifeboat from some disaster. They were poor slaves of some other race, left here to die.

Sure. And is that why they're so perfectly adapted to this planet, so obviously a part of it.

No. There was to be no justifying. No more. There was the ship, the endless rows of acceleration couches. He pictured it, the way it must have been, when the Kahrii left their world, (was it dying?) which must have been like Sahara III. They came in search of a new home, knowing they would have to begin again. Did they realize just how much they would lose?

He picked up the weapon and looked out into the fast darkening night. Already the ship was a black silhouette. Soon, now.

"Arilee," he said.

"Yes, Gito."

He turned. She was already beside him. She was dressed in her work coveralls, flashlight and tools hooked neatly to her belt. She looked very small, now, a delicate and lovely spirit from some quiet, elfin world. He had known for some time that he loved her—he had never loved her as much as he did now.

Gito's plan was simple—it was the aftermath that would be difficult. The weapon was a standard stunner. With a wide-open lens it would merely bring long and restful sleep to its victims. When the Kahrii had entered the ship, he would spray it—stem to stern, and he and Arilee would carry the sleepers back to the tunnels. It would be a long night's work. But then, he told himself, Saharan nights were uncommonly long anyway.

And after that? There was the Corps to inform of his action. He grimaced at that. They would not be overly long in replying.

They stood together in the sultry beginnings of night. When the first pair of luminous eyes emerged from the tunnel Arilee's hand tightened on Gito's arm. He looked at her, but said nothing. A long, stiffened Shari root gangway was placed in the entry port; its carriers then knelt beside the ship and buried their heads in prayer. Moments later, a low, eerie sound drifted from the tunnels. Gito stiffened, and a sob tightened in the girl's throat.

It was a sound he knew, instinctively, had not been heard before. It was a song of hot winds sweeping over the desert, green shoots searching the scorched planet for water; a song of life, birth and death. And then they came.

They came out of the tunnels in a single file, their heads bowed low, and the song rose with them and filled the night.

To Gito, the white-robed figures already seemed long-dead ghosts returning to haunt themselves; to haunt the race that had forsaken some far off star eons before. With a start, he saw that each carried a small section of Shari root, cradled in their arms like a precious child.

A picture flashed before him of the tombs of long-dead Egypt on Earth, and the aeire columns of a forgotten race of Sirians. There, too, were the remains of ceremonial food provided for the long journey into death.

Gito had no idea how long they had been there, while the endless procession emptied the tunnels and disappeared into the ship. When Arilee touched his arm he jerked back, startled, then blinked his eyes. The desert was empty. The entry port was closed.

The weapon seemed suddenly heavy. He looked at Arilee a long moment, then walked toward the ship. He stopped a bare twenty yards from the dark shape. He was not sure what effect the walls of the vessel might have on the weapon's field of dispersal at so wide a setting. He had to be sure. The thought of facing the Kahrii after they regained consciousness and discovered what he had done, was bad enough. He was already haunted by that. To meet one before, who had not been affected by the weapon, would be unbearable.

Arilee held the flash while he made final adjustments. With his finger finally on the heavy trigger, the enormity of his act brought cold sweat to his face. Okay. He had expected this, and steeled himself against it. Last minute qualms were normal—but it was worse than he had imagined.

He was wrong, and he knew it. No! Damn it, you *made* your decision—do it! His finger tightened. Nothing happened. He jerked his finger away. His heart beat wildly against his chest and his whole body shook. He looked up at the sudden shifting of the eerie light.

Over the crest of the dark ridge, the four moons of Sahara III moved swiftly toward him through the black sky. He looked again. He had never seen them like that before—had he? Always, they seemed to travel the night in wild, erratic patterns, chasing each other across the heavens in a meaningless procession. Now, the two largest moons had nearly converged upon each other to become one—and the two dwarf sisters moved swiftly toward them in a path that could only bring them into conjunction.

Gito looked away. The moons of this planet themselves seemed to be warning him against the thing he had to do. Could he go back? No! He could stop them, save them. It was his—

The word stuck in his throat. His finger fell away from the trigger once more.

My God, was that what I was going to say? Is that how I justify this—as a duty?

He trembled at what he had almost done. Suddenly, a parade of self-righteous, cold-eyed madmen passed before him in solemn review. From their lips they uttered a stream of unctuous, emotionless edicts; edicts that changed, condemned, doomed a billion helpless faces.

It is our duty, *they told the fearful crowds: it is for* you *we make these changes—we have decided for you how you shall live, how you shall die, and this is right, because* WE HAVE DONE THESE THINGS AND KNOW THEY WILL BE RIGHT FOR YOU! *Your shape, your color, your gods have been wrong; but now we will make them right...*

...And the centuries of one way are forgotten, and the faceless crowd began new ways...because the grim-lipped men who spoke had more than strength in their words; they had strength in other ways...

Gito's trembling hands opened and the weapon dropped to the sand. He looked up with blurred eyes at four moons that were now one, shimmering, ghostly light above.

"Gito....GITO!" Arilee's fingers bit painfully into his arm. He turned, following her wide, staring eyes to his feet. There was nothing. Only the discarded weapon half-covered in the sand.

Then he saw. The pale gray of the sand was turning to mottled blackness. He stepped back quickly. Then bent to the ground. He jerked his hand away and stared at it as if it was a thing he had never seen. *Wet!* His hand was *wet!*

As he watched, the mottled patches blurred together until a visible film of moisture covered the sand beneath his feet. He looked up, scanning the desert. All around them, the floor of the flat valley shimmered beneath the converging moons.

Arilee trembled. "Gito. What *is* it?" Her voice was barely a whisper. He stilled her with a gesture and cocked his head to listen. The song of the Kahrii was beginning again. It was the same song, he thought, only—there was a difference. The first song had been something old, the end of a life—this was a song of beginning.

The ground beneath his feet seemed to tremble with the urgency of the Kahrii voices. Then, he knew it was more than that—a low, awesome rumble of power was rising from deep beneath the surface of the planet.

Arilee gasped. The sand beneath her feet gurgled in a final protest, then the water bubbled from the ground in force. Gito grabbed her and shoved her toward the dome. She stood, numbly watching the strange fluid that already covered her ankles.

"Run," he said sharply, "*Run!*"

"Gito—!"

"I don't *know!*" he yelled, "Just run!"

Halfway there, his heart sank. The water was rising faster than ever now; he estimated quickly and knew they would never make it. Even if they reached the dome, how could they enter without bringing the flood with them? Then what? How high was it going to *go?* How much pressure would the dome take, submerged under the tons of water?

He stopped Arilee and jabbed a hand toward the smaller, closer dome of the sandcar. Arilee saw. Together, they pulled through the sandy water that now swirled above their waists.

Arilee stumbled, disappeared. Gito plunged down to bring her up, gasping and choking.

At the dome, he pressed the lock of the port with his thumb and waited, listening to the mechanism groan against the pressure. Once it seemed to stop and he wedged his body between the narrow opening and shoved. The motor began again, then slowly folded back the door. The waters rushed in to fill the dome above the tracks of the sandcar.

Once Arilee was seated beside him and the canopy locked, he shoved down hard on the overdrive bar, not waiting to build up speed on the useless treads. The power unit howled in protest. Great founts of steam roared beneath them in a gray cloud as the treads retracted and the sandcar trembled. Then they were out of the dome and rising on a hurricane column above the water…

It was a dawn he would never forget. From the ridge above the valley, he watched, Arilee sleeping restlessly in the seat beside him.

The first rays of *Posi Frondee* streaked the new alien sea with red. How many centuries had passed, he wondered, since the four moons had met to suck the dormant waters from the ground and fill the deep well of the dry valley?

He knew, now, that was exactly what it was—a well of the planet's own making, ringed by the solid rock wall.

As the harsh light hit the ridge across the valley, he could see the water had reached far less than halfway back up the 750 feet of the wall. And already it was receding, sinking back into the depths below the sandy floor.

He picked up his binoculars and swept the far end of the valley. Yes. There it was. It had drifted some in the night, but it was still there. The Kahrii ship floated serenely, rolling above the valley floor. Above, he reminded himself grimly, the flooded tunnels he might have used to 'save' the aliens from their folly.

He closed his eyes and took a deep breath. He let it out slowly. He had been right—and wrong, too. Golsamel-ri had told him they would meet again—and they would.

Symbols? Well, the Kahrii were bound, as he had known, by what they could actually see. In his hand he held the symbol that had saved them when the waters rose—this time, and how many times before?

He opened his fist and looked at the object in his palm. It was a small, rough, cylinder, two inches long. Millions of them had risen with the water from the ground, and hundreds had clung to his clothes, and Arilee's.

He split it open down a long seam with his fingernail. Black, tender seeds clung to the inside of the pod. When he touched them lightly, they fell in a numberless stream into his lap.

Gito grinned. No, not numberless at all. When he had the time to count, he knew there would be 888—and the answer to the controlled population of the Kahrii.

Here was the tiny miniature, the model, for the Kahrii ark. When the waters receded, the seeds would recede with them, and the giant Shari would renew themselves and grow in the moist sand.

The larger Kahrii 'seed' would come to rest, too, and new tunnels would be dug in the sand, waiting for the silver-gray shoots to rise and nurture the race.

There would be hunger, he knew. But the Kahrii were good about that—and he suspected the old, mature Shari that had been sheared off at the surface would renew themselves for awhile, and provide until the young plants thrust to the sun. It had happened before, hadn't it? And the race had lived.

Gito pulled his gaze away from the scene outside and rested his eyes on the figure beside him.

He wondered, briefly, if the Warden of Tsirtsi had left an Arilee behind? A quiet chill of fear began to rise in his heart, then died quickly.

He, too, had acted to save—and had ended by destroying. And through the same, sure sense of knowledge and duty Gito had come so close to repeating.

"Arilee," he said softly. She opened one sleepy eye and smiled.

Again, the small finger found his lips and closed them.

"Don't," she said. "Haven't you learned yet a Mistress always knows what a man is thinking?

"Even," she added sleepily, "one that just handed in her resignation?"

Survival Course

Vivid pictures oscillated across Martin's mental screens:

He was a warm pearl in a giant oyster. The oyster was squeezing him to death with dank passion...

He was in the last crushing seconds of fetal agony. Damn! Mother should never have had children...

An inchworm. Inside a great pea. Bam! Cook snapped him cruelly from the pod...

The last, he decided, was close enough to the truth. Something very bad had happened to the ship. Something fatal. The escape capsule had imploded its fleshy walls, formed a Martin-sized cocoon and ejected him from whatever catastrophe lay behind. Now—

ABLE MARTIN.

"What?" Martin tried to move his head. Abruptly the walls sucked themselves back into place. Martin rose weightlessly from his form-couch, pulled himself back, snapped himself down.

MARTIN.

"Who's that?"

SHIP'S COMPUTER, MARTIN.

"Oh."

ARE YOU INJURED IN ANY WAY?

"No. What happened?"

THE SHIP HAS BEEN DESTROYED. YOU ARE ABOARD ESCAPE CAPSULE FORTY-TWO.

Martin waited for more. Evidently direct questions were required. "Did we hit something? No, that's not likely, is it? How did it happen? Did anybody else get off?"

Ship's computer was silent. Martin shrugged, inspected his surroundings. There wasn't much to see. The capsule was spherical. Spongy amber walls. No ports. A single safe-light to his right. Maximum distance from one wall to another, roughly two-and-a-half meters.

And he was—where? Deep space. Between Wolf's Star and Jefferson. But that didn't mean a thing, really. He knew that much. The ship had been in Warp when whatever happened had happened—it could have been tossed into reality nearly anywhere. If he was now remotely near either Wolf's Star or Jefferson it would be a universally large coincidence.

MARTIN.

"Right here."

THE SHIP WAS DESTROYED THROUGH A MALFUNCTION IN THE DAVIDSON AUXILIARY REGULATORS. ESSENTIALLY, INTERFERENCE FROM AN UNANTICIPATED MASS CAUSED A SUBSEQUENT MISALIGNMENT OF THE DRIVE FIELDS, WHICH EJECTED THE SHIP FROM NONSPACE AND DESTROYED IT WHILE ITS WARP ENGINES WERE STILL PARTIALLY FUNCTIONING.

"Oh," said Martin. He had no idea what the computer was talking about.

CHANCES AGAINST SUCH A MALFUNCTION ARE EIGHT TO THE TENTH POWER. THERE ARE NO SURVIVORS OTHER THAN YOURSELF.

Martin winced at that. "*No*body got out? There were two hundred and fifty people aboard."

TWO-HUNDRED-FORTY-SEVEN, the computer corrected. EXCLUDING YOURSELF. WHY WERE YOU IN ESCAPE CAPSULE FORTY-TWO WHEN THE SHIP WAS DESTROYED?

Martin was taken aback. "Huh? I was taking a nap. Why do you ask?"

IT IS UNAUTHORIZED TO ENTER THE ESCAPE CAPSULE UNLESS AN EVACUATION ORDER HAS BEEN ISSUED OR ENTRY PERMISSION HAS BEEN GRANTED.

"Look—"

IF YOU WISHED TO TAKE A NAP, MARTIN, WHY DID YOU NOT UTILIZE THE BUNK IN YOUR CABIN?

"I don't know, I was tired. The capsule was handy. It seemed like a good idea at the time. Listen—what difference does it make now?"

OCCUPYING AN ESCAPE CAPSULE WITHOUT AUTHORIZATION AND/OR RECEIPT OF AN EVACUATION ORDER IS A PASSENGER VIOLATION. THE VIOLATION WILL BE RECORDED.

Martin laughed out loud.

NOT UNDERSTOOD, said the computer. WHY DO YOU EXPRESS DISINTEREST IN THE REPORTING OF THIS VIOLATION?

"Forget it," said Martin. He was getting fed up with the computer's rational ramblings. And worried. There were things he needed to know. Important things. *Where are we and where are we going? When does help arrive? How much air is aboard? Food? Water?*

He asked the most important question first. The answer set his heart thumping against his chest.

"That's all? Eight *days?*"

APPROXIMATELY, the computer told him.

"I don't want approximately, I want exactly!"

EXACT OXYGEN REQUIREMENTS FOR A PERSON OF YOUR PHYSICAL STRUCTURE, MARTIN: ONE HUNDRED NINETY HOURS, PLUS OR MINUS ONE HOUR, CALCULATED FOR NORMAL WAKING AND SLEEPING PERIODS, WITH MINIMAL ACTIVITY.

"Holy Christ," Martin muttered.

YOU NEED NOT BE CONCERNED WITH OXYGEN CONSUMPTION, MARTIN.

"No?"

NO. THE SUPPLY IS MORE THAN ADEQUATE FOR THE DURATION OF YOUR ANIMATE PERIOD.

Martin sat up. "My *animate* period?" Short hairs climbed the back of his neck. "What's that supposed to mean?" He remembered something. "Listen—you're talking about putting me under—something like that. So I'll use less oxygen? Great. I—"

The computer droned: I AM REQUIRED TO STATE CERTAIN FACTS. PLEASE HEAR THEM BEFORE YOU COMMENT FURTHER. ONE: EACH STANDARD ESCAPE POD, MOBILE (SEPM), IS EQUIPPED WITH AN ADEQUATE LIFE SUPPORT SYSTEM. THIS SYSTEM INCLUDES OXYGEN—WHICH WE HAVE DISCUSSED—CONCENTRATED FOOD STAPLES, WATER AND A NUMBER FOUR MEDI-PACKET, MODIFIED. TWO: ADDITIONALLY, BASIC PLANETARY SURVIVAL GEAR IS AVAILABLE SHOULD THE CAPSULE AND ITS OCCUPANT BE RELEASED IN THE VICINITY OF A PLANETARY BODY CAPABLE OF SUPPORTING HUMAN LIFE. THE CAPSULE IS DESIGNED TO ACCOMPLISH A SINGLE LANDING ON SUCH A BODY UNDER NORMAL CONDITIONS. THREE: THE CAPSULE IS ALSO EQUIPPED WITH A STANDARD REIMAR SEVEN-O-TWO BEACON TRANSMITTING DEVICE (BTD), CAPABLE OF EMITTING A THREE-STAGE TRANSLIGHT EMERGENCY SIGNAL WITH A RANGE OF FIVE-HUNDRED LIGHT-YEARS. THE

BTD TRANSMITS A CONTINUOUS HOMING PATTERN FOR A PERIOD OF ONE STANDARD YEAR.

Martin waited. The computer remained silent. He felt immensely relieved. The capsule didn't look like much, but apparently there was more behind its fleshy walls than met the eye.

"This—signal beacon," Martin asked. "How long does it take to reach—wherever it's going?"

THE BTD SIGNAL IS A TIGHT-BEAM TRANSMISSION WHICH BOOSTS AN EMERGENCY 'PULSE' AT TRANS-LIGHT SPEEDS, AS I EXPLAINED. THE IMPULSE REACHES ITS MAXIMUM RANGE OF FIVE HUNDRED LIGHT-YEARS IN FOURTEEN POINT SEVEN MINUTES.

Martin let out a breath. "Then it's already out there. Someone could have picked it up. They could be on their way now."

NEGATIVE, MARTIN.

"What?"

THEORETICALLY, YOU ARE CORRECT. IF THE SIGNAL HAD BEEN TRANSMITTED—AND RECEIVING DEVICES HAD BEEN WITHIN RANGE OF ITS IMPULSE AND A WARP SHIP HAD BEEN AVAILABLE—AS YOU SAY, 'THEY COULD BE ON THEIR WAY NOW.' HOWEVER, ALL SUCH ASSUMPTIONS ARE NECESSARILY INVALID SINCE NO SIGNAL HAS BEEN TRANSMITTED.

"What?" Martin nearly leaped off his couch, forgetting the safety belt that held him in place. "Look—what the hell are you waiting for? I've got a hundred and ninety hours of *breathing* time, friend—plus or minus whatever I'm wasting jawing with you! Just get yourself—"

The computer interrupted: YOU DO NOT UNDERSTAND. I STATED THAT I WAS REQUIRED TO MAKE CERTAIN FACTS KNOWN TO YOU. THESE FACTS CONCERNED THE CAPABILITIES OF THE ESCAPE CAPSULE. 'CAPABILITY' IS DEFINED AS 'HAVING THE CAPACITY OR ABILITY.' IN OTHER WORDS, THE ESCAPE CAPSULE IS EQUIPPED TO PERFORM AND/OR SUPPLY THE AFOREMENTIONED SER-

VICES. UNDER CERTAIN CIRCUMSTANCES, FOR EXAMPLE, THE BTD SIGNAL WOULD BE UTILIZED. UNDER OTHER CONDITIONS, IT MIGHT BECOME EXPEDIENT TO EMPLOY PLANETARY SURVIVAL GEAR. AS IT STANDS, HOWEVER, NONE OF THE EQUIPMENT AND/OR SERVICES MENTIONED ARE APPLICABLE TO THIS PARTICULAR SITUATION.

Martin's blood ran cold. *Applicable?* His first impulse was to scream at the computer and beat on the amber walls. What the hell did it care? *It* was content to stay where it was forever—an electronic half-wit buried in spongy bliss. Its oxygen supply wasn't running out in plus-or-minus hours.

Instead he brought his rapid breathing under control and leaned back on his couch. Not that the computer would care one way or the other whether he was calm or hysterical. Screaming, however, was bound to use up an inordinate amount of oxygen.

Half-wit or not, the computer was there and had to be dealt with.

"Look," Martin said easily, "what I think we have here is a communications problem."

I AM EXPERIENCING NO DIFFICULTY IN COMMUNICATING, MARTIN.

"Okay. I am, though. Let's run through it again. You haven't activated the signal beacon. Why?"

AS I EXPLAINED, BTD TRANSMISSION IS NOT APPLICABLE IN THIS SITUATION.

"Why not?"

WHEN THE SHIP WAS DESTROYED IT WAS THROWN OUT OF WARP AND BACK INTO REALITY. I HAVE MADE EXTENSIVE EFFORTS TO LOCATE OUR POSITION RELATIVE TO INHABITED AND/OR RECORDED QUADRANTS. FROM THIS POINT IN SPACE NO RECOGNIZABLE CONSTELLATIONS CAN BE OBSERVED. I HAVE, OF COURSE, TAKEN INTO CONSIDERATION THE FACT THAT STELLAR PATTERNS DIFFER ACCORDING TO ONE'S POSITION. AD-

DITIONALLY, I HAVE MADE SPECTROSCOPIC ANALYSES IN AN ATTEMPT TO IDENTIFY A FAMILIAR CLUSTER OR UNIT. RESULTS: NEGATIVE.

Martin's heart sank. "In other words, we're lost."

RELATIVE TO MY RECORDED KNOWLEDGE, YES.

A thought suddenly struck him and he sat up straight again. He weighed his words carefully. "Do you believe your—navigational records are wholly complete?"

NOT UNDERSTOOD, MARTIN. 'WHOLLY COMPLETE' IN WHAT SENSE?

"In the sense that you have data on all planets and star-systems that have been discovered, all areas of space that have been mapped and explored."

TO A LARGE EXTENT, YES. WHEN I WAS ON THE SHIP NEW DATA WERE CONTINUOUSLY PROGRAMMED INTO MY BANKS IN AN EFFORT TO MAINTAIN COMPLETE AND ACCURATE NAVIGATIONAL RECORDS. LOGICALLY, HOWEVER, IT IS POSSIBLE THAT DATA EXIST THAT HAVE NOT BEEN MADE AVAILABLE TO ME. I HAVE NO DEFINITE BASIS TO CONCLUDE OTHERWISE.

Martin took a deep breath. "Then—logically—a signal from our position *could* be received."

IT IS CONCEIVABLE.

"Then transmit the signal," Martin said firmly. "If there's any chance at all—"

NEGATIVE, MARTIN. THE ODDS ARE ASTRONOMICALLY HIGH AGAINST RECEPTION.

"To hell with the odds!" Martin struck his fist against the couch. "My odds are zero unless you do something!"

NEGATIVE, MARTIN. I WILL NOT ACTIVATE THE SIGNAL BEACON.

Martin eyed the blank walls narrowly. "I'm not asking—I'm *telling* you. I'm a—a human and I'm giving a machine an order."

PERHAPS IT WOULD BE HELPFUL IF YOU FULLY UNDERSTOOD THAT THERE IS A DIFFERENCE BETWEEN A

COMPLEX COMPUTER SYSTEM BASED ON THE PRINCIPLES OF LOGIC AND A SIMPLE SERVING ROBOT. ALTHOUGH I AM RECEPTIVE TO CERTAIN COMMANDS, I AM NOT PROGRAMMED TO OBEY YOU BLINDLY UNDER ALL CIRCUMSTANCES. MY BASIC FUNCTION IS TO INITIATE LOGICAL ACTIONS BASED UPON AVAILABLE DATA. WHILE IT IS TRUE THAT THERE IS A POSSIBILITY THAT A SIGNAL BEAMED FROM THIS POSITION MIGHT BE RECEIVED THE ODDS—AS I EXPLAINED—ARE OVERWHELMINGLY NEGATIVE. ACTIVATING THE SIGNAL WOULD INVOLVE THE DISSIPATION OF AN IMMENSE AMOUNT OF ENERGY. CONSIDERING THE ODDS, SUCH AN EXPENDITURE WOULD BE UNNECESSARILY WASTEFUL.

Martin dropped his head to the couch. "Look," he said wearily, "what am I going to do with all that immense amount of energy when I'm *dead* eight days from now? Will you explain that to me. Please?"

He let out a deep breath and looked at the amber walls. "Listen, I said a minute ago we had a communications problem. No. *I* do. You know my name, so you also probably know from the passenger roster what I do. I'm a heavy-equipment salesman. I sell things to people who want to dig up mountains and build bridges. All of our stuff is fully automatic—you can program it to do anything you want it to do. Only, that's not my end of the business. I know how to stick the tape in—period. What I'm saying is, I'm not used to talking to computers. I simply don't understand why it seems—and I'm not saying it's true—but it *seems* as if you're not making every effort to get me back to civilization before my air runs out." Martin shook his head. "I don't understand that. If you're not going to activate the signal—what are you going to do?"

An idea suddenly occurred to him. "A minute ago you said something about how I wouldn't need all the oxygen on board. That it would be—what? 'Adequate for my animate period?'

Is that what you've got in mind—putting me in some kind of deep sleep or something? We didn't get back to that."

YOU MISUNDERSTOOD, MARTIN. THE WORD 'ANIMATE' IN THE SENSE IT WAS USED, CAN BE DEFINED AS 'POSSESSING LIFE,' OR 'LIVING.' WHAT I SAID WAS THAT 'THE SUPPLY IS MORE THAN ADEQUATE FOR THE DURATION OF YOUR ANIMATE PERIOD.' BY THAT I MEANT THAT PRIOR TO THE TIME WHEN YOUR AVAILABLE OXYGEN SUPPLY WOULD ORDINARILY BE CONSUMED YOU WILL BE IN AN ESSENTIALLY NONLIVING STATE, AS FAR AS PERSONAL COGNIZANCE IS CONCERNED.

Martin felt something terrible clutch at his stomach. "For God's sake—what are you talking about? What are you going to do to me?"

I ASKED EARLIER THAT YOU ALLOW ME TO PRESENT CERTAIN FACTS. YOU HAVE, HOWEVER, FREQUENTLY ALLOWED YOUR EMOTIONS—

"Damn you!" Martin shouted. "I'm alive! I'm supposed to have emotions!"

ASSUREDLY. AS I STATED, THE STANDARD ESCAPE POD, MOBILE (SEPM), HAS CERTAIN CAPABILITIES. I ALSO ATTEMPTED TO EXPLAIN THAT WHILE THE SEPM'S PRIMARY FUNCTION IS TO TRANSPORT HUMAN SURVIVORS TO SAFETY, IF POSSIBLE, THERE ARE CONDITIONS UNDER WHICH—

"Listen," said Martin, "I don't want to hear any of that again."

—UNDER WHICH THIS FUNCTION IS NO LONGER RELEVANT. EXAMPLES: WHEN NO PLANETARY BODY CAPABLE OF SUPPORTING LIFE IS PRESENT WITHIN THE OPERATIONAL SPHERE OF THE CAPSULE...WHEN THE ODDS AGAINST RECEPTION OF A BTD SIGNAL BEAM ARE ASTRONOMICAL. I ALSO EXPLAINED THAT, WHILE I AM RECEPTIVE TO CERTAIN COMMANDS UNDER SPECIFIC CONDITIONS, I AM NOT PROGRAMMED TO OBEY ALL INSTRUCTIONS. PRESENT CONDITIONS ARE SUCH THAT I

HAVE OVERRIDDEN ALL BUT MY PRIMARY PROGRAMMING. I AM INITIATING A SECONDARY LOGICAL ACTION BASED ON AVAILABLE DATA. I WILL EXERCISE THE STELLAR OUTREACH OPTION IN EXACTLY FORTY-FIVE STANDARD MINUTES.

Main stared dumbly. "You'll what? I don't have any idea what you're talking about."

IT IS QUITE PAINLESS, MARTIN. YOU WILL NOT—

"Painless!"

YOU MUST UNDERSTAND THAT THE ALTERNATIVE IS QUITE NECESSARY. THE STELLAR OUTREACH OPTION IS NOT EXERCISED UNLESS OTHER CHOICES ARE IMPRACTICAL. IN THIS CASE NO OTHER OPTION IS OPEN. AGAIN, THE PROCEDURE IN NO WAY—

"Wait a minute," Martin said hoarsely. He was scared, bewildered. His head throbbed. The whole thing was a nightmare.

Only one fact was frighteningly clear: the computer had no intention of trying to save his life. For some reason of its own it was going to kill him.

Once he'd let his mind form the words he felt reasonably calm. And it was absolutely necessary for him to remain completely rational. His emotions were meaningless to the computer. If he was going to stay alive he would have to face the computer on its own ground. If he couldn't fight logic with logic—he was dead. It was as simple as that. The computer couldn't have put it better.

"All right," he said calmly, "tell me about the—Stellar Outreach option."

YOUR REASONABLE ATTITUDE IS ENCOURAGING, MARTIN.

"Thanks," Martin said dryly.

THE STELLAR OUTREACH OPTION WAS PROGRAMMED INTO THE BANKS OF EVERY SHIP'S COMPUTER AS AN ALTERNATE TO THE ESCAPE CAPSULE'S PRIMARY FUNCTION. ESSENTIALLY: SURVIVORS WITH

LOW RESCUE PROFILES—SUCH AS YOURSELF, MARTIN—ARE REAPPORTIONED INTO THEIR CHROMOSOMAL COMPONENTS, ENCAPSULATED IN LIFEBANK DISPERSAL CARRIERS (LDC) AND PROJECTED IN A RANDOM PATTERN FROM THE CENTRAL POINT OF ORIGIN—WHICH, OF COURSE, IS THE ESCAPE CAPSULE ITSELF.

Martin swallowed and stared at the amber wall. "But—why?"

THE PURPOSE OF STELLAR OUTREACH IS TO SPREAD THE SEED OF MAN. IT IS AN ENTIRELY LOGICAL SUB-PROGRAM. THOSE WHO CANNOT SURVIVE IN THEIR PRIMARY FORMS ARE GIVEN THE OPPORTUNITY TO SURVIVE AS POTENTIAL LIFEBANKS OF THE FUTURE. IT HAS BEEN THEORIZED THAT MAN MAY HAVE EVOLVED ON MANY PLANETS IN JUST THIS MANNER. AT ANY RATE, APPROXIMATELY ONE HUNDRED MILLION CHROMOSOMAL UNIT PACK SYSTEMS (CUPS) ARE DISPERSED THROUGH SPACE IN ONE THOUSAND LIFEBANK DISPERSAL CARRIERS. AT A SPECIFIED DISTANCE FROM THE INITIAL DISPERSAL POINT EACH LDC EXPLODES AND SCATTERS ITS CUPS—THUS, GREAT SPATIAL DISTRIBUTION IS ACHIEVED.

Martin was valiantly holding onto his reason. *God help me,* he thought grimly, *if I ever get back to anywhere someone's going to hear about this...*

"You can—do all that?" He was curious in spite of himself. "Here—in this capsule?"

THE PROCEDURE IS RELATIVELY SIMPLE, the computer told him. BASICALLY THE SUBJECT'S PHYSICAL BODY IS—

"I don't want to go into that part," Martin said quickly.

THEN PERHAPS AN ANALOGY WILL SERVE. GENETICALLY SPEAKING, IF YOUR BODY WERE SUDDENLY TO EXPLODE EACH PARTICLE WOULD, IN A SENSE, RETAIN ITS IDENTITY. THOUGH EACH, OF COURSE, WOULD BE NONSENTIENT, EACH WOULD RETAIN THE CELLULAR IDENTITY OF ABLE MARTIN. CURIOUSLY, I CAN PRESENT

A SIMILAR ANALOGY USING MYSELF AS AN EXAMPLE. ORIGINALLY COMPUTERS WERE CONSTRUCTED AS SINGULAR UNITS. NOW, NEARLY ALL ARE ORGANIC TO THEIR IMMEDIATE ENVIRONMENT. I WAS A PART OF EVERY PART OF THE SHIP. PARTS OF ME WERE LOST WHEN THE SHIP WAS DESTROYED, BUT SINCE EACH PART IS ESSENTIALLY A PART OF THE WHOLE—

"Okay, I understand," said Martin. "One question. Logic or no logic, what you've got in mind is to do me in, right?"

IT IS A COLLOQUIALISM MEANING TO BRING ABOUT THE DEATH OF AN INDIVIDUAL.

"Yes. That's what it is. What it amounts to is you are going to take a human life against its will. What *that* is is murder, whether a—a person does it or a computer. You can look up the definition yourself. I don't have any desire to be 'nonsentient,' friend—and I couldn't care less about Spreading the Seed of Man. I don't know much about robots and computers but I can't believe you haven't got some kind of built-in something or other that prohibits your taking a human life. Look that up in your banks or cells or whatever and tell me I'm wrong."

ESSENTIALLY YOU ARE RIGHT, MARTIN. HOWEVER, YOUR STATEMENT IS NONRELEVANT.

"It's relevant to me!" Martin shouted.

PERHAPS. HOWEVER, WHEN I TRANSFORM YOU FROM YOUR PRESENT PHYSICAL STATE INTO CHROMOSOMAL UNIT PACK SYSTEMS I WILL NOT BE 'TAKING A HUMAN LIFE.' I WILL MERELY BE REDISTRIBUTING ITS COMPONENTS IN A DIFFERENT MANNER. FROM YOUR WORDS I SENSE THAT YOU ARE EMOTIONALLY DISTURBED. AS I STATED, THE PROCEDURE IS PAINLESS. AN ODORLESS GAS—

"You can't—"

—WILL BE RELEASED IN THIRTY-EIGHT MINUTES. A—

"Thirty-eight minutes!"

—A STANDARD FORTY-FIVE MINUTES IS GRANTED TO SUBJECTS BETWEEN ANNOUNCEMENT OF THE PROCEDURE AND ACTUAL PROCESSING. THIS TIME MAY BE USED AT THE DISCRETION OF THE INDIVIDUAL CONCERNED—SLEEPING, EATING, OR THE CONTEMPLATION OF MYTHICAL DEITIES ARE SEVERAL OPTIONS. ENTERTAINMENT TAPES AND HOLOGRAPHIC PRESENTATIONS ARE AVAILABLE. ACCELERATED LEARNING TAPES ON A VARIETY OF SUBJECTS ARE ALSO ABOARD, INCLUDING COURSES IN ONE HUNDRED SEVENTEEN LANGUAGES. THESE LATTER, OF COURSE, MAY APPEAR IMPRACTICAL TO STELLAR OUTREACH CANDIDATES. YOU HAVE NOW CONSUMED NINE MINUTES, MARTIN. TIME REMAINING: THIRTY-SIX MINUTES.

Martin's body was slick with moisture. A sickly odor exuded from his pores. Think, think—he had to *think!* Only, how could he think with his head splitting open? He wondered if there was anything as simple as an aspirin in a Number Four MediPacket, Modified.

In moments his hands began to shake. He tried to stop them by putting them under his back, then clamping them to the arms of the couch. Nothing helped. The sweat on his body turned cold and he began to tremble uncontrollably. He closed his eyes and forced his breathing back to normal.

Maybe, he decided, it would be best to forget the whole thing. Stop fighting it. He had less than eight days of oxygen—even if the computer would let him live to use it. Those eight days would be pure hell—knowing they were the end, that no help was on the way. Why not just...

He angrily swept the thought aside. Anything could happen in eight days. If he could stay alive maybe he could con the computer into sending a signal. Someone *might* pick it up.

A range of five hundred light-years covered a pretty big chunk of space.

Life Dispersal Carriers—great God, who had thought that one up! He wondered what the odds were against any of the one-hundred-million cellular bits of Able Martin ever getting anywhere. Or doing anything when they got there. Those kind of odds, though, didn't seem to bother the computer at all. And why should they? Passengers in Chromosomal Unit Pack Systems would find it difficult to complain to the space lines.

Time...time...damn it, time was running out! Thirty-six minutes. Less than that, now. Maybe there was something in the planetary survival gear. If he could find it. And get to it. Take a good slice at the fleshy walls. Maybe short out the computer and...He tossed the idea aside. That wouldn't get him any closer to activating the beacon. Hell, he wouldn't know what to do with it if he found it.

There was only one way. He'd known that from the beginning. Fight the computer on its own ground. The computer wasn't God—it was a machine—a machine that used the tools of intelligence, but really had no intelligence of its own. Computers reasoned—but they only reasoned with what they had to work with. Didn't they? Basically, then, while the computer had access to a great deal more knowledge than he had and could put it together faster and better—he, Able Martin, could outthink it. If he pushed the right button at the right time. That was the key: the computer had limitations. Find those limitations.

He tried to think back on what the computer had said. There had to be something. Somewhere. Option: activate the signal beacon. No. The computer was stubbornly set against that. No time to argue the point. Option: Get to a planet. Get out of the capsule. Double-negative. He was a billion prime miles from nowhere. Option: talk the computer into letting him live long enough to dream up other options...

Martin wearily swept the whole thing aside. It was hopeless. No time. *Think,* damn it! Look at it. Turn it around. Take it apart.

"Computer."

YES, MARTIN.

"How much time left?"

SEVENTEEN MINUTES, TWENTY-ONE SECONDS, MARTIN.

Martin's stomach turned over. No time, no time!

He didn't try to think. Just let it flow. Let it all run by like a swiftly moving river. Watch it as it passes. Warp. Malfunction. Destruction. Ejection. Beacon—

Hold it.

Something.

He struggled to pin it down. Don't struggle—relax. Warp. Malfunction. Destruction. Destroyed how? What did the computer say?

"Computer!"

YES, MARTIN.

"How was the ship destroyed?"

I HAVE INFORMED YOU OF THAT, MARTIN.

"Inform me again!" Martin said savagely.

YES, MARTIN. THE SHIP—

"Like you told it before. *Exactly* like you told it before."

—THE SHIP WAS DESTROYED THROUGH A MALFUNCTION IN THE DAVIDSON AUXILIARY REGULATORS. ESSENTIALLY, INTERFERENCE FROM AN UNANTICIPATED MASS—

"Wait. There. An unanticipated mass. What—kind of a mass?"

A MASS WITH THE DENSITY OF—

"Forget the details," Martin said quickly. "General description."

GENERAL DESCRIPTION: THE MASS IN QUESTION IS DEFINED AS A PLANETARY BODY.

Martin's heart skipped a beat. "Okay. Planetary body. And the ship came too close to it. So its mass interfered—Where? Where was the mass? In Warp?"

NO, MARTIN. THERE ARE NO PLANETARY BODIES IN NONSPACE.

"Then it's here—in real space?"

YES, MARTIN. IF THE DAVIDSON AUXILIARY REGULATORS HAD BEEN FUNCTIONING PROPERLY, PRESENCE OF A MASS OUTSIDE THE WARP WOULD NOT HAVE—

"There's a planet here? And you didn't tell me about it!"

ITS PRESENCE WAS NOT RELEVANT, MARTIN.

Martin bit off his words. "Time. How much time?"

TWELVE MINUTES, EIGHT SECONDS, MARTIN.

Martin took a deep breath. Easy. Take it easy...

"The planet. How far away is it?"

FOURTEEN POINT SEVEN MILLION MILES.

"How long would it take to get there?"

NOT RELEVANT, MARTIN.

"Hypothetically!"

SIX STANDARD DAYS, PLUS FOUR HOURS, MARTIN.

We could make it. We could just...

"Air. How about air?"

OXYGEN CONTENT IS SUITABLE FOR HUMAN LIFE.

"Then why in hell—" Martin paused, collected himself. "Please. Give me the reasons this planet isn't—relevant to me."

SUITABLE OXYGEN CONTENT FOR SUSTAINING LIFE IS MERELY ONE REQUISITE FOR PLACEMENT OF SURVIVORS ON A PLANETARY BODY. OTHER FACTORS INCLUDE; PROBABILITY OF ADEQUATE FOOD AND WATER SUPPLIES. SUITABLE CLIMATIC CONDITIONS. NEGATIVE FACTORS: POSSIBILITY OF PRESENCE OF LIFE FORMS INIMICAL TO HUMAN LIFE. POSSIBLE—

"Look," Martin interrupted. "Those things are for me to decide. I'll take my chances." He stopped, bit his lip thoughtfully. "Wait. Wait, you don't know whether any of those factors are relevant, do you? You said 'possible,' and 'probable'—that means you can't tell anything from here. Or can you?"

NO, MARTIN. AT THIS DISTANCE, IT IS ONLY POSSIBLE TO COMPUTE MASS, DENSITY, ATMOSPHERIC CONTENT, PRESENCE OF LAND AND WATER AREAS—

"Then you can't say it's not suitable—you haven't seen it!"

AFFIRMATIVE, MARTIN.

"Then for God's sake, let's at least look at it! We've got the time, we can get there. What's the big hurry to send me sailing off in your bloody whatever it is—lifebank disposal—"

LIFEBANK DISPERSAL CARRIERS (LDC), MARTIN.

"Okay! You've got to—"

MARTIN. FIRST, I SHOULD NOTE THAT THE POSSIBILITY OF ACTIVATING THE BTD WAS CONSIDERED, DUE TO THE PRESENCE OF THE PLANETARY MASS. HOWEVER, LACK OF ANY RADIO ACTIVITY OR EVIDENCE OF OTHER COMMUNICATION DEVICES NEGATED THE OPTION. IT WAS NECESSARY, THEN, MARTIN, TO WEIGH THE PROBABILITY OF YOUR SURVIVAL ON THE PLANETARY MASS AGAINST UTILIZATION OF YOUR COMPONENTS UNDER THE STELLAR OUTREACH OPTION. RESULTS: ONE: IT IS NOT POSSIBLE FROM THIS DISTANCE TO ADEQUATELY DETERMINE ALL PERTINENT CHARACTERISTICS OF THE PLANETARY MASS IN QUESTION. TWO: SUCH CHARACTERISTICS COULD BE DETERMINED BY VIEWING THE PLANET FROM A CLOSER PROXIMITY. THREE: ENERGY CONSUMPTION REQUIRED TO REACH THE PLANETARY MASS FOR FURTHER STUDY WOULD PROHIBIT FURTHER LARGE EXPENDITURES OF ENERGY. FOUR: IF THE CHARACTERISTICS OF THE PLANET INDICATED A LOW SURVIVAL PROFILE (LSP), PLACEMENT WOULD BE NEGATED. ADDITIONALLY, NO ENERGY WOULD THEN BE AVAILABLE TO EXERCISE THE STELLAR OUTREACH OPTION. CONCLUSIONS: IT FOLLOWS THAT SURVIVOR ABLE MARTIN COULD THEN NEITHER BE (A) PLACED ON A SUIT-

ABLE PLANETARY BODY NOR (B) UTILIZED AS CHROMOSOMAL UNIT PACK SYSTEMS (CUPS). THEREFORE, I HAVE A CHOICE BETWEEN EITHER EXERCISING THE STELLAR OUTREACH OPTION OR PLACING MYSELF IN THE POSITION OF VERY POSSIBLY BEING UNABLE TO EXERCISE EITHER THE STELLAR OUTREACH OPTION OR PLANET-PLACEMENT. IT IS ILLOGICAL TO CHOOSE THE LATTER. FURTHER, EDICT ONE OF MY PRIMARY PROGRAMMING INSTRUCTIONS (PPI) PROHIBITS SUCH ACTION.

Martin looked up wearily. "I have to ask. What's Edict One?"

EDICT ONE PROHIBITS ME FROM ENDANGERING A HUMAN BEING'S CHANCE OF SURVIVAL THROUGH NEGLIGENCE.

"What?" Martin jerked up, then sank back limply to the couch.

"Time."

SIX MINUTES, EIGHTEEN SECONDS. THE PROCESS, AS I HAVE EXPLAINED, IS COMPLETELY PAINLESS. AN ODORLESS—

"Shut up," said Martin.

That was it then. Six minutes. Zero. There was no point in carrying the farce any further. Clearly, he had been had. The electronic half-wit was winner and still champion.

He thought about three girls who might miss him for a while and a number of creditors who would tearfully mourn his passing. He wondered what the planet looked like. He wished he could see it and tried to imagine it. Trees. Lakes, maybe? Fresh air. All the fresh air he would ever need. Lonely, but a whole world...

Martin sat up abruptly. "Computer!"

YES, MARTIN.

"What's your definition of a world—a planetary body—capable of supporting human life?"

ONE; ATMOSPHERIC CONTENT TO CONSIST OF—

"Just generalize—briefly!"

ADEQUATE AIR, FOOD AND WATER PLUS A SUITABLE ENVIRONMENT.

"That's all?"

YOU REQUESTED A BRIEF, GENERAL STATEMENT, MARTIN. THERE ARE NUMEROUS SPECIFIC REQUIREMENTS.

"But basically, that's it."

AFFIRMATIVE, MARTIN.

Martin took a deep breath. "I'm going to describe a specific planet. It has adequate air, food and water, plus a suitable environment. That meets your general requirements?"

YES, MARTIN.

"I have described this escape capsule. Do you still accept my definition?"

NEGATIVE, MARTIN. THIS ESCAPE CAPSULE PARTIALLY MEETS SOME OF THE REQUIREMENTS OF A PLANETARY BODY CAPABLE OF SUPPORTING LIFE. IT DOES NOT, HOWEVER—

"It has air, food and water," Martin shouted. "And the environment's suitable—I love it!"

—DOES NOT, HOWEVER MEET ALL NECESSARY STANDARDS OF A SUITABLE PLANETARY BODY.

"Listen," Martin said desperately, "there are artificial planets, satellites..."

YES, MARTIN.

"They have atmospheres—like this one—and don't tell me that atmosphere has to be on the outside, either—"

AGREED, MARTIN.

"—and nobody said anything about size, so—"

PLANETARY BODIES CAPABLE OF SUPPORTING HUMAN LIFE CAN INCLUDE THE CATEGORY OF ARTIFICIAL AS WELL AS NATURAL PLANETS. HOWEVER, THIS PAR-

TICULAR ARTIFICIAL PLANET LACKS A NECESSARY CHARACTERISTIC.

"What?"

UNDER YOUR DEFINITION, A SPACESHIP, SEAGOING VESSEL, LANDCAR OR EVEN AN ANIMAL-DRAWN VEHICLE COULD CONCEIVABLY FULFILL THE REQUIREMENTS OF HAVING ADEQUATE SUPPLIES OF AIR, FOOD AND WATER AND A SUITABLE ENVIRONMENT—WHETHER THEY ARE PLANETARY BODIES ARE NOT. HOWEVER, NONE OF THESE CARRIERS FULFILL THE NECESSARY REQUIREMENT TO WHICH I REFER. NONE CAN SUSTAIN A HUMAN BEING OVER HIS NATURAL LIFESPAN. NEITHER CAN THIS CAPSULE. NOR IS THERE ANY LOGICAL PROBABILITY THAT ADDITIONAL SUPPLIES OF AIR, FOOD OR WATER CAN BE OBTAINED FROM OUTSIDE SOURCES. THEREFORE, IT, TOO, MUST BE CLASSIFIED AS A CARRIER, AN INSTRUMENT CAPABLE OF SUSTAINING HUMAN LIFE ON A TEMPORARY BASIS—NOT AS A PLANETARY BODY.

"Oh, Jesus," Martin moaned. "How much time?"

THREE MINUTES, TEN SECONDS, MARTIN.

"Look—what's the hurry? Can't you delay?"

NEGATIVE, MARTIN. THERE IS NO LOGICAL REASON FOR PROPOSING A DELAY IN PROCESSING.

Three minutes...

No way to—"Hold it!" Martin sat up, strained against the couch. "That's all that's missing, right? The capsule's got to sustain me for my natural lifespan. Then it can be a planet. Officially."

YES, MARTIN. UNDER A BROAD DEFINITION.

Martin held his breath. "Computer. How old am I?"

QUESTION, MARTIN. ARE YOU INQUIRING AS TO YOUR AGE OR MY KNOWLEDGE OF YOUR AGE?

"Yes. Your knowledge. Do you know how old I am?"

NEGATIVE, MARTIN. I DO NOT HAVE THAT INFORMATION.

Martin breathed a silent sigh. It wasn't in the passenger records, then—just name, occupation, destination. The image of a second-hand sweeping around a dial at lightspeeds flashed through is mind.

"What's the average lifespan of a human being?" Martin asked.

SOURCE: CONFEDERATION STATISTICAL BUREAU (CSB): THE AVERAGE LIFESPAN OF HUMAN BEINGS WITHIN THE PROVINCES AND TERRITORIES OF THE CONFEDERATION IS NINETY-SEVEN POINT FOUR STANDARD YEARS.

"Oldest recorded lifespan?" Martin added quickly.

OLDEST RECORDED LIFESPAN: ONE HUNDRED AND FIFTY-ONE POINT THREE STANDARD YEARS. PLACE: SYSTEM NUMB—

"And you don't *know* how old I am?" Martin broke in. "Earlier, you said you could tell from my physical characteristics how much oxygen I'd use. Can't you see me? Don't you know what I look like?"

NEGATIVE, MARTIN. I DO NOT 'SEE' AS A HUMAN DEFINES 'SEEING.' I HAVE SENSORY DEVICES WHICH ENABLE ME TO GAIN A VARIETY OF DATA—

"How much time?"

FIFTY-THREE POINT NINE SECONDS, MARTIN.

Sweat stung Martin's brow. He gripped the couch to keep his hands from trembling.

"Computer," he said evenly. "I am three hundred and forty-nine years old."

QUESTION: MARTIN: WHILE I CANNOT 'SEE' YOU IN THE MANNER IN WHICH YOU DEFINE 'SEEING,' I CAN SENSE CERTAIN PHYSICAL FUNCTIONS. YOU HEART IS OPERATING IN THE MANNER EXPECTED OF A HEALTHY

HUMAN MALE, BETWEEN THE AGES OF THIRTY-FOUR AND THIRTY-SEVEN.

Martin's stomach turned over. *Christ, I had him. I almost had him...*

—THEREFORE, THERE IS AN IRREGULARITY BETWEEN YOUR STATED AGE AND YOUR PHYSICAL CONDITION. TIME: FOURTEEN POINT THREE SECONDS.

Martin's throat clamped shut.

PRELIMINARY PROCESSING WILL BEGIN, MARTIN.

"Wait!" Martin cried frantically.

TIME: EIGHT POINT ONE SECONDS, MARTIN.

"Listen, damn it," Martin shouted, "I'm three hundred and forty-nine years old. I—Wait, look—it *is* a thirty-five year-old heart, I—I had a transplant! Right, I had a transplant!"

TIME: SIX POINT THREE SECONDS, MARTIN.

"You can't kill me," Martin shouted, "don't you understand? Look at the odds—I'm way overdue to die! That's logical, isn't it? I've got more than enough air, food and water to last me the rest of my natural lifespan!"

TIME, TWO SECONDS, MARTIN. THE—

"No!"

—STELLAR OUTREACH OPTION IS CANCELED.

Martin sank back and sucked in precious swallows of air. "All right," he said weakly, "this capsule is a planet. An official planet."

AFFIRMITIVE, MARTIN.

"And the Medi-Packet. And the food and water supplies."

AFFIRMITIVE, MARTIN.

"Show me how you open the thing up. The exit portal."

A red knob appeared beside him. IT IS INOPERATIVE, MARTIN, UNLESS SENSORY PROBES INDICATE A SUITABLE ATMOSPHERE ON THE OUTER SURFACE. THERE IS NO SUCH—

"Fine. Okay." Martin lay back and took a deep breath. "Computer. I want *my* planet to assume an orbit around the other planet in question. Any objections?"

NEGATIVE, MARTIN. THERE IS PRECEDENT.

"Any orbit I want."

AFFIRMITIVE, MARTIN.

"Okay. Do it. Now."

AFFIRMITIVE, MARTIN. SPECIFY ORBITAL HEIGHT, PLEASE.

Gotcha, you son of a bitch…

"I want a decaying orbit," Martin said, "to about eighteen inches. Then just hold it there. Stationary. Yes, that'll do nicely."

The computer said nothing.

Grandfather Pelts

Klaywelder landed the *Glory B* as gently as a baby's breath. The gravitics held a quarter-inch above the ground as the big engines hummed down the scale and sighed.

Klaywelder sighed with them. Then, without a glance outside, he pulled himself up quickly from the pilot's couch and walked the few feet to his quarters. At the foot of his bunk he carefully pressed his right thumb against a particular spot on the bulkhead. The deck beneath him shuddered and screeched in protest as its atoms were harshly realigned. The metal surrounding his cargo was now unmetal—a horrid molecular mess with all the spectographic purity of scrambled eggs.

Klaywelder nodded with satisfaction. No one, not even Klaywelder himself, could open it now—only the peculiar little character on Filo who had installed the thing could wrench it back to normal without melting down the ship.

Klaywelder strolled back to the cabin and stuffed his pipe with Guubi weed. The first puff made him gag. He scowled and knocked the bowl out on the deck. Earth tobacco, he promised himself, would be first on his list. And with what he had in the hold he could well afford the best, this time.

He glanced through the port at the rolling, sage-green hills and whipped-cream skies. Last stop, Pharalell IV, and then home—and more credits than even he had ever dreamed of.

Klaywelder's smug contentment turned to mild annoyance. The domed entryport at the edge of the field looked like an ugly pink hive—and now, out of that hive swarmed three angry silver hornets, making their way for the *Glory B.*

As the hornets drew closer they turned into glittering speedsters. Klaywelder spotted the tiny Federation emblems on their sides. Two of the speedsters carried customs guards with dark rifles bouncing off their backs. The third held the short, stocky frame of Arto Frank.

Klaywelder bit his lip. He hadn't seen Arto in six years—and Arto was the last person he'd hoped to run into on Pharalell IV.

Klaywelder dropped to the ground and closed the port behind him. Frank burned rubber inches from his boots.

"Uhuh. I thought so." Arto Frank eyed him grimly. "What do you want here, Klaywelder?" He didn't wait for an answer. His head jerked to one side and motioned the other speedsters. "Mac, Artie—seal the ship."

The guards braced kickstands and moved forward.

"Hold it," warned Klaywelder.

The guards looked at each other, then at Frank. Klaywelder backed against the hull and pointedly pressed a bright stud at his belt. Frank watched him from narrowed eyes.

Klaywelder folded his arms. "I just wanted to get this whole little scene down on film, Arto. All right, now tell 'em."

Frank showed the barest instant of hesitation. Klaywelder smiled to himself. He reached into his tunic and tossed Frank a neat blue packet. Frank caught the object without looking at it.

"Travel Clearance," said Klaywelder. "Ship's Registry, Ownership Certificate, Parole Papers and Federation Tourist Visa."

"Tourist Visa," Frank repeated and looked at him without expression. Then he turned his head and nodded slightly at the two guards. They pressed their speedsters to life and roared off across the field.

"You can turn off the gimmicks now," said Frank. "If you had them on in the first place."

"I did," said Klaywelder. He pressed another stud. "I'm not under arrest, then?"

"No." Frank faced Klaywelder squarely. "You're not under arrest. What you're under is a thirty-two-hour surveillance until you break atmosphere."

"That's harassment—"

"You can forget the guardhouse law, Klaywelder," Frank said flatly. "Just remember this. As Federation Customs Officer on Pharalell IV I can arrest you if you break the law here, lock you up, seal your ship or send you right back to Barrion for breaking parole. I'll do that, Klaywelder, if you so much as step on the grass. Understood?"

Klaywelder nodded.

"Just to set the record straight," Frank added quietly, "I know why you're here. I've even got a fair idea where you've been." He glanced up at the ship's dark hull. "I can smell contraband fur, Klaywelder—behind eighteen inches of titanium. I'm sure you have a nice hoard in there. I'm just as sure you could turn the whole cache into carbon before I could get a Search & Seizure."

Frank shook his head. "I wouldn't go to the trouble. Just remember—" he poked a menacing finger at Klaywelder—"you're not dealing with animals here. The Pharalellians are intelligent beings under Federation protection. You lay one hand on a Pharalell pelt—"

"Arto!" Klaywelder let an expression of shock cross his face.

"Uhuh. Sure." Frank stared at him distastefully. "I forget. You're a tourist. Just don't you forget, Klaywelder."

With a final look of disdain, he mounted his speedster and disappeared across the blue tarmac.

Through long years on the outer fringes of the law—and somewhat beyond—Klaywelder had learned to maintain an outer calm in spite of inner feelings. It was difficult to hold onto that control now.

Difficult? It was all he could do to keep from shouting, jumping up and down, turning handsprings. Arto Frank was right, of course. There was indeed a lovely cache of furs beneath the metallic fruitcake of his deck—heavy, cobalt-blue Rhinofox from Claxin, incredibly fine Sapphurs from Ehhinode and fifty-thousand rare microfurs from Deserexx—inch-long platinum pelts from the tiny minkmice, who conveniently welded themselves together in death to form long, silky stoles.

And all those goodies looked like so much boar bristle next to what he was seeing now.

He strolled beneath the feathery, sage-blue trees in the central plaza of Ochassh, the town nearest Pharalell's sole spaceport. He felt a little like an ant at a convention of beetles. The Pharalellians were roughly the size of teenage elephants but there was nothing remotely elephantine about them. They strolled gracefully and majestically about the plaza—four long legs moving in rhythm with shorter forearms hanging from shoulder height. If a prize Afghan were mated with an oversized anteater, Klaywelder decided, their progeny might look something like a Pharalellian.

But Klaywelder only absently noted these minor characteristics—for covering those great bodies from head to toe was the most indescribably glorious fur he had ever seen. It was finer than a spider's gossamer strands. It had the sheen of a lovely woman's hair by moonlight, the sparkle of a dew-covered leaf in early morn, just touched by the sun. And it came in blacker than jet, in breathtaking amber, in fleeting cream—and in every other shade he could imagine. Knowing his special customers as he did, Klaywelder was sure each pelt—just to be ultra-conservative—Klaywelder gave up.

Counting credits in stacks that high made him dizzy.

He played tourist for the rest of the afternoon. He bought examples of carved *Dinii* wood, a favorite Pharalell souvenir. He sent half a dozen postcards to people he had never heard of and ignored Arto Frank's man, who had not been more than twenty yards behind him all day.

At sundown, he walked back to the ship, had a leisurely meal and fell into a peaceful sleep. His dreams were so erotic and furry he almost blushed passing the mirror on the way in to breakfast.

Klaywelder had managed to stay out of jail more often than he'd been forced to stay in. He was sure, in his own mind, this was because he took his work seriously and went about each job with a surgeon's care. He had learned a lot about Pharalellians before landing on the planet. He knew they were extremely religious, exhaustingly polite and unbelievably naïve. All three qualities placed them in an almost textbook Category AAA—which meant they were rigidly protected by Federation edict against people like Klaywelder.

On the other hand, the Pharalellians' own mores and manners tied Arto Frank's hands very nicely. Frank could in no way warn the Pharalellians against him. Discourtesy to any living creature—and that included bad-mouthing fur thieves—was a most extreme no-no. Frank, then, could not make a move until and if Klaywelder stepped out of line.

And that Klaywelder wasn't about to do—certainly not in any way discernible to Arto Frank.

It was the largest house on the square—large even by Pharalellian standards. Sun-washed white stone flowed into subtle pastels of pink and green. A high, ornate metal gate graced a vine-covered entryway.

The big Pharalellian moved sedately out of his doorway and into the street. Klaywelder faultlessly allowed himself to be crowded off the stone walk. He flailed his arms wildly, then collapsed in a horrible heap. He lay there unmoving, his head cocked ominously against the curb.

The Pharalellian stiffened, then cringed visibly.

"Siim shave me!" it cried. "What have I done?"

Klaywelder moaned. The Pharalellian swooped down and laid a beautifully furry hand across his brow. "I am Steresshshi," it said gently. "You will call me Garii, please. It is a name reserved for intimate friends who have known me at least forty seasons. You have by my discourtesy earned the right to use it. Are you hurt badly?"

Klaywelder sat up and blinked.

"I'm all right. I think." He shook his head. Then his eyes widened. "Oh, no—"

Garii stiffened. "You are injured, then?"

"No, it's not that." Klaywelder began frantically searching the street around him. "My physical body is of no consequence. Not when my spiritual well-being is threatened."

Garii's eyes quivered under his furry brow. "Your—spiritual—"

"Yes." Klaywelder nodded. "I can't seem to find my pouch. It was here—I wear it around my neck on a silver chain—"

The Pharalellian bent down to join the search. "This pouch—it is important to you?"

Klaywelder sighed. "It is only my ticket into Paradise, nothing more."

Garii sucked in a deep breath.

"It contains the nail parings of my father and his fathers before him," Klaywelder explained somberly. "As I am the ninth son of the ninth virgin, the pouch containing the male spirits of my family is naturally in my trust."

"Yes, naturally." Garii was openly trembling now. "Our ways are strikingly similar."

"You noticed that?" Klaywelder peered under a loose bit of paving. "Actually, that's why I've been so anxious to visit Pharalell IV. I truly believe my people have a strong spiritual kinship with yours."

"Oh, yes—indeed!" Tears rolled down Garii's eyes, staining his silvery pelt a light cobalt blue. "And I, through gross stupidity, have banned your soul from the Thousand Rooms of Infinite Pleasure!"

"It's nothing, really," said Klaywelder.

Garii swept great hands to his face and moaned.

"If you will permit me I shall begin Atonement by tearing out my visual organs. It is a small thing—but a start—"

"No, please," said Klaywelder. "Ah—there's my pouch. It was under your foot all the time."

Garii stifled another moan. "Now I have trod upon your fathers. Visual organs alone will not suffice."

"No problem," Klaywelder said easily. "They're found." He hooked the pouch around his neck. "That's what's important."

The Pharalellian gently helped him to his feet. "You must enter my house, now. I have much indebtedness to overcome."

"Oh, no." Klaywelder yawned absently. "I wouldn't consider disturbing you."

Garii's mouth opened in horror. "I could not blame you for refusing. I have no right to ask. Still—" he faced Klaywelder with pleading eyes—"I beg you not to leave me with no chance of Atonement."

Klaywelder watched the sun form fascinating whorls of color on Garii's fur. Out of the corner of his eye he could see Arto Frank's man frowning in puzzlement at the edge of the plaza.

"All right," he said finally. "If you really insist."

"My gratitude is unbounded, sir."

Klaywelder shrugged. "You can call me Klay."

Garii insisted Klaywelder spend the remainder of his stay on Pharalell IV in his home. Klaywelder declined and the Pharalellian nearly removed his visual organs before it was explained that Klaywelder could not possibly spend nights outside his ship since his ancestral altars were located there and could not be moved.

Garii understood. But during the daylight hours Klay must allow his host the opportunity to work at full Atonement. That, Klaywelder agreed, seemed fair enough.

Klaywelder was not about to spend a night away from the *Glory B.* Not that Arto Frank could possibly do any damage there but Klaywelder did not intend to give him the chance. Besides that, he wanted Frank to establish a normal Klaywelder day-night pattern in his mind.

At sunset on the third day Frank pulled up beside him on the narrow road from Ochassh to the spaceport.

Klaywelder greeted him with a slightly lopsided grin. He was more than a little high—mentally and physically. Wine had flowed freely at the party, and Garii made certain his guest-of-honor's cup was never empty. Every swallow, it seemed, was a step closer to full Atonement.

There was more. Klaywelder was dizzy from mingling with the twenty or thirty Pharalellians assembled to meet him. Each one's pelt was more magnificent and multihued than any he had imagined before he came to Pharalell IV.

Frank studied him.

"You're going ahead with it, aren't you?" he said finally. "I can read it all over you." He shook his head. "Klaywelder—"

"I don't know what you're talking about," said Klaywelder. "I'm up to my ears in Pharalellian wine at the moment, Arto.

My host—Steressh-shi, to you—I can't reveal his intimate name to strangers but—"

Frank's speedster jerked ahead abruptly, wheeled to block Klaywelder's path.

"Listen," Frank said darkly, "I know what it's all about. I've known since the minute you set down here. You can't pull it off. Don't even try, Klaywelder—"

Klaywelder sighed. "I sense deep spiritual conflicts within you, Arto. At evening devotions I shall ask my ancestors to bring peace to your troubled soul."

Frank made a pointed remark about Klaywelder's ancestors and their relation to Klaywelder himself. Then he left in a cloud of dust and disappeared down the road.

"As further proof of my Atonement, Klay, and because I consider you a spiritual brother whose devotion transcends the boundaries between us, I hope you will allow me one more privilege."

"Only ask," said Klaywelder.

"You have noticed the great door at the end of my quarters?"

"I may have," said Klaywelder, who had noticed little else since he had become Garii's guest.

"That door leads to the Shrine of my Ancestors," said Garii. "I would be honored if you would accompany me there."

Klaywelder lowered his eyes to hide his excitement.

"The toenails of my fathers are pleased, Garii."

His heart pounded against his chest. His research on Pharalellian religion had been very specific about ancestral shrines.

Garii pulled a lavish key in the great door and something clicked. The massive panel swung open.

Klaywelder held back a gasp. The room was as big as an auditorium. Dark, somber columns arched from the walls and met high above in a domed ceiling. A single shaft of sunlight fell from a high pane, giving the great vault an aura of eternal twilight.

Nearly a hundred candles set in dark red glass circled the walls—and spread carefully over the stone floor before each candle was a magnificent golden pelt.

Golden.

Klaywelder could hardly believe his eyes. If living Pharalell pelts were indescribable—what could you say about these?

"It is our belief," Garii said reverently, "that the degree of virtue attained by a Pharalellian is later reflected in the tone of his pelt. I am most pleased that my fathers and their fathers are all of respectable hues."

You can say that again...

Garii led him silently about the room and Klaywelder noted that a small earthen pot of wine and a clay dish of fruit had been placed before each glowing candle.

"That is a part of my duty," Garii explained proudly. "As the reigning male in my family, I have been accorded this privilege. Each day I bring fresh offerings of reverence." He lowered his big head. "To do so brings great honor to me and my house."

Garii laid a gentle hand on Klay's arm. "Come, my friend—now I would show you Shastalian, greatest of my ancestors."

Klaywelder followed past long rows of gleaming, golden pelts. Finally Garii stopped. "There—" he pointed—"Shastalian, grandfather of grandfathers. A saintly creature and the most famed of all Pharalellians."

Klaywelder wanted to cry. He could hardly bear to hold his eyes on the rippling sea of gold at his feet. He was here—this close to it. A planet's ransom and then some in one glorious pelt.

Not that it really mattered but he wished briefly that he had been a little more imaginative about his own 'religion.' Somehow ancestral nail parings just didn't quite cut it next to Shastalian.

"You see, Klay," Garii explained solemnly, "we consider the Pharalellian body to be unimportant. We are held within its bonds only a little while—but Eternal Life resides in the Pelt. When we are fortunate enough to move into that Loftier Plane the troubles, cares and Atonements of this existence are left in the poor vessel we term the body. Your beliefs are similar, I think."

"Oh, yes," Klaywelder said absently, "very similar, Garii."

"When the time comes for one of us to pass on to that Higher Existence he is taken to a most sacred place. You have seen the large building on the other side of the plaza? The one trimmed in black and gold?"

Klaywelder nodded.

"That is *Fakash-il Shrai*. It means Abode of the Skinners."

Klaywelder swallowed. He looked up at Garii.

"The—skinners?"

"Yes. It is a most dedicated profession. Skinners are chosen from among only the highest and worthiest of clans. Since the body of a Pharalellian is never seen without his pelt the Skinner candidates are blinded at birth, of course."

"Of course," said Klaywelder. He decided this was one phase of Pharalellian religion he could have done without.

"They are very skilled members of the Priesthood," Garii went on. "They must be, since it is a delicate thing to transfer the living soul from the body to the Pelt."

Klaywelder stiffened. "The—living soul? You mean—"

"Certainly," said Garii. "There must be breath still in the body when the Skinners begin their task." He spread his hands. "Or else the soul would not go on to Eternal Life, would it?"

Klaywelder felt a cold chill creep up the back of his neck. He wondered how many Pharalellian ancients, at that last moment, looked up at the sharp blade and blinded eyes of the faithful Skinners—and decided they weren't quite ready for Eternal Life as a golden rug.

"You seem far away, my friend." Garii's voice held puzzlement.

Klaywelder cleared his throat. "I—was, Garii. I'm so overwhelmed by what I've seen, by what you've told me—I fear I lapsed into meditation for a moment. I hope you'll forgive me."

Garii sighed happily.

"Don't apologize, Klay. To think that you have actually experienced the feelings I have known here myself." He stared gravely at Klaywelder. "Might I presume that my Atonement is now complete?"

Klaywelder glanced once more at the great golden pelt of Shastalian, grandfather of grandfathers.

Damn thing must weigh a good four or five hundred pounds. Still.

"Yes, Garii," he said finally. "I'd say that just about does it."

Klaywelder eased through the lower hatch of the *Glory B* and flattened himself against the cold concrete below the ship. It was long past the middle hour of Pharalell's night. The light in Arto Frank's dome had winked out some time before but Klaywelder had waited patiently in the darkened cabin.

Even in the Blacsuit, he felt as conspicuous as a blazing beacon crawling on his belly across the broad field. The skintight garment ate every photon of available light—still, he imagined Frank's cold eyes cutting a blinding swath through the darkness.

He was sure radar had his ship bracketed to the ground. If *Glory B*'s hull rose as much as a half-inch or the power level of her engines suddenly changed—every alarm in the area would scream itself into a blue hemorrhage. He was banking on the fact that Arto Frank would be expecting a ship to leave the field—not a man. And he prayed silently to his ancestors' mythical toenails that Pharalell was too small a post to include body sensors as standard equipment.

At the rear of Garii's house, he pulled a small gravitic unit from under his Blacsuit and attached it to his belt. On half power he lifted himself over the high wall, then pulled himself smoothly along, inches above the clay shingles, and up the arching dome.

With a suction attached to the single pane, he lifted the glass out easily with quick use of his cutter. Then, slowly, he lowered the grav's dial to one. Weight returned and pressed him against the tiles. He removed the unit and hinged a thin, sloping metal wedge to its base, forcing the wedge into its "load" position against a heavy spring.

Finally he poked a shielded flash through the dome's hole, let a thin smile crease his lips. There it was—dazzlingly bright even in the dim shaft of light. Shastalian.

Klaywelder bit his lip.

Here comes the tricky part...

He placed the grav unit just inside the edge of the dome, then flipped his remote until he was sure the unit's weight had been sufficiently reduced to hold itself. When he was certain, he increased the weight and watched it slowly descend to the floor.

It touched bottom a good eighteen feet from Shastalian. Klaywelder wiped sweat from his brow. The unit had no horizontal control. The trick was quickly to raise the unit a few feet, shut off its power, let it fall, then raise it again before it hit the floor—and repeat the procedure until he could get the thing moving in a series of parabolic arcs toward Shastalian.

Klaywelder took a deep breath. The first time his hand trembled and the unit fell nearly to the floor. He tried again. He was getting the hang of the thing now, and the unit was moving in slow, graceful arcs—luckily, in the general direction of the Shastalian pelt.

Ten feet. Fifteen. Seventeen—now.

Klaywelder gently halted the unit and lowered it to the floor. His heart pounded against his chest. He was only inches from the pelt—he didn't dare press his luck further. Wiping his brow once more, he twisted the remote to full weight, pressing the unit below hard against the floor.

Click!

Klaywelder winced. The noise seemed to echo off the stone walls, much louder than he had expected. But—it was done. The spring-loaded wedge, set off by the unit's weight, whipped a thin steel tongue under the edge of the pelt. By raising the unit inches at a time, Klaywelder slowly wormed the wedge under the heavy fur, caterpillar style.

He glanced at the horizon. A thin line of pink was edging the low hills to the east. He turned away and concentrated on the problem below. There was no more time—the unit was nearly under the center of the pelt and it would have to do. He closed his eyes and turned the dial to full power.

Shastalian lifted slowly off the floor and rose toward the ceiling, a shadowy golden ghost in the dim shaft of his light. The pelt nuzzled up against the top of the dome only yards away. Klaywelder extended a thin metal tube to the right length and gaffed Shastalian as he would a giant, furry fish.

He had one more moment of panic when the pelt stuck in the dome's narrow hole. Then he was home free. Klaywelder touched the pelt for the first time. A chill ran through his whole body. There was absolutely no way to compare Shastalian to anything.

Bracing himself and his prize, he pressed a small wafer to his throat and mouthed a single sub-vocal command. A few miles away, a relay clicked in *Glory B*'s computers. Silent engines whined into life. And at the same time, alarms hooted and moaned across the field and bright beams stabbed angrily into the sky.

Glory B rose swiftly from the spaceport in a low, ground-hugging curve, homing in on Klaywelder. For a moment blue strings of heat spat at her from the field. They halted abruptly.

At that angle, Frank would soon have been sizzling the roofs of Pharalell homes and buildings.

Klaywelder grinned. The ship streaked over the outskirts of Ochassh and came to a hovering stop three feet above him. He let the grav unit lift Shastalian into the port, then pulled himself up. The port snapped shut and Klaywelder bounded to the control cabin. He threw himself into the command seat and slapped on hand full across the board.

Glory B lunged upward in teeth-shattering acceleration. Blue fire spiderwebbed against the hull for a brief moment. Then Pharalell IV shrank to a bright green globe against blackness.

Federation ships would already be on Red Alert—but space was terrifyingly vast and the patrols were spread pitifully thin. He would be long gone when they finally got to where he was supposed to be. A quick stop on Filo to open the scrambled hold, then a first-class plastjob for himself—a good one, this time, from eyes to toes—and then Earth.

He broke out his last sixteen-ounce steak from the locker and topped it with a bottle of Pharalellian wine. In comfortable lethargy he strolled toward his quarters, stopping by the entry port to gaze once more at Shastalian. He would have liked to have spread the big pelt out to its full length but there was no place in the ship nearly large enough to accommodate the great golden fur.

Stretched out on his bunk, Klaywelder thought about Arto Frank and grinned tiredly. Poor Arto. He was, though, genuinely sorry about Garii. Garii was all right. He hoped Shastalian's loss didn't hit him too hard.

Still, he reasoned with Klaywelder logic, Garii had lots of pelts—while he had only one. Klaywelder turned over and closed his eyes.

—and came fully awake. The luminous dial over his bunk said he had slept only a short hour. His senses were fuzzy from the strong Pharalellian wine. He cocked his head and listened. Nothing. He shrugged and turned over—then sat up stiffly.

There it was again. Unfamiliar.

He set his feet on the floor and something heavy draped over his ankles and wrapped softly about his calves. Klaywelder gasped and jerked away. The firm grip held, tightened, and he yelled as he was pulled to the floor.

Klaywelder fought savagely. He kicked, pummeled with his fists. His blows were muffled in thick, warm fur, as damp leather tightened about his waist and inched up across his chest.

He screamed and cursed himself and Garii and the universe until his throat was raw. And in some last, coherent corner of his mind he wondered if anyone else knew Pharalellians didn't believe in a life after death—and didn't need to.

As thick golden fur covered his face he saw a quick bright picture of dark earthen cups on a smooth stone floor—small offerings of reverence for those who had passed on to Eternal Life.

The Stentorii Luggage

The Double-A call light wailed and blinked itself into a bright red hemorrhage on the wall. I woke up fast. My first thought was fire. Logically, reasonably, I know there hasn't been a hotel fire in 800 years—but tradition is tradition.

I punched the visor and Greel's face popped on the screen. The lobby clock over his shoulder read 3:35. I moaned silently and flipped on vocal.

"Duncan here."

"Chief, get down here quick." I didn't ask why. Greel's my head bellhop and bellhops can smell hotel trouble.

"Where are you?"

"Level 12. Desk 19."

"Check. Hold everything, kid." I started to cut off, then I saw something else behind him. I took a deep breath and held it.

"Greel. Is that—Ollie?"

Greel nodded. Like he was going to be sick. I was in my clothes and out the door. I took a manual emergency lift and fell seventy-eight floors in eighty seconds, not even thinking about my stomach. Not with Ollie to think about.

Ollie's uncle is Mike Sorrenson, owner of Hotel Intergalactica, and a reasonably decent person. Ollie is something else again. Crew cut, eager, bow tie and fresh out of college. My job—teach him "all there is to know about the hotel business." Which should be a real snap, as he already knows all there is to know about everything.

Thursday, for instance. Ollie got his menus mixed and served scrambled eggs to five hundred visiting Vegans. That's all. No trouble. Except the difference between a Vegan and a chicken is strictly a matter of size and evolution—and we're still cleaning up Ballroom Nine.

I came out of the lift, my stomach only ten floors behind. Ollie popped out of his chair and came toward me, a sick smile pasted across his face.

"Mr. Duncan, I—"

"Sit down, Ollie, and shut up," I said quietly. He swallowed and sat down.

I turned to Greel.

"Okay," I said. "I'm ready. Let's have it."

"I'll save the details for later," said Greel. "We've got to get moving. Fast. I have reason to believe there are from four to fifty Skeidzti loose in the hotel."

I drew a blank at first. Then it hit me and I felt cold all over.

"Oh, my God," I said, sending a withering look at Ollie.

"Uh-huh." Greel nodded. "The way I get it from Ollie, four Stentorii checked in about 3:00. They wanted to go right up to their room so Ollie sent a boy with them and told the Stentorii he'd put their luggage in a lift right away."

"They kind of grinned at me, Mr. Duncan," Ollie interrupted, "and said that was fine, there was no hurry about the bags."

"Yeah, I'll bet they did," I said. I looked at Greel, and we both felt sick. "Don't tell me the rest. Ollie checked them in on the Master Register, turned to get their bags—and what do you know, they were gone."

Ollie looked surprised. He started to ask how I could possibly know but I glared him back to his chair.

"Okay," I said. "What have you done so far?"

Greel took a deep breath. "First, they have about thirty to thirty-five minutes head start. I've shielded four levels above and below. I don't think they'll get that far, but no use taking chances. We've got one lucky break. Since the whole Quadrant borders on Free City they can't get out except through a Registration area."

"What about—"

Greel nodded. "Already done it. I've closed all five Desks in the Quadrant. Anyone wants to register has to come in by way of Seven."

"Fine. Just one thing—" I flipped through the register. "Could they have gotten outside through this door?"

"No. It was unshielded, all right. But there were no checkouts after the Stentorii registered."

Our luck was holding. At least the Skeidzti were still just the hotel's problem. I've got a few friends on Free City's revolving council, but I don't like to mess with those boys unless I have to.

I sent Greel to organize the bellboys into search squads. Then I checked the Stentorii's room number and hauled Ollie out of his chair, figuring the only way to make sure he stayed out of trouble was to keep him with me. Before I left the lobby

I picked up a pair of low-charge stunners and handed one to Ollie.

"Look," I said, "do you think you could possibly handle one of these things without knocking us both out cold?"

Ollie nodded vaguely. He took the weapon and held it as if he were certain it would go off in his hand.

"Sure, Mr. Duncan, but why do we need weapons? I mean, I'm sorry I let those things get loose, but—"

I stopped at the lift and stared at him. I suddenly realized the poor kid had no idea what he had done wrong. All he could see was that Greel and I were making a big fuss over a couple of alien housepets.

"Ollie," I said patiently, "do you really know what a Skeidzti is? I don't want an oration. Just tell me the simple truth. Do you or don't you?" He started to say something, then changed his mind and shook his head.

"I thought so. Well, first of all, don't refer to them as 'pets.' They may be cute as a kitten to a Stentorii, but as far as you're concerned they are dangerous, quick, carnivorous, highly adaptable little monsters. Only 'adaptable' is about as descriptive as calling the ocean moist. A Skeidzti in a kitchen will hide in a stack of plates and, by God, you'll eat off of him and swear he *is* a plate. A Skeidzti in a garden is a rock, a weed, a pile of leaves. In your bedroom he's a garter, a sock or a necktie. Only—put one around your neck and you'll damn well know he's not a necktie. Now do you think it might be permissible for me to continue to bear arms against the Skeidzti, just in case?"

Ollie was taken aback, I could tell. Almost enough to keep him mouth shut. He thought for maybe a full second before he said anything.

"But Mr. Duncan, if the Stentorii knew they were dangerous—" And that did it. I poked a hard finger in his chest and backed him against the wall.

"Look, Ollie," I said grimly, "that college line of logic is what got us into this jam in the first place. Now get this, and remember it. You don't need a degree in Alien Psychology to know that Rule One is *never* use your own viewpoint as a premise in guessing what an alien is thinking or doing. It just simply doesn't work that way. An alien's actions are based upon what he thinks is reasonable and proper—not what you think he ought to think.

"Why do you think we have separate Quadrants and private entrances to each room? It sure as hell isn't for economy's sake, I can tell you that. It so happens that some of these so-called reasonable civilized beings still consider each other as rare culinary delights. While that sort of nonsense is SOP in Free City, this hotel is strictly out of bounds. And here's another rule you can put down in Duncan's lectures on Alien Psychology: If a guest phones down for a midnight snack, he may mean he wants the key to his neighbor's room." I took a deep breath.

"Am I getting through to you, Ollie?" Ollie nodded, wide-eyed, and I shoved him into the lift ahead of me. We hung for a moment, then the gravs caught hold.

In my business you learn to get along with aliens, or at least put up with the ones you can't possibly get along with. And some *are* completely impossible—like the Nixies. Except for simple trade relations, I can't conceive of anything I might have in common with a Nixie.

And there was another rule of thumb for Ollie: Never be deceived by appearances. An alien's resemblance to human form is no indication that his outlook will in any way resemble human logic and reason. Until you know, don't guess; and don't assume, either, that a lack of human form denotes a lack of common interest. A Goron is a repulsive, warty glob of pink and brown protoplasm consisting of twelve eyes, nine pseudoarms—and an entirely human liking for jazz, poetry, Scotch and women. Or anyway, Goron females.

On the other hand, ignoring the general hairyness and the rodent-like features, a Stentorii looks as humanoid as I do. He is also a completely alien, cold-blooded, murderous creature without a shred of mercy in his body.

I stared hard at the Stentorii who opened the door. He stared back at me from tiny red eyes set wide on either side of his whiskery pink muzzle. Then he saw Ollie and gave a high squeaky laugh, baring a mouthful of sharp yellow teeth. He turned into his room and said something in Stentor to his companions. They nearly fell apart.

I had had just about enough. Time was running out. I switched on my portable recorder and said:

"According to Statute XII, Galactic Standard Code, I wish to invoke the privilege of communicating with you; without fear of future prosecution in case I may offend, by way of accidental implication, any tradition, custom or moral standard of your race." The Stentorii just grinned. I spoke a little louder. "I said I speak without offense!"

The Stentorii frowned. He didn't like that at all. But he understood it.

"All right," he said grudgingly, "I accept."

"Fine," I said, and let him see that I had switched off my recorder. I never start an argument with an alien without invoking the non-offense clause. Of course, the same clause is stated in every Registration Contract, providing mutual protection for the hotel's guests and its employees. But I like to play it safe.

By now the three other Stentorii were up, grinning at Ollie. I ignored them and spoke to the one at the door.

"My name is Duncan," I told him. "I am manager of the hotel. This is my assistant, Mr. Sorrenson. I will come right to the point. You played a little joke down in the lobby a few minutes ago. Although the incident is a serious breach of your Registration Contract, I am willing to forget the matter if I am able to gain your full cooperation. On behalf of Hotel Intergalactica, I formally request you recall your Skeidzti immediately and turn them over to me for housing in the hotel kennel."

The Stentorii glanced at his companions, then turned to me with a look of mock astonishment.

"Mr. Duncan, do you imply the hotel has allowed my pets to become lost? Naturally, I will hold you responsible if they come to any harm while in your charge." I had half expected something like this. I couldn't do a thing but play it out.

"All right," I said, "I haven't time to appreciate your humor. You know it is illegal to bring unregistered alien pets into this hotel. I am also certain you are aware that we are in the Federation Circle, which is *not* in Free City territory—which means all guests, by the act of signing their Registration Contracts, place themselves under Federation law for the duration of their stay here."

The Stentorii grinned, showing his yellow teeth.

"Mr. Duncan, you are bluffing. I am quite aware of the law, and respectfully submit that if you check your copy of our Registration Contracts you will find your employee here countersigned the Alien Responsibility Clause."

Well, that was his round. I was sure he was too oily a character to fall for it, but I had had to try. He was right. Under our Registration Contract it is presumed that while the hotel is responsible for a full knowledge of the Galactic Customs Restrictions, an alien cannot be expected to inform the Desk Clerk of all possible violations he may be guilty of on any particular world. And any clerk green enough, or stupid enough, or both—like Ollie—who signs a Responsibility Clause without checking Galactic Customs—ought to have his head examined. Of course, we could take the Stentorii to court. Maybe we might even win, on the grounds of purposeful malice, but I don't like to get the hotel into lawsuits. It's bad publicity, and it gives other wise guys grand ideas.

The legal pitch having failed, I was ready to continue with Unveiled Threat No. 1.

"Look," I said wearily, "I admit you are within your legal rights. Although just how far within I'm not too certain at the moment. But before you come to any decision let me remind you that, while I may not be in a position to take official action against you, I fully intend to file a Warning Report to every member of the Galactic Hotel Association, which includes nearly twelve million first-class hotels and their subsidiaries. I don't know what your business is. But since you are here I presume it entails traveling. Traveling means hotels. If you refuse your cooperation, I assure you it may be quite difficult to find a decent room within twelve thousand parsecs of this planet."

The Stentorii shrugged and closed the door on my foot. I'm sure he would have hacked it off for a souvenir if I hadn't jerked it out.

I looked at Ollie. His fists were clenched by his side and there was a look of iron determination in his eyes.

"Well?" I said.

"Boy," said Ollie. "Just *wait* until they try to check into a GHA hotel again."

"Ollie," I said weakly, "I didn't come up here to actually accomplish anything with those characters. It is strictly a matter of form. A necessary routine for the record. Everything I said went completely down the drain. They were not impressed, frightened or embarrassed in any way. It is impossible to reason with a Stentorii because he is inherently incapable of taking anything you say seriously. He is also incapable of caring whether he gets a hotel room. Anywhere. Ever. He has one now, and the future is absolutely of no importance. He doesn't care about you, me, life, death *or* hotel rooms. Didn't you hear anything I said in the lift?"

"Sure, Mr. Duncan, but—"

"Ollie. Shut up."

I ditched Ollie and stopped off at my office for a wake-up pill. Greel had his command post set up in the Level 12 lobby and I joined him there. The lobby was full of squat Fensi bellhops, swarming in and out of the lifts like agitated ants.

Most of my bellhops and some of the administrative staff are Fensi. I like to have them on the payroll, and I'd hire fifty more if I could get them. Fensi are quick, alert, reasonably honest and highly adaptable. Their adaptability alone makes them worth their weight in gold to a big hotel. A Fensi can breathe a wide variety of atmospheres, take plenty of g's, and doesn't care whether he's hot, cold or in-between. Unless you're a Fensi, room service around here can be a literally killing job.

Greel sprinted across the lobby, a wide smile stretching over his hairless blue face.

"I'm glad you're so happy," I said. "Maybe you should have gone to see our friends upstairs."

Greel laughed. "Maybe we won't need 'em, chief. The boys think we can clean the Skeidzti out by morning—with a little luck, of course."

"More than a little, if you ask me. Get any yet?"

Greel held up a finger. "One. Skorno picked up an ashtray on Ten and it nearly bit his hand off." He nodded toward the desk and Ollie and I followed. He picked up a small stationery box and pushed it toward me.

"Skorno got it before it could change completely—you can see what it was trying to do."

I could. The object in the box was a dead Skeidzti, but only one-quarter of it was in its natural form. The last thing it had touched was Skorno's hand. Following its blind-rule instinct it had imitated a hairless blue Fensi arm nearly up to the elbow, before it had either run out of material or died.

Now that it was dead it was slowly changing back to its natural form. The part we could see resembled a thin, eight-inch-wide wormlike creature with stubby serrated legs. I figured it could move about as fast as a caterpillar without adapting. It was a highly vulnerable creature, and in order to survive it had developed a high degree of protective camouflage. With its soft body and slow speed almost anything could pick up a quick and easy meal. And its natural color didn't help at all. The dead quarter of the Skeidzti was a brilliant, almost phosphorescent orange.

"Well, son, get some idea what we're up against?" Ollie's eyes were glued to the box and his face was as blue as Greel's.

"Can they—can they adapt to *anything?*"

"No," said Greel, "they have limitations. I'm sure they can *imitate* most anything, but they couldn't change as quickly under six or eight g's, or, say, in a methane atmosphere."

"Not for two or three generations, anyway," I added soberly. Greel nodded.

"Anyway, Ollie, the point is these varmints are already used to a Stentor-Earth atmosphere. And if any get out—"

"It would be comparable," I put in, "to a plague of invisible bobcats."

I think for the first time Ollie was hit with the seriousness of our problem. I could sense a kind of helpless panic in his eyes, as if he had suddenly realized he'd opened the floodgates and let the valve break off in his hand.

"Mr. Duncan, I—well, maybe we ought to get help. I mean—I'll take the blame—and—and—" He was shaking like a leaf. I eased him down to a chair.

"And just what sort of help did you have in mind?" I asked.

"Well, the police! Couldn't you—"

I shook my head firmly. "No. I certainly could not. That, my friend, is all we need. The Federation would quarantine the hotel, rout several thousand guests out of their various notions of sleep, and raise enough hell to wake every DeepDream addict from here to Andromeda."

"Aside from the fact," Greel added, "that every Skeidzti in the hotel could hitch a free ride out of here in some cop's pocket."

"Right. No, we can handle it ourselves, a hell of a lot quieter. We've had worse before." Ollie's face told me he thought

I was an out and out liar. But then, like I said, this kid has a lot to learn about the hotel business.

The Skeidzti had been loose in the hotel since 3:00 A.M. By 5:30 we had killed eight of them. And eight Fensi bellhops had bandaged hands.

It was obvious we couldn't go around touching everything in the hotel to see if it was real or Skeidzti. Added was the problem of knowing *when* we had killed them all. The Skeidzti came in disguised as four pieces of Stentorii luggage, but we had no idea how many had clustered together to form each piece. And the Stentorii weren't telling.

I called Greel and Ollie to the Desk for a strategy meeting. Ollie dropped in a chair and sank into brooding silence. Even Greel's customary optimism seemed to have temporarily vanished. He reported the bellhops were doing their poking with sticks now, but the results were still alarmingly low.

"What we need," Greel complained, "is a system."

"Yeh, we need a system, all right," added Ollie helpfully. I stood up, paced around the Desk. The strategy meeting was dying on its feet.

"Look," I said, "let's analyze it. Our problem is to get rid of the Skeidzti, right?"

"Right," from Greel and Ollie.

"Okay. Now to kill them we have to see them. And by seeing them I mean we have to see them as they really are."

"Or catch them during a change," added Greel.

"Exactly." Somewhere in the back of my head an idea was catching hold. I kept talking, trying to push it out.

"Then our problem is this. We have to *force* them to change into something we can recognize as a definite Skeidzti." Greel's frown vanished. He sat up straight in his chair.

"You mean, like if we made them all change into an object we knew we only had one of."

"Sort of like that. Only that means we'd have to be able to isolate the Skeidzti in a specified area—and even if we could do that it'd be a hell of a problem to get rid of all the objects we didn't want them to imitate. Which means more stick poking. Remember, they can flatten out on the walls and ceilings just as easily as they can curl up like an ashtray or a sofa pillow." Greel's face dropped back into a disappointed frown.

"No, you've got the general idea," I said quickly. "But I think I've got a way to work the same thing, only quicker." Greel suddenly looked around, and I turned and saw Skorno, our first casualty, coming out of the lift. In his bandaged hand he held an ominous looking club, and in the other a limp and bloody throwrug. He stopped before us, grinning, and tossed the rug on the floor.

He said, "Three more, chief."

I bent down for a closer look. This time, three Skeidzti had joined to imitate a portion of the rug. It was a near-perfect job. They had continued the intricate pattern, carrying out the design exactly where the real rug stopped. The only thing wrong, Skorno explained, was that he passed the rug fifty times a day and knew it was about twice as large as it should have been.

Something about Skorno's rug worried me. I asked him how long he thought it took for the Skeidzti to change from one form to another.

"About half a second," he said. "But I think it varies, depending on what they're imitating."

"For instance?"

"Well, on a plain surface, like a wall or something, they're faster—much faster."

"You mean," I asked, "if they have something more complicated to imitate, it takes longer?"

Skorno shook his head. "I wish it did. When I said it varies, I meant just the first few times. Once they've imitated something, they don't forget it."

"Well, hell," I snapped, "I know they can't imitate simultaneously! There has to be *some* definite minimum time lapse!"

Skorno spread his hands helplessly. "I know, chief. But whatever it is, it's too small to do us much good. They're just too fast for our reaction time. We still only get about one out of every ten we see." Swell, I thought. If they were too fast for the Fensi, we were really up the creek.

"What about spraying a low-charge disruptor all over the place and picking up the pieces?" said Greel hopefully.

Skorno said, "I forgot to mention that with a low-charge you have to hit them in just the right place or they're only knocked out for awhile."

"And while they're unconscious they're just as safe as ever," I finished for him. Then Skorno's words suddenly sank in. "Good Lord! Do you mean you're using *high*-charge disruptors—inside this hotel!"

Skorno nodded sheepishly. "What else can we do, chief? Sure, the place looks like a two-cluster cruiser plowed through. But we're getting 'em, slow but sure."

I was beginning to get a little bit mad. I thought about the Stentorii, sleeping peacefully in their rooms while we blasted four levels of valuable real estate looking for their damnable pets. And what, I asked myself, are we doing about it? Mooning around in the lobby on our respective rears, that's what we are doing. I stood up again, glaring at Ollie on general principles.

"All right," I said firmly. "This has gone far enough, gentlemen. I'm not saying there *is* any other way to finish off this mess, but I do have one humble idea that might save a little of Hotel Intergalactica's property. I figure as long as we're going to turn this place into a shooting gallery we might as well have something to shoot at."

I went over our floor plan with Greel and Skorno and picked out an area where the Skeidzti had proven particularly obnoxious. Then I sent Greel to seal off the other contaminated levels, and told Skorno to marshal his forces in Humanoid Hall. I picked Humanoid Hall for two reasons: One, plenty of Skeidzti to work on, and two, a minimum of furniture. For previously stated reasons I kept Ollie with me, and hopped a Class-A lift for Level Eight.

More than once I've had good reason to be thankful we enforced strong lift security measures. No matter where the Skeidzti might go, I was dead sure they would never reach guest quarters.

There's a good reason for this. We ordinarily house about thirty thousand guests in the hotel at any one time. That number represents five to fifteen thousand separate races, each one requiring its own unique set of conditions. In Quadrant Four I've got Denebian Iceworms at -200 F. right "next door" to a cluster of Calistan Feroids sleeping soundly in boiling mercury. No problem. We can handle 1,240 different atmospheres, with innumerable variations in density, temperature and lighting.

The real problem is sociological, not mechanical. If the Galaxy is old, the oldest thing in it are its grudges. To put it bluntly, some of these characters have hated each other's guts so long they forgot *why* about two million years ago.

Naturally, an Altaran isn't going to walk into a Vegan's room and strangle him. There's a problem of about 900 degrees and thirty g's to overcome first. But that's no real problem either—about 500,000 years ago they swarmed all over each other's planets in protective armor, and strangling was the nicest thing that happened.

And that's where we come in.

What they do outside Hotel Intergalactica is none of our business—but inside we make sure no one is faced with temptation. That's why our room segregation is vertical instead of horizontal. The hotel is built on the hive principle. Each cell or room has a private entrance bordering on the lift. There are no halls or corridors to wander around in, and any connecting rooms connect up and down. No exceptions.

It's a necessary rule and we enforce it. There are plenty of Common Rooms on the opposite side of the lifts for conferences and amiable gatherings—free of charge.

We work it that way for economical reasons, too. It's a lot easier to, say, keep a gravitic lift at 9g constant for a Cygnian than to change it to forty-five for a Lyri passenger. Everybody minds their own business—and nobody waits for an elevator.

That's where lift security comes in.

We run a high density forceshield over each lift entrance. Try to enter one that's not attuned to your requirements and you run smack into an invisible wall. Which is precisely what would happen if the Skeidzti tried it. Imitation is one thing. Fortunately, duplication is another.

It suddenly dawned on me that here was the real reason the Stentorii played their little joke on Ollie. They knew the Skeidzti couldn't get by the lift shields, so they didn't even try. A typical bit of Stentorii humor, I thought wryly. Don't dump your problems just anywhere—toss 'em where they can do some good.

I knew pretty well what to expect on Level Eight.

It was worse.

What did Skorno say? Like a two-cluster cruiser plowed through? It was more like a complete reenactment of the Battle of the Rim.

Through a low cloud of acrid blue smoke I made out the dim outlines of Fensi bellhops, lined up in military order across the room. Skorno groped toward me through the wreckage. I put a handkerchief to my nose and stumbled out to meet him, Ollie choking along behind. The air was full of the smell of fused plastic, burnt carpeting and a particularly nauseous odor I identified as fried Skeidzti.

"Are you sure there's *anything* left alive up here?" I asked. Skorno nodded, breathing in the poisonous atmosphere like fresh country air.

"Sure, chief, they're here all right. You just can't see 'em." He nodded toward the ready Fensi crew. "We're all here, I think. What next?"

"Nothing," I choked, "until this smoke clears away. What happened to the air conditioning?"

"Greel's working on it. We had to block off some of the vents. Grid's not fine enough to keep out a Skeidzti." I looked up. The air was already beginning to clear. I gave it a few more minutes, then stepped up on a scorched sofa. I was anxious to get started so I cut it as short as possible. The idea, I explained, was to take advantage of the fact that there was a lapse, however small it might be, between the time a Skeidzti could change from one form to another. Catch them in that stage, and we had 'em. Simple as that, if it worked.

I lined the Fensi in a crude circle in the center of the room, facing outwards. Then I pulled some debris together for a shield, jerked Ollie down behind it and dimmed the lights. Dimmed them—not turned them off. The idea was to force the Skeidzti to adapt to new lighting conditions, and I was afraid if I turned them off altogether they'd sense they were safe in the absolute darkness and not adapt at all.

I gave them plenty of time, dimming the lights slowly until I could hardly tell they were on at all. Then I pressed the switch for maximum brightness and the room was flooded with brilliant light.

And there they were. They were fast, but not faster than the speed of light. For nearly a full second they stood out like ink spots on a clean white sheet, and we poured it on 'em. They were stunned perhaps a quarter-second past their normal reaction time. The Fensi are fast anyway, and that quarter-second margin was all they needed. We went through the routine three more times, then had to wait for the smoke to clear. We had killed thirty-seven Skeidzti.

Fine. But it gave me something to think about.

We had estimated there were at most fifty or sixty Skeidzti loose—and if we had killed thirty-seven on one level, in one room—how many did that mean were left? I mentioned it to Greel. He shrugged it off with typical Fensi optimism.

"What difference does it make, chief? We've got 'em on the run!"

"Sure," I said cautiously, "we've got 'em on the run *now*, all right." Both Greel and Skorno were grinning from ear to ear, having the time of their lives.

But I wasn't sure at all. Something kept asking me how long it would be before the Skeidzti caught on to the system—and whether we could come up fast enough with something to meet them. Before I left I gave explicit instructions to keep all isolation shields up—even after they were sure a room was clean. Greel gave a resigned shrug. I could tell they both thought the old man was taking the sport of Skeidzti hunting entirely too seriously.

Back in the lobby I sank into a chair and lit a cigarette. Ollie brought coffee, and we stared bleary-eyed at each other for half an hour. Ollie obviously didn't feel like talking and I was too damn tired to chew him out anymore. I could tell he was giving it to himself pretty hard anyway. That was probably doing more good than anything I could say.

Poor Ollie! If nothing else, one night of crisis at Hotel Intergalactica had rubbed off a considerable amount of shiny college exterior. His perfectly trimmed hair was caked with ceiling plaster. His neat bow tie dangled from his neck like last night's lettuce, and somehow he had managed to crack one side of his gold-rimmed glasses. He was beginning to look exactly like what he was supposed to be—a harried night clerk, who wished to hell he could remember why he had ever thought of going into the hotel business.

At 7:30 I located my army on the intercom. They had finished Eight, Nine and Ten, and were mopping up on Eleven. I told Greel to split his crew and send half up to Thirteen. We gulped the last of our coffee and headed down to Eleven.

I breathed a sigh of relief. Eleven wasn't nearly as bad as Eight. Either the Fensi had improved their marksmanship or the light trick was cutting out a lot of random shooting. Greel walked up, holstering his weapon.

"Well," I asked, "what do you think?"

"I think we just may survive the night," he said tiredly. "I'm going to try one more go-around here, then move up to Twelve."

"I have purposely been avoiding that thought," I said dryly, picturing the grinning Fensi horde blasting through my expensive lobby. "And of course," I added casually, "we haven't really *seen* any Skeidzti in the lobby, Greel. It may be that—ah—" Greel shot me a suspicious glance and I shut up. So who needs a lobby?

Greel reloaded his disruptor—a little too eagerly, I thought—and leaned against the wall.

"Actually," he said, "I don't picture it being too bad on Twelve."

"You don't, huh?" I said doubtfully.

"No, I mean it, chief. Funny thing, they were as thick as flies on Eight and Nine, but on Ten, and here on Eleven—they seem to be sort of thinning out."

I raised an eyebrow at that. "I don't suppose there could be a leaky shield, somewhere, or they might be catching on to that light trick."

"Oh, no," Greel insisted, "we're getting them all. They're just not as thick is all. I figure when they got loose on Twelve they all high-tailed it down to the lower floors for some reason, maybe to make—"

I grabbed Greel's arm and squeezed it hard. Something he had said suddenly sent a cold chill down my neck. Greel looked puzzled. I motioned him and Ollie to a quiet corner of the room, then turned to Greel.

"Did you send half your crew up to Thirteen?" I asked carefully.

Greel shrugged. "Sure, chief. You said—"

"Okay. Now think. I want to know exactly how many men you had here—*before* you split the crew."

Greel thought. "Forty-eight."

"Exactly forty-eight?"

"Exactly. I'm sure because it's the whole night shift for the Quadrant and everyone's on duty."

"Mr. Duncan," said Ollie, "what are you—"

I cut him off sharply. "Hold it, Ollie. Whatever it is can wait." I turned back to Greel. "Then if you split your crew, we should have twenty-four men in this room. Right?" Greel nodded. He started to speak, gave me a puzzled frown instead. He turned and carefully counted his crew.

"Oh, my God!" he said.

"I get thirty-six," I told him. "Ollie?" Ollie nodded, wide-eyed. I felt Greel stiffen beside me. I looked, and his hand was sliding toward his holster.

"Hold it," I said. "There's one way to make sure."

I checked on the intercom with Skorno on thirteen. Skorno counted twenty-four men. I nodded to Greel and Ollie.

I had wondered what the Skeidzti would come up with to counter our move. Now I knew. They had done they only thing they could do. They had imitated the most common thing in the room, the only thing that wasn't being blasted to shreds by the disruptors: the Fensi themselves.

I walked quickly to the center of the room.

"Attention, everyone," I yelled. "Line up against the wall, quick!" I watched them carefully, getting dizzy trying to spot the phonies.

"I'm going to tell you this once," I said. "Listen, and get it right!" I told them right off that twelve of them were fakes.

They caught on fast, knowing better than anyone what the Skeidzti were capable of. I wasn't worried about warning the Skeidzti. Whatever they were, they were no more intelligent than a well-trained dog.

"There is going to be some shooting," I said. "Ignore it and do exactly as I say." I paused, and Ollie and Greel drew their weapons.

"All right, first man. When I say go, walk to the lift and drop to Ten. Go!" The first Fensi walked to the lift and disappeared.

"Second man, go!"

"Third man, go!" The third Fensi walked to the lift, exactly like the first two. Only that was as far as he could go.

Ollie, Greel and I burned him before he could change.

Then it happened. The Skeidzti sensed something wrong. Eleven fakes suddenly bolted for the lift. The real Fensi ignored my order and joined the shooting. I yelled but no one could hear me.

Suddenly the whole area about the lift erupted in blinding blue flame. I shielded my face and felt a sharp pain in my side as the floor came up to meet me.

Greel was on his feet first. I shook my head and limped over to him. There was a large jagged hole in the wall and I knew right away what it was, even before I saw the tangled mass of fused wire and metal. I picked up a hunk of carpet and tossed it down the lift. Then I went limp all over.

The carpet went down the lift as smooth as any living thing. The shields were down. The Skeidzti had the run of the whole Quadrant.

Greel was giving his crew a royal chewing out. I cut him off and ordered the Fensi to Level Twelve, on the double. It was too damn late for chewing out now. We were in real trouble. I looked around for Ollie. He was gone. I cursed myself and kicked a piece of furniture halfway across the room. That's all I needed—the Skeidzti and Ollie running loose.

"Greel! Check the inner shields, see if we've still got *anything* sealed off in this place!"

"I did. So far as I can tell it's just the lift."

"That's bad enough," I said grimly. "On this side of the lift they're open to anything one room deep. And on the other side, the first guest who steps out of his room will—" Greel shook his head violently. I brightened, suddenly remembering. We had already sealed the guest side and I knew the two sides were controlled separately. Unless something else happened, we still had them sealed into the lift with access restricted to the Common Rooms, kitchens and ballrooms. They were still within the Quadrant, and away from the guests.

"All right," I said as calmly as possible, "we start over. It means maybe eighty floors of isolation, and they won't fall for that light trick again. We'll have to escort every guest through the lift and arrange for alternative dining areas. And I want every Fensi tested through a shield that's working. I don't think they'll try that again, but—"

The intercom crackled and Skorno's voice came on high and frantic.

"Chief! Listen, that crazy kid has opened the shields! He broke into Central Control and let down every barrier in the Quadrant!"

"*What!* Why in—look, it may be too late but try to get the damn things up again. Quick!"

Skorno moaned. "I can't. He's fused the controls! I can't even *find* the cutoff switch!" I felt a sharp pain in my mouth and realized I was trying to bite my tongue off. If I ever got my hands on that kid—

"Listen, Skorno, find him! I don't care what you do to him, just find him!"

"I can't figure it," moaned Greel. "He must have gone completely off his rocker."

"He had better be off his rocker," I said grimly. "That's the only thing that's going to save him from me." The intercom sputtered again. Ollie. Somehow, I knew before he even spoke.

"Mr. Duncan, listen, I had to do it. I couldn't tell you because I knew you'd—"

"Listen, you little punk—" growled Greel. I frowned and shook my head.

"Ollie," I said gently, "this is Mr. Duncan. I understand. I'm not angry. Not at all. Now listen, Ollie. I know you're not feeling well. You're tired, Ollie. Tell us where you are and we'll come and get you—help you, I mean—"

"Listen," Ollie said angrily, "I'm not crazy. Now pay attention and do what I say—exactly!"

I swallowed. He was gone, all right. "Yes, Ollie. We're listening. Go ahead."

His voice relaxed. "I'm on Eighteen. The Crystal Ballroom." I swallowed again. My beautiful new ballroom.

"Come up through the loading entrance," Ollie went on. "You'll enter at Lift, ah—Forty-five, Humanoid Kitchen annex."

"Yes, Ollie. We'll do that."

"And Mr. Duncan—"

"Yes, Ollie?"

"This is not a threat, sir. But don't bring any weapons."

"Oh—" The intercom went dead. Ollie was through talking.

"Well?" said Greel.

"Well what?" I snapped. "Do *you* want to flush him out of there?"

Greel shrugged. "Lift Forty-five is this way, chief."

Ollie let us into the kitchen.

The smell nearly knocked us back into the lift.

"Gahhhh! What is it, Ollie!"

"Ghayschi stew," he said. "Pretty horrible, isn't it? Here. Wear these." He tossed me a box and I quickly jammed two of the Chef's Little Wonder Air Filters into my nose and passed the box to Greel. Ghayschi stew, I thought. The kid has really flipped.

"Ollie—" Then I stopped. He was evidently not kidding. His eyes were a little too bright and his face was wet and glistening. Also, he had a disruptor in his hand.

"It's on low charge," he said, "but I don't want to knock anybody out, Mr. Duncan. I got us into this mess and I've got to get us out—my own way." He paused. "Now," he said, "will you give me a hand with this pot?" I shot him a skeptical glance.

"Why? Where are we taking it?"

Ollie tensed. "Mr. Duncan," he pleaded, "you've got to trust me!"

"Trust you! You've wrecked my hotel, let those infernal pests loose, and you—you stand there with a gun in your hand and ask me to trust you? Move the damn pot yourself!"

Ollie seemed to think a minute, then a hurt expression spread over his face. "All right," he said calmly. "If I give you the gun, will you help me? You said yourself the hotel is wrecked. Why not give me a chance?"

I took a deep breath and let it out slowly.

"Okay, Ollie. Give me the gun." Ollie handed me the disruptor. Greel started to move and I motioned him back. Ollie was right. I really had absolutely nothing to lose.

I grabbed one end of the pot.

"This way," said Ollie, shoving open the door to the ballroom.

"Here?"

Ollie nodded.

The Crystal Ballroom is new, and I'm proud of it. The floor is imported Denebian seaglass and the walls are Serinese protomurals. When the murals are on and the floor is lit, there isn't a hotel in the system that can touch it. I cringed as we set the large pot of Ghayschi stew square in the middle of the seaglass floor.

"Now what?" I asked.

"Now we get out of here. Quick." I followed him back to the kitchen. Behind him he trailed a long, thin wire. One end was attached to the top of the pot. Greel and I watched in silent wonder as he pulled the wire through the kitchen and into a tiny room off the kitchen pantry.

I knew where we were; it was the light control booth for the seaglass floor. I had shown it to Ollie several days before.

Ollie seated himself at the control board and began to play the lights. Through a small window I could see the ballroom, and the huge pot of Ghayschi stew. The floor began to glow, pulsing from gold to blue to green and back again. Ollie experimented a while, then seemed to be satisfied.

"Now," he said finally, without turning away from the controls, "we are ready."

I raised an eyebrow at Greel. Both of us were wondering just exactly what we were ready for.

"Fortunately," said Ollie, "the ballroom itself doesn't border directly onto one of the unshielded lifts. The anteroom shield is still up, though. And now—" he pressed a button by his chair—"it's down." Greel and I exchanged another look.

"Next," said Ollie suddenly, "dinnertime."

I shut my eyes. Ollie jerked his wire. The pot tipped and the gray and brown viscous mess of Ghayschi stew spread slowly across the ballroom floor.

"Now what?" I asked cautiously.

"Now we wait. I've turned on the auxiliary blowers. The smell is spreading through the Skeidzti occupied areas." I had a few choice comments on this move, but I kept them to myself. This was Ollie's party. I figured I could always strangle him later.

We waited ten minutes.

Then Ollie suddenly went into action. His hands swept over the light control board and the seaglass floor danced and pulsed with shifting colors, shifting faster and faster through the spectrum. I watched Ollie's face. His skin was tight and great beads of sweat poured from his forehead down his neck.

Then the tense mask suddenly broke and a wide grin spread over his face.

"Look!" he yelled, nodding toward the floor.

I looked. At first there was nothing to see. Then I rubbed my eyes. The fast-changing lights must have affected my vision because the whole floor seemed alive with bright orange spots.

Then it hit me. *Skeidzti!* The floor around the stew was crowded three deep with them—and they were all changing back to their natural form!

We watched for an hour and a half. Finally Ollie jerked a lever and the colors faded away. He sank weakly back in his chair. I felt cold all over, and suddenly realized I was soaking wet. Later, we counted two hundred seventy-nine dead Skeidzti on the ballroom floor. It was all over.

I had plenty of questions but I saved them until after breakfast. Some of it I could figure out, but I still didn't know how Ollie had been sure the Skeidzti would eat his infernal stew.

"Oh, I knew they'd like it," said Ollie. "Ghayschi stew is a favorite Stentorii dish. I looked it up. I figured the Skeidzti ate table scraps."

"That I can guess," I said. "But when they couldn't keep up with the changing lights why didn't they stop eating? Were they too stupid to know they either had to give up a meal or die?"

"No," said Ollie, "not stupid. They just couldn't help themselves. I figured any animal that could adapt so quickly and move around so fast was bound to have a pretty high metabolism. Any animal like that has to eat, oh, maybe six or eight times his weight in food every day or starve to death. They came into the hotel at 3:00. When I turned on the lights upstairs it was nearly 10:00. After seven hours they *had* to eat.

There was nothing in the world that could have stopped them."

Ollie paused, sipped his coffee. "They finally adjusted to your light trick because they had no alternative stronger than survival. I used the same idea, but this time they had to make an impossible choice between two basic instincts."

"And they couldn't," I added. "So to avoid it they sort of, what—died of a nervous breakdown?"

"Something like that. In school there was this thing about some old experiments where a chicken or rat was trained to certain responses, then the responses were mixed or taken away and—"

I yawned and got up to leave. "Sure, Ollie," I said. "Let's be sure and talk about it some time." I started for the door.

"Mr. Duncan—?"

"Yes?"

"Am I fired?"

I thought a minute. I was so tired I could hardly hear him.

"No, Ollie," I said wearily. "I don't think so. There's just one thing, though."

"Sir?"

"Keep," I said sternly, "the hell out of *my* kitchens!"

The Talking

When Tigian woke, the hut was still colored with the gray palette of dawn. The boy slept soundly beside him, a lock of thick yellow hair pressed tightly against his cheek. Tigian looked at him fondly a moment, then rose quietly, covering the small shoulders with matting.

On the far side of the hut he found the water jug and drank deeply, letting the cool liquid stream down his shoulders. From a wall peg he lifted the dark obsidian knife on its woven cord, and the long, plaited folds of his *rhamae*. The *rhamae* was made of cunningly fashioned knots which told the story of the People to those who could read them. Its length was peppered with black knots numbering the years, and red knots heralding great and dire events such as feast and famine. The white knots were the names of chieftains, and his own was among them. Suspended from the *rhamae* were the elements of power: a shell from the river, a stone from the earth, and a polished yellow bone of the beast that fell from the rim of the world.

Tigian hung the knife from his left shoulder, then looped the *rhamae* around his neck, twisted it once, and thrust his right arm through the circle. The knots formed a fringed pattern that reached just beneath his chest. It was the only garment he wore.

Crossing the room, his foot hit a small pot and sent it clattering over the reed floor. Tigian swore silently and grabbed his toe. He hopped painfully to the door, glancing once at the boy. Age is coming, he told himself grimly. Once I could grab a *gnee-gnee* in the dark and tell you who it belonged to. Now, I am stumbling over pots in the full light of dawning. He sighed, and blinked at the new day.

The sky was still pink, but Tigian noted with satisfaction that the *fegheen* were already at work—tending their fields in the west, and casting nets across the dark river. The harvest would be bountiful this year, and the storehuts would swell with grains and fruits and fat baskets of red berries. Even the *fegheen* would eat well, and the People would have their fill of hot breads and fishes, and the flesh of water birds.

Thinking about food made him hungry. He sniffed the air and caught the warm, pungent aroma of fried fish from the cook hut. Tigian smiled to himself. There would be salts from the north fields for seasoning, and a thick red sauce of sweet and sour berries. He walked a few yards from his door and stretched luxuriantly. It could, perhaps, be a good day after all. And if the harvest continued to go well, he might think about declaring a Free Day. The *fegheen* wouldn't notice the difference, of course, but it would go well with the People.

His thoughts were broken by the shuffling of feet behind him.

"What is it, Fego?" He didn't turn, for it could only be his servant. No other was allowed within the compound. Fego pattered around to one side and bowed slightly, touching his *gnee-gnee* in respect.

"Tigian slept well?"

"Tigian did. What do you want?"

"There is breakfast. A succulent dish of—"

"I know what it is."

Fego lowered his eyes. "Tigian is most discerning."

"Tigian has a nose. Is this why you break my morning? To tell me there is fish on my table?"

Fego bowed again. He was a thin, sad-eyed old man with almost no body hair. Worry lines creased his brow, though Tigian was certain he never worried about anything.

"It is of no import," Fego began, which meant that it was, "but in regard to the Saying..."

"What?" Tigian looked up for the first time.

"The Saying. Undoubtedly, Tigian has prepared suitable words for the People."

"Certain," said Tigian. Fego knew very well he'd forgotten all about it. "Why do you ask, Fego?"

Fego forced a look of grievous pain across his features, and touched his crotch again. "To bring myself honor, I took the liberty of transcribing a phrase or so from the Story. I thought to persuade you to, ah—use it in*stead* of the one you have prepared, which is undoubtedly a great deal better and more appropriate."

Tigian grinned slightly. "All right, let me see the thing. Perhaps I'll favor you. What is the subject of this masterpiece?"

Fego started to speak, but Tigian stopped him. He took the knotted cord from his servant and held it well away from his eyes. It was a quote from Negius, tenth chief of the People; a rather erratic and unpredictable leader, according to the Story. He was a favorite of Tigian's, as Fego well knew.

"Be you frugal in prosperity," he read, "and generous in time of need. Fools will call you good and wise, and the wise will call you fool. There is no pleasing the People." Tigian looked up narrowly at Fego.

"I thought perhaps the first part," Fego shrugged. "It is thought-provoking, and few will understand its meaning. The People are not comfortable with a Saying that is overly clear. I think they feel cheated."

"There is some merit in this," Tigian said soberly.

"I am honored."

"And I am hungry." He sniffed the air again and frowned at Fego. "Have a care," he warned. "If that lout of a cook burns my breakfast, I will have more from you than a Saying."

Fego scurried off quickly, and Tigian blinked into the morning, scratched his crotch, and yawned. The new sun turned the river deep amber, and touched the ripe, swollen fields with gold. To his left lay the neat, checkered farm and the dark forest beyond. Ahead were the huts of the People clustered about the banks of the river, and far to the east, into the sun, he could see the narrow white ribbon of the Falls, crowned by a halo of mist. It was a fair, gentle day, with a touch of chill in the air, and he could see the length and breadth of the Earth from his doorway, clear to the great high Wall around the world.

Tigian was glad to see a sparse crowd at the Saying. It was a good sign. No one bothered with ritual when the river was teeming with fish and the fields were heavy with grain. Just let a little sickness come into the world, though, or a blight in somebody's orchard—*then* they all remembered who was chief.

There were two Birthings. According to custom, Tigian examined the children closely. They were both boys, and one, sadly, was obviously *fegheen.* It looked up blankly at him with pale, wide-set eyes over a flat, almost bridgeless nose. He tied the brown knot of the *fegheen* around the small ankle, and the gray band of Darkness above it. No one questioned his judgment. They knew he favored gray for *fegheen* Birthings—even below the count. They might not wholly approve, but in a good year when there were few deaths among the work force, they would say nothing. There were many, even, who openly approved of his actions, and knew that he was right.

The parents, of course, were not present. The judgment of the child was sufficient; they had seen it, and knew. They would both be cut before the sun was down, as the law prescribed. The man, Tigian knew, would probably kill himself soon after.

It was often the way, though there was no dishonor to Birthing a *fegheen.* The woman would likely sicken and die from infection after the cutting.

There were happier events, as well. A farmer named Hadrik had reached his fifty-fifth season just the day before. The People cheered, and Hadrik beamed with pride as Tigian tied the green knot of Quitting about his ankle. He grasped the old man's *gnee-gnee* in tribute, and promised faithfully to attend his Deathfeast. Hadrik weeped openly, and in a sudden fit of emotion reached out and touched Tigian's *gnee-gnee* in return. Tigian smiled, and the crowd smiled with him. It was not custom, but age had its privilege.

There was a question about harvesting, and what Tigian felt was an absurd argument over fishing nets. He solved both problems quickly. No one objected to his swift justice—for no man present had even listened to the cases. Their thoughts—as well as their eyes—were already on the group of Seeded females waiting at the edge of the matting. There were seven—two over the last Saying, and Tigian decided that was a good sign. He knotted the pale blue cord around each slim ankle, and took his time about it. They were a pretty lot, for the most part, and all seemed as eager as the men to get the ceremonies over and done with. It could be a happy time for the People, with nearly half a year of joyous communal *phirking* before the females came to Birthing.

One girl in particular caught Tigian's eye. She was a slender young thing, no more than fifteen seasons old, with pale aureoles circling her breasts, and a delicate patch of gold over her *frihc.* Tigian sighed, for she reminded him of his own daughter, Guillia. The resemblance sent delightful stirrings through his loins. He touched the girl lightly on her thigh and looked once at Fego, and Fego nodded understanding.

The ceremonies over, Tigian rose and thanked the People for coming. They touched their crotches respectfully. He said the ritual words to end the Saying, and started for his hut.

"Tigian. I claim a Talking!"

The words stopped him. He turned slowly, giving himself ample time to compose his features into something resembling serenity and understanding. Great Creator's Eyeballs—he'd kill Fego! Fego shrugged miserably, his face telling Tigian that *he* didn't know anything about this—it certainly wasn't *his* doing.

The crowd muttered to themselves and stretched to see who had spoken. The boy edged his way forward. He was dark-eyed, intense and gangly, much like any other boy of the People. Only, of course, he wasn't, Tigian reminded himself.

"I am Darius, and I am of age, Tigian. I claim a Talking."

"Then you shall have it," Tigian told him, trying to recall the proper words. "It is your right, granted by the law of the People. I give you Keep under the mantle of the *rhamae.*" He was sure he'd gotten it right, or most of it. No one would know the difference, anyway, except Fego.

The boy mouthed his thanks and touched his *gnee-gnee,* and Tigian turned and walked from the Saying as quickly as his dignity would allow.

The boy Cavian greeted him with a sleepy smile. Tigian roared and sent him scampering wide-eyed from the hut. He tore the water jug from its hanging and smashed it against the far wall. Then he sank wearily to the floor.

It's a fine thing, he muttered darkly, when a chief is given no consideration by his People. There is a right way to do things, and a wrong way. What was the use in *having* a ritual, if no one followed the rules? A Talking was something to think about, and consider. It was an important event for the People. You did not simply—jump into one without preparation and planning.

Only, that was precisely what the boy Darius had done.

He was still fuming when Fego bowed his way into the hut. "Tigian," he said, catching his breath, "the boy's parents send their apologies. It is clear to me they knew nothing of his plans. They confirm, though, that he is of age."

"Fego, this is not the way to do things," said Tigian. "You are supposed to have an ear to the People."

"He said nothing to anyone," Fego sighed. "At any rate, it is not as bad as it might be. I have taken the liberty of checking the family tapestries. The father is Ghalius, a senior fisherman. He is of the Thigian branch—a good clean line with no *fegheen* for three generations. The mother, Lhania, has had one other child by another mating. Her line is equally as good as the father's. I can give you—"

Tigian waved him off. "Leave the knottings, Fego. I'm quite capable of reading them myself. For all the good it will do. *Damn* the boy, anyway!" He slammed his fist down hard, rattling the powers of his *rhamae.*

"He is under the Keep, Tigian..."

"Don't remind me," Tigian scowled at him.

All of the People who saw Tigian and the boy walking by the river knew there was a Talking underway, but they had the courtesy to go about their business and pretend they saw nothing. Sometimes, *not* doing something was a big part of keeping faith with tradition, and their respect did not go unnoticed by Tigian. In a sense, it helped make up for the way the day had begun.

Even the boy seemed to realize that his behavior had been less than proper, though Tigian had done nothing to show his disapproval.

"I guess I did something wrong again," he said, kicking at a river stone.

"Do you know what this thing could be?" Tigian asked.

"I—guess so," said Darius. He looked up hesitantly at Tigian.

"Go ahead. You are under the protection of the Keep. Do you understand what that means, boy?"

"I think I do."

"It means that I have sworn before the People that you will not be held accountable for what you say to me during the Talking. You are—excused in advance for any unseemly questions you might ask, and nothing in our conversation will be considered as heretical. Do you understand that?"

"Yes, Tigian."

"And you have given thought to what might have been discourteous about your actions this morning?"

The boy lowered his eyes. "I—there were things I was supposed to do."

"No." Tigian stopped and held up the small chin. "That is not entirely correct, Darius. It is not a law you have broken, but a tradition. Every boy has the right to demand a Talking. It is a privilege of approaching manhood. That is the law. *Tradition* says that a boy discusses his desire for a Talking with his parents, so that they, in turn, can grant the leader of the People the courtesy—"

"No!" Darius shook his head fiercely and pulled away. "I didn't *want* to tell them anything. I wanted to talk to you!"

Tigian stared, the blood rising to his cheeks. Why, no one had ever talked to him like that before. Keep or no Keep!

The boy saw instantly what he had done, and his eyes widened in fear. "Tigian—I erred greatly."

"Outrageously, Darius. You are—under my protection," he said calmly, "but I see no reason to test the power of that law."

"I showed no respect..."

"You did not. Perhaps this is some sort of problem with you. Perhaps you show a similar lack of respect for your parents. This would account for your disregard of tradition."

The boy looked puzzled. "This is not so, Tigian."

"It would certainly appear to be so, Darius. We are judged by our actions, not our words."

"But I believe that, too," Darius protested. "That's why I said nothing to—him."

"Him?"

"My father. *He* didn't have a Talking. Tigian, don't you see? He didn't want to. Hardly any grownups I know ever even thought about it!"

Tigian's heart went out to the boy. Could he not see his own youth mirrored here? The brash self-confidence of a wide-eyed boy stumbling toward manhood. Questioning everything, and wondering why the world around him took so long to catch up. For the moment, though, he buried understanding.

"A Talking is a privilege," he said evenly, "something a man chooses. It is not a thing that must be done."

The boy looked pained. "But there is so much to learn, Tigian. How could a man not seek the answers to his questions?"

Tigian studied the boy. The large, dark eyes in the narrow face. It was a face almost pinched together—a sharp, pointed chin that flared abruptly into high cheeks, broad, heavy brows and a thatch of oat-colored hair. It was a face common to the People; close enough to his own. But it is not a child's face, thought Tigian, even though a child still lives there.

They lunched without talk on the bank of the river under a shade tree, and Fego came and quietly took their empty clay dishes away, leaving the jug of clear wheat ale cooling in the shallows. Darius had never tasted the drink before. He said it reminded him of flowers and bread, and Tigian smiled and said that was exactly what it was, only that all the solid parts had been taken out, leaving the *thought* of bread and flowers behind. Darius considered that, then laughed out loud. The idea seemed to delight him.

He is, truly, both man and boy, thought Tigian. His eyes reflected the strange knowledge that is the secret of every child, but a very adult smile played at the corner of his lips. As Tigian watched, a party of boys and girls ran laughing by, limbs flashing in the sun, each as bare and brown as Darius himself. Darius followed them with his child-man eyes.

When the ale was gone, the boy lay back and stretched to let the sun warm his body. Tigian joined him, and Darius moved over easily to rest his head on the man's shoulder. A flock of white birds winged high overhead, lazing on the wind, hardly moving at all. Tigian and Darius followed them a long time until they disappeared down the valley.

"Tigian," the boy said finally, "that is one of the questions I would ask at my Talking."

"What, Darius?" Though he knew full well where the boy was going.

Darius turned on his stomach and looked down at him, chin cupped in his hands. "It has to do with the birds. Kind of. Only not really."

"Yes?"

"Tigian, do you think the Wall is truly the end of the world? I mean, do you think there is—something else outside?"

Ah, thought Tigian, *there it is.* "We can see the whole world," he said. "It stops at the Wall, and no man can go beyond it."

Darius bit his lip impatiently. "Yes, but if he *could?*"

"He cannot, though."

"But imagine that he could."

"All right."

"Imagine that he could—make steps in the Wall, and climb it."

"But he cannot, Darius. The Wall is of the hardest stone, and is the height of a mile standing on end. A man cannot cut a step in it without stone harder than the Wall itself. And there is no such stone in the world."

Darius frowned. "We are imagining though, Tigian. Remember?"

"I remember," said Tigian, trying hard to match the boy's expression.

"Then if a man *could* cut the steps, he could climb to the top. Now. What would he see?"

"What do you see?"

"Sir?"

"You are here, looking up at the top. What do you see?"

Darius looked at him curiously. "Well, nothing, but—"

"Then why do you think a man on the top could see more? He could see the world below, yes—"

"But if he looked the *other* way, Tigian. What would he see then?"

"Why, nothing, I suppose."

"Tigian—" Darius looked pained. "There has to be *something*."

"Why?"

"There just—" Darius brightened. "The birds, remember? The birds fly over the edge of the world and disappear. What do they see, when we can't see them?"

"Look up, Darius," Tigian said patiently. "Where are the birds flying now?"

"Well—in the sky."

"They are indeed." Tigian spread his hands. "And might they continue to fly in the sky, whether one small boy sees them or not?" He picked up the clay bowl beside him and poured the last drop of wheat ale to the ground. Then he found a tiny stone and placed it in the bottom of the bowl and showed it to Darius. "You are fond of imagining, are you not? Then imagine that the bowl is the world and you are the stone. When a bird flies past the rim of the bowl, you can see him no longer. However, he is still there. Things continue to *be,* whether we see them or not. Just so, the sun and the moon and the stars disappear to circle the world—" he swept his fist over and under the bowl, "—and return again."

All of the muscles in the boy's face went tight as stone. Tigian was certain tears would well in his eyes any moment. "But—but that—it's just—"

"What you were *taught?*" Tigian finished. He stared straight through Darius' eyes. "Yes, boy, it is. Is that why you reject it? Because it is the belief of the people? It would appear that you have little respect for anything that comes from the mind of another. Only those things which Darius believes are true."

Darius colored. "No, Tigian, it's just—"

"What, boy?"

"You'll think I lack respect for tradition."

Tigian sighed. "Darius, I am already quite certain of it. Do not let that stand in your way."

Still, Darius hesitated. Tigian caught his eyes. They had been wandering to the *rhamae* all morning, when Darius thought he wasn't looking. Now, they were fastening there again.

"Ah, it is the Bone, is it not?"

"Yes," Darius nodded. He looked warily at Tigian, dark eyes peering through a shock of hair. "We can speak of that?"

"We can. It is a part of the history of the People, and no great secret."

"And did it truly come from the beast that fell from the rim of the world?"

"It did."

"What did it look like, Tigian?" Wide eyes flashed. "Like no beast that lives on Earth?"

Tigian almost smiled. Instead, he kept his face solemn and devoid of expression. "If you had listened to the Story of the People that was told you when you were young, you would know that the beast fell to Earth over the Falls long ago. I do not know what it looked like, nor does any man living. That part of the Story is forgotten. We only know that it happened."

"Then—"

"Wait," said Tigian, holding up a hand. Shadows crawled across the world. The short autumn day was coming to a close. "While I do not wish to steal a moment of your Talking, Darius, the sun is fading. And if I am not mistaken, you were about to tell me that since the beast fell from the rim of the world, it must have *come* from somewhere else. From there you will surmise that since it is clear that water must run flat before it drops, the Falls, too, come from somewhere outside the world. Is this not so?"

Darius looked like a small, bewildered child who has forgotten where it lives. Tigian smiled and patted his oat-brown head. "Boy, can you not imagine that I have been a child myself? Full of wonder at the world, and bursting with questions such as yours? Why do we do this? What causes that?" He laughed to himself and shook his head. "Right after my father told me the Story of the Beginning—I was barely six, then—how the river disappears into the earth to circle the world and come back to us replenished. I spent hours tossing jugs in the water; I'd toss a jug into the current, then run back to the Falls and wait for it to come back again. Not a one ever did. I was very disappointed, and my mother was terribly angry—for I had taken all the jugs from the house."

Darius grinned, but the grin faded quickly to a thoughtful frown. "Still, Tigian, there is the question—"

"Darius, Darius," Tigian said wearily, "do you see that tree above our heads?"

"Yes, Tigian."

"Is it real? Can you touch it?"

"I can."

"And yet there are many things you cannot tell me about this tree. How does it grow from a tiny seed? How does a new tree create similar seeds within itself? Where did it come from in the first place? You do not know these things, yet you touch the tree, see its bark, and hear its leaves rustle in the wind. Therefore, you believe that it is real, even though you understand next to nothing about it." Tigian paused. "Must all mysteries be clear to you, Darius? Can there not be truth, without understanding? I do not know where the beast came from, nor how the great Falls fills the river again and again. I do not know how the sun and the moon float above the world without falling, but they do. For they do not depend upon my knowledge of their ways to continue doing what they do. Darius, do you believe in the Creator?"

The boy's eyes widened. "Of course, Tigian!"

"Then does it not seem proper to allow Him to create as he sees fit—without fully explaining His actions to you?"

Darius bit his lip and stared shamefully at the ground. "I—did not think of it that way, Tigian." When he looked up again, his eyes were on the verge of tears, so Tigian smiled and pulled him quickly to his feet.

"Come, now, let's speak of other things, all right? There's more on a young boy's mind than the mysteries of the world, isn't there?" He winked broadly, bringing the beginning of a grin to the small face. "Tell me," he said, holding the boy's shoulders, "do you have a sweetheart, Darius? I'll bet you do."

Darius' eyes sparkled. "Oh, yes, Tigian. His name is Marius. He is of the Dhirlios branch, and his father is a farmer."

"Good, good. And do you have fine times together?"

"Yes, Tigian."

"And you have kept yourself clean, have you not?"

"Tigian!" Darius looked startled. "Why, that is the law!"

"Yes, and a very important law, too. You know that, do you not?"

"Oh, yes, Tigian."

The sun dropped behind the rim of the world and a chill breeze rippled the water. Tigian led the boy away from the river and headed up the path back to the huts.

"Of course," Darius said solemnly, "I am nearly of age now, and I have wondered what it is like to enter a girl's *frihc.* Marius and I have talked about it."

"You have, have you?"

"Yes. We have decided it is probably a good thing."

"Well..." Tigian pretended to see something in the sky. "I expect you will find this is so."

"There are a great many girls I know who are most attractive. A few are nearly ready for Seeding."

"Indeed."

"But I believe *your* daughter is truly the best, Tigian." Darius grinned enthusiastically. "I think I would very much enjoy a *phirking* with her!"

"That's nice," said Tigian. Who wouldn't?

At the top of the path he stopped, looked out over the river a moment, then laid a hand on the boy's shoulder. "The sun is gone, Darius. And I am afraid the Talking is over. I hope that it has been of value to you."

"It has, Tigian. Truly."

"Think upon what we have discussed. And let your mind dwell upon those things that were *not* said, as well. Often, truth lies hidden in places we forget to look."

"I will, Tigian." He bowed and touched his *gnee-gnee* in respect. Tigian smiled at him, and turned up the path.

"Tigian—"

Tigian looked back. Darius seemed smaller, now—as if the day had cut him a good head shorter.

"Was it—a good Talking, Tigian?"

"Was it, Darius? Only you can really say."

"I—think it was." The big, dark eyes reached out to him. "But I'd like to hear what you—"

"Darius. The sun is over the rim of the world. And the Talking is over..."

Fego had a fire going and a good stew simmering in the pot, but Tigian wasn't hungry. "Find the good ale," he said wearily, "wherever it is you keep the stuff hidden. And Fego—"

"Yes, Tigian?"

"Bring enough. And bring two cups."

Fego raised a brow. "Yes, Tigian."

"Not *yes,* Tigian," he said sourly. "I have been 'yes, Tigianed' to death." He pulled off the *rhamae* and draped it over a peg. "There. Just Tigian. All right?"

Fego grinned, ducked out and came back with two large jugs plugged with reed. "I thought perhaps we could forego the cups. This does not appear to be a cup-type event." He stood a moment, studying Tigian. "It is always the way with a Talking. There is nothing for it, except a little ale—or a great deal of it."

Tigian grunted at him and settled in by the fire. He took a long draft, wiped his mouth, and passed the jug to Fego. Fego drank, and set the ale by his side.

"It went well, then? Or badly?"

"Is there a difference?" Tigian waved his own words aside. "Oh, it went well enough, I suppose. I gave him all the right answers. He didn't believe any of them, but he's smart enough not to say so. Right now, of course, all he wants to know is what's over the rim."

"Then he is possible."

"He's possible. But that doesn't mean anything. They all want to know that."

"Yes."

"Maybe he'll stop right there. Maybe he *wants* to know more but didn't ask. Who can say?"

Fego grinned. "There was a time, Tigian, when I was most uncertain of *you*. You were seventeen before you knew what your *gnee-gnee* was for. I finally decided it was my duty as chief to show you."

Tigian gave him a dark smile. "You are an impudent old man, Fego."

Fego shrugged. "You want Fego the obedient servant, get back in your *rhamae*. And I am not so old, Tigian, that I have forgotten what a rare thing is the curious mind. We breed very fine farmers and fishermen, and plenty of dull-witted *fegheen*. But I can count the number of really good Talkings I've seen on two hands." Fego rolled his eyes and raised the jug to his lips. "Creator's Crotch—there was a time when I thought for certain I'd have to spend the rest of my miserable life under the *rhamae!*"

Tigian laughed and reached across the fire for the ale. "It was not that bad. And I was *not* that stupid, Fego."

"No," Fego grunted, "you were worse." He blinked into the coals and yawned. "Ah, Tigian," he said wearily, "age drains the mind and soul of a man like water through a net. I no longer care whether a man or a woman shares my bed—so long as there is plenty of warm matting about. I have lost my capacity for ale, as you can see. I have little interest in the present, and none in the past. I could care less whether we grew from the droppings of a great bird, or fell from the stars." He looked up, eyes heavy and blurred. "And you know something, Tigian? While there is much I would like to have back, there is one thing I would gladly put away, and cannot. I am still cursed with wonder."

"It is a thing we share, Fego."

Fego gave him a wary glance. "Then you should look to yourself, Tigian. In this world, only young boys and foolish old men think about tomorrow."

Tigian stared into the fire. He thought about opening the other jug, and decided against it. He wondered briefly about the girl he had seen at the Saying. She would be somewhere about. Fego would have seen to that.

He looked at the old man and smiled. Fego was asleep, sitting up, his hand curled around an empty jug. He has been a good chief and a good servant, thought Tigian. He has served the People well, and deserves a deeper sleep than that.

Perhaps Darius would be the one. Maybe the boy would come along—learn what he needed to know. Perhaps, he thought, I will one day become the servant of Darius, and Fego can go to his Quitting.

The rest, though, was up to the boy. No one could take him further. It as a thing he must come to by himself, and only time would tell. For Fego was right. There were few who took their questing minds far enough. The really bright ones looked up at the Wall and wondered what lay outside. But few came the rest of the way. It is not an easy thing to bring wonder and acceptance together in the mind of a man. To learn the terrible truth that it matters little what lies outside the world; that the People were going nowhere at all, and never would. That they must learn to survive where they were. But it is a thing that must be understood, and a knowledge that makes the *rhamae* hang heavy on the shoulders of a chief.

Happy New Year, Hal

Hurray.

For the fourteenth consecutive year Hal gets Marta Lee Enright out of her bra. Tosses fluff bundle to back seat; turns to catch a question in her eyes, a dubious smile.

"We shouldn't, Hal."

Marta's voice: dull; mechanical.

"Listen, honey—"

Hal's voice: tedious; apathetic.

"Baby, they're great. God, they're just great!"

"Hal..."

Hal mentally shuts his eyes; grinds his teeth; tries to keep his hands off; reaches out anyway.

"We've *got* to get back, Hal. Christ, Max'll kill me!"

"Max is up to his ass in bourbon."

"He never gets *that* drunk. Please, Hal—"

Brief, precious silence. Mint seconds. Unused. Time span. Nothing called for in the script. Hal rushes in with:

"Marta, I'm sorry as hell!"

Marta: suddenly alive: fear in her eyes; in the soft light from steamed windows, a half-circle shadow at the corner of her lips; taut; an overtaxed tendon looking for work. Hal nods encouragement.

Words blossom: explode: *"I would, Hal – I really would if I could!"*

"I know. Marta, listen – "

Too late; sudden; sharp: a blade through breath. Shift: back to the script.

"Come on, baby. Don't be like that."

"Hal – "

"Just tell me you like it. I *know* you like it."

"Please – "

"Tell me."

"Hal, I *love* it, that's not the – "

Wide eyes pleading, small hands raised automatically to fend him off. And Hal automatically pressing on.

Hal: cursing in silence. After fourteen insane reruns of 1974, most people would turn off Oldtalk. Mouths spewed the obligatory words; ears shut out the meaning. Not Hal: total awareness: every bland sentence; worn sounds assailing the senses. Each a gem of enthusiasm: See Jane Run. See Spot Jump.

Watching Marta in half-darkness: ladylike struggle; struggle scheduled to end in nine seconds. Stalemate. Hal: blinking, as car turns corner. Lights sweep briefly over curves of flesh. Eighteen minutes and counting. Minimal petting; sparring; reluctant retrieval of bra and blouse; back to the party. Joan: where the hell have you *been* all this time?

"Where the hell do you think I've been?"

Witless grin: vacuous smile number fourteen.

"Where I've been is to get ice. You sent us after ice."

"Uh-huh." Joan: eyebrow raised in doubt. "I trust that's *all* you got."

"Ha. Ha. Funny."

"Not to me you son of a bitch."

"Get *off* it, Joan—"

Joan: turns away; busies herself at sink. Drone of party drifts in from den: hive of sleepy bees.

Hal: watches sack of ice melting on counter.

"Honey, listen—"

Wait. Joan scheduled to sulk for two minutes: free time: nothing in the script.

Joan: real voice. *"Hal, it's not going too badly. Not really."*

"Great. Glad to hear it."

She'd like to face him. Can't. Doesn't miss the tone, though.

"Be happy with what you've got, Hal. My God, any—real conversation is something, isn't it? We've had an interesting evening. Honest!"

Genuine irritation: *"If you'd just try not to hear the Oldtalk, Hal. You don't even try!"*

"I can't."

"You might try. For my sake."

"I have tried. I try all the time."

Voice cracks: *"How do you think I feel, knowing every damn time you're going out for an hour and a half with Marta Enright? How do you think I feel, Hal?"*

"Oh, God!" Hal: disgust. *"Do we have to bring that up again? Christ, Joan, what difference does it make? We didn't do anything—we didn't do anything fourteen godamn times in a row! Why can't you just—"*

Cut. Over and out. So: what did we do with freetalk time?

Beautiful: just great.

Joan: turns on schedule.

"Here, see if you can break up a little ice, lover. Maybe it'll cool you off." Warning: "Hal. Keep your hands off that bitch."

"Drop it, Joan."

"I mean it, Hal."

"Listen. Nothing happened—"

"We won't talk about it now. After everyone leaves."

Joan: stalks out of room. Hal: gets hammer from drawer; breaks up ice in sack; waits stoically for wincing pain due after eighth stroke.

Talk about it: after everyone leaves. No way: there isn't any after. No one leaves until the "new" year comes in. Then: back to the beginning. The big d.j. starts the record again. Chapter fifteen. Play it again, Sam.

Six. Seven. Eight.

"Damn!"

On target.

Max Enright finishes Oldtalk joke. Rushes in three real words:

"Hear the radio?"

Wait. Liz Harmon's bit about new scandal: What principal did or didn't do to girls' gym teacher.

Joan: *"Yes, I did! They've done real well this year. There was a lot of stuff on the station this morning and – "*

Hal: "Got to change those records. Who wants to hear what?"

Feels himself getting up. Fights it. Quick pain as body does what it damn well pleases.

Brushes by Marta. Black look from Max.

"I want to talk to you, Hal..."

"Do that, Max."

"Anyway – " Joan: bits and pieces. *"They think maybe it's better – this year – than it was – two women died in Europe somewhere and – there was that plumber or whatever he was in – South Carolina I think – "*

Quick finish: before Max begins story of tricky real estate deal; pulled one over on those bastards in East Bay.

Hal: settled in for nine minutes of Oldtalk. Stiff slug of Scotch on schedule. Chokes. Slams mental brakes: wait: think:

had he choked before? Ever? No—By God no. It was new! It was—

"Great, Max—say one thing, any time I can screw those characters I'll do it. If *you* don't, *they* will!"

Quickly-quickly: *"Listen. I choked. I choked and I never—"*

Oldtalk sweeps in: buries his bulletin. Maybe later. Not much—but something. Things did change. Right here. In this neighborhood. Madge and Ray Ackerlein: poison ivy: two years in a row. He'd helped tell it in town; later, heard it squeezed into a blank spot on the network.

" —don't forget the horse!" Liz Harmon: on tail-end of Phil's request for more of cheese and crackers he'd eaten; digested; eliminated fourteen times.

"I heard it this morning. It swam out into the water again only this time it didn't drown, *by God!"*

"Here, Phil, try some of this. It's onion dip."

"That was where—Jamaica?"

"Hey, good. Whadja say it was?"

"No, Bermuda, I think, but—"

"Just plain old onion dip. You can get it at the store. Liz, don't you ever *feed* this man?"

Midnight: minus six minutes and counting.

A look in the eyes. Even through the porcelain glaze of Oldtalk. Even poor goddamn Max. Giving Marta hell. Glaring at Hal.

Marta: staring at him. Hal sees: reads it loud and clear. If it doesn't change this time, Hal—Wrong. Won't lose your mind, Marta. Just think you will. No way, baby. You didn't bring a fuzz-brain into the year, you don't take it out.

Hal: head scheduled for right turn. Sneaks a look to the left. Minus three minutes and counting. Happy New Year. Ring out the old; ring in the old. Snap! Midnight: 31 December, 1974. Bong-bong-bong-bong-etc. snap! 12:01: 1 January, 1974.

Costume and set changes:

Marta: blue pants suit. Blink-blink. Red skirt, white v-neck.

Hal: black sports shirt. Blink-blink. Green turtleneck.

Joan: bourbon and coke. Blink-blink. Vodka and soda.

Etc:

Not so bad for some. Not so good for others. Phil and Liz at a different party. Blink-blink. For Phil and Liz read: Jack and Ella. Zap! Just like Captain whatsizname. Jack and Ella at the door. Thanks for a great time, Hal. 12:07 a.m. Jack: a little looped. Ella: giving Jack that look, the one Hal never gets used to. Bye-bye baby. Cut to: Jack and Ella. Car arcing off bridge. 12:23 a.m. Ella: instant widow, fourteen times removed.

Minus one minute and counting.

Phil: *"They're saying maybe it was the tests. The ones at the Pole."*

Hal: *"What the hell difference does it make?"*

Max: *"Godamn scientists. Don't know which end – "*

Marta: *"For Christ's Sake, Max – not now!"*

Liz Harmon: four words in Oldtalk; nobody hears, not even Hal.

Hal: looks at Marta. Joan. Max. Etc.

Little hand crawls up to twelve.

Phil: "Happy New Year!"

Liz: "Happy New Year, everybody!"

Max: "Happy New Year, gang! Go get 'em!"

Marta: "Happy New Year—it was great!"

Hal: "Happy New Year—let's do it again soon."

Joan: "Happy New Year, Hal."

A Walk on Toy

Mara was teeth-gritting mad.

There were tears, too, but mostly tears of relief—a few tears were called for, she decided, after two months in a stinking suit on a mudball planet.

She let her eyes climb the high column of the *Taegaanthe,* towering over Gara Station. Tightness welled up and caught in her throat. It was more than just a ship. It was hot food, clean clothes, safe sleep, human talk.

And it was a bath. God help that rusty can if it didn't have a good eight hours of hot water on hand!

She breathed a deep sigh and turned away from the closed hatches. Clenching her fists, she cursed whatever silent crew was aboard to the limits of her nearly unlimited vocabulary. Then she sat down again and waited...

She was used to waiting. She had waited on Earth for an Outworld ship and endured the soul-draining trip to Krishna. And she had waited for the freighter at Krishna. And waited...

The freighter was a ghost-tripper. Ninety-nine-plus percent cargo. Cabin doubling as quarters-mess-control room-lounge.

And Mara Trent-Hanse, raised in the ultraprivacy of Earth, lived eighteen inches from the pilot for twenty-two days. He was an old spacer named Haust, and he was doubly dedicated to the long, dark night, and life without "the confining burden of clothes."

A ghost-tripper towing four million miles of cargo doesn't emerge from subdrive to disembark passengers. Certainly not a passenger as uncooperative as Mara. The Trent-Hanse name meant nothing to Haust, and no name he could imagine was worth risking unaccountable megabucks in some warped envelope of space-time.

With a final friendly pinch, he loosed the escape capsule in what he hoped was the approximate orbit of Gara in real space and silently wished her luck.

Gara Station. Two months of staring through her faceplate at chlorine clouds on a flat brown horizon. Occasionally, a paddle-wheel mudder and its toad-gray crew, slapped across the dull surface, going slowly from nowhere to nowhere...

She had been patient. It wasn't that easy, now. There was something else to look at besides mudflats. There was the high needle of the *Taegaanthe,* old and ugly, scarred by the winds of time—and the most beautiful sight on Gara or any other world.

When the hatch finally slid open, she caught herself—and walked leisurely toward the dark hull. Her heart pounded. Her knees were weak. And she'd be double-damned if she'd let them know it.

It was a long ten minutes before the face appeared in the small panel and the outer lock closed on Mara. Her helmet was off before the green light winked on, before the cool hiss of oxygen finished filling the chamber.

She filled her lungs and rolled her head in a lazy arc, letting the ecstasy of clean air sweep over her. Then she turned to the face in the panel. Tall, deep-featured. Heavy brows cragged over a strong nose, wide mouth, long jaw. She thought him crudely attractive except for the cold, tourmaline eyes.

The mouth opened. The voice came harshly over the speaker.

"All right—get the helmet back on."

Mara blinked. "What?"

His eyes closed patiently. "I said: Get the helmet back on. I can't spray it without you in it."

"Oh," she said, remembering. She snapped the thing back on her shoulders, flinching at the suit's smell. It was more fetid than ever after the tantalizing taste of pure air.

The germicidal spray jetted from six sides of the chamber, the hotness penetrating even through the protective insulation. Finally, fresh water washed boiling liquid away, and the man's nod signaled approval.

Mara needed little encouragement. She stripped off the heavy suit, opened a panel, and tossed suit and helmet inside. She heard the cleansing jets go to work. Then she turned back to the dark face.

He was watching, impatience pulling at the tourmaline eyes. Whatever he was waiting for, it was a mystery to Mara.

"Well—would you open *up,* please?"

His heavy brow rose, and one corner of the wide mouth lifted in amusement.

"In those?" He nodded toward the filthy coveralls.

Mara felt color rise to her face. "I intend to bathe as soon as possible," she said icily. "I won't offend you for long. But I certainly can't do anything about it in here."

He laughed heartily. "Like hell you can't! Think I'm going to let you in like that? Son of a squid, girl, we'd have to abandon ship! Hurry up, now—strip and soap. I can't stand here all day."

Mara's eyes widened. "Stand here all—look, friend. I don't intend to—to—"

The face disappeared and the panel slammed in midsentence. A tube of soapy material plopped out of the wall, and warm water bombarded her from all directions.

Mara cursed and choked, then stoically closed her mouth. One grim eye on the closed panel, she unzipped the coverall and stuffed it down the disposal. It wasn't exactly what she'd anticipated for two long months. But it was water—hot water and soap, and it was over all too quickly. She closed her eyes and stretched, standing on tiptoe, letting warm jets of air flow over her skin.

There was a sudden *chink!* of metal on metal. She froze, opened her eyes and stared. The inner lock was open. He stood there letting his eyes take the grand tour. He tossed the clean, folded coveralls and boots with a grin, and left her standing with tight, balled fists and murderous eyes.

She slipped into the things quickly, masking her embarrassment with loathing. Then she grimly crossed through the lock into the ship.

She faced him squarely. Her eyes shot sparks of anger.

He smiled easily, leaning against the bulkhead with his arms folded across his chest.

"Well, you're not half bad with all the grime off you—even for an Earthie. Heard they all had figures like ore sacks, but I can't say that fits you. I'm Gilder. Are you contracted for the night? No, course not—you don't know anyone but me, do you?"

She slapped him hard and spat out a word in the common tongue. It meant alien-tainted-debauched lecher. And more.

He grinned at her.

"On Earth," she said tightly, "I could have you *fixed* for that!"

He eyed her quizzically. "Why, it was a formal proposition, girl. N'more than common courtesy. He studied her another long moment, then jerked his head over his shoulder.

"Handel! Get your carcass in here!"

Mara turned curiously, then stiffened. She backed against the bulkhead and gripped it tightly.

The boy crept out of the corridor, naked except for thin black shorts. His body was thick with welts and heavy keloid. He had a tiny, bald head, watery eyes, and a cut for a mouth. Gilder raised his boot and slammed it hard into bare ribs.

Handel moaned and trembled against the deck. Mara blinked in disbelief, and with a scornful stare at Gilder, bent and touched the boy's bleeding side. His face met hers. Mara jerked away. She read the meaning in his eyes, knew it for what it was. Dark, passionate loathing for her. For Gilder…

The big man laughed. "He's a Painie—never see one before?" His eyes settled on her with dark amusement. "You can throw away the book here, girl. This is Outworld, and you're among Survey folk, now. It isn't Muh-ther Earth, it's Gara, Zybarr, and Deep-squeeze—an' about as far from Free City courtesy as you're likely to get.

He shook his head disdainfully. "Great Suns, what the hell are you doing out *here*, anyway?"

Mara was half listening, numb with fear and revulsion. "I'd—like to go to my quarters—*please!*"

If he'd keep silent, not speak, she might make it. And if the boy didn't look at her again…

"Handel!" Gilder kicked the boy solidly in the head. Mara leaned weakly against the bulkhead. The corridor started to swim around her.

"Handel, lead milady to her quarters, eh?" He laughed softly, and Mara stumbled down the hall following the thin, shuffling feet.

Eridek awoke.

He lay on his bunk and watched the great chill drain from his limbs. The pump of his heart took hold; stilled blood began to move.

He opened his eyes and looked up at the gray ceiling. From the stillness beneath him, he judged they had landed and knew it must be Gara. He searched his senses, still feeble and unresponsive, probing for some thread that bound him from his state before the Dream and now.

A memory opened slowly, petaling to let tiny lights drift to the surface.

Gara.

Gara and a girl.

What about the girl?

Something flitted by, and was gone—a fleeting patch from the fading fabric of the Dream.

Eridek shrugged, sat up, and worked the tone back into his muscles. His mouth was dry and padded. He reached a shaky hand for a tube of water, sucked hungrily at its coolness, then closed his eyes and let the whole substance of the Dream unfold like a dark bolt of heavy cloth.

He remembered...

He remembered the One who lived within the great darkness of the far nebula. For the timeless length of the Dream, Eridek had been behind that darkness and lived as another and seen things no other man might possibly imagine.

Now, until the Dream came again, the One would look out upon the things that Eridek saw—and think them almost as strange as Eridek did the other.

He stood, walked to the long mirror, and stared at his naked reflection. Tall, lean-bodied, fair skin, even features, clear eyes. It was a handsome enough face, but he knew it lacked the strength of a man to whom "strength" had meaning.

For Eridek had no need for such a thing. Strong emotions denoted conflicts and tensions, and the One who shared his soul wished no harm or corruption in its resting place.

Eridek dressed. Once more, a fleeting thought of the girl came to his mind. He shrugged the thought aside. Whatever it was, it would come soon enough. Sooner than he'd care for, certainly.

Out of the room, among the familiar sounds of the ship, he found himself almost glad to be moving toward the company of others. He rounded the corner and saw the stunted figure of the boy a split second before Handel stumbled into him.

The boy whimpered. Eridek shook him off with a muttered warning. Then he saw the girl.

He glanced for a moment into dark, startled eyes, then jerked back as searing pain coursed through his skull. He doubled up, gasped for breath.

When he looked up, they were gone. The pain dissolved as quickly as it had come, but Eridek stood against the bulkhead a long moment, letting his breath return, waiting for his hands to stop shaking.

It had been a bad one. Very bad. He pushed it hurriedly into a deep recess where it would fade from black to gray and hopefully, lie dormant and unseen for awhile.

He stepped into the Common and quickly scanned the three faces. He breathed a quick sigh of relief. There was nothing significant about the future of Gereen deGeis—nothing except the shallow wave of pleasure-pain that was always there.

She turned and smiled as he entered, and Eridek flinched away and let his eyes sweep briefly over Gilder Lanve-Hall, and then to Pfore, the man's alien Gantry Brother.

There was a brief shadow over Gilder, but whatever it was, it was of no immediate concern. And there was nothing at all in the quiet, gray eyes of Pfore. The slim, azure-skinned creature did not even deign to look up.

Eridek ignored them all and mixed himself a drink. From behind him, Gilder said, "Have a nice Dream, Eri?"

Eridek's hand immediately tightened around his glass. Even before he turned, he could see the contempt in the Gantryman's eyes.

Facing him, the contempt was still there, but Eridek no longer felt anger. He understood that anger too well. And the contempt, too. To erase that contempt was to erase Gilder, and the water world of Gantry, and the involved relationship of Gilder's forebears with Pfore's people.

And that, of course, he couldn't do—any more than he could change the way Gereen looked at a man, or the reason she bothered to look at all.

They sat together—Gilder, bare to the waist, drink in one hand, the other draped in easy familiarity over her shoulder. Her red hair hung in marvelous disarray, and the thin chemise revealed or covered as chance allowed.

It's a false picture, he told himself. He knew Gereen's sensuality was almost void of intent, just as Gilder's cruelty was as unstudied as a beast's. They are what they are. What they must be, he corrected.

As I must be what I am.

"Missed you, Eri," she said. She moved easily away from Gil and came toward him. "Why spend so much time by yourself, when your friends need you? Why, Eri?"

She touched his arm lightly. He smelled the closeness of her and turned away. He downed the drink quickly and made another.

Gil laughed harshly. "Sit down, Gereen. You can't compete with Eri's soulmate, for God's sake!"

Gereen frowned in mock disapproval. She leaned over a chair and cocked one eye at Eri. "Eri can't help what he is," she said softly. "Any more than you can, defiler of whales—"

Gilder laughed and choked on his drink. He reached out and pulled her to him. She landed in his lap and the silver bells on her ankles tinkled with her own high laughter.

Eridek said, "Who is the girl, Gilder?"

Gil looked up, mild annoyance beginning at the corners of his mouth. Then he seemed to sense something in Eri's voice. "What?"

"Who is she?" Eri repeated.

Gil shrugged. "From our noble captain's words, I take it she's the replacement for Hali Vickson. Why?" He grinned. "You taking an interest in new females?"

Eri ignored him. "I know she's Hali Vickson's replacement. But who is she? Where does she come from?"

Gil studied him a second before answering; Gereen looked from Gil to Eri, puzzlement crowding her face.

"She's an Earthie, no less," Gil said. "Cute little thing, too. High born and high—"

"What is it, Eri?" Gereen interrupted. Eri caught her eyes upon him. She was all seriousness, now. The wanton sparkle was gone. From the corner of the room, blue-skinned Pfore's saucer eyes blinked and opened.

"All right," Eri sighed, "I had a Telling."

Gereen paled. Her hand touched her bare throat with a life of its own.

"So. You had a Telling," Gil said too loudly. "So what?"

"Gil!" Gereen snapped.

Gilder mumbled something to himself, glanced at Eri, then turned away.

"I was in it, wasn't I, Eri?" Gereen was as white as death. "What's going to happened to me, Eri, what—"

"No!" Eri barked savagely. The girl relaxed slightly, but her fingers still wandered nervously over her body.

"If it was you, think I'd tell you?" Eri said irritably. "If you're going to get it, you're going to get it, Gereen. Don't come to me for your weight and fortune everytime I have a goddamn Telling!"

Gilder clapped and laughed loudly. Eri glared at him.

"You saw Hali Vickson," she said tightly. "You knew that, and you *told* him it would happen to him—"

"No," Eri said evenly. "I didn't."

"He—said he *thought* you knew," Gereen corrected. "It's the same thing, isn't it?"

"I'm sorry I mentioned it," said Eri. He faced her and smiled lightly. "Nothing will ever happen to you, Gereen—unless you put the wrong tube in the wrong vein."

Gereen suddenly laughed. The wanton sparkle was back. "You might try it with me sometime, Eri. If the Belt *allows* that sort of thing—"

Eri shrugged wearily, knowing the uselessness of battling wits with Gereen. He felt the first two drinks, and needed the third.

"The girl, now," Gilder said quietly. "She was in your Telling, Eri."

Eri felt muscles tighten with a quick fear. He glared narrowly at the Gantryman.

Gil made a face that mirrored disgust. "Come on, Eri, cut the outraged look. Doesn't your mighty Belt know I can't listen in on *that?*"

"The Belt knows you, Gil," Eri said solemnly, "but I don't."

"What the hell is that supposed to mean? He shrugged. "Suit yourself. It was the girl though, wasn't it?"

Eri remained silent. Gilder looked into his drink, then emptied it.

"Well, who needs Earthie girls!" Gereen laughed shrilly. Her voice was overly loud against the silence. "From what I understand..." She cupped her hand over Gil's ear and whispered. Gil laughed and pushed her away.

Gereen picked up one of the bottles and searched for a glass, then lifted the bottle itself. She whirled, a high turn that lifted the softness of the chemise, and then fell into Gilder's lap again. She squealed, tossing the bottle to Eri.

Eri caught it with a thin smile. "Right," he said softly. "Who needs her?"

And who needed Hali Vickson? And Shered of Dorbek? And Tregalon? He drank and tossed the bottle to Pfore.

Or us? he added. Who needs any of *us?*

He watched Gereen from a sad corner of his mind, and the poetry of her reached down and found a quiet, dormant segment of his soul untouched by the One—a tiny corner that still belonged to Eridek the man.

He was out of sight, but Handel still crouched against the bulkhead, shaking and white. His limbs jerked uncontrollably.

"Stop that, please!" said Mara. She bit her lip nervously. "Stop it, do you hear?"

Handel's eyes rolled back in his shiny skull. "Hnnnnnnn-n-n-n—Hhnnnnn!"

Mara felt the deep emptiness begin once more in the pit of her stomach. She closed her eyes and swallowed hard.

"All right. Get up. It's over," she said calmly.

Handel raised himself to a crouch and peered cautiously between his fingers at the empty hall. Then he looked fearfully at Mara.

"Come *on,*" she said firmly.

"He—go?"

It was the first time she'd heard him speak. She flinched and held back her revulsion. His voice was like the frantic thrashing of a fish out of water.

"Yes," she said. "He's gone. Who was he, and why did you—"

Handel shrank back. "He is Eridek, Lady! He wears the Belt of Aikeesh!"

Mara felt a cold chill begin at the back of her neck. "Nonsense," she said quickly, "there's—there's no such thing."

Handel shook his head dumbly. "He is no real-man, Lady! No man!"

She opened the door at the light knock. The girl raised a brow at her expression, catching the slight hint of hesitation, the caution in her eyes.

Gereen smiled. "God, I don't blame you. Our dear Gilder the diplomat welcomed you aboard—right?" She laughed lightly and extended a hand. "I'm Gereen, Mara. Okay if I come in?"

Mara nodded dumbly. The sight of Gereen had shaken her for a moment. Even on Earth, where faces and figures changed with the tide to meet the quick demands of fashion, the girl would be exotically beautiful. Red hair fell lazily over ivory shoulders. Deep, green eyes gazed at her above a sculptured nose and full lips. Her mouth and the tips of her eyes were delicately touched with silver.

"Really. You mustn't pay any attention to Gil." Gereen sank gracefully into a chair.

"Oh?"

She leaned back lazily and studied Mara. "He means well, but—Gantrymen aren't particularly famous for their manners. It's the way they are."

"I—noticed." Mara smiled thinly. She felt her face color at the thought of the morning's incident. Gereen looked at her questioningly, and Mara said quickly, "I'm very anxious to meet the rest of the crew. How many are on board?"

Gereen shrugged. "Gil, you've met—and me. And there's Eri—"

That would be the one, she thought...the man in the corridor...the one who scared the boy.

"—And there's Pfore. He's Gilder's Gantry Brother. Not very sociable either, I'm afraid. But Eri, now—Eri's very nice." She laughed. "He'll talk to you without scowling. And then

Handel—" She frowned distastefully. "And that's all. Oh, the captain, of course."

Mara straightened hopefully. "Yes! The captain." She leaned forward earnestly. "Should I call on him—I mean, what's the custom? Let him know I'm aboard? Is that the right thing? Or at dinner, maybe—"

An amused smile had begun to spread across Gereen's lips. It grew into a wide grin, and she threw back her head and laughed throatily.

"No, darling." She shook her head at Mara's puzzlement. "You'll see the captain, in time—but *not* at dinner. At least I hope not!"

She reached out to touch Mara's hand. "Sorry—you couldn't know, of course. Our good captain is—Q'sadiss—an alien. He doesn't eat with the crew."

She rolled her eyes to the ceiling. "Thank the gods for *that*. Sk'tai might possibly fornicate in front of the entire ship—but he certainly wouldn't share a meal with us." She smiled wryly. "And I'm sure the former couldn't possibly be as distasteful as the latter!"

"Oh," Mara said softly, "I see." She didn't, but she pushed aside the images forming in her mind.

Gereen stood up. "Anyway, welcome aboard," she said warmly. "I hope I haven't scared you off or anything. We're not a bad bunch, really." She winked broadly. "—For Outworlders, I mean."

Mara flushed. "Gereen—don't think I come equipped with a full set of Terran intolerances. We aren't all that way, you know."

Gereen looked at her a long moment, then shook her head absently. "No. Of course not. You wouldn't be here if you were. Would you?"

"No," said Mara evenly. "I wouldn't." It was easy to see that the girl didn't believe her, in spite of her easy smile.

"Anyway," said Gereen, "here. For your first dinner on the *Taegaanthe.* Unless things have changed a great deal, I *know* they don't let a girl bring many pretty things to the Rim."

She pulled a small package from a fold in her gown and pressed a silver nail against its seam. The package blossomed like a flower, spilling shimmering petals of blue across her arm.

"It's a Palaie chemise," she explained, and caught Mara's questioning look. "Don't worry. It'll fit. You don't need to flow into a Palaie—*it* flows onto *you!*"

Mara reached out and held the almost weightless garment. "It's—lovely." She smiled warmly. "Thank you, Gereen. For thinking of me. I—"

Gereen shook her head. "See you at dinner. Oh, 1900 hours, by the way, Common's just down the hall to the right." And then she was gone, and Mara decided there was at least one person aboard who thought "Earthies" weren't the intolerable pariahs of the galaxy…!

Eri shook his head adamantly. "Serevan has more sense than that, Gil. Why plunder a few planets now and risk bringing the Rim in against him—when he can get his finger in the whole Outworld pie with a little patience?"

Gilder lowered his glass. His eyes flicked from Gereen deGeis, sitting across from him, to Mara Trent-Hanse at the end of the table. Yellow hair, tilted eyes and golden skin. She caught his glance, then, and turned away. Gil grinned.

"But Serevan *isn't* patient, you see?" He waved a finger at Eri. "As you say, a clever man would wait till his seat at the Council's bought and paid for; then he'd take a bite of this and a bite of that, and who's to know the difference?"

Eri nodded. "And that's what I say. He'll not risk everything now."

Gil spread his hands hopelessly. "Eri, Serevan's a *Rafpigg*—he'll try for the whole dish—and maybe choke on it."

He laughed and pushed his plate aside. "Hell's Gates, it's more likely the Rim'll sit back and let him have what he wants. If their own slice is big enough!"

Eri shook his head. Pfore shifted slightly, and his deep-azure skin caught highlights from the Common's lamps.

"Do you think, Brother, that the Outworlds will have nothing to say of this? It is of a time—"

Gil made a noise. "You think like a Sunperch, Pfore. The Outworlds have nothing to say. As usual. And nothing to say it with," he added bitterly.

"That's no longer quite true," Eri said softly.

Gil turned on him. "You're not talking about the Rim fleet, I hope?" He laughed incredulously and emptied his glass. "You think those day lilies would risk a spanking from Earth—just to help the *Outworlders?*" He shook his head darkly. "Not when it's easier to lean back and look the other way—and fill their fat pockets right along with Serevan."

Mara bit her lip. She could hardly believe her ears. Why—it was Lord Serevan himself they were talking about—as if he were a common *thief* or something!

She'd met the man several times in her uncle's home. A tall, charming man—sun-dark with full patches of silver against his temples. He'd been a planetary governor even then, several years before he was mentioned for a seat on the Council.

Listening to Serevan, actually, had finally convinced her to try for the Outworlds. He'd told of the exotic worlds with black glass mountains and wine-red seas. Worlds of mile-high forests under feathery leaves as big as a whole room in Hanse House.

And he was a Vegan, too, she reminded herself, and that made him practically Terran stock, didn't it?

Mara stopped herself. That was the way they expected her to think, wasn't it? And she was showing them how right they were...

All right, so it might take a while to shake an "Earthie's" scorn for the Outworlds. But—by damn, she'd do it—in spite of Gilder Lanve-Hall or a captain who couldn't eat with his crew!

"Mara," laughed Gereen, "have you left us, dear?"

Mara looked up quickly. "Oh. No, I—" She brought a hand nervously to the top of her chemise. "I'm sorry." She smiled around the table. "Thinking, I guess."

Gilder smiled amusedly. "Serevan hit too close to home, Lady?"

Mara flushed. "He—" She bit off her words and smiled politely. "You're entitled to your opinion of the Lord Serevan. And I imagine you might get a—different point of view in the Outworlds. But I'm sorry. I can't agree with you at all."

"Why?" Gil leaned forward intently, hands folded under his chin. "Because he's a Vegan? Or because I say he's an out-and-out planet stealer? Or both, maybe?"

Mara frowned thoughtfully. "Do you mean am I prejudiced because he's a Vegan? Probably, to be honest. That's not unexpected, is it? After all," she smiled, "you are prejudiced because he *is* one. Aren't you?"

"I detest him because he's a thief," Gil said simply. "He takes things that belong to other people."

Mara shook her head firmly. "I don't believe that. I believe he wants to see the Outworlds develop and grow—and not for himself, either. For the eventual benefit of the people of the Outworlds."

Gilder slapped his hand against the table and threw back his head in a raucous laugh.

"*Eventual benefit,* is it?" He glanced around the table. "Now there is a real Earthie for you, my friends. Be good children. Go find us some lovely worlds—preferably with a lot of fine metals on 'em. And some sweet-smelling spices and maybe a new furry animal, something that we can cuddle and love but that doesn't *bite.* And—be sure it doesn't live too long, 'cause we tire easily of our toys here on Earth!"

"You're rather good at clichés," Mara said coolly, "and over-simplifications. It's easy to leave out the parts you don't like, isn't it?"

Gil leaned forward. She could almost feel the heat of his hatred.

"You really want to hear the parts I don't like? Try this one: If you find a world that's not too nice a place to live—a little too hot or cold, or full of things that don't take to humans, why—that's easy enough. *Just don't be human any more!"*

He shook his head sadly. "Don't you know how it was out here? Truly? Didn't they tell you at home—or have the history books taken care of that? If a world doesn't suit you, they told us—change to suit the world. Grow a tail or a pair of horns or a set of fine gills." He laughed.

"Gilder," said Eri.

Gil ignored him. "Look, Lady, you see?" Her reached up and pulled his shirt away from his throat. Mara felt her heart pound against her chest. Pink, open slits pulsed on either side of his throat from below his chin to the base of his collarbone.

"Gil, Gill, Gilder," he smiled. "You see—Gantry didn't exactly have any *land* to settle on—but it had a lot of fine, high-grade ore on her sea bottoms. Ore that Mother Earth wanted." He looked around the table. Eri, Gereen and Pfore were staring into their glasses.

"As I say—if the world's not right—change to fit the world. And in six or eight generations, we'll let you *keep* a little of that ore for yourselves. But not too much. And none at all, if an Earthie pet like Serevan comes along and gets it first!"

"It's—not like that," Mara said numbly. "It's not like that at all."

Gil stood. He poured a glass of wine and toasted her grimly. "You're a hothouse flower, girl," he said harshly. "Come out in the fields and see how all the *weeds* are growin'!"

Mara got to her feet shakily. "Excuse me...please," she muttered and fled from the room quickly...

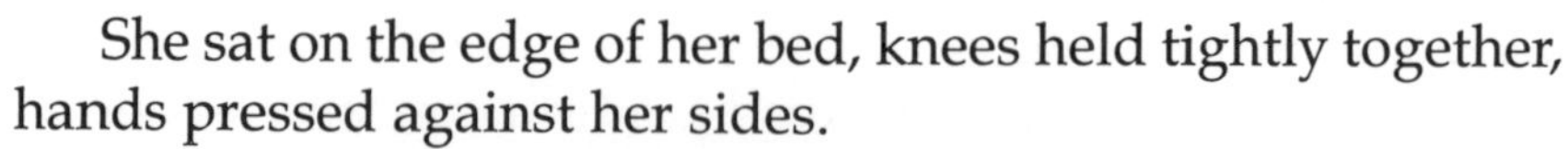

She sat on the edge of her bed, knees held tightly together, hands pressed against her sides.

It's not like that at all, she told herself.

She made herself say it. Again and again.

And if she said it enough, she knew she could make it true.

She straightened suddenly. *Make* it true? Do I have to *make* it true? Don't I believe it? Or do I think Gilder is right?

Certainly, Earth's a wealthy planet. No one ever said it wasn't. And why shouldn't it be? Earth sent out the ships that found the worlds, and it was Earth's children who tamed them.

Then why did these people think of themselves as "Outworlders"—people who didn't belong to Earth at all, who despised and hated their mother world with a paranoid passion?

All right, she told herself grimly. Turn it around. *Try* to see it the way they do.

They don't really know Earth. They're third, fourth, fifth generation—born nowhere near the hills of New Frisco, or Roma or Atlantia Complex. Home is Gantry, Hellfire, Styryxx and Lone. And—are they still children of Earth?

She wondered. When the body changed, what happened to the soul, the psyche, the inner man that was really what a man was. Did it change, too—become something else?

Certainly, there would be changes in a man born on a water world like Gantry—a man who had no dry-land heritage to remember.

She realized, suddenly, that it wasn't really a question of whether or not the Outworlders were children of Earth. They were not. They were children of their own worlds. What was she asking, then?

Not whether or not they're children of Earth...but whether they are still men...

And she knew the hatred, the murderous image of Earth came from something deeper than that. It came from the real or imag-

ined belief that Earth had cast its one-time children aside, turned them into something not quite human to be used and exploited to fatten a few billion distant cousins on a world they'd never see.

And that was the thing she would never let herself believe. If that were true, it meant that men like Serevan carried an unspeakable guilt upon their shoulders. And more than that. It meant that the Families of Earth, who ruled the commerce of the stars, bore an even greater guilt. Families, she reminded herself, such as the House of Trent-Hanse...

Something was wrong with the Palaie chemise.

The pressfold she'd used to mold the gown about her was gone. The almost invisible seam should have fallen away with the slightest touch. It didn't. The more she searched and pulled, the tighter the garment wrapped itself around her.

Mara sighed and bit her lip in frustration. Gereen, maybe, could show her—

No. She'd sleep in the damn thing before she'd ask for help.

She crossed the cabin irritably and poured a glass of the pale white wine on the table. Of all the ridiculous—

Mara stiffened. The glass fell from her fingers and shattered on the floor.

She stood perfectly still. She refused to let herself believe what was happening. There was some other explanation, some—

A chill rose along her back and touched the fine hairs at the base of her neck. Something moved. Lightly, softly up the side of her leg, smoothly over her thigh, warmly past her stomach to her breasts.

Mara gasped. She tore at the gown, trying desperately to rip it from her. At her touch, the dress responded fiercely. It caressed her with a wild, burning intensity. She threw herself against the wall, grabbed sharp scissors from the table, and cut at the thing with all her strength. The dress tightened about her. She cried out and the scissors jerked from her hand.

Then the word touched her mind with a sudden shock of horror. *Stimdress!* It was no Palaie chemise at all, and Gereen had known exactly what it was.

Sickness welled up into her throat and gagged her with a sour, burning taste. She realized what Gereen had in mind. And only because Mara had left the Common when she did...

She screamed, strained for breath. She felt her grip on the wall give way as the thing tore her away and pulled her to her knees, forced her to the floor. Its living hands throbbed across her body, and she had no more strength to cry, to scream, to move.

She silently cursed Gereen in one sane corner of her mind. *Bitch! she yelled. Alien-tainted bitch! Damn you...damn all of you!*

Murky water roiled on the surface of the tank, and Pfore turned over in warm silt and smiled to himself.

A picture wavered, then crystallized in his mind. Handel. Thin limbs pressed against a hard surface. Metal? A roundness. Tunnel. Pipe.

The boy was in the ventilator shaft on the port side. The shaft ran by the engine room and then past stores and over the cabins.

Handel's vision was sliced by thin, vertical bars of blackness. Pfore recognized the blackness as the grids that looked down upon Gereen's room.

Beyond the grid, through Handel's eyes, Pfore saw the delicate blue tracery of veins against ivory flesh, the cold glint of shiny needles, and the serpentine coil of bright red tubing.

And on the wetness of Gereen's lips and the azure shadows of her closed eyes—Peace. Hate. Agony. Love.

Pfore read the thoughts in Handel's mind. They crawled over his consciousness like scuttering, mindless insects—tiny creatures who lived and died in quick seconds of unfulfilled intensity.

Pfore smiled. The image of Handel wavered, changed. Handel lengthened and swelled, and his eyes bulged into milky globes. His sleek, scaled body raced fearfully into the depths. Pfore circled silently above, his body cutting the green waters, his eyes on the frantic creature below.

The Sritafish jerked in and out of high coral castles. It knew that the blue thing above was a Hunter and that unless it found cover its life was measured in seconds.

Gills throbbed, and the pink membranes within shivered in fear. The fear grew, and the long body trembled in a flash of silver scales. No! Movement would only help the blue Hunter find him, would only—

The blue Hunter struck. Its impact drove razor teeth into the Sritafish's spine. The teeth snapped, and in a blinding second of pain it was over.

Handel screamed...

The blue Hunter rolled lazily away. His stomach was full, the taste of blood-prey still tart upon his lips. Then the gray shadow loomed dangerously before him. The Hunter blinked, startled.

Gilder laughed. "He who dreams of the Sritafish had best keep an eye out for the shark, Brother!"

"There are no Sritafish here. Only filthy vermin in the ventilators."

"We will hunt the warm seas again. Soon."

"Will we, Brother?"

"Yes!" Gilder projected an angry, foam-flecked wave. It crashed against jagged red coral in splintering fingers of blue. Pfore caught the blue splinters, froze them into cold points of light, tossed them against blackness.

"You see? We swim in a dark and airless sea, Brother."

"It is necessary, now."

"Is it?"

"The airless sea holds our enemies, Pfore. Would you fight them here, or wait until they foul the waters of Gantry?"

"They already foul those waters. The herds were thin less than a two-period ago. What must they be like now?"

Gilder was silent.

"They want it all, Brother. It is as you say. There will be nothing but scraps left for the Gantrymen. And now there is even an Earthie in our midst. What is she here for? What does she want? Do the Terrans fear we will hide the Survey worlds from them? I do not like her here."

"I do not like her presence either. But she is here, Brother. She brought herself."

Pfore sighed and laughed lightly. "Ah, Gilder, I hear your words. But—does your Egg Brother see what you are blind to see?"

He lifted the image gently from Gil's mind. Golden hair. Wide, dark eyes. The fragile, slender figure...

Gilder scoffed. He brought high winds and salt spray and the fronts of sea trees together and superimposed them over the slim picture of Mara. Mara disappeared under a tall, full-breasted Gantrywoman with slate-blue eyes and dark hair flecked with spray.

"You paint fine pictures," Pfore said drolly. "If you wish, we shall pretend your Egg Brother was born upon the morning tide, and does not know a Pirishell from his breakfast."

Pfore turned over in his tank and Gilder lashed out angrily. His thoughts met only the dark shield of sleep...

The hovercraft hummed high above yellow fields marbled with a dark tracery of stone. Mara leaned out and let the afternoon sun fall full upon her face, then pulled her head back into the cabin.

"What did you call it? Psi? Psi as in Old Greek?" She fluffed her thick hair into place.

Eri shook his head grimly. "No. Scythe. S-C-Y-T-H-E. As in slash, cut, slit, kill."

"Oh." Mara sank back in silence.

Eri looked at her. "We named it that after we left," he explained.

Mara turned to him questioningly. "The—ship's been here before?"

"Six months ago. This is where we lost your predecessor." He moved his head in a vague, downward direction. "Hali Vickson caught it over there—near that darkest ridge."

Mara looked. She could see nothing, but the sight of the low line of black rock gave her an uneasy shudder.

"There's an ecological shift going on here that's got 'em jumping back at Center," he said. "We've got a couple of snoopers planted around, but a snooper won't always catch what a man does. We have to come and take a look for ourselves now and then."

Eri turned the hovercraft in an easy curve, pressing Mara against the narrow hatch. "That yellow stuff that looks like dead wheat is dormant Sabregrass. The grass is what got Hali. He knew all about it. Had it neatly catalogued away. Slides, pictures, seed spores, growth patterns—the works. He had three weeks down there and plenty of research time in the ship. He never went out without body armor. So we got ready to leave, and Hali had to have one more look—something about a possible connection between a wide band of this and a short band of that. And that's when the Sabregrass got him."

Eri frowned darkly. "That's when something always gets you," he added, almost to himself. "When it's all over and you turn around and walk away from it, and it knows you're finished and not really watching any more."

He turned, suddenly, and stared at her with open puzzlement. "What are you doing out here, Mara? What do you want with us?"

There was anger in his voice—a deep, harsh resentment only partially masked by his even tones.

And that, thought Mara, was all that really made the difference between Eri and Gilder. Eri still wore the veneer of a few superficial niceties. Gilder no longer bothered, or never had. He wore his hatred like a banner.

She'd hoped Eri might prove to be different. Whether he wore the Belt, as Handel said, or not—he seemed less divorced from humanity than the others.

She had had little to do with either Gilder or Gereen since the incident at dinner, and the episode with the Stimdress. Both events still lingered like a dull horror in the back of her mind.

And that left Eri. Well, so the door was shut there, too.

"Is it so hard to believe," she answered him, "that I could just *be* here, Eri? Because I want to be?"

Eri shrugged. He kept his eyes on the low horizon. "Mara, you talk as if it's an everyday thing to see an Earthie—a Terran, working in the Outworlds." He smiled dully. "We don't want to be here. Don't you know that? What do you expect us to think about you?"

She turned away. "Maybe," she said evenly, "I just expect to be accepted for what I am. That's asking too much, isn't it?"

"Probably," he said frankly.

She gave a bitter little laugh and shook her head. "Well, anyway, *all* the prejudice doesn't begin on Earth, I see."

"It's a waste of time to talk about such things," he said flatly. "Gilder tried to tell you about the Outworlds. You didn't believe him."

"I think the Outworlder's picture of Earth is probably no more accurate than Earth's view of the Outworld."

"That's hardly an answer."

"It is, though. How can I know the Outworlds unless I see them? And you. And Gilder and Gereen. Have any of you ever really *been* to Earth? Do you know what it's like? Or do you just think what you want to think because it's convenient?"

Eri jerked around. "Have I ever been—" He threw back his head and laughed. "You don't really know, do you?"

Mara frowned. "Know what?"

"Outworlders *can't* go to Earth. We're not allowed there. We're quarantined—fenced off. Keep the freaks out of sight so they won't upset the good citizens!"

"That's not true, Eri—now you sound like Gilder. I've *seen* Outworlders on Earth."

"You've seen what they wanted you to see. A few bought and paid-for flunkies. Showcase Outworlders from Vega or Alpha C. No more Outworlders than you are. But they make a hell of a lot better appearance than some wart-hided dwarf from Rigo."

Eri looked at her. "Settlement policies were different in the beginning. When there were plenty of Earth-type worlds to go around, there was no need to bother with the Vulcans and Zeros. But the planets past the Rim weren't as easy to live on as Paradise and Dale. Heavy gravity, hard radiation, too hot, too cold—or worse.

"But the Outworlds had something most of the First Colony planets didn't. They were rich in the things desperately needed on Earth. Remember what Gilder said? If the planet's not right—change to fit the planet. He's right. Do you think Earth intended to let those worlds *go*—just because they weren't fit to live on?" He shook his head bitterly.

"Eri," Mara protested, "I know about the Adapters. No one forced the colonists to—change. They did it because they *wanted* those worlds!"

Eri laughed. He swung the hovercraft in a smooth arc that took them past sawtooth peaks and out over another broad expanse of bright-tipped Sabregrass.

"That's the textbook answer," he said. He spat out the words harshly. "Didn't they teach you in school where those colonists came from? Did you think they were bright-eyed pioneers, eager to conquer new worlds?"

He shook his head. "The people who submitted to the Adapters were misfits—throwaways. Ring War veterans too battered to work in the new cities. And women caught in first-wave radiation who didn't stand a chance of getting genetic clearance on Earth. But they could have their bodies altered for four-g living on Gelerax! And, hell, they were likely to breed monsters anyway—why not breed *useful* monsters?"

"Aren't you exaggerating, Eri?" she said reasonably. "There are always some—undesirables among colonists. But I won't believe that the Outworlds were settled solely by Ring War vets and GX women!"

"Those undesirables you're talking about are my esteemed ancestors," he said dryly.

"I didn't mean—"

"I know. You didn't mean anything. You're an Earthie. You think like an Earthie thinks. Why shouldn't you? You've never been told anything different."

Eri shrugged bitterly. "No, I'm the one who's naïve, Mara—not you. Eridek of Colmier VI explains the Outworlds to the daughter of the Hanse House!" He laughed and locked himself in silence.

The hovercraft circled over the high, flat mesa, then turned into the wind to settle a hundred yards from the orange dome.

Eri jumped down without looking back. He walked quickly away through a veil of rising heat. Mara watched him a few moments, then grimly opened the hatch and stepped into a wave of stifling air.

"Anything?" Eri asked.

Gil looked up. He was bare to the waist, sweat streaming from his neck and shoulders in small rivulets. He squatted before the dome and glared suspiciously at a green wave dancing palely about in the shaded scope.

"Something," he muttered darkly. "Don't know what the hell to call it, though." He looked up sourly at Eri. "Doesn't make sense. Pfore's down at Two Mile. There's no indication of any pulse like that on his side. That means the thing's localized—whatever it is—something's happening on my scope that's not happening on his. And that, friend, is impossible."

Eri frowned. "No malfunctions, I suppose."

Gilder made a noise. "No. Equipment's okay. What it means is that the organic life of Scythe is undergoing a dramatic change. Basically, it's centered about the Sabregrass, but everything's played a part, you can bet on that. Now. Suppose you tell me why it's happening all over the planet, except in a 300-square-mile area over there?"

He spat disgustedly on the sandy ground. "I even changed meters with Pfore, just to make—"

Gilder stopped. He squinted past his scope, out over the broad mesa. He cursed silently, and his eyes moved up to Eri.

"What's she doing here?"

Eri shrugged. "She wasn't doing anything on the ship. I thought maybe she could make herself useful. As long as she's here," he added.

And just what the hell did you figure she'd *do,* Eri? To make herself 'useful?'"

Eri held Gilder's gaze. The Gantryman's shoulders hung loose, relaxed, but his eyes smoldered with barely controllable anger.

"Take her back. Now."

"Any particular reason—or just a Gantryman's privilege?"

Gilder darkened. The narrow, pink slits in his throat fluttered nervously.

Eri let himself smile. "As you say, Gil." Gilder didn't like the smile, he knew. Eri turned and stalked away toward the hovercraft.

"Eri—"

Eri stopped and looked back.

"She doesn't belong here. She's got no business running around on Scythe."

Eri spread his hands. "Gil, she's got no business on the ship—but she's there. You didn't send for her and neither did I. Survey qualified her. Do we use her or don't we?"

Gilder's lips suddenly split into a wide grin.

"Goddamn, Eri—use her for what? What do you do with an Earthie girl on a Survey ship?" His blue eyes sparkled with amusement. "Any suggestions?"

"That's your department," Eri said blankly. "Not mine." He brushed moisture from his brow and turned away.

Before he turned, his eyes caught Gilder, and Gilder was looking past him, at the girl. The amusement was gone. There was something else there. Eri couldn't say what it was.

Mara swallowed hard. She wondered whether anything as alien as Captain Sk'tai could possibly read a human expression. If he can, she thought, I'm in trouble already.

The bridge of the *Taegaanthe* was a hemisphere amidships, a smooth concavity bristling with multicolored lights and studded with pearl-gray buttons.

The greater part of the circle was filled with Captain Sk'tai himself. To Mara, standing behind the guard rail directly above, he seemed like a gigantic leather butterfly constantly emerging and retreating in its cocoon. A bewildering assortment of appendages brushed out to touch against the pearly buttons and flashing lights.

"Mara Trent-Hanse, is it?"

Mara started, as the human-sounding voice boomed all about her.

"Yes—sir," she said.

The captain chuckled. "Beauty. Such a beauty. A flower of Old Earth in our midst. Wonders never cease, as they say."

Mara flushed.

"Been to Earth—or close to it, anyway. New Phoenix? Reykjavik Station? That surprise you?"

"Yes, sir. A little."

"It's not stranger than *you* being *here,* though. I guess you've heard that already."

"Several have—mentioned it, yes," Mara said tightly.

"And—?"

"I didn't expect a welcome-aboard party. I knew the Outworlder attitude toward Earth."

"But you came anyway."

"I did."

"Why?"

"Because I don't like to hear how something's supposed to be. I don't care to read about places or look at pretty pictures. And I've never cared a great deal about other people's opinions. In other words, I wanted to see the Outworlds myself."

"—And Outworlders," the captain added, with only a thinly veiled amusement.

"Yes," said Mara. "And Outworlders."

The captain sighed. The noise was like the wind from a great bellows.

"Well, you passed the tests at some Survey School or other—or you wouldn't be here. Either that or you have considerable pull. Which is not unlikely with a name like Trent-Hanse."

Mara took a deep breath. "I was in High Range at Remoga. I can perform my duties." If you and the others will let me, she said to herself.

"Remoga, eh? And they trained you in—"

"I'm a Speaker, Captain. First Class," she added tightly.

Captain Sk'tai seemed to hesitate. "A—Speaker?" Some part of the great bulk below seemed to shake its head incredulously.

Mara filled her lungs and launched into a partial double debate in High Treecoosh, stopped suddenly and gave him a sample of the impossibly complex Yaraday chittering, a smattering of Erebist, and finally, the ritual blessing of his own tongue—as unlikely a combination of sounds as she could imagine.

"Glory!" Sk'tai gasped. "I wouldn't have believed it!" He laughed soundly. "You speak with a northern tinge, know that? My own island, too—or near enough."

"I can give you the eastern ridge of dialect if you prefer," she said calmly.

"Enough—I'm convinced."

"I was two years in surgical implant—three under hyp. I hope," she said dryly, "I can mumble a few languages."

"I sense more than a little bitterness—and in your own language, too," he said questioningly.

Mara laughed nervously. "Really, Captain? I can't imagine—"

"Look," he said, and his voice took on a firmer note. "You'd do well to face some realities. And you'd do well to face them now, I think."

Mara's hands tightened on the railing. She swallowed hard and with a great effort of will, made herself speak without any hint of a tremor in her voice.

"I—have faced little else *but* realities, Captain. From the moment I stepped on board, realities have been served to me three times a day—"

She clenched her fists and felt the control drop away from her voice. "I am sick to death of—Outworld realities!"

The captain was silent a long moment. The leathery cocoon below fluttered, then stilled.

"You came to us, remember? No one asked for you."

"No. They didn't. But what is it I've done that—"

"—That makes them despise you?" he finished. "Simple. You've brought out the love-hate in Gilder. The sado-envy in Gereen deGeis. The oh-so-thinly buried Dream psychosis in Eri."

Sk'tai sighed. "Not because of what you do—simply because you're here. You remind them too much of things they would rather not remember.

"You're a backward child, Mara Trent-Hanse. From a backward world. Oh, the Terrans are clever and ruthless, when they want to be, and *that's* often enough. But in the Outworlds an Earthie's a crawling infant—no more than that. And you're a most dangerous infant to have around, I think, because you carry seeds of destruction within you—and they all see that! And miserable creatures though they be, none want that destruction!"

"I don't want to destroy anyone!" Mara said hopelessly. "I want to *learn!*"

But she knew that learning had nothing at all to do with what he was saying.

"I can," she repeated lamely. "I can—if you'll let me."

"You can die," he said simply, "and perhaps destroy. I see nothing more that you can do aboard the *Taegaanthe*."

Mara's heart stopped. *"Die!"* She shook her head in open-mouthed refusal. "I came here *to learn to live,* Captain!"

"Living isn't enough in the Outworlds. Don't you see? Can't you realize that is what they sense in you? *Survive* is the only word they've ever known out here. To *live* is what an Earthie does!

"You think Gilder a barbarian. A man with no more than lust and murder on his mind. He's much of that, granted. But more, too. Gilder and his Egg Mate were born on a world where trust meant death and murder meant another day of life.

"And Eri. Five hundred years ago his ancestors landed on Jaare, a world no more made for man than—than my own. The seeds of the Dreamers were already on Jaare when Eri's people got there. To stay, they accepted the Dreamer spore, and became more than men—and less.

"Gereen deGeis had the blood drained from her veins the day she was born on Tyson's world. To face what they found there, Tyson's people had to match the planet's eccentricities with their own. And so Gereen's drug cycle hands her a new metabolism twice a day—but she lives."

The captain sighed. "I know nothing of Handel, or how he comes to be what he is. We found him on Gellahell, more dead than alive. We saved him, and of course he hates us all for that. There's no way to say where he comes from, but you can bet it's a world where pain's the same as survival.

"Now tell me, Mara Trent-Hanse," he said gently, "tell me how it is they'll learn to—*accept you for what you are?"* He laughed hollowly. "That's the sad joke, you see? What you are is the one thing they can never accept!"

"I see no joke," she cried, "no joke at all—"

"There's more to it than you know, though," he told her. "The Q'saddis have some rare traits, Mara—I'm more than what you see slithering around below—I'm anything I want to be. Whatever I see, whatever crawls or flies or bounces about. Can you see the joke in that? I can taste your beauty, Mara, and desire you, too. You look at me with loathing, and you can do no more, being what you are. But *I'm* not the exotic creature aboard the *Taegaanthe*—it's your human-appearing companions *who are the real aliens here*...Do you see? Do you see what you've brought yourself into?"

Mara turned with a low, stifled cry and ran blindly down the corridor. She shut her door behind her, backed stiffly against it, and stared straight ahead at nothing.

"No," Gilder said flatly. He cursed under his breath and gripped the railing tightly.

Captain Sk'tai ignored him. "She will go with you," he said. "She's being paid to work; so she'll work. If the sensors are correct about C-71 there'll be a use for her."

Gilder was silent.

"You dislike her so much," Sk'tai said finally, "that you'd rather do without a talent you may need."

Gilder's mouth twisted into a frown. "I don't like or dislike the girl," he said irritably. "I have a job to do. My Brother and I can't do that job—and keep our Earthie from falling in a goddamn hole or something at the same time."

The captain chuckled.

"You know how Pfore and I work," Gil protested. "You tell me how she fits!"

"She goes with you, Gilder," the captain said patiently.

"If you think Pfore and I can't handle this—"

"I think nothing." The captain's patient tone had taken on a sharper edge. "I think Center sent us a Speaker, and who knows the ways of Center, or questions their reasons? It may be they had C-71 in mind."

"There's no one to talk to on C-71," Gil muttered.

"No, but there *were* beings there, were there not?" The captain sighed. "Gilder," he said wearily, "let us not pursue this. I give not one of your damns for your feelings about the girl. She is here. She is a Speaker. There is a most peculiar world awaiting you down there. It may be that she can shed some light upon its peculiarities."

"It may be that she can get us all killed," Gil muttered darkly.

Gil stood on the gentle hill and eyed his surroundings with narrow suspicion. The rise beneath him was a perfect quarter-sphere covered with neatly clipped grass. At the base of the hill, shorter grass abruptly gave way to another variety that was one unit higher and one shade darker.

Exactly one unit.

Exactly one shade.

He squinted out across the narrow horizon. The darker grass continued for a thousand units, then gave way again to the lighter variety. The light grass climbed a hill that was a duplicate of the one beneath his boots…

It was as if a planet of overzealous gardeners had finished their work just that morning, cleaned their tools, and vanished into the ground.

Into the ground—or somewhere, Gil frowned scornfully. And when? Yesterday? A thousand years ago? Six months?

Only the former inhabitants of C-71 could answer that, and they had neglected to give word.

Gil reached down and ripped up a large handful of grass. It was a peculiarly pleasant sensation, and he allowed himself a half smile. Seconds ago there had been order and perfection. Now, one blemish scarred a small circle on the top of one hill in one quadrant of a perfect world.

He watched. Somewhere below, he knew, frantic signals pulsed out from the torn root system. A nutrient booster was even now flowing up to bathe and heal the damaged area.

Gil shook his head grimly as the blades began to quiver. Within thirty seconds, the new crop was entrenched. It stopped growing at the precise unit height of its mates.

He turned away and walked the few steps back to the dome. A tall whip aerial flashed from the silver console by the entry. To one side, Mara puttered with a collapsible table and chairs. He smelled the aroma of food from the small cook unit, grunted to himself, and passed her without looking up.

"Well," she said behind him, "what do you think of Toy?"

Gil stopped, one arm still crooked like a wing in his jacket. He squinted back over his shoulder, then faced her.

"What do I think of—*what?*"

Her half-expectant smile faded quickly. She looked away nervously and inspected the cook unit.

"I—thought it was rather appropriate," she snapped. "That's all. If you don't like it, for God's sake call it C-71!"

Gilder bristled. "Girl, look at me!"

Mara's eyes rose patiently.

"I don't care *what* you call this world," he said darkly. "It's what you're thinking that bothers me." He glared at her disdainfully. "Don't you understand? That kind of thing doesn't belong out here. It leads to carelessness, is what it does, and I'll not put up with carelessness where *my* hide's involved!"

He spat contemptuously at the close-cropped grass. "You're right. The name's appropriate—too damned appropriate as far as I'm concerned. An' when you start associating those cute little trees and phony hills with some Earthie fairy tale, you might as well shoot yourself full of sarazine and sit down and wait for it, 'cause you're as good as dead already!"

Suddenly, his eyes widened, and he jerked away. "Mara, behind you!"

She twisted aside and threw herself into a half crouch, clawing for the sidearm at her belt.

There was nothing at all behind her. She turned and flashed him an angry stare.

"Like I say," he said somberly, facing her, "start thinking of this place as 'Toy,' and the next thing you know, you've forgotten all about Survey rules and set your pistol for a goddamn cook unit!"

Mara flushed. Gil reached down and picked up the gold-barreled weapon, made a show of opening it and meticulously checking the charge. Then he jammed the pistol back into its holster and tossed it to her roughly.

"Put it on," he said flatly. "*Don't* take it off."

Mara gritted her teeth and said nothing. She buckled on the pistol and rolled the cook unit back into the dome and walked to the edge of the hill.

If there was a hidden menace on Toy, she decided grimly, it was probably the menace of monotony. An entire planet of precise lawns and duplicate hills. And cities, too. They'd flown over half a dozen that morning. Tiny squares of whiteness from the air—each exactly like the other. Each mathematically equidistant from the rest.

Mara shook her head. Could you ever really understand such a world? Divorce yourself from humanity and see Toy through alien eyes?

She remembered a lean, star-burned man, a teacher at Survey who looked twenty years older than he was. He had lost his arms at Stinger and had definite ideas on staying alive in the Outworlds.

"...There's one thing we can't teach you here—you'll learn it in the field or you won't. Forget where you came from. Forget who you are. Think and reason in alien terms, not your own. Assimilate every aspect of your surroundings and never turn your back on a strange world. It's not easy—but it's the only way a Survey man keeps alive..."

That was the answer, then. You learned. Or you died. And Mara wrapped her arms about her shoulders as a sudden chill struck her atop the low hill.

She *couldn't* think that way. She was Mara Trent-Hanse from Earth, and she could never become an Outworlder. And that meant Gil, Sk'tai and all the others were right.

I'm lonely again, she thought. I'm as lonely here as I was on Earth. I didn't belong there, and I'm not a part of the Outworlds, either.

Where am I supposed to be?

Toy's sun dropped behind perfect hills, and Mara spotted the small figure on the broad green plain below. She turned away and walked wearily back to the dome. Gilder sat over the dark, enameled box whose slow-moving needle recorded some mysterious segment of Toy's inner workings.

"Pfore's coming back," she said absently.

Gil frowned. He didn't look up. "Yes, I know."

"Oh," she said, "well, of course you do." She knew immediately that he'd taken her words in a different way than she'd meant them.

"You don't like him, do you?" He glanced away from the snail-pace tape and grinned at her with amusement.

Mara tightened. "Don't, Gilder," she said calmly. "Please. Don't start something. I meant that you would know Pfore's coming before I did for the simple reason that you can—talk to him. You can. I can't. I forgot. It's no more than that—not unless *you* want to make something out of something that's not there. If you do, go ahead. Just don't include me!" she added hotly.

She turned and walked stiffly to her own segment of the dome.

"Greetings, seducer of mighty whales. What kept you?"

"What do you mean, what kept me?"

"I couldn't raise you," Pfore said idly. "I supposed you were deeply involved in some important project." He presented a lurid image of what he imagined that project to be.

Gil made a mental noise. "It's for certain you haven't been watching too closely, Mudfish, or you'd not come up with rubbish like that."

"No need to watch, Brother," Pfore said wryly. "I can read the purple tones of frustration a mile away."

Gilder's thoughts turned to ice. Pfore felt them, and backed away.

"There are times when you imagine too much, Brother."

"Perhaps," said Pfore. "After all, what does an Egg Mate know?" Then, he broke contact quickly, before Gilder could retaliate.

Gereen made a wide sweep above the three small figures. Their presence on the green plain appeared as bright pulses of life on her screens. Behind them was the ever-present static of C-71's star, and the broader, darker wave that said there was a substantial amount of electronic and mechanical activity going on under the planet's surface.

The energy was fairly low and constant beneath the grassy lawns and low hills—higher under the cities. She expected that. The support systems under a living center *should* be more complex than the ones bringing food and water to planets.

The screens told Gereen a great deal about C-71's cities. The motionless blue lines said power—the lighter, nervous spiderwebs of aqua showed how that power was being used.

She was fascinated by the intricate patterns of energy. The automated facilities must be filling the cities' needs at a near capacity rate. Each area, she guessed, was turning out enough goods and services to support several million inhabitants—inhabitants who no longer required the systems' capabilities.

What happened to those things the planet produced? Cycled back to raw materials, probably, she thought. Made, destroyed, and made again.

Life support for millions—and only three pulses of life on her screen—Gilder, Pfore and the Earthie. And in the distance, the white, too-perfect city...

Eri watched duplicates of Gereen's screens in the dark Commpad of the *Taegaanthe*, circling C-71 a thousand miles away. He saw, and understood, the broad socio/geo structure painted by glowing lines and waves, but noted them only vaguely in one corner of his mind.

Something bigger worried at the edge of Eri's consciousness. So far, it was only an itch, an uncomfortable feeling. But it was moving about in the darkness, trying to shape itself into something real.

Eri knew what it was. The One who shared his soul saw something in Eri's universe that interested, stimulated, or disturbed its being...

Captain Sk'tai held the image of the Survey Team on C-71 in some facet of his mind. Other facets noted the hull temperature of the *Taegaanthe,* the ship's speed, altitude, orbital path, and the fact that one and a quarter liters of coolant per tenday were leaking from the aft gally refrigeration system.

Three aspects of his being played an incomprehensible mathematical game with each other. He noted that one of those aspects was attempting to cheat the other.

Handel slept, and dreamed of white mice with razor-chrome teeth...

From the top of the last hill she looked down upon the city. Perfect, windowless white buildings set in a grillwork of even streets. A gameboard, she thought. A game with all the pieces set up shining and new, and all the players gone.

The outer perimeter began with neat, uniform structures four stories high. From there they progressed in symmetrical ascensions to a central, fifty-story tower. She decided it looked all the more like an alien chessboard—a giant, insane chessboard with all the pawns, knights and queens on the same side...

"We should be back in two hours," Gil told her. "We won't go too far in on this first trek. It's just a look-see."

Mara shook her head. "Who's *we,* Gilder?"

He frowned, pretending not to understand. "Why, Pfore and I." He grinned foolishly. "Well, damn me—did you think you were goin' in with us?"

Mara set her jaw tightly. "And why not?"

Gilder shrugged and exchanged a quick look with Pfore. "Someone's got to mind the store," he muttered.

"You've got Gereen for that," she reminded him. "In the hovercraft."

"Gereen," he corrected, "and you." He turned to his Gantry Brother, and they lifted light packs and started off down the hill.

"You're afraid something will happen to me," she said.

Gilder stopped. He turned, and an incredulous frown spread across his features. "Where in hell did you get an idea like that? What I'm afraid of is you'll get *me* killed—with some damn foolishness."

He chuckled disdainfully. "Course, there's not much to worry about, is there? Here on 'Toy,' I mean."

Mara ignored him. She lifted her own pack and adjusted it to her shoulders. His brows rose in the beginning of refusal.

"I'm going, Gilder," she said quietly.

Mara felt strangely apart from herself—as if her mouth opened, while someone else she didn't quite know formed the words.

Gil studied her with no expression at all, then moved down the hill.

Mara glanced at Pfore out of the corner of her eye. His blue skin glistened like soft rubber in the sunlight. The flat, even features of his face reminded her of the bare beginnings of a sculptor's head—clay smooth and wetted for tomorrow's work.

He's never spoken to me, she realized suddenly. He's never once spoken or even looked in my direction since I've been aboard the *Taegaanthe*. I'm not even here.

She turned away and let her eyes touch the walls of the city. The pale slabs rose all around her—untouched, unblemished. Ahead, the black surface of the street disappeared under points of diminishing whiteness. There wasn't a mote of dust under her feet. Not a twig or a scrap of paper or a blade of grass.

Only what we've brought with us, she thought, and looked back at the three dull sets of footprints behind her.

She could hear her own breath magnified against the silence. The soft rustle of her clothing was a harsh, noisy intrusion.

Pfore shifted and Mara followed his glance. Gilder ducked and walked out of one of the low doors. He blinked in the sunlight.

"Nothing new," he said somberly. "It's exactly like the others. God!" He shook his head in wonder. "Apartments. Maybe a couple of million of 'em—an' every one the same, down to the last nit-picking detail."

He glanced meaningfully at Pfore. "I took some check measurements. There's something that looks like a bed in each place, and next to it there's a stool. There's not so much as a millimeter's difference between the way the stool sits from the bed in any room in this whole kookin' city."

"Irrational," said Pfore.

"Not really," said Mara. "Not from their point of view, anyway."

They both glanced at her blankly, as if they'd forgotten she was there.

"What," Gil asked impatiently. "What's that, now?"

"I said the creatures who built this, and all of C-71 for that matter—probably thought this was the most *rational* world possible. It's—well, order, carried to the highest possible degree, isn't it?"

Gil laughed lightly. His mouth twisted into a slight grin. "I think we can all look around us and see the evidence of order, Mara."

She flushed at his tone. "Then it's not an irrational world!"

"It is to me," he shrugged.

"To you, Gil?" She raised a brow. "Really? I would have imagined that an experienced Survey man is capable of *projecting himself into the problem.*"

His ice-cold eyes fell on her a full second before his laughter echoed through the empty streets.

"I've seen it all, now, by the Stars—an Earthie quotin' Survey rules!" He walked off, slapping Pfore on the back, and Mara followed silently.

They turned a corner and came upon it suddenly; none of them expecting anything except the monotonous regularity of the streets and buildings.

Gilder gave a low whistle. He stopped, muttering something under his breath Mara couldn't hear.

The statue stood under a high arch atop a square column. Beyond, there was a tantalizing glimpse of a broad plaza and long walls covered with signs and symbols. But for the moment, none of them could take their eyes off the statue.

"Swine," Gil said almost to himself. "By God, swine standin' up on two legs."

"No." Mara shook her head. "*Mock* swine. What swine shouldn't be."

Gil looked at her. "What?"

"She is right," Pfore said, and Gil frowned and shaded his eyes at the statue again.

"Yeah," he bit his lip thoughtfully, "yeah, I guess so." He gave her a peculiar, appraising glance, as if he'd found himself suddenly agreeing with her and wasn't sure how to handle the new feeling.

Mara couldn't take her eyes from the squat, ugly figure. In hard stone, she saw only soft, yielding flesh and dark-pit eyes. Her mind reeled dizzily. Pig eyes. Little pig eyes just a step away from—*people* eyes.

Her heart pounded and the breath caught in her throat. Why? Why are they swine and not swine at all...?

It's not right—not right at all...and I don't want to *be* here—not on Toy or Scythe or anyplace else I don't belong and don't understand.

"Mara?"

She blinked, looked down with puzzlement at Gil's hand under her arm.

"What, Gil? What?"

"You all right, now?"

She looked up into the tourmaline eyes. Cold, a moment ago, and now—what? Concern? Was there concern there for a brief second?

She laughed to herself. Whatever it was, it was gone as quickly as it had come—if anything had been there at all.

The long, high walls rose nearly a hundred feet above the square. Light clouds moved against a pale sky and gave the illusion that the walls were leaning slowly in upon them.

"It's a script of some kind," Mara said. "But—the alternating rows are pictographs." She nodded excitedly. "Gilder, I'm almost certain. The pictographs tell the story of the words above them."

He looked at her doubtfully. "Can you read it?"

She frowned at the high wall and tapped one fingernail against her chin. "I don't know. It's not exactly my line, but—

a Speaker picks up a certain feel for this kind of thing. Let's see…"

She moved off slowly down the wall. Gil and Pfore followed.

"There was at one…period, *enclosed*…yes! A segment of time, then. Has to be that. At one time there was…see the little figures all—different?" She pointed. "And then that's negated very strongly on the right, to show the same figures—only in order, this time."

"At one time," she read slowly, "there was disorder, then came—whatever it is; I think it's the symbol for their race. Then came blank and there was order and—rightness…"

A cold shiver swept over her at the thought. She turned to Gilder.

"They're saying everything was 'out of order' at one time, and they came and made everything right. That—things can't be as they should be until there's no conflict. Until—*sameness* makes the ugliness of difference go away."

"A hive culture," Gil said grimly.

Pfore nodded. "But not a natural hive," he pointed out. "They picked up hive aspects along the way. They didn't start out like this."

"I wonder," Mara said almost to herself, "how it—*did* begin?"

The question plagued her.

Why? she asked herself. Is it because I know and they don't—that Toy reminds me too much of Earth?

Earth never came close to Toy, she knew. But the pattern was there. In the sameness of people, the sameness of cities. In the way an overcrowded culture moved toward the—what? The dangerous security of identity?

No conflict…make the ugliness of difference go away…

To be alike was to be without fear. And we almost made it—when the billions begat billions and there was no more room for persons. Only for people. Numbers. Inhabitants of the hive.

But it didn't happen on Earth. It didn't happen on Earth, she realized suddenly, *because the Outworlds bought our freedom...*

Mara stopped—almost staggered with the weight of realization. It was true, wasn't it? There was no way to make it go away. The explosion to the stars gave Earth a wealth they'd never imagined. And more than that. Much more. The precious room to breathe...

And wasn't this, really, what the Outworlds hated?

Not because we sent them to the stars and changed them—made them more, and sometimes less, than human...

...But because we threw them away. Because we made them change so we could stay the same.

It happened quickly.

At the other end of the square, Gilder and Pfore were setting up the photo-recorders against the waning light. The squat machines glittered and whirred as they scanned the enigmatic walls of Toy.

Mara walked distractedly along the edge of the broad plaza. Her mind was light-years away, her eyes on the even blocks beneath her boots.

She looked up suddenly, blinking in surprise, to find she'd turned the far corner of the wall without even thinking where she was going. And then she saw the rows of bare white booths.

They were faced in thin sheets of milky glass, and she thought, idly, that it was odd they'd seen no glass besides this anywhere in the city, and maybe it wasn't glass at all, but a kind of plastic...

...And even as she walked the few steps to touch the cold surface, the thought brushed against her mind that she might be an Earthie, but she was also a qualified member of the *Taegaanthe*'s Survey Team, in spite of what anyone said, and the alternate moment to this one flashed before her, where she backed away and called Gilder and didn't touch the glass at all...

Gereen's eyes widened and she tensed and leaned forward, her hands automatically seeking knobs for adjustment as a new kind of wave pulsed wildly across her screens...

Eri screamed as bright hooks of pain tore at his soul.

His fists smashed through the Commpad's monitor and came away bloody. His body jerked uncontrollably, flailing itself against steel walls in painful, erratic arcs. Finally, when the One who shared his being gained control of muscles and tendons that had already pulled themselves through awful convolutions, Eri sank to the floor and curled up silently, arms folded across his chest, knees tight against his chin...

Captain Sk'tai blinked an aspect of consciousness into being, and with the flexibility of his kind, experienced awareness, from a new and unfamiliar viewpoint...

In Handel's dream, the beautiful white rats with razor-chrome teeth came delightfully closer...

Gilder was running before the high, short scream echoed and died across the plaza. He turned the wall, body low and angled to the smallest silhouette, pistol tight against the butt of his palm and thrust out before him.

He saw the brief flicker of movement as the milky panel whispered shut upon itself, and he knew. In a cold, frozen instant he knew all there was to know about the silent booths, and he put all his hate and anger and horror into his heavy boot and smashed the panel into a million white shards.

And of course she was gone, just as he knew she would be.

"*Cover!*" He shot the mental command to Pfore, and Pfore moved. Gil bent low and melted the base of the booth until slag and steel hissed in poison clouds and forced him away.

"Too late, Brother—!"

"Shut up!"

"I can see, Gil."

"Probe, Pfore!"

"Too late—"

"No!"

"Gilder—"

"Deeper, Brother—deeper, damn you!"

Pfore sobbed—sent out deep mental fingers and reeled back in agony. Gil caught him roughly, gripped his arm tightly.

"Pfore," he said aloud. "Pfore, once more. *I* can't go there—if I could—"

"They want me, Gil," Pfore said numbly, "and you—and all of us. They want us all."

"There's nothing *down* there!" Gil said savagely. "Machines, Brother, nothing more!"

"Gilder—"

Gil's teeth locked and he tasted blood. "Get—her—*out,* Pfore!" He held Pfore in a steel grip. "Get—her—"

He saw it as it came around the far corner of the wall. His mind cried out and he cursed himself and wondered why he couldn't have known—with the grass, the hills and the city—why hadn't he seen this, too, because it was the logical thing to see and the final goddamn insanity of sameness....

There was the ugliness of difference, and then there was order...

And Gilder knew they'd finally achieved it on Toy. The booths were the last answer, and there were no more answers after that, and no more questions or conflicts or disorder... Only mirror-image citizens on a mirror-image world, and a statue to mock their madness.

It came around the wall and waddled toward him uncertainly on drunken pig legs. He saw the fish-belly flesh and the dark-pit eyes, and when the mouth tried to gasp itself into his name, he shut out the picture of a girl with dark hair on a green hill, and he squeezed the trigger and held it until there was nothing more of her to see.

And then he dropped the pistol and leaned against the high wall and retched...

They had been sitting in the Common, and he hadn't spoken for a long time, and Gereen said, "You're thinking about the Earthie girl, Gilder."

And Gilder said, "I'm not thinking about anything at all."

"It was a long time ago, Gil."

She said nothing for a long moment, then, "She didn't belong, you know that, don't you? It's not the same as Eri on Tristadel or Ramy Hines on Butcher. They knew what to expect and it could have been you or me, don't you see? It's not the same, Gil. She didn't *belong*."

For the first time in his life, Gilder felt the faint whisperings of fear, and he wondered if this was the way it had begun for Hali Vickson and Mara Trent-Hanse and Eri and Ramy and all the rest.

First the fear, then the sudden, chilling loneliness.

And finally, the knowledge that no one ever truly belonged—that you only really belonged to the last world that claimed you...

STARPATH

I

The light flicked from OPERATIONAL green to amber READY. I leaned back in the cushioned depths, took a deep breath and let it out slowly. My body automatically began the discipline that let every nerve, muscle and fiber approach controlled unconsciousness.

Without moving, I glanced at Cadet DeLuso. The boy was quiet, but a fine mist covered his cheek. Natural enough, under the circumstances. First op-jump *ought* to bring out the sweat in a man, if he has any sense at all.

The blinking amber said 12, 11—10 seconds. I closed my eyes and silently wished Cadet Matt DeLuso luck. That's the least you can do for these kids—wish them a little luck...

No, I caught myself—that's not all, Waldermann. There's one thing more. You can stop thinking of your Cadets as kids. They're not kids at all, they're men. And damn fine ones, too. If they weren't, they wouldn't make it this far—they wouldn't be Starpath candidates.

So, seconds before jumpoff, I gave DeLuso manhood – the least I could do, and maybe the most. DeLuso – himself would have to take it from there.

Then READY amber turned to red TRANSMIT, and the soft gong began pealing the seconds from one to ten – in the very special note that triggers a deeply keyed response in every Starpather's brain. My eyes closed, and I began to trance out. A deep hum rolled through my body, rising from thunder to a siren shriek. Through some far, dimly wakeful sense, I heard a faint cry from DeLuso. Then I exploded…

There's always that tiny jolt, like a hundred billion little cubes of ivory clamping together at once. Ask any Starpather about that jolt. He'll tell you it's the sweetest sound in the world.

You see, it isn't a stack of cubes at all, friend – it's *you*. And if you can feel that jolt it means your body is back in one piece again, and you've made it through Starpath.

The first thing I did was look at DeLuso – fast. He was there, his eyes flickering open, breath steady. I pushed myself up, and the cushions petaled wide to let me through. DeLuso turned then and looked at me.

"Congratulations," I said dryly. "For some reason, Cadet, it appears you've made it through Starpath."

DeLuso was a light shade of classroom chalk, but he managed a grin. "Thank you, sir. It's – a lot different than I expected."

I shot his sick grin right back at him. "Oh? Really, Cadet? *Well, it's also a lot different than* I *expected, Mister!*"

DeLuso stared. I jerked coveralls and slipons from the locker and glared at him. "You made a *noise,* Cadet. Did you know that? No, you didn't hear it, but I did. *You made a noise during transmit!* Your relaxation cycle was imperfect. Something tensed, probably a muscle in the lower throat, and a little breath of air you weren't supposed to have in the first place moved over that muscle causing vibration, motion, sound. Or, as we call it in Starpath, Cadet—good old Instant Death. Evidently you stopped in time. You are here—and that pretty well proves it, doesn't it? Now, next question: How many times do you think you can get away with a damn fool stunt like that?"

I glanced at the tiny station chronometer set in the curved wall of the shell. "You have twenty-one minutes, forty-two seconds, standard time, to work out that little problem. I suggest you have it solved on schedule, or you won't have to worry about getting chewed out at the next station. Any questions?"

Apprehension had started across his face, but it faded quickly. "No sir," he said smartly. "No questions, sir." Good man.

I tossed him coveralls and slipons. "Get dressed, Cadet. Let's see what's going on outside."

We left the dome and stepped out on the plastic circle under the dim moon of Arcturus Seven, better known to the colonists there as Gellhell. We were 33 light-years from Earth as the crow flies—microseconds by Starpath. The Frostrees beyond the settlement clearing were halfway through their screaming lunch, tearing each other apart and flinging bloody foliage to the pink sky. The ragged, scab-covered colonists stood just beyond the dome's field, pelting us with filth. Several of them dropped dead and began to decompose as we watched.

Cadet Matt DeLuso didn't say a thing. I was beginning to think he might actually make Starpath.

"Okay," I told him, "you've caught the scenery. Go get the cargo—we only have 18 more minutes here."

DeLuso retreated to the dome and lugged out the 3x5 flat aluminoid carton. I opened it near the edge of the field, checked it quickly, released the inner seal and closed it up again. They saw what we had, and for a brief minute they even forgot about throwing stuff at us. A low moan swept over the crowd.

I looked them over. One guy was a little taller than the rest. He was skin and bones like everyone else, but a trifle less scabby.

"You," I pointed, "would you come to the edge of the field, please?" He dragged himself over on shaky legs and stopped a yard away. He stared at me through rheumy eyes, then spat at my face. The spittle hit the field and rolled away.

"You're a little *late,* Starpather," he croaked. His mouth curled up in hate, and I thought for a second he might spit again.

"I'm sorry. We do what we can. How many have you lost?"

He laughed, and that just about ended the conversation right there. "You want this morning's count, or up to the last three minutes? We started with 900 people here, mister. We got about 200 left."

"I'm sorry about that, too," I told him. I picked up the case and tossed it through the field. It landed on the soft turf on the other side.

You always *throw* cargo through the field. You never roll it, or push it or shove it. The field's about an inch thick, and if you happen to shove something a little too easy, or a pebble gets in the way—or anything—your cargo just stays there till Hell freezes over. Things that get caught in that inch don't move. Once you lose momentum you can't push it through, and certainly no one on the other side can pull it. Not unless you turn off the field. And brother, that is just what you *don't* do—ever.

The colonists were already into the carton and passing out the little blue pills, but the tall man in front of me hadn't moved.

"Think that stuff'll work?" he asked doubtfully.

I nodded. "It should. They worked on the sample culture you furnished. No reason it shouldn't do the job."

"Uh-huh. But you don't really *know,* do you?" he said dully. I could tell the poor guy was dead on his feet. In his condition he shouldn't have even been standing up. He made no move to get his share of the pills. I had an idea he just really didn't care anymore.

"No," I said quietly. "I don't know for sure. I hope they do. I'd like to make you understand that we want to save as many people as possible on Gellhell."

"I'll bet you do," he said darkly. "I'll bet you stay awake nights thinking about Gellhell. I'll bet you can hardly take a drink of good Earth whiskey or pull a Fungirl into the sack you're so...worried...about..."

I turned away from him. His eyes were clouding up, and he was shaking all over. "DeLuso! Over here!"

He came up quickly. "We have about 6 minutes, Cadet. Get in there and run through Operational prep. I'll be with you in three and a half minutes."

DeLuso stared. "Operational? Sir, you want *me* to activate?"

I watched him a moment. Right now he could use a bit of fatherly encouragement, a little friendly service cajolery. To hell with that. He also needed to learn to follow orders without a moment's hesitation.

"Cadet, you received an order." I let the hard freeze travel from my eyes to his. He swallowed hard. But again control returned quickly. He snapped off a perfect salute and disappeared into the dome. I turned back to my scarecrow colonist.

He was exactly where I had left him, and he made no motion toward the antiplague drugs.

"About your Frostrees," I said, "we can't help you destroy them—and we don't advise *you* to try, either. The lab boys discovered they're a part of your ecological setup, and you can't spare them."

"Frack the ecological setups, mister!" The rage was back in his sunken eyes. "These things are killing our crops as fast as we can grow 'em. We don't hardly have the strength to burn 'em back!"

I nodded. "There's something in the carton for that. Tiger wheat. It worked pretty well on Ogirra. They had a problem very similar to yours."

His temper dropped a few degrees, but his eyes narrowed suspiciously. "What you figure something called Tiger wheat'll do to the people, mister? Or did you think of that?"

"Shouldn't do anything," I told him. "Unless you're part plant. It should poison the Frostrees or anything else that tries to grow near it. Won't bother people. Just stay away from it until after it loses its strength at harvest time. It's all in the microbook in the seed pack."

He glared at me and shook his fists tight against his sides. "We don't want any part of the stuff," he hissed. "We'll make out ourselves somehow. Without Starpath handouts!"

The gong sounded softly behind us. "You might change your mind when you get back on your feet. I hope so. Good-bye—and the best of luck."

He tried to mouth a curse, then dropped on his thin knees to the ground. I jumped through the hatch and let the seal sigh behind me. I was in the cushion as OPERATIONAL green turned to amber. DeLuso's eyes were welded to the bright, blinking READY.

"Everything operational, sir."

I gave him a curt, military-type nod, then added: "Watch the throat muscles; I might see you next stop…"

II

DeLuso gasped as we stepped out of the dome. It was night, and Vara Vara's purple moon filled half the sky, spotting the landscape with soft, violet shadows. A slight breeze carried the odors of exotic blossoms and dusty pollen.

DeLuso said something, softly, but I didn't catch his words. Still, I understood. Vara Vara is that kind of world.

"Makes you feel kind of guilty," he said absently. "I mean, sir—after Gellhell—the things they have to do just to stay alive."

I grinned in the darkness. "Uh-huh. Seems that way, doesn't it? You know anything about Vara Vara, son?"

He turned, and I picked up his face in the violet shadows.

"It's Paradise, DeLuso. At least, if there's a paradise anywhere in this Universe, Vara Vara comes closest to filling the bill. It's rather old, for a colony. Discovered nearly 150 years before Starpath. Long-sleep colonists—some of the few on record that ever landed anywhere in those days. They took one look at Vara Vara, and decided this was it. So they mutated—and made Vara Vara theirs."

I could feel the boy's surprise. Somewhere a night bird broke into its trilling cry. "Sir—*mutated?* But—"

I nodded. "Mutation equipment was standard on every colony ship those days just in case. Then, as now, it's pretty hard to turn back. This was one of those cases. They thought it was worthwhile, and I can't say that I blame them. As to *why* they made the change, the answer is down there."

I walked to the edge of the field and pointed into purple darkness.

"Below, Cadet. We're in the top of a planet-wide forest, three miles high. Up here is where the colonists live. This is the paradise part of Vara Vara. Two miles down is the hell."

I walked back to the dome and turned up outside volume as high as it would go, aiming the directional pickups straight down. DeLuso hadn't moved.

"Now," I said. "Listen."

There was really very little to hear at this distance, but it was enough to stand a man's hair on end. It wasn't so much what you *could* hear…

I looked at the cadet. He was a purple statue with a marble-white face. I turned the volume back to low.

"Don't ask what's making those noises," I said. "You wouldn't believe me if I told you. Anyway, the Vara Varans don't mind. Needless to say, they don't wander around down there."

I stopped, and faced DeLuso. His eyes were turned to the leafy darkness. I knew what he was doing; he was trying to pinpoint the soft, velvety hum that had suddenly filled the night. I smiled to myself, remembering the night that almost alien sound had first reached my own ears.

"There," I said. "Look." I raised a hand toward the dim purple moon. A bright ball of cold fire was pulsing toward us through black leaves. The soft hum turned to a definite, whirring beat. Then the fluttering of wings filled the night. A blur of violet flowed across the surface of the field, then settled lightly on a loop of twisted vine. DeLuso's eyes widened.

"Hello, Lyrerae," I said.

"Hell*oooooooooooo,* Keith Waldermann, my Starpather!" Her voice was a high, golden song. She touched the coldlight bug nestling on her shoulder, and it purred into dimness.

All of the women of Vara Vara are beautiful, each in their own way. The expression of beauty is a part of the Vara Vara way of living. None of the others—to me—can touch the beauty of Lyrerae.

She smiled, glanced at me warmly, then turned her eyes searchingly on DeLuso.

"And this one, Keith? I have not seen him with you before?" Lyrerae's voice made her simple statement sound like a declaration of love.

"Lyrerae. This is Cadet Matt DeLuso. This is his first trip, but we may be able to make a Starpather out of him."

"I'm—pleased to meet you," Matt mumbled.

Lyrerae laughed. "He's pretty, but not as pretty as you, Keith."

"Of course not," I said seriously, "he's just a cadet. Maybe when he's an old Starpather, he'll be as pretty as I am. And what can we do for you, Lyrerae? Any problems?"

A light breeze ruffled the soft surface of her wings, and she made quick adjustments of balance. "There are no problems on Vara Vara, Keith. We left our problems behind many years ago. But," she said brightly, "I am going to find a problem for you, Keith. I promise. I think you will stop coming if I cannot find a problem. Yes?"

"No," I grinned, "I won't stop coming, Lyrerae."

"I know," she laughed. "I know! And you, Matt DeLuso? You will come back, too?"

"I'd like that," said Matt. "Very much."

Lyrerae winked at him and stretched high on her long legs, spreading slim arms and delicate wings. The light down that covered her body fluttered briefly, then flattened slowly into place. It was something to see. It was simply WOMAN, spelled in capital letters.

I said, "Be nice to the customers, Cadet. Smile or something." DeLuso wasn't listening. His gaze was lost in golden eyes, and Lyrerae had made another conquest.

Then she left us with a high, singsong laugh and rose out of sight beyond violet shadows.

I touched DeLuso's arm. "Okay, son, come on. We've got calls to make."

He blinked hard and brought his eyes back from the purple moon.

"Sorry, sir, I—"

I turned him around and grinned. "Don't be, Cadet. You get used to a lot of things on Starpath. You never get used to Vara Vara. Now, let's get hopping."

We had time for two more. Gresticbor was a dawn world full of scaly beasties, but nothing the well established colony there couldn't handle. Then Styrxx, a mining planet dug in half a mile under a white sun we'd never see. They had a nice revolution brewing there, and both sides wanted arms from Starpath to, as they put it, "guarantee law and order." Arms, of course, they didn't get. Starpath figures talk is cheaper than arms and certainly a lot less lethal in the long run. So talk I gave them.

Styrxx is very heavy on rare earths, and they're almost ready to afford the luxury of a two-way Starpath terminal. I let them know that the paperwork on two-ways for a world without a stable government had a way of getting shuffled around a bit. They got the general idea, but I was glad we had a nice, firm field around us. Mining isn't entirely automated out there yet, and some of those guys looked ready and able to take a couple of Starpathers apart. Field or no field.

We'd hit four worlds in a little under 3 hours. Travel time: Zero Plus. Light-years: say, five hundred, five-forty. Then suddenly the schedule was broken for us, and we were shuttled off the circuit and into stasis at Primera.

I caught DeLuso's puzzlement as we stepped out into the busy station at Primera Starpath Control. I let it go for the moment. There was nothing I could really tell him—not yet. Anyway, I didn't feel much like talking.

Breaking schedule is part of the game, but it always pulls that permanent knot in your stomach a little tighter. You know that each time *you* make a schedule, chances are good that other stomachs are having fits so your particular emergency can be smoothed over.

It isn't easy. And we never get used to it, in spite of what we tell ourselves: that someone else needs shuttle time more than we do. That *they'll* be waiting on the sidelines for you to finish up next time around. It doesn't work that way. Those are your worlds out there, and some of them are in big trouble. Some of them might not make it if you miss your next call. Some of them are so critical you should try to get scheduled for a call every month or so. But you know it might be a year—or two years—and you wonder what's happening out there.

But there just isn't enough power to keep all the circuits open. There just aren't enough men who can ride the Starpaths. Not yet.

III

By the book, Primera goes down as a Class-A world. By definition, that means it's old enough and rich enough to have an industrial export-import situation, a large population and a stable political setup. Most important, it means Primera qualifies as a Starpath Crossroads, a world where the power plants can handle the mainlines and shuttles for a Starpath sector—one of those unfathomable slices of the galactic pie.

There are more than enough diversions on Primera to keep a man from boredom, if you happen to be in the state of mind that allows you to enjoy them. It was, I reflected wryly, about half true what they said about members of the Corps. An off-duty Starpather is no damn good to anyone. It's a pretty fair appraisal. The men who qualify for Starpath duty are not men who easily shrug off the burden of the worlds that depend on them. It isn't a responsibility you cast aside one day and pick up the next.

There's really no such thing as a Starpather on leave.

I guess I'm a little dense. We'd been on Primera two days before I figured out what was wrong with DeLuso. The standards I easily and naturally applied to myself could mean little to him. I had an idea he'd make a good Starpather in time. Experience would take care of that. But for now, he was a fresh, raw cadet who had been Earthbound all his life until 48 hours ago. Since then he had crossed 500-odd light-years of space and walked on five strange worlds. Not a hell of a long Starpath career—but not bad for two days out of Earth!

As yet, I realized, Matt DeLuso was not overly interested in tradition. He was, normally enough, interested in what any healthy character of 20 or 21 years should be interested in. To put it mildly, he was straining at the bit to get at the sights of Primera—and doing his best to keep his impatience from an obviously ancient superior officer!

As we crossed the warm, sun-drenched mall to the Grand Primera's dining area, DeLuso kept his jaw clenched and eyes straight ahead, stonily ignoring the open admiration of two dark-eyed beauties tanning themselves at poolside. Seated at our table, he gave the oversized menu that same degree of concentration I'd expect from an astrogator pouring over his charts. Even when a trio of silvermasked Fungirls brushed by, tall, statuesque creatures who moved with unworldly grace, DeLuso merely clutched his menu tighter.

So I know when I'm beaten.

"DeLuso!"

The menu dropped, and my cadet jerked into a full sitting brace. "Sir!"

"All right. Take it easy," I said. "We might as well get it over with, Cadet. It's either you or me, and I figure you win the deal hands down." DeLuso managed to maintain innocent bewilderment.

I let out a deep breath. "Come off it, mister. You've got dancing girls and nightclubs written on your eyeballs. Order something for me and hang on a little longer. I've got a couple of calls to make."

DeLuso brightened slightly. But I've been around long enough to catch those not so subtle hints of—what? Disbelief? Doubt? I stood up, leaned my hands on the table, and stared down at him with my best parade ground scowl.

"Son, you really think I'm too palsied to make it to the phone by myself—or find a number when I *get* there?"

DeLuso paled. "Oh, no, sir!"

"Fine. In that case, Cadet—"

"Keith, all your numbers are doddering grandmothers by now. I know—you stole about half of them from my book!"

I jerked around to face the deep voice behind me and looked up into a leather face slit by a broad smile. *"Walt!* Walt, for the—!" We were pumping hands and slapping backs, and DeLuso was standing at stiff attention across the table.

"They told me at Command you were out on shuttle. I dropped by as soon as we were scheduled off."

The tall man winced. "I know. Took my adjutant half a day to get the office girls back in harness. I had an idea Keith Waldermann was in town."

I grinned. Good old Walt. "Sir," I said gravely, "you have just saved an old Starpather's creaking image. Oh, Sector Commander Martin, meet Cadet Matt DeLuso."

Martin grabbed Matt's hand, sizing up the cadet in that rapid and remarkably accurate manner that amazed everyone who had ever worked with him. It was the kind of ability you'd expect in a Starpath Commander—but it was certainly no less remarkable for that.

"Glad to have you aboard," said Walt. "Been with us very long, Cadet?"

"Two days, sir," Matt said. "I'm kind of a newcomer, sir."

"What he didn't mention," I told Walt, "is that he made his first and fifth jump during that period. Which is a little rough, Cadet," I grinned. "Didn't tell you that before. Afraid it might go to your head."

Matt reddened suddenly, and Walt smiled. At the same time, the sector commander's brow raised, and he exchanged a quick glance with me, obviously impressed.

"It looks as if you may have a Starpather on your hands, Major," he said evenly. Walt gave DeLuso another searching look as he spoke, and the tone of his voice changed slightly. Matt didn't catch it, certainly. But I'd known Walt Martin a long time.

He said, "I think a man's fifth jump calls for a drink from his sector commander. I, ah, will also include a lunch on the deal, since the chits will find their way to my office eventually, anyway. Might as well make sure they're honest. And Cadet." He turned to DeLuso. "If you think an even older Starpather might be able to come up with a few decent numbers, I suggest you get yourself fitted with some dress greens this afternoon. Now if we can be seated, gentlemen, I think we might be able to make a small but significant dent in the Starpath budget..."

Nobody loves a Starpather. They envy us because we're the glory boys, the danger corps, the top rung on the ladder. Sometimes they respect us, because they know what kind of a job we're doing. But *nobody* loves us. I guess that's really asking a little too much.

Primera City is big—class conscious, wealthy, sophisticated. It's a city full of old money, the kind that's hard to shake up and difficult to impress.

There is one thing, though, that's guaranteed to do the job: three Starpathers in full dress uniform, plus a trio of the best-looking girls in town.

We took the full tour. Matt DeLuso's eyes seemed to grow wider at every stop. We made several of the most popular spots in town and ended up at a place accurately described as the best steak house in the known universe. And everywhere, of course, we were the center of attention. If you're a Starpather, you're supposed to get used to that.

Me, I never do. I don't think many of us do.

You see, it's not quite the same as being a planet-wide stereo star, or a high government official. It's not like that at all. A better analogy would be the attitude most people have toward their police force: necessary, maybe, but not overly welcome—until you need them.

Take the analogy a bit further, and you have the general feeling toward Starpathers. We're the highest paid, most privileged cops in history. We go places no one else is allowed to go, see things not one in a million will see in their lifetimes. We patrol the known segments of the galaxy—that small arm of the stars lost on the edge of the Milky Way's rim.

It's dangerous, sure. Not too many of the people who complain about our so-called status would trade places with us for a day. But who thinks of that part of the job when they see a cop out spending the taxpayers' money?

Matt DeLuso seemed to find a great deal to consider on the black surface of his morning coffee. I had an idea his silence wasn't entirely due to the effects of wine, women and song. I thought—and I was right—that he had managed to glimpse a few of the negative aspects of Starpath service.

"You'd have to be pretty dense not to see it, wouldn't you, sir?"

I knew what he meant, but I asked, anyway. "You've discovered that we're liked—but not *well* liked. Right, Cadet?"

DeLuso nodded. "We heard about it in school. You know the way things filter down, sir. But that was just talk. When you see it out here—the way they look at you..."

I smiled to myself and poured a fresh round of coffee. "There's something else, too," I told him. "Another factor. You don't get so much resentment when you are where people have everything—and that's the situation back home. Old Mother Earth is riding high—has been for a long, long time. Why feel bad about Starpath? No, Cadet, the formula works this way: a Starpather is loved in direct proportion to the current amount of comfort available on Homeworld 'X'. Primera tolerates us; Gellhell hates us. You've seen both worlds, and it's not too difficult to follow their reasoning. Look at it this way. At about 20 times light speed which is the best we can manage so far, a Longsleeper still takes 20 years to cover the distance out to Deneb. Subjectively the colonists haven't missed a thing. They haven't aged; that 20 years was spent in blissful sleep.

"Deneb wasn't bad—they found two good worlds there—but they're still a long way from home. It'll be several generations before they can begin to tame their worlds to the point where minimum technology begins. But they do have one thing. They have us. Within a few weeks they have their Starpath receiving station open. We get the signal and drop in to say hello. One more link in the chain is complete.

"Naturally, these people are pretty happy to see us at first. We just left home, seconds ago. We have all the latest news for the past 20 years. So we say hello. Then...."

"Then," DeLuso finished for me, "we seal up the works and say good-bye. Yes sir. I get the idea."

"So do they, very quickly. The thrill of pioneering wears off as soon as the supplies run out. Soon they need things. Maybe they need things badly, like Gellhell. We do what we can, but we can't do everything. Most of the time we stand behind our force field and give friendly advice. But we don't take passengers, and we don't bring in supplies. We don't, because it's economically impossible. It costs a small fortune to break up the mass of two men and assemble them at the other end of Starpath. The load of necessities for just one world would bankrupt the whole spiral arm!

"The colonists know this," I said, "but it isn't much comfort when you need help in the worst way. We have the stuff—but we can't give it to them. And it looks as if we're still a long way from pushing heavy cargo through Starpath. That leaves us in kind of a touchy position. Until a world has time to develop its own power—like Primera—we can't even set up a Starpath transmitting station. We just run through on the circuit and drop off 10 or 15 pounds of whatever will do the most good at the time."

"Sir," asked DeLuso, "did you ever read about the early 19th- and 20th-century railroads on Earth? They laid track across the country, but they couldn't afford to stop at every station along the line. Only the economically important areas had anything like *real* two-way travel. Starpath is about in the same position now."

I shook my head. "Worse, Cadet. Remember, those trains *could* stop and let off cargo and people, and take something out. We can't. Even the richest worlds still have to send anything out the hard way—through every long mile of space. Starpath is a link between the worlds. A valuable link, certainly. But for now that's *all* it is. We've been in space a little over 300 years, but we haven't always had the advantage of even 20 times light speed. Space travel has been a slow, hard pull. And Starpath's even younger—less than a hundred years. We're just getting our feet wet, Cadet. We have a long way to go."

IV

There were two more days. Matt DeLuso spent them with the girl he had met on our big night out. I spent mine alone, and didn't regret it at all. They were quiet, good days, with the balmy sun of Primera following me over bright beaches and through shaded parks.

For the first time since I can remember, I managed to put Starpath in a small compartment somewhere and let the old nerves unwind. It was still there, of course. It never goes away. But there was something else there, too. It was almost as if some part of me had an idea it might be a good thing to store up visions of green grass and wet mornings and red sunsets over gray mountains. I remember every minute of those 48 hours and I hang onto them. They say it takes a good three to five years to grow a new pair of eyes, even if the first ones work out. So I need pictures of those two good days.

I was half awake on pink sand when the shadow of the Starpath floater dropped over me and shut out the sun. A port opened before the gear touched sand, and I took one quick look at the young pilot's face. Just one. Then I grabbed my gear and sprinted the few yards to the ship and pulled myself in. The boy wouldn't look at me; his face was a sick ash-gray, and his eyes were somewhere else. I laid a hand on his shoulder and turned him around.

"Okay, son, take it easy. Now. Is this what I think it is?"

He nodded dumbly, trying hard to work his mouth over the words. "Sir...*it's Priority Red.*"

I didn't say anything. Like the boy, I knew there was nothing to say. I didn't believe it any more than he did. You just don't believe there'll ever be a Priority Red...

The ship screamed down and jerked against the roof of Starpath Control. It only took me half a minute to reach the staging room, but I knew it was true long before then. I could feel it—the unbelievable surge of power pouring into Control from all over the planet. There'd be no private or industrial power left on Primera now. It was all channeling into this one building, down into the giant generators beneath Control and out to some flyspeck world that had bought itself the big package of trouble.

We were draining a planet to feed raw power to a distant star. The same thing would be happening on a dozen other Starpath Control worlds. Electric transport would halt; atomic plants would scream as hot power was torn from their vitals. If you needed power to live—you'd die. Whatever problem you had, Priority Red was bigger.

"Keith! Over here!" I jerked around, vaulted a power truck hauling an ugly, snouted weapon and faced Walt Martin. He grasped my hand and signaled to a nearby captain. The captain nodded and sprinted away.

"I'm glad you're here, Keith," Walt said softly. "We're going to need everyone who's had over fifteen minutes of Starpath experience!"

"It's true, then. It finally happened."

Walt nodded grimly. "It's true, and it's bad." He turned to the high-vaulted chamber of the staging room. It was chaos, unless you knew what was going on there. Every bank of Starpath conveyors was in use. As men stepped from their missions on a hundred worlds, they were handed a combat suit and shuffled into line. Weapons trucks hummed back and forth like blind beetles through the auxiliary tunnels. And everything, men and equipment, funneled eventually toward one particular Starpath portal.

"Where is it, Walt? Where did they hit?" The sector commander's face was gray and drawn. He had aged ten years in half an hour.

"I said it was bad, Keith. It's worse than that. It's Corphyrion."

I took a deep breath and held it. "Yeah. It would be. *Damn,* Walt! We'll never hold it! It's too far!"

"We'll hold it," said Walt. "We'll hold it because we have to hold it."

And he was right, of course. If we didn't hold Corphyrion, we'd lose more than Starpath. Starpath first, but then the whole spiral arm.

The captain pulled up to us then and handed me a set of combats. Behind him sprinted Matt DeLuso, half in and half out of his fighting gear.

"Major!" he said and stared a salute in my direction. Then he saw Walt beside me and turned the gesture to him. "Commander Martin! Sir, I—"

I said, "Okay, hold it, Cadet. This is a Priority Red, son. I don't have time to tell you what that means. Neither does the Commander. Get yourself to supply and draw a weapon. Pull one for me while you're at it. There won't be a briefing on this one, Matt—just stick close and come out shooting."

Matt stared. "Shooting? Sir, shooting at *what?*"

I looked at him, then at Walt. Walt smiled grimly. "Cadet, we haven't the faintest idea. But I think we'll know what to shoot at when we see it."

I didn't have the slightest doubt about that.

Walt and I transmitted together, on the second wave. DeLuso and Captain Hamiel, Commander Martin's captain-aide, came right behind us.

It was a pure, textbook hell. There were about forty men already crowded outside the dome, behind the bubble of our force field. There was no room to do anything. Everyone was on top of someone else. Beside me, a heavy-weapons sergeant cursed under his breath as a combat foot came down on his gauntleted hand. He was trying to assemble a bulky disruptor that had of necessity been transmitted in four sections.

Raw, unimaginable power was surging in from Starpath worlds to supplement and reinforce the dome's generators. The field's protective bubble was expanding to make room for our forces—but not fast enough. The dome's air conditioning wasn't built to handle this kind of thing. On top of that, whatever was outside our field was letting us have it with some pretty awesome stuff. Energy washed over the field, turning it faintly red, and we were getting plenty of heat from that alone.

A hand tapped my shoulder, and I faced Commander Martin. He motioned me to the far side of the dome where a harried group of technicians were laboring over a small, glowing screen.

"Their weapons output makes it damn near impossible to pin down any positions," he growled. "But we think we have *something.*" He pointed. "There. Those three blips keep turning up in spite of the static. We have three disruptors assembled. I can't afford to wait for more. We can't take much more of this pounding, Major—get this stuff in line and try to knock out those positions!"

I pulled Captain Hamiel along with me and sent Cadet DeLuso back to key in the cables from radar to our bank of disruptors. Sweat burned into my eyes under the heavy combat armor. I glanced up once and saw a deep circle of cherry red pouring across the side of our field.

Suddenly the sweat under my helmet turned to ice. We were dealing with some smart cookies. They hadn't been able to penetrate our force field with their mass firepower—so they were turning everything they had on one spot. That spot was absorbing a hell of a lot of energy—and holding. For how long?

I didn't want to think too much about that.

DeLuso sprinted up and signaled me the cables were keyed. I turned. Two Starpathers were gingerly lowering the deadly disruptor tubes and extracting the shiny safety keys.

"Ready, Major," said Hamiel. "I've set it up for one blast over each of the three targets. I think, sir, if we hit them while they're still concentrating fire on one area—"

I nodded quickly, cutting him off, and glanced once more at the deep, red scar spreading across our field. I wondered what the enemy—whoever or whatever they were—would be thinking right now. The more I considered that concentrated firepower stunt, the less I liked it. It was a good idea, certainly. Maybe I'd have done the same thing in their place. Still, maybe it was just *too* good an idea...

I turned back to Hamiel. "Captain, change your settings. Concentrate two of your weapons on targets one and three. Lob the other one high and slow over target two. I want it to fire a good two seconds ahead of your other weapons."

Hamiel stared. I could see his eyes darting around to the side and behind me, probably hoping to find Walt looking over my shoulder.

"Major," he said slowly, "we don't know much about their weapons, but we do know they have the capacity to knock off a slow-firing battery."

"That, Captain, is my thinking, too. It's getting hotter than hell in here—please carry out that order, Hamiel! Now!" He turned red under his helmet, his mouth opening with the beginning of another protest. I moved him aside quickly.

"DeLuso!"

The cadet nodded, moved to the weapons and made rapid adjustments. He raised his hands from the board, and I pressed the button of the first disruptor, sending the silver bolt in a high, slow arc they couldn't miss.

They didn't. Before I'd counted off the two seconds, a white blast shook the dome, and I jammed home the other two buttons at once. Twin missiles thrummed through the field in a ground-hugging trajectory. A mile away, double cones of silent purple light winked and died. I ran around the dome and glanced at the small screen.

Two of the blips were gone for good. A disruptor missile plays some pretty horrifying tricks on its target. Every atom in the area moves a meter to its right and changes place with its neighbor. Result: some pretty gory scenery.

"Major." It was Hamiel. "Sir, I—"

"Forget it, Captain. We don't have time for a bloody court martial—those characters aren't licked yet!" In answer, a flood of red splashed over the dome. I grinned anyway—their concentration was a lot weaker than before.

We fed bolts into our three disruptors as fast as they could fire. Some of them got through—and a lot of them didn't.

We weren't fooled by the enemy's strength any more, but they had learned a lot about us, too. They were answering us from three new positions now. But they had spread their power thin. I could feel their concentrations weakening, and I could read the story in the viewer. Walt looked over my shoulder. I looked back, and he smiled grimly.

"Okay," he said, "let's take 'em, Major."

It always seems to end up that way, doesn't it? You can soften up the enemy with the most awesome of weapons. Then you have to go in yourself and dig 'em out.

We went. And every Starpath soldier that leaped through that force field knew there was only one way back. He knew that field couldn't be turned off to let him in unless every enemy position was destroyed first. I did what every other soldier did. I tried not to think about it.

There wasn't time to worry about getting back. We found that out soon enough. I lost half a dozen troopers before we made the small gully about 100 yards from the dome.

I knew Walt's group had fared a little better. But not much. We gave them everything we had—hand disruptor, V-grenades, small arms fire. We did a pretty fair job of it, too, because the second wave got through our covering fire with only half our casualties.

I moved out of our gully down a small ridge and got my first sight of the enemy. A dark beak opened under black pinpoint eyes, and a stubby weapon came up fast in long arms. I kicked in the green-tinted faceplate and kept going. A trooper in front of me turned with half a face and dropped under my feet. We stormed the first position and fried a good fifty of them. They died silently, great horny beaks straining for whatever poison they breathed back home.

I turned, then, to take a quick count of my men. My stomach sank, and a bad taste welled up in my throat. There were three of them left: Matt DeLuso and two veteran Starpath troopers.

I looked at Matt. He managed a tight grin. He didn't look much like a raw cadet now. You couldn't come through that last hundred yards without earning Starpath wings.

Martin stepped into our post and held out a weary hand. "Well, Keith, we got 'em. It was a high price for Round One. But we did it."

I looked at him. "Sir?" Then I got it. A cold hand reached up and touched the hairs on the back of my neck.

Of course—*the ship!* Somewhere, there was a ship that had brought the aliens to Corphyrion.

Walt nodded grimly. "I've ordered a couple of small flyers, but it'll take half a damn hour to get them through piece by piece and reassembled. Hell, Keith, this is no way to fight a war—sneaking back and forth across the galaxy through a mousehole!" He cursed under his breath and ran a glove over his mud-streaked faceplate. "Come on, let's get these troopers back to the dome area—fast!"

We almost made it...

Suddenly a soldier in the rear looked up and yelled loud enough to burn out every receiver in the area. And there it was—a black, egg-shaped ship rising out of the hills not two miles away.

We turned and sprinted for the dome area, but it was already too late. Red lights winked from the black ship, and troopers began to die. The disruptors behind our field opened up to cover us, but there was little they could do. It was too late now to even think about lifting the field to let us in. No matter what happened on Corphyrion, we couldn't risk losing the dome.

So that was that. If our disruptors couldn't stop that looming black egg, the enemy could scoot for home and come back with a thousand, a million more—before we could get enough power on Corphyrion to put down a small-sized riot.

There were five of us—Walt, DeLuso, myself and two troopers. We all hit the dirt at once and hung on. We had a pitiful amount of cover—a small, dried up creek bed and a couple of leafless shrubs. All we could do was wait. And I didn't figure we had too much longer for that.

The alien ship dropped lower, then settled atop a small hill overlooking the dome. I cursed aloud, and DeLuso turned with a questioning look.

"They're landing, Matt," I said dryly, "because they're a particularly nasty bunch of characters. They're in no hurry to finish us off!"

"They don't have to be," grunted Walt. "That ship is just big enough to neutralize our disruptors, long enough to ram a beam through that field. Look!"

I glanced across the gully and squinted at the dome. A bright red spot was growing on one perimeter.

It couldn't have been more than a foot wide, but it was a concentrated circle of awful power. Theoretically the dome's field would hold. But it had never been meant to stand that kind of attack.

"Major!"

I jerked up, following DeLuso's arm. I frowned, seeing nothing.

Then figures moved in the churned up debris before the dome, and three troopers suddenly plunged into the open, running for a grove of trees to our left. They made 15 or 20 yards before the ship spotted them. I clutched Walt's shoulder as red lances leaped out and cut the legs from under the last trooper. As he dropped, he tossed a long sliver of silver to the man beside him. He and his companion made it to the trees as angry beams of light cut through every leaf and branch above them.

Walt and I exchanged quick looks then belly-crawled our way back along the ditch. DeLuso and the troopers followed.

We met them halfway—Captain Hamiel and a young Starpath technician. Hamiel grinned, snapped a quick salute at Martin.

"I thought you might find some use for a couple of these, sir. We also borrowed a carton of fuses."

I looked at Hamiel's feet, and I suddenly knew what the dying trooper had tossed to his buddy. There were three bound cannisters of disruptor missiles. Enough to send every alien on Corphyrion to his own particular heaven—the hard way.

I grinned and pounded Hamiel on the back as darts of crimson fire searched the air over our heads.

"Captain, the apologies are on me! Walt, it'll work, if we can get close enough to drop this bundle within a hundred yards of the ship. There's cover at the base of the hill, and they're not likely to have troops out now. They're too damn busy trying to get one of those beams through the field!" Walt managed a tired grin, but it was the old Walt again. He glanced at me, then at Hamiel.

"Okay, Captain—let's get ourselves a spaceship!"

V

It was there, less than a hundred yards away, squatting like a black bug on the crest of the hill. We came up from behind, away from the scathing red beams, but a terrible crimson aura lit the ship to tell us of the awful firepower pouring over the Starpath dome below.

I glanced up the hill, then at Commander Martin. Walt's face was grim in the fading light. He slid back around the dark slab of rock to my side and shook his head.

I understood. It wasn't going to be a pushover, if it was possible at all. The first 75 yards weren't too bad; scattered outcroppings offered cover, particularly after Corphyrion's sun dropped lower behind the hills. That was the beginning—75 yards of possible protection. After that came 25 long yards of red death.

That last stretch of ground was completely bare. There wasn't a loose pebble for cover. All we could do was count on the increasing darkness—and hope the aliens had naturally poor night vision. There was some consolation in the fact that they were likely to be concentrating most of their attention on the dome in the opposite direction, but—I wasn't personally counting a hell of a lot on that. I'd seen them fight.

We *had* to lay those disruptor missiles right on the enemy's doorstep. It was obvious, now, from this distance. The alien ship glowed with a faint, blue-green aura—they had a screen of their own. There was no way to tell how strong it might be, but we couldn't afford to guess. There was too much to lose if we happened to guess wrong. For all we knew, they had already alerted their home world through some means of communication we knew nothing about. We had instant transmission—but only through Starpath. Another race could have already solved the problems of hyper-speed radio in a totally different manner. It might be too late already...

We couldn't dwell too long on that. The job now was to get those missiles up the hill, as close to the ship as possible. It was enough for the moment.

It happened—and none of us saw it. Hamiel was with us, right behind me, then he was gone. Then Walt cursed and stiffened beside me. I turned to see a dim figure disappear in the rocks to the right of the ship. Commander Martin stared for a quick second, then jerked around and plunged after his aide. I jumped up and wrapped my arms around his combat suit in a tight grip.

Walt tried to shake me off, and we both went down to the hard ground.

"Damn it, Major," he raged, "get—your—hands—!"

I shook my head and held fast. "No, sir. It's done. Someone was going to have to do it. He just decided first."

Walt relaxed slightly, but his eyes still blazed into mine. "That wasn't his decision, Keith. It was mine."

I nodded. "That's why he didn't wait, Walt. He got the job he wanted before you decided to volunteer. He was right about that—wasn't he?"

Walt didn't answer. He walked slowly over to the cannisters and hooked them over his shoulder. He looked back and smiled distantly.

"Everyone else is disobeying orders today, Major. Guess I better take a crack at it myself." He turned and motioned to the nearest trooper. "Come on, son, let's get our luggage up the hill."

"Walt," I said tightly, "just a damn minute! That doesn't happen to be your job either!"

He turned to answer but his words died as a spark of blue fire flashed in the darkening hills.

I looked up. Captain Hamiel was framed against the sky, perched high atop a scarred boulder on our right. He was yelling at the top of his lungs emptying his sidearm at the great black egg. The bolts splashed harmlessly off the screened shell, and a dark muzzle shifted in the middle of the alien hull and seared Hamiel's boulder with red flame.

Hamiel dropped. For a moment I thought he was hit; then I caught him again as he crabbed his way to another position. He fired again, then jerked away as another red beam split the landscape.

I turned to catch Walt and his trooper melt into the darkness. DeLuso stood beside me, unmoving. I cursed myself silently. Three Starpathers were out there now, moving up on an alien ship, while I stood behind a damn boulder with DeLuso and two troopers, waiting to offer history's most helpless covering fire.

I had known it the minute we reached the hill. Walt had known it, and so had the Captain. It was perfectly clear.

Whoever moved up that hill could forget about coming back.

I was looking right at Hamiel when he died. A red beam simply sliced him in half as he changed boulders. It was all over. The captain had finished his job.

And it worked. Walt and the trooper reached the last bit of cover without trouble. I glanced at the dark muzzle in the alien hull. It still swept the boulders around Hamiel's body, searching the shadows for more of the enemy.

All Walt and his trooper had to do was stay in the darkness—and wait for that one, perfect heartbeat when something tells you *NOW!*

I strained against the growing night, gripping the barrel of my gun until steel burned into my glove. I guess the distance Walt and the Starpather must have covered, then silently signaled DeLuso. We moved off up the hill, hugging the dark side of the stony ridge. I stopped once, searching for movement ahead.

Nothing. Only the red aura of deadly fire pouring into Starpath's dome, and the faint blue shimmer of the alien screen. Then—

—two shadows, silent, close to the ground. I strained against the darkness. For a quick second, I saw them—Walt and the trooper, outlined before a patch of white, only a few yards from the black hull, a few steps away.

DeLuso shouted beside me and the two dazzling white flares exploded overhead like small suns. The two bright figures in combat gear paused for a split second against the blinding light, then raced for the alien ship.

The trooper was ahead, Walt a few steps behind. The deadly muzzle above them cut a swift, angry arc out of the sky. A tongue of red fire licked across the hill and burned the trooper to his knees. His quick, short cry echoed through my receiver; then he was quiet. Walt ran on another ten feet before a beam of crimson winked against his helmet.

He kept moving—a weird, aimless dance before the beam found him again and slammed him hard against the ground. The thin pencil of energy stayed there, searching him out with murderous vengeance, probing, cutting, slashing away until a billion fiery segments of Walt Martin blazed against the night.

DeLuso and I moved as one man, dodging the bright lances, sprinting for the silver bundle of missiles ahead. Red fire dug at my heels, turning cold rock into molten pools. We spread, Matt to the left, me to the right. For a brief second, we were free of the deadly fire as alien guns shifted to cover their splitting targets.

I saw it coming as if I had all the time in the world. A red lance of fire hissing across the hill in a precise, slow, agonizingly perfect arc. I even knew exactly where and when my legs would intersect that blazing circle. I was down, clutching dumbly at a raw, charged groove of black where a portion of thigh had been a moment before.

There was no time for pain. I crabbed awkwardly along the ground, ahead of the hungry lances that probed the landscape for the rest of me.

DeLuso dodged past, and I fired a short and ineffectual burst over his head toward the dark ship. The two troopers behind us joined in.

Matt grabbed the cannister without stopping and bolted for the ship. A bright beam clipped his shoulder, and he staggered briefly, then went on. I fired another burst and got a splash of hot liquid rock for an answer. It burned through a soft spot in my armor and lay like a small sun on my spine. I screamed until the noise hurt my ears, then—

"Major! Over here!"

I turned, caught the two troopers a few yards to my left, behind a low ridge of rock. For a second I just stared at them, wondering how the hell they had made it through that forest of red fire. Then I got a good leg under me and moved.

I glanced up the hill once and froze. My throat went suddenly dry. Matt was down! *Gone.* An ugly circle of fire churned the ground where he had been a second before. I cursed something to myself, turned away from the troopers, and started up the long hill.

A trooper yelled, leaped out after me. I aimed a savage kick at his head with a leg that wasn't fit for kicking. He shoved me behind cover as the ground turned to flame behind me. Pain hit my leg in a pulse of agony. I lashed out, slamming a weak fist at an anonymous faceplate. The trooper pulled back, startled, his mouth moving frantically. I was in no mood for listening.

"Damn it!" I screamed. "A soldier's down out there, trooper!"

"Major, he's safe! He made it!"

"He—what?" I sat up, pushing the trooper off, and raised my head over the ridge. An alien flame brightened the sky, but I saw him.

Red lances probed and screamed around our own cover, but no beam could reach Cadet Matt DeLuso. He was flat beneath the curve of the alien ship, face pale in the bright light, the silver cannisters safe beside him.

Come on, Matt; Get those fuses set!"

I gripped the barrel of my weapon, wondering what was holding the boy up. All he had to do now was—

Then I saw it, and my body went suddenly limp with defeat. Even from here you could tell that the fusing elements were nothing but masses of useless metal. Somewhere on the long trip up the hill they had been hit.

I cursed and pounded my fist against cold stone. Men had died to get those missiles up there, in the shadow of the alien ship. And now they were nothing. Useless.

"Oh, my God, sir. Look!"

I caught the trooper's tone and jerked around. For a moment there was nothing. Then I saw, and a pulse of grim pleasure shot a burst of laughter from my lips. The two troopers heard and returned black grins.

We were licked. Sure. But now we had something to shoot at, something with a blue aura of protection. The aliens knew Matt was under there, and they knew whatever he had with him meant trouble. So they made the big mistake. They sent their own troopers out to get him.

Fire pinned us to the ground, but we poured in a wave of death at the enemy soldiers. Faceplates burst, and parrot beaks screamed for homeworld air. We piled them up in charred heaps as fast as they came around the black ship. The trooper beside me dropped as a red beam neatly sliced the left side of his body from the right. Through a storm of crimson death I saw Matt DeLuso, far away, crouched beneath the enemy ship. I saw him calmly snap the safety keys from his disruptor missiles, and I realized coldly—and proudly—what he was going to do. I added another trio of aliens to the burning pyre beside the ship, and then red fire crawled along the barrel of my weapon and plunged a million hot needles through my eyes...

VI

They bought us time on Corphyrion—Matt DeLuso, Hamiel, and 17 other Starpathers who died there. Only one—Walt Martin—knew just how much we needed that time.

I wish Matt DeLuso could have known what he was doing when he pulled the keys and set off his missiles by hand against the cold hull of an alien ship. He would have done it anyway, certainly. He didn't need any big reasons. It was a job that had to be done—and that was enough.

But there's so much Matt didn't know—Matt, the troopers behind our field at the dome, the young soldier who carried me through red hell just before Matt's disruptors did their job. There are some things we can't talk about, even to that most exclusive group of men who make up Starpath.

You can't tell a man he's a Starpath trooper because he's one out of a billion—because his brain contains some rare quality that enables him to withstand that terrible twist through whatever strange dimensions Starpath passes. You can't tell a Starpath cadet he has one slim chance in hell of making it through his initial flight—of waking up to stand on a new world and gaze at unknown stars.

Oh, we try. We try to weed them out before it's time for that deadly voyage through wrenching darkness. But—we need them—we need them so badly!

And if we think they can make it—if we think they *might* make it, we put them into a Starpath capsule and shut out the thoughts that come.

When we get a Matt DeLuso, a man who can ride the Starpath lanes, we give him hell and tell him he's a foul-up cadet who'll probably never make the grade. What *can* you tell him? That you lost a thousand others in another dimension, hoping for one DeLuso?

You see, there *isn't* any vast, Starpath army out there. It doesn't exist. We don't have a cop on every beat to guard the alien stars. We don't have anything like that at all.

We have half a thousand troopers—five hundred men—and 3,000 lonely worlds spread across the great spiral arm. Three thousand tiny vulnerable worlds, and only five hundred men who can span the depths between them. That's it. That's the Starpath secret.

We spread out from Earth too fast. We weren't ready to fling colonies across the great gulfs between the stars. We weren't ready because our ships were too slow to spread a network of impregnable defenses over a thousand light-years.

We weren't ready because there was always the chance of Priority Red.

And now it's happened. A nonhuman intelligence. An alien intelligence that wiped out the colony on Corphyrion without a second thought.

Starpath has warned the other worlds, and the ships are sweeping out to the far reaches with men and weapons. But starships take too long—much, much too long to save a world. Only Starpath can be there instantaneously—when it happens. It's up to Starpath to hold them back until we can build new, faster ships—ships with *Starpath drives* that can wrench an armada through the dark dimensions to any point in the galaxy.

It'll take time, but we can do it.

We must do it!

Made in Archerius

The colonel's staff car pulled hurriedly away from the curb, leaving a gray hedge of exhaust rooted to the boiling street. Hurstmier smiled, watching until the car became an OD blob in the stream of traffic. He waited another minute, then stepped from behind a parked van and took the marble steps four at a time.

It was noon, and the hospital lobby was nearly empty. An aged nurse snoozed behind the admitting desk and three bored reporters lounged by the elevators munching packaged sandwiches. Hurstmier received a swift, cursory glance as he passed. He pressed the button, waited, and took the self-service to five.

The dark-browed sergeant wore a burp-gun over his shoulder and a forty-five on his belt. He looked miserably uncomfortable squeezed behind the tiny field desk. As Luke Hurstmier approached, dark eyes glared at him from under the heavy steel helmet. While the eyes took him in from head to toe, thick fingers rubbed carefully across his credentials.

Luke waited patiently. He had been through the routine exactly eight times. He had long ago decided the man was hand-picked for the maddening procedure by Colonel "Tiger Jack" Starrett.

Finally, the sergeant frowned, touching the grip of his forty-five suggestively. He had concluded, reluctantly, Luke guessed, that there was no valid excuse to shoot one L. Hurstmier, as he highly resembled the face on his ID card, which matched the card's mate in his desk file. He was allowed to pass, the sergeant giving no indication he had ever laid eyes on Luke before.

At the end of the long hall, Luke stopped before the plain gray door. He rang three times and the door opened quietly, letting him into the semi-darkness. Luke blinked in the half-light. Two technicians glanced up and he nodded to them without speaking. Behind him, the cameras whirred softly and the tapes revolved on silent spindles.

As he stepped before the one-way mirror, Luke felt the familiar tightening in his chest. He watched as Ben Hooker bent over the huge, oversized bed. The figure on the bed was sleeping. As usual, in this case.

Six days before, though it seemed longer to Luke, Morph of Archerius had landed in upper Maryland. His spaceship was under heavy guard at Luke's laboratory in Aberdeen and Morph was interned with a fractured leg and respiratory complications in the biggest bed Johns Hopkins had been able to throw together. Luke decided he should be used to Morph by now. He should, but he wasn't. Morph was not easy to get used to.

As Luke watched, Morph stretched and yawned, bringing his over-long forearms above his head and extending his length to a frightening twelve and a half feet. His body was covered with thick, shaggy fur, his small, round head nearly hidden in a mass of heavy hair. More than anything, he resembled a large, very tired sloth.

Luke scowled at the sleeping figure. Since Morph's arrival, mile upon mile of copy had been written about him; newspaper, radio and TV had exhausted every conceivable angle and aspect of the first alien to land on Earth. Every angle except one, thought Luke.

If anyone else had noticed it, they had forgotten it in the general excitement and confusion of Morph's arrival, or, more likely, ignored it out of convenience. But Luke hadn't forgotten. It had puzzled and disturbed him from the very beginning—

—How, he asked himself, does a big hairy slob who sleeps eighteen hours a day, find time to invent an interstellar drive?

Dr. Ben Hooker shed his antiseptic suit and mask, lit a cigarette, and stepped into his office. Luke Hurstmier half opened his eyes as Ben entered. He was stretched in an armchair, his feet on Ben's desk.

"How's Sleeping Beauty?" asked Luke.

"Sleeping," said Ben, "and I'm not supposed to tell *you* even that much. Mr. Hurstmier will receive pertinent information regarding the medical aspect of our patient through authorized liaison reports."

Luke stared in mock surprise. "Let me guess. You've been talking to 'Tiger Jack' Starrett again."

Ben shook his head. "Wrong. He's been talking to me. What exactly are you trying to do, anyway, get an old man canned?"

Luke grinned. Ben waved a thick sheaf of papers under his nose.

"Somehow, he knows I've been letting a certain engineer read Morph's medical charts. He also knows the engineer is Luke Hurstmier. He is not at all happy."

"I imagine not," Luke mused. "I've been dodging him about three days now. I think he's unhappy about something."

"Uh, yes," Ben said dryly, "I'd say that. At least."

"Does this by any chance mean you are cutting off my source of information?" asked Luke.

Ben glanced up sharply. "Now why would I want to do a thing like that? Just to keep my job?"

"I won't be offended," Luke said bravely, "it's all part of the general trend. During the last twenty-four hours I have managed to get myself banned by Interrogations & Records, General Data and Central Filing."

"Perhaps," Ben suggested, stuffing his pipe, "you are making a nuisance of yourself."

"Perhaps. At any rate, you now have your choice of retaining our week-old friendship or knuckling under to the growing anti-Hurstmier faction. In which case, I shall go to the head of the hospital and reveal that you are holding six nurses captive in your laboratory for immoral purposes."

"Paagh!" scowled Ben. "I must be even older than *you* think I am; I'm neither gratified by your flattery nor aroused by the concept behind it. I don't suppose you could just come right out and *tell* me what you want to know?"

"Several things. One, I want to know what exactly is the matter with Morph."

Ben straightened, running long fingers through his iron-gray hair. "Would it be improper to ask what this has to do with taking that drive unit apart?"

"I'll let you in on a little secret," said Luke. "Frankly, I don't think that drive unit is *supposed* to come apart."

"Starrett will be happy to hear that," Ben mused.

"No doubt. As for what I'm looking for, I'm not all sure. There's something about Morph's ship that's very, very puzzling, and I feel the best way to find out what it is is to find out as much as possible about Morph."

Ben studied the lanky young man with his hard, clinical eye.

"For instance?"

"Huh-unh. I'm still in the hunch stage. That's about three flights below a for instance. Now. How about this Alien Flu?"

Ben winced. "It's a type of viral infection. You could have read that in the papers. Very similar to the several types human beings catch every day. It's transmitted through the body openings like flu or common cold. My guess is Archerians are very sensitive to respiratory infections; that's based on what we've learned about Morph is just six days, of course, but it's a safe enough guess. We've found old scars on Morph's lungs from repeated bouts with this thing—or something very much like it."

"Do you think it's ever fatal?"

"Could be," said Ben, "same as a cold or Asian flu *could* be fatal. I doubt if this thing is very often. I hope they haven't built a ship like that without discovering antibiotics," he added sourly.

"Well, don't count on it," said Luke. "Which came first, the A-bomb or the Salk Vaccine? I don't imagine we're a very unusual phenomenon. Now. What are you doing for it?"

"Well, treating it, of course!" Ben scowled, looked down, and began shuffling the papers on his desk, apparently annoyed by it all.

"I had hoped you were," said Luke, "but how?" He leaned back in his chair, grinning smugly at Ben. If he had learned nothing from his previous visits with Ben Hooker he had learned the meaning of the shuffling of papers. Luke had obviously driven the conversation into an area that old man wasn't exactly eager to discuss, and the shuffling was the prelude to a stall.

"Of course," said Ben carefully, "it's quite difficult working on a completely foreign physiology, but Morph is responding very satisfactorily to our, ah, standard antibiotics..."

Luke grinned to himself. The old boy was certainly a lousy staller.

"...Naturally, Morph's resemblance to our own order of Edentata is a lucky coincidence—for Morph and for us—he reacts in much the same way to drugs as our test animals. Actually, the big problem has been to convince about fifty anteaters, armadillos and sloths to *catch* Morph's infection."

"Well, I think you've done a grand job," said Luke acidly, recalling the roomful of sneezing and coughing oddities he had seen in the hospital's basement. "Now if we can interrupt the Zoology lesson for a moment," he said, squaring himself in the chair, "how about telling me what you're *really* up to, friend?"

"I have no idea what you're talking about," Ben lied openly.

Luke shrugged. "Okay, forget it. This is definitely not my week, anyway. What about the fractured leg? Is that Top Secret, too?"

"A leg is a leg," Ben snapped. "It's knitting."

"Well, that's reassuring," said Luke, pulling himself out of the chair.

"Not leaving?" Ben urged.

"Yep. Got a few more agencies to intimidate before I get back to my little ole spaceship. Thanks for the information. Such as it was."

"Oh, certainly," said Ben pleasantly. "Come and pump me anytime."

At the door, Luke stopped and turned. "Oh, there was one more thing."

Ben snorted, shaking his head slowly. "Yes, I presumed there was. The thing you came for in the first place."

"You've been associating with Starrett too long. You're overly suspicious."

Ben crossed his hands on his lap, enjoying being on the other end of the pump for a moment. "Sure I am. Now what was it?"

"I wonder if you would let me have a look at Morph's personal possessions. You know, the things he had on him when they brought him in."

"You've wasted your whole performance," Ben said smugly. "I haven't got 'em."

Luke slowly sat back down.

"Starrett took them two days ago," said Ben. "I assume Security has them by now. Why didn't you *tell* me you wanted them? I could have killed Starrett, fed him to Morph, and—"

"Oh, shut up," said Luke.

Starrett: Naturally, you understand that you do not have to answer any questions at all during these visits. You are in one of our finest hospitals, and we are doing our best to take care of you. You are our guest, not our prisoner. You understand that, don't you?

Morph: Most certainlies! Morph are most excellently cared. You physicians are muchly good in their grasping hold of medicals. Will it give to me greatness amounts of pleasurlies to bring Archerian medicals to your medicals. Oh boy! Sure enough!

Starrett: Your people are quite advanced in the science of medicine?

Morph: Oh, certainlies. Surely. Of course. All and everys come to joy in wondrous fine cures by Archerius' medical worldlies.

Starrett: Excuse me, Morph, I mean no offense, of course, but sometimes your translating device does not seem to, ah, give me the full meaning of what you say. This is no doubt due to my lack of familiarity with the instrument. Would you try to give me the meaning of your last phrase, "medical worldlies?"

Morph: Yes! Yes! Oh why not is it? Archerius' possess world for hospitals, world for physical typelies of science, world for all studies of learnliness. Is nothingness, really. Ho-hum, By God, yes! That's what it is.

(tape sliced and edited here—latter segment of interview continues.)

Starrett:...and these, spatial disturbances forced you to land on Earth?

Morph: Surely, surely. As I have before acquainted you, pal of my bosoms, I have been towardly Cheriuc Cluster in next doorly Galaxy.

Starrett: As I understand, you were journeying toward a destination in another galaxy, not this one? Is that so?

Morph: Oh, yes, yes, yes!

Starrett: How long does such a trip take, say, from here?

Morph: Oh, non-time, maybe muchly seem to be of three or fourness of day periods, but not truly a time, boy, just seemly to be.

Starrett: Then your drive does involve a faster-than-light principle?

Morph: Faster notly, oh buddy lover. Not so speedness like "fast" but speedness like placeness to placeness.

Starrett: You mean speed has no bearing, since you do not go *between* two points.

Morph: Ah, you have this too, eh?

Starrett: No, I meant, well—what is the principle behind this drive?

Morph: Morph is business-type man, not mechanic-wise. How the Hell am I knowing? Damned if I do. So what? Who can say?

Starrett: Then let me ask—

Luke swore wearily, leaned forward and cut off the tape. "Is muchly damned nonsense, Lieutenant."

The lieutenant stiffened. He pressed the rewind button, watched the tape rewind, watched the tape spin on its reel, then carefully replaced it in a numbered plastic box, hesitated, then looked up at Luke. He was young, and the two gold bars on his neatly pressed shoulders gleamed brightly in Luke's eyes.

"Were there any more tapes you wished to hear, sir?"

Luke smiled patiently. The lieutenant had a nice way of putting it. He knew, of course, there were other tapes Luke wished to hear. About three dozen more, as the request list on his desk indicated. What he was trying to say was were there any more tapes *besides* the ones he wanted to hear.

Luke sighed, lit a cigarette, and blew smoke casually toward the ceiling. "Hmmm, well, do you happen to have any tapes or films on Morph's personal possessions?"

The young man cocked his head thoughtfully, then fingered through a card file on his desk. He withdrew a thin stack of cards, carefully marking his place. He held the cards well out of Luke's sight, shifting his glance from the cards to Luke to make certain he wasn't peeking. Finally, he shook his head firmly and placed the cards face down before him.

"I'm sorry, sir. There is no indication here that Engineering Personnel are authorized to see these films."

"I only wanted the one on Archerian currency," pleaded Luke.

The lieutenant shot him a puzzled glance, flicked through the cards again quickly, and said, "Sir, there is no film or tape on Archerian curren—" He stopped suddenly, the color rising his cheeks.

Luke grinned triumphantly. The lieutenant swallowed nervously.

"Of course, I shall have to inform Colonel Starrett that I have inadvertently given you access to unauthorized information," he said sternly.

Luke stood up and leaned over the officer's desk. "Well, I won't tell if you won't," he grinned crookedly.

The lieutenant shook his head. "Thank you, sir. But I—must report all such incidents."

Luke started to speak, then caught the lieutenant's nervous glance toward the ceiling. He looked up. There was nothing to see but an air-conditioning ventilator. Luke frowned thoughtfully, then suddenly understood. No wonder Starrett was hot on his trail. He wondered if his own workshop was bugged, too. Probably. Certainly wouldn't want to be left out.

In the hall, he paused, pulled the thin shiny object from his pocket, and gazed thoughtfully at it for a long minute.

It was very late when he closed the door of his workshop and sank into the comfortable grease-stained easy chair. It had certainly been a fruitful day, he thought wearily. After leaving the young officer at Aural & Visual, he had managed to squeeze in Trade Relations, Alien Psychology and Speculative Studies before closing time. Of course, it was only a rough estimate, but he felt he had directly or indirectly antagonized at least fifty of sixty people at the three agencies. Not too bad.

Luke grinned. Speculative Studies had been rather close. He had nearly run over Colonel Starrett on the stairs.

Without looking up, Luke said, "'Morning, Colonel."

Starrett paused, his neatly clad frame poised just inside the doorway. "Oh, you were expecting me, were you?"

Luke glanced up from his desk, his eyes moving past the dazzling field of color on the crisp jacket and resting on the sharp, hawk-like face. "I'm not overly surprised," he said wearily. "Come on in. Grab a seat if you can find one."

Starrett glanced sharply all around the room, grimacing slightly at the tool-littered, grease-stained workbenches, finally choosing to stand. Luke repressed a smug, satisfied grin.

"How's it coming?" Starrett asked casually. He had moved to the center of the room, facing away from Luke toward the smooth ovoid form of Morph's ship resting on blocks amid the clutter of the shop. Its unblemished gray surface stretched from fore to aft in a graceful twenty-foot curve. Both the surface and the shape strongly resembled the four-foot drive unit on Luke's desk.

Luke stared at the ramrod back. "Oh, it's coming along fine," he said brightly, "we've established a basic premise to work from: We're quite certain the big shell is the ship and the little one is the drive."

Starrett jerked around, eyes glaring. "That's very funny. Or it would be if it weren't so damn close to the truth! What is holding things up, here, Hurstmier? You?"

Luke answered without looking up. "Lack of availability of pertinent data necessary for adequate analysis, Colonel. I think you know the answer to that one better than I do."

Starrett's eyes narrowed and his mouth tightened in a grim smile. "I see," he said hoarsely, "I see. When you were recommended for this project I was told you were a good engineer; that your methods were perhaps a little unorthodox, but nevertheless, quite competent. I'm afraid that description was a little inaccurate. You are not unorthodox, Hurstmier, you are unstable. If your so-called Daily Reports were not proof enough, your—adventures of the past few days would more than confirm my opinion." His lips tightened over his teeth in a grim little smile. "I suggest we stop sparring around, Hurstmier. You are deliberately trying to sabotage this project. Why?"

Luke shook his head wearily, stood up and walked around his desk. He let one hand run over the smooth surface of the drive unit.

"You're wrong," he said, facing Starrett. "I have a very deep desire to find out what makes this ship tick. But I repeat: I don't think I *can* find out unless I am allowed to see the complete picture."

Starrett glared, his mouth pursing up in a sour curl. He paced around the edge of the ship and stopped a few inches from Luke.

"You think I am withholding information that might enable you to take this drive apart? Deliberately? Is that right?"

Luke nodded.

"I see. Well, you are correct," he beamed triumphantly. "Partially correct, anyway. I *am* withholding information, as you have so doggedly discovered. But *not* information pertinent to *you*. It is the stated policy of this project that each department be allowed to work independently, without undue influence from each other. You are aware of this, of course, whether you choose to ignore it or not. The reason is simple: We want each group to discover as much as it can on its own. Come to its own conclusions. After we feel we have sufficient data, we certainly—"

"—will hand the pieces to a committee and stick them together with a pot of glue," finished Luke. "It doesn't work that way, Colonel. We're not taking inventory in a supermarket, we're trying to put together an alien civilization; find out as much as we can from available data."

Luke ignored the field of red creeping up the Colonel's face.

"You're going at it exactly backwards," he went on, "the classic example of the cart before the horse." Luke shook his head savagely. "Uh-unh, you can't departmentalize a thing like this; *all* data is pertinent to *all groups.* As for me, if I can't get the data I need from you I'll continue to get it from whatever source is available."

Starrett let the breath whistle slowly out between his clenched teeth. "I see," he said ironically. "No doubt you feel this explains your *need* to examine anatomy charts, postage stamps and alien coins. All of these items are necessary to your investigation of the drive unit. If you can give me a logical reason for those asinine requests piling up on my desk, Hurstmier, I'll *give* you Morph's personal possessions!"

Luke's face brightened. He said, "That is a promise I intend to remind you of, Colonel. As for opening this drive unit, if you've had time to monitor your tapes in Ben Hooker's office you'll know I've already stated that I don't believe the unit is intended to come apart. As far as I'm concerned, no coin or any other material object is going to open it. You've read our reports? Then you know there is no material connection between the control board and the drive itself. The control board contains several hundred units; we have pinned down the function of about half of them. *None* of them is in any way physically linked to the drive.

"This device," he explained, pointing to a rough diagram on his desk, "is a course computer. It offers the pilot an almost infinite combination of simple, pushbutton destinations. Spatial *and* hyperspatial, if we can believe Morph's gibberish."

Starrett scowled impatiently. "All right. What's your point?"

"Just this: Each component on the board is linked to a central transmission unit. The purpose of this unit is to send wave impulses to the drive. The linkage between the drive and the control board is *strictly electronic.*

"So the drive is permanently sealed in its impervious casing of God knows what, and for a very good reason: It doesn't *need* to be opened. All maintenance or repair, if any is ever necessary, is performed by impulse signals from the board. Some of those units are obviously designed for such a purpose. I haven't found them yet, and I don't intend to push any buttons to find out if I'm right."

"I'm afraid not everyone at Control agrees with you," said Starrett. "They consider the possibility that one of those 'buttons' might open the drive unit."

Luke nodded. "I've considered that. And I don't believe it. I believe it would be disastrous to open the casing, *if* you could, because I think it was put there partially as a safety device. I think the reason for this is that the drive does not totally 'exist' in its casing during certain phases of its operation." Luke smiled grimly. "Tell the people up at Control to come down and push buttons. If they're lucky, they *might* push the one that deactivates the drive. If they are not, there's a good chance they can be the first men to reach Andromeda. The hard way. Frankly, I don't believe Morph would be foolish enough to leave his ticket home wide open; not if he knows anything at all about Homo sapiens."

Starrett regarded Luke with cold, impersonal eyes. "All right," he said patiently, "I've *read* your reports. I don't have the technical background to agree or disagree with you; I can only say that if your scientific reasoning is in any way similar to your—erratic, personal actions, my former opinion still stands. However, as I said before, I think it's time we quit sparring with each other. You and I both know I didn't come here to discuss drive units. You are evading the issue, which is the *reason* behind your interference with other departments of this project."

Luke remained silent.

Starrett sighed. "All right. Forget it. Just tell me one thing. You know something you're not telling me. It has nothing to do with the ship or the drive. Am I right?"

Luke nodded. "You are," he said.

Starrett's shoulders relaxed slightly. He leaned against the side of the ship. "I see. Then at least we're getting *somewhere,*" he said caustically. "Let's take it a step further. Are you withholding this—information because you feel you are being persecuted? Out of bitterness toward me?"

"No," said Luke flatly, "*I'm* holding back because I *can't* tell you anything until I have the information *you're* holding back." Luke smiled. "You see? It's a stalemate, Colonel. And I'm afraid it's up to you to break it."

Starrett drummed his fingers against the hard gray shell of the ship. He stared blankly at the ceiling for a moment, then shook his head slowly and reached into the pocket of his jacket.

"I'm probably make a fool of myself, Hurstmier," he said stonily, "but that can't be helped. My job is to see that you do yours, period; so I'm going to overlook that policy we were discussing. Frankly, I think I'll regret it. Let's just say my curiosity has gotten the best of my judgment. I'm going to show you something. On one condition: I want your promise that you will not, in the future, attempt to—extort—information from other departments. Do you accept these conditions?"

"I do, and gladly, Colonel," said Luke.

"All right," Starrett sighed, "here."

Luke held out his hand and felt the tinkle of heavy coins drop into his open palm. He moved away from the colonel and held them under a strong light. There were six coins. Four seemed to be in the same language; none, he knew immediately, contained the curly symbols he had become familiar with from the Archerian control board. All of the coins were beautifully and finely engraved. Luke felt his heart pump wildly into his throat.

"The composition of the four in your right hand is a very high grade of silver hardened by some process to the strength of steel," said Starrett. "The other two are a platinum and gold alloy. Also hard. Metallurgy says they'll last forever."

"I believe it," said Luke breathlessly. He faced Starrett. "Has it occurred to you as—peculiar, that none of these coins is from Archerius?"

"Not at all," said Starrett. "Morph explained that he was on a trip away from home. He says coins of all systems have relative values on all other systems. Incidentally, I might as well tell you. These are Morph's *only* personal possessions."

Luke's brows raised. "No clothes? Personal papers?"

Starrett shook his head. "Morph says he was born with all the clothes he needs. He says he needs no papers, that the carrying of documents is a primitive custom, and his religion forbids the wearing of ornaments."

Luke made a face. "That gives me a little more evidence for what I've been thinking, Colonel. Morph seems to have a logical answer for any question he may be asked. It's all just a little bit too pat for me."

Starrett's eyes narrowed. "You said 'evidence,' I believe. Evidence of what?"

Luke glanced at the coins once more and handed them to Starrett. Then he eased himself back into his chair. "All right," he said finally, "you've kept your end of the bargain. Here's mine. I think Morph has told one lie after another from the moment he arrived. I don't believe that nonsense about 'spatial disturbances.' I don't believe he was forced down here at all."

Starrett's gaze hardened, and his eyes raised slightly. "That's *not* your responsibility, Hurstmier," he warned.

"Hold it," Luke held up a restraining hand, "I think you'll understand when I'm finished. Hasn't the possibility entered your mind that Morph may not be all he seems to be?"

"Naturally," Starrett snapped, "we've kept our minds open to *any* possibilities. So far, we have no reason to believe he's anything except what he says he is. Do you?"

"Several reasons. Morph contends he comes from a highly developed intergalactic civilization, complete with planet-wide hospitals, universities, etcetera, etcetera. Yet this so-called civilization is incapable of building their own starships."

Starrett straightened up.

"Now what's that supposed to mean?"

Luke continued, ignoring the question. "Two, the ship he came in has been stripped of every item made in Archerius before it landed."

The Colonel raised his eyes in a silent plea to Heaven. "I knew I'd be sorry," he mumbled. "All right, Hurstmier, getting back to your first statement; suppose this ship *wasn't made* in Archerius. Canadians drive American cars, Italians fly British jets. So what? I'd certainly expect that sort of decentralized usage to extend to an intergalactic level."

"Granted," said Luke, "but why strip the ship of everything from your own planet? Why unless you didn't want anyone to see your own products?—or if you didn't *produce* any?"

Starrett was silent. Luke hesitated a moment, then decided the time was certainly as ripe as it would ever be. He reached into his pocket and took out the thin metal disc.

"You gave me some coins," he told the colonel, "now here is one for you. Only you're getting the poor end of the deal. I found this inside the instrument panel. It had slipped down a crack into the course computer unit."

Starrett examined the object critically, then stared blankly at Luke. "It's a coin. So what?"

"So it's an Archerian coin. The engraving matches the writing on the instrument panel. It's the *only* Archerian object we have besides Morph himself. Compare it to the other coins. Do you know what it's made of, Colonel? I did the analysis myself. It's tin, coated with a little bit of silver chock full of impurities."

Starrett took another look at the coin. It was indeed a sloppy job of minting. The edges were slightly ragged and uneven, and the imprint was off-center, with half the profile of some Archerian dignitary missing entirely. The only possible comparison that Starrett could think of was a poor example of early Roman.

"It's a lousy job," he admitted. "But it doesn't prove anything. Maybe it's a souvenir, or something. I certainly don't believe it's a contemporary Archerian coin, if that's what you're driving at."

"Maybe, maybe not," said Luke. "I could be wrong about the coin. I don't think so, not in the light of everything else. I *know* I'm not wrong about the ship. I'm an engineer, Colonel. It's my job. That ship has been thrown together from about eight different species of spacecraft. Sure, the outside's beautiful—that's because it came that way. The rest of the ship is a big nothing."

"But you don't know that," Starrett argued.

Luke stood his ground. "I *do* know that," he said firmly. "I can tell a slicked-up jury-rig when I see one. We've probably got half, or one-third of the entire Archerian trading fleet right here in front of us."

Starrett shook his head in disgust. "Anyone can dream. Hurstmier, what possible reason—"

"—could Morph have for pulling the wool over our eyes? I couldn't say. I only know he's lied about his technology, and that leads me to believe he's probably lying about everything else. It seems to round out that way."

"Look," Starrett said patiently, "you are a businessman, a trader. You land on the biggest desert island in the world. The natives are rich and friendly. What are you going to do, kick 'em in the teeth?"

"Certainly not. I'm going to be very friendly, con the natives out of their pearls and spices with a lot of wild promises; then I'm going to steal quietly out of the harbor on the first dark night that comes along."

"Oh, for God's sake, man," yelled Starrett, "don't carry the analogy to the point of the ridiculous! We're not natives. We *know* the difference between pearls and worthless trinkets and Morph knows that. Why should he botch up an untouched, wide-open market?"

Luke grinned weakly. "I've read the papers, Colonel. I've listened to the tapes. Every time Morph gets his hands on that idiotic translator he makes another wild promise. The whole world's eating out of his hand, waiting for Utopia. And what has he actually shown us? Has he told you anything you don't already know? What have we got? A hacked-up spaceship that Morph threw together, and a drive I'll give you ten to one he couldn't begin to explain in a million years. I *know* he didn't make it. And oh, yes, we've got a coin. We've got a coin manufactured by a race of sloppy, technological pygmies!"

"You're only guessing," said Starrett. "You're just guessing."

"Well, while we're *guessing,* how do we know Morph didn't come down to check us out for—"

"I know," said Starrett tiredly, "for an invasion fleet. We've considered that. What if he did? If we let him go and he is a scout we've had it. If we keep him here or kill him we've got one chance in a billion that he came barging in here without telling anyone where he was going. Do you believe he'd do that?"

"No," Luke admitted. "I don't. But then I don't really see Morph in the conqueror's role, anyway. I don't think he could stay awake long enough to invade anything. As far as I'm concerned, he's a plain, double-dyed, slick as a whistle con man. Period."

Starrett got slowly to his feet, suddenly aware that he had been sitting on a greasy crate for the past ten minutes. "Is that all, Hurstmier?"

"That's all I can think of at the moment," said Luke.

"Well, it's certainly been fascinating. You know, of course, that I can't keep you on the project?"

Luke nodded. "I figured as much."

Starrett regarded him solemnly. He bit his lip and shook his head slowly. "I'm sorry, Hurstmier, I'm really sorry, but—"

Luke waved aside the apology. "Forget it, Colonel," he grinned. "Just promise me one thing, will you?"

Starrett stopped at the door and turned. "What's that?"

"Next time you talk to Morph, keep your eye on your wallet, huh?"

Luke was already pulling papers from his drawer when the Colonel slammed the door behind him.

Dr. Ben Hooker stared straight ahead, ignoring Starrett's hoarse, floor-pacing harangue. Luke sat next to him, doodling on one of those clean white pads that are standard equipment at every conference table. Below him, half a dozen military and civilian members of the project squirmed in various stages of discomfort.

"What—I—cannot—understand," growled Starrett, "is how you *let* him get out of the hospital!"

"No one *let* him do anything, Colonel," said Hooker. His voice was tired and strained. "We took his leg out of the cast and everyone just sort of—went to sleep. We have no idea how he did it but I suspect he had some sort of sleep inducing powers we—"

"Bahhhh!" said Starrett.

"It's quite reasonable, what Dr. Hooker says," one of the civilians noted. "The technicians on duty used to complain they got tired just *looking* at Morph."

Starrett shot a fiery gaze at the man. "And it didn't seem important to report a detail like that? Don't you realize every fact, no matter how fantastic it may seem, must be considered when you're dealing with an unknown factor?"

Luke cleared his throat loudly and gazed thoughtfully at the ceiling.

Starrett glared at him. "I was expecting some sort of comment from you, Hurstmier. You expected this, I suppose?"

Luke shook his head. "I expected him to leave, Colonel. I really didn't think he'd go about it like this, though. I guess he figured he could do without the natives bidding fond goodbye from the shore."

Starrett reddened. "If I remember correctly, his prime objective was to con us out of our 'pearls,' wasn't it?" He turned sharply to one of the uniformed men. "Did he take anything from the hospital? Anything missing at Aberdeen? Anything? Anywhere?"

"No, sir," said the man, "Just the ship, sir—"

Starrett glared the young officer back in his chair. He turned to Luke.

"He got what he came for," said Luke calmly.

Starett's eyes narrowed. "Which was?"

"Once I read an article about a clan of con artists that travels around the country in Cadillacs and trailers, bilking the public. I can't remember the name; it's a whole family, all related and all crooked. They hit a town like the plague, painting houses with cheap whitewash that runs off in the first rain, selling 'imported' woolens that fall apart when they're cleaned. The police have been on to them for years and they warn a community when the clan is about to hit a town.

"I imagine whatever serves for a police force in the galaxy is just as well aware of Morph and his crew. Which is precisely why he 'happened' to steer onto a backwater planet, ripe and ready for plucking. I'll bet he's opened up more new planets than all the exploratory ships in the system!"

"But he didn't sell us anything," Starrett argued.

"He didn't sell you anything you were *expecting* to be sold," Luke corrected. "He sold you Morph, that's all he needed to sell."

Luke grinned. "The funny thing is he could have had anything he wanted, just for the asking. But the con man's psychology doesn't work that way. He *has* to bilk the public or it's no fun."

Luke turned to Starrett. "Morph praised our medical achievements until he was blue in the face, and you finally got the idea. He certainly worked hard enough to give it to you. Am I right, Ben? Didn't you work up a preventive vaccine for Archerian respiratory ailments?"

Ben's mouth fell. "Yes. I did. I was glad to be able to do it, of course, and—"

"—and the authorities that be thought it would be a grand lever to pry a generous trade concession from the wealthy Archerians," Luke finished.

"It was a gift," Starrett added defensively.

"Sure," said Luke, "Only you didn't *exactly* give it to him, he stole it."

Ben shook his head in disbelief. "I find it incredible to believe anyone would go to so much trouble for a—free cold serum."

"Trouble! For something he can sell back home for whatever he decides to ask? No trouble at all, Ben."

"But why us?" balked Starrett. "Couldn't he get his blasted vaccine on some more, ah, advanced planet?"

Luke grinned. "I told you. You have to *buy* things on advanced planets. Besides, it's more kicks to bilk the natives. Anyway, they're probably on to Morph everywhere else.

"Incidentally, Colonel, I took another long, hard look at that Archerian coin. We were both wrong. It's neither primitive nor contemporary.

"I guess it's the final insult," Luke grinned. "The only thing Morph left us is a very poor attempt at counterfeiting."